THE GREATEST WORK OF THE DAY.] 1D. [A BEAUTIFUL ENGRAVING WILL BE PRESENTED GRATIS.

JOLLY DOGS

OF LONDON;

THE TWO ROADS OF LIFE.

OFFICES—NEWSAGENTS' PUBLISHING COMPANY, LIMITED, 147, FLEET ST.

PRICE ONE PENNY.

GIVEN AWAY WITH Nos. 1 AND 2 OF THE "JOLLY DOGS OF LONDON."

THE JOLLY DOGS OF LONDON.—ONE O'CLOCK IN THE MORNING.

DEATH OF A JOLLY DOG

THE MORNING.

THE JOLLY DOGS OF LONDON;

OR, THE TWO ROADS OF LIFE.

"YOU'RE MY PRISONER, RICHARD RENSHAW."—*See page 2.*

PROLOGUE.

SHOWING HOW A JOLLY DOG GOT MUZZLED.

"SLAP BANG! HERE WE ARE AGAIN! WHAT JOLLY DOGS ARE WE! With a fal-lal-la (Look out, ole f'llah, can't ye paddle yer own canoe?) fal-lal-la ('Ware, lamp-posts!) fal-lal-lal-la (Steer by the coal-gratings—good as a railway) fal-lal-la (Down with that opposition party!) WHAT JOLLY DOGS ARE WE!"

Making night hideous with this popular refrain, yelled at the highest pitch of their strained voices, three jolly dogs—sad dogs, nevertheless—came reeling along the pavement of a dark retired street, just as the church clocks were striking one.

Two of them were decidedly handsome dogs, the third appeared low-bred, and a puppy.

They were all drunken dogs, and had much ado to keep on their legs.

"Oh! confound this, Neddy, let's have a new version,"

No. 1.

laughed one of the noisy libertines, a tall, slight fellow with pale face, perfect features, rich dark curls, pencilled moustache, and a pair of fine dark eyes. "Let's have some words new and original, and more to the purpose."

And he burst forth, impromptu, in a deep mellow voice—

"Oh! we're a crew of jolly dogs
　　Who never can get cross,
　And loud as dogs we yelp and yell
　　New trash not worth a toss.
At music-halls so jolly oh! jolly oh! jolly oh!
　Where nought but bosh is jolly oh!
What jolly fools are we!

　We roar, we rave, we whoop oh! ah!
　We laugh ha! ha! We leap and squeal
　Slap bang! Here we are again!
　What silly fools are we!

NOTE.—*The Right of Dramatising and Translating is Reserved by the Author.*

" Chorus, cheerful pups.

> Fal-lal-la! fal-lal-la!
> Fal-lal-la! fal-lal-la!
> Slap bang! here we are again!
> What jolly dogs are we!'

" Ha! ha! ha! Hoo—hooray!"

Under the black brow of a tall, gloomy building, two stern-faced men, closely wrapped in their heavy overcoats, are lurking, keeping an eager glance fixed on the roysterers.

" That's our man."

" Aye, Clincher, I know his voice, the rogue sings well; but he'll soon change his tune, I fancy. Yes; that's Dick Renshaw; I've long watched him. I knew how it would end; he's been 'keeping a book,' 'seeing life,' 'living fast,' and going full tilt to the devil for the last twelvemonth. Take care to grab him tight, he's a determined young scoundrel."

" But the others?"

" The one's a pigeon—his name's Jemmy Gimp, a draper's assistant. He came in for his uncle's fortune, and the others are 'wringing him out.' He's not implicated."

" But the other is?"

" Yes, that's Edgar Wenlock, Gentleman Dick's fellow-clerk and accomplice. The case isn't so strong against him; unless the other plays booty, he'll get off; but we must nab them both."

" S—sh! they come!"

The three young roués were now staggering towards the place where the police officers lay in ambush.

" What say, magnificent bricks?" cried Renshaw, huskily. " S'pose we get up a sensation. Let's rouse the respectable inhabitants, the snoozing drones of this genteel quarter, and make 'em parade in their fatigue dress and nightcaps. Are you game?"

" Primed up. How's it to be done?"

" Let's sing the 'Firemen's Chorus,' and perform the accompaniment on the knockers and bells. Jolly Dogs, follow your leader. Fiah!—fiah!—fiah!"

Rat—tat—a-rat-a-tat. Ring—a-ring-a-ding.

" Hooray! Fiah!—fiah! Duncan, awake! Fiah!—fiah!"

The two detectives rushed from their hiding-place, and each collared his man.

" Deah boy, how are ye?" laughed Renshaw, struggling with his captor. " Glad to see me? Well, don't hug a fellow so tight. What going to shtand, Robert? Come, I say, forty bob will look as pretty in your hand as in the beak's. Let's go; we're gentlemen. It's all right, we'll put down."

" You're my prisoner, Richard Renshaw."

" Phew! you know my name, then," whispered the young profligate, as if suddenly sobered, " and the charge, drunk and disorderly. Is that the notion?"

" No; I arrest you on a charge of forgery and embezzlement."

" At old Mammonson's?"

" Yes; surrender. You'd better come quietly; I'll call a cab."

" Very obliging. But, hark ye, detective, fifty quid, on the nail in an hour, if you let me go!"

" Not for fifty thousand! Come, give it up; it's no use struggling, you're drunk; I shall hurt you."

" Very considerate; but mind yourself, old hawk, I'm dangerous!"

The Jolly Dog, uttering a fierce growl, seized the officer by the collar, and a desperate struggle ensued.

Meanwhile Gimp and Wenlock had mastered the other constable, and had thrown him heavily on the stone curb.

" Rescue, Jemmy! strike him behind, Ned! Rescue!" gasped Renshaw, as he wrestled savagely.

Wenlock, whose cheek was ashy pale, whose limbs tottered with dismay, muttered in his companion's ear,

" Better yield, Dick; it's blown at last; it's about the checks."

" What then, you cur!" growled the other. " Will you desert me? Dash you, then, take that!"

Exerting all his strength he whirled off the constable, who fell against Wenlock, and with him rolled into the gutter.

Like a speeding shaft shot from a giant's bow, Renshaw flew along the street, leaving his hat rolling in the road behind him.

" Stop thief! stop thief!"

Renshaw turned his head.

The officers were hotly pursuing him.

His comrades had disappeared.

Renshaw paused.

He drew a clasp knife.

He clapped the keen edge of the blade to his throat.

" The game's up," he muttered. " Shall I escape by the one sure means—by the 'leap in the dark?' I dare not, the light of conscience glimmers down the fearful abyss into which I should plunge! No, no; apart from the profane act of self-murder, it is not such as I who dare face death! Courage, Dick, you're not caught yet!"

He dashed down the knife with a horrible shudder, and once more he rushed madly onwards.

" Stop him! stop thief!" shouted his pursuers.

Sharply turning a corner he confronted a policeman.

The man seized him.

There was another desperate struggle, but it was not long sustained.

The detectives, now accompanied by a crowd of half-dressed inhabitants of the neighbourhood, surrounded the prisoner.

The steel rings clicked round his wrists.

He smote his forehead with the hard handcuffs.

" That'll stop his night-howling for awhile, the young vagabond!" cried one of the bystanders, shivering in his shirt-sleeves, " waking quiet folks at this hour. Yah! so much for being 'a Jolly Dog.' "

" He's muzzled now, anyways," rejoined another.

" Call a cab, some of you," said the detective.

A four-wheeler rattled up.

" Stand clear," said the officer. " Come, Mr. Renshaw, you must sing your next solo in the cells at Bow Street."

————

The intent and purpose of the present bold, thrilling, and sensational romance is *pure*. The object is to contrast the meanness and wretchedness of criminal life, the madness and misery of "fast" life, and particularly the folly, vulgarity, and profligacy of "Jolly Doggism," with the peace, happiness, and comfort of honesty and steadiness. The chief incidents are really true, though strung together in the form of an intensely exciting work of fiction.

BOOK I.

CHAPTER I.

A CRY IN THE DARK.

A DENSE fog hovers over the broad, deep breast of the dark Thames.

Gliding swiftly and silently, a small boat is urged along by a sturdy fellow, who pulls hard against the swift, strong tide, fast running down.

Another man, standing erect in the bows, holds aloft a red, flaring link, and shading his smarting eyes with his left hand, peers heedfully ahead through the mirky, filmy mist.

" Hold water!"

The oarsman held the boat at rest.

She drifts astern in the rushing current.

The man who holds the torch steps lightly from thwart to thwart, and seats himself in the stern-sheets.

" Go on steady, mate."

The man rowing lets the oar-blades slip lightly into the stream, and pulls strongly.

By the glare of the link the men's faces appear grimed with coal-dust, coarse and hard-featured, and stolid in expression.

They are bargemen, who are steering for an old hulk, moored in the mid-stream, and their purpose is to fire a danger-light on board her to serve as a warning beacon to craft moving on the river.

"Phew! a cuss on this 'farnal fog," said the oarsman. "Hand o'er the 'bacca-box, mate."

The man steering complied, having first slipped a quid into his own mouth.

"'Taint pleasant, nohows," he remarked, his voice sounding faint and hollow. "'Twas lucky for that poor stray lass as the fog didn't fall till daybreak."

"Aye, 'twas so, Beamish," said the other, "though, arter all, it's but one less out o' hundreds as is drowned in course o' the year. Poor young soul! Respectable-looking, warn't she?"

"Werry much so, mate. 'Struth! one might say, reg'lar gentry."

"Mayhap there'll be a reward offered?"

"No, 'spects not. Clothes seems good mater'al, but old and rent, and mud-stained; hands white as lilies, but no weddin'-ring. The awful old story, I'm 'feared."

"Ah, a governess, or a unfortnit, belikes."

"Unfortnit enough, Hogan, Lor' knows. Wife says the poor lass be sure to die off. On'y a job for the parish coffun-maker, when all's done. Well, death's the best release for a many poor sinners; the cold grave ain't so cold as the stranger's hearth to the homeless and starvin', who has nought to depend on but the hard crusts of human charity."

"Can't say as 'tain't true, mate. Did she leap off the bridge?"

"No, sprang from the bank at high water, down by the old wharf. My boy, Shem—fine lad, that—though, by luck, I'm his father."

"A boy to be proud on."

"Aye, he is so. Well, mate, Shem were lyin' asleep in the lighter, awaitin' for the steam-tug, as didn't come arter all, along o' this dirty fog, when he hearn a sloush, and lookin' o'er the lee-side, saw a gal, with a child still gripped in her arms, a flound'rin' in deep water. Her clothes kep' her afloat, but the tide was runnin' hard and fast. It were on'y arter most supperhuman exartions that Shem managed to get her into a boat towed to the lighter. The poor young mother seemed to lose fortitood, and kep' the babe above water, though she herself were half drownded, and a screamin' piteous. When got into the boat she become quite onsensible, but the child were all right. Oh, the babe will do well enough. The purtiest, comic'list little creetur, Hogan, as ever come smilin' into a world of sorrow."

"Boy or girl?"

"Gurl; a fine gurl. Sech a pair of eyes! blue as the skies—which, it seems, as we're never to see agen. Cuss the fog! it anigh chokes me."

"And what 'll become o' the poor little thing if s'pose the mother dies?" asked Hogan, when his mate had ceased coughing. "Send it to the workhouse, I spects?"

"Well, my wife, she says, no; and she mostly has it all her own way."

"You'll find the child a burden and a charge, I'm 'fraid."

"May be, times is hard; but Shem's a growin' up, and bless my heart, but somehows I don't like the thoughts of partin' wi' the winsome little rogue."

"But won't the gal tell ye who she is, and where she comes from?"

"Lor bless yer eyes, Hogan, the poor creetur's mind is all adrift. She lies moanin' and moanin', but as onconscious as if she were a lyin' in the bed of the river."

"But has she no letters on her?"

"Ne'er a one"

"And no marks on her clothes?"

"Well, there is a fine cambric handkerchief, but the corner's part torn off; howsoever, one word remains, which is 'Earl,' and as Shem's given to callin' the wee fairy thing 'Elfie,' he shall stand godfather for the poor little waif, and we'll call her 'Elfie Earl.'"

"Queer name, though. I should say Jane or Sushanner."

"Wife think's it pretty, and Shem's pleased with it too; and don't matter to me, I likes 'em to have their own way; it's allers best, I must own, God bless 'em, for better wife than my Martha, or better son than my Shem—"

"Hold hard a moment, mate. I thinks we're nearin' the lighter. If we don't keep a weather eye open, we may run astern of her; so starn off."

Proceeding very carefully, within a few moments they found themselves floating under the dark hull.

Beamish clambered on board the barge, and lighted a blazing fire in an iron chafing dish.

The red glare shone lurid and fierce through the hovering fog.

He got down into the boat again, and taking one of the oars with his companion, began to pull briskly in shore.

They turned the boat, and drifted swiftly along the rushing tide, the thick and inky stream plashing drearily beneath the gunwale.

"Goin' straight home, Beamish, arter we put in shore?"

"No, mate; tell the truth, that poor lass gives me the dismals. I shall turn into the 'Coal-whipper's Arms' for a hour or so, jest to smoke a pipe, and enjoy a little 'armony."

"Anythin' on there to-night?"

"Yes, a raffle and a 'friendly lead' for poor Tom Coke's widder."

"I'll go wi' ye, then. I put in for the watch."

"And so did I. I should be mighty proud for my Shem to sport a ticker like any other gen'leman. Hist!"

Muffled by the close and heavy vapours, came faintly the wild shriek of some human being in mortal agony.

The men rested on the rowlocks, and stared aghast at each other.

Again a terrible cry as of one in a death struggle.

"Man overboard!" said Hogan, rising.

"You'll be overboard, too, if you don't sit down, mate, Trim the boat; now then! Hark ye!"

A third and yet more thrilling scream.

"Shiver my topmast! if drownin' people ain't as common in these 'ere waters as tad-poles in a marsh-pond!" gasped Beamish.

Hogan, who was still on his feet, arched his fingers round his lips, and hallooed in the direction from which the cry had sounded.

"Yo, ho! yo ho! where away? Sing out agen, you in distress—yo, ho!"

"Help, for God's sake!—help, help!" shrieked a voice from the water.

The cry sounded nearer.

"Starn all! Light another link, Beamish!"

Again the men shouted.

They received no answer.

"Poor wretch. Depend on't, Hogan, he's gone under."

"Where are we now, think ye?"

"Off Millbank Gaol!"

"Ha!"

The lurid glare of the flaming torches flashes bright on the black and surging waters which roll on beneath their murky mantle of fog.

A hand is suddenly tossed up through the muddy stream, then arms, then white and distorted features.

The next moment the boat heels over, and its occupants give a yell of alarm.

The drowning man has fixed a convulsive grasp upon her bows.

Beamish drags him into the boat.

His head falls back on the huge man's shoulder, and his limbs droop.

He sinks down upon the gratings.

The torches flare down upon him as he lies senseless and motionless.

He is tall and slim, dressed in a close-fitting suit of coarse grey surge, his black hair is close-cropped, and one leg, the trouser being rolled to the knee, is bare, and stained with slime and blood, and the torchlight glints on a cold, bright, steel ring encircling the ankle.

The men exchange meaning glances.

"Millbank," says Hogan, quietly giving a tug at the oar to turn the boat in that direction. "He's a convict escaped. Shall's take him back? there'll be a reward, perhaps."

"No, no, poor devil, no," whispers Beamish, hoarsely. "'Taint in natur'! The old wharf, mate, on the Lambeth side. Give him up? Cuss me, if I've the heart to do it."

CHAPTER II.

THE FAIR ACTRESS HOLDS A LEVEE—LOVE AND JEALOUSY—A QUARREL AND AN EXPLANATION—CONFESSION—THE DREAM—THE SURPRISE—CREMORNE!

THE curtain rises to merry music.

A gay and dazzling scene.

In a pretty room, showily furnished, and lighted brilliantly, a party of young gentlemen and ladies are lounging upon damask chairs, couches, and sociables, listening with rapt attention to a dark-eyed, pale-faced youth, who, seated at a grand piano, is playing and singing in admirable style.

She whose beauty was the theme of the musician's song—a lovely girl, with eyes of liquid blue, and wavy hair of richest gold—reclined languidly, surrounded by a group of gallant admirers, who joined in the chorus with great enthusiasm.

*   *   *   *   *

SOLO.

Who when Love accoutred came,
  Bearing all his burning lances,
Forged in passion's fiercest flame,
  Quelled him with her lightest glances;
That to Venus straight he flies,
  Swears 'tis useless to deceive her,
Owns one beam of those blue eyes
  Worth the contents of his quiver.
Who is this our peerless queen?

CHORUS.
Angeline!—bright Angeline!

"Bravo!—bravissimo! Well done, Leoni!" was the general exclamation.

The fair girl rose, and, sweeping gracefully across the room, laid her soft hand coyly on the shoulder of the blushing and trembling youth.

"That's very pretty of you," she said; "you must teach me how to thank you."

The young musician tried to answer; but speech failed him, he blushed and stammered incoherently.

Nevertheless, the blue eyes dilated, and a ravishing smile lit on the lips of scarlet.

An exclamation of disgust broke from a tall, good-looking fellow, who, with his arms listlessly folded, was leaning against the wall in a vacant corner of the room.

"What's the row, Ned?" enquired a companion seated beside him.

The question was put in an under-tone, rather needlessly so, however, as all the rest of the company were laughing and chatting together.

"What ails you, Ned? You look like the ghost of Lord Lovel."

"Pshaw! yet it does make a fellow feel mad."

"What does?"

"Poor young Leoni. With all the fervour he inherits from his Italian father, with his rare talents, that he should be wrecked and ruined by that artful flirt."

"Come, Ned, don't be too hard upon poor Angeline; she is a woman of the world, a charming actress both on and off the stage, and, any fellow with common sense knowing this, will act accordingly, and worship her as something very dazzling and divine, but immeasurably out of reach."

"Curse her! Don't speak of her. You need not look so glum. I know I'm her guest to-night, and silence is the best mercy I can show the heartless jilt."

"Show mercy to yourself, my boy," returned his companion, gravely. "You are in love with her; quit her, hate her, if you please, but never allow yourself to be deceived about a thing that must be patent to your good sense; in hard, true words, that you can never marry her."

"My wife? She my wife? Rather——"

He could not finish the sentence, but turned terribly pale, and gnashed his teeth.

"By Jove, Ned, your serious phiz for the moment startled me into seriousness; but, tell truth, you really are not so deeply smitten?"

"Smitten? Yes, with disgust at her absurd arrogance."

"Phew! you certainly do appear to be in disgrace this evening. She cut you dead at your entrance, and since has not blessed you with a single glance, though she appears to be unusually gracious."

"We have quarrelled."

"The deuce you have, my boy? Deem yourself favoured; there are few that Angeline Lablonde would deign to quarrel with."

"I'd be off, George, but the party will break up soon."

"Yes, some of the fellows, and most of the girls have to play in the after pieces. I and Lyddy are going to Cremorne; perhaps we can prevail upon her supreme loveliness to go with us. Come you, too, and I'll fetch Humphrey Puffy. It will be jolly."

"Not I."

"Bah! don't be a muff, Ned. By the simplicity of Venus's doves, I'm ashamed of ye."

With a laugh, George Grant, for that was his name, turned away, and mingled with the company, who were now gathered about their fair hostess taking their adieux.

The room being cleared of all the assembly except a dark, gentle-looking girl, George conversed a moment with Angeline Lablonde, and then, gallantly bowing, withdrew to the piano with this lady.

Angeline swept majestically towards a gilded couch on which her lover had dejectedly thrown himself.

"Edgar, you are mad!" she exclaimed, in a tone of fierceness, at the same time seating herself by his side, and leaning her soft cheek on her hand.

"Mad, Angeline? I must be, for I believed in you, Angeline. I would have staked my soul on your truth; you told me once that you loved me, you led me on with your siren smiles, and then, at last, when—when—oh, G—d!—when I had thrown all down at your feet, my reputation, my common honesty, when I became what I am, you—you treat me as if I were a mere inanimate thing, a toy without life or feeling, to be cast away like a broken fan or a soiled glove. What have I done, Angeline? I dare not think of it. But for what have I sacrificed more a million-fold than life? For love—pure, fervent love; and that love you make your mock, your profit in the base, base sense. You have ruined me!"

Angeline shuddered at this vehemence. Then a radiant gleam of scorn flashed in her bright blue eyes, and she drew herself up with an air of disdain.

Edgar had buried his head in the damask pillow, which was strewn with his rich black and glossy curls.

"Pity me, Angeline!" he murmured, brokenly. "You are incapable of love; but pity me, pity me! Your commiseration shall comfort me when I am a convicted felon and a prisoner."

"Just Heaven! what have you done? What are you raving about?"

"Nothing, nothing," returned Edgar, wearily, "at least, nothing for which I shall be assailed from without. I am cunning, as well as criminal."

"I pity you," replied Angeline; "yes, indeed, I pity you."

"My own dearest," he murmured, with intense fervour, starting up, and seizing her hands. "Oh, but that is not enough. Say—say that you love me!"

"Man, are you really mad?" cried Angeline, fiercely. "Ah," she continued, in a regretful tone, "you are weak and foolish; you have no self-controul."

"What do you mean!"

"Mean, Edgar? Why, mon enfant, be advised; you know you do—you take too much of that heady champagne."

And she burst into a low, provoking laugh.

"Love you?" she re-commenced, after a long pause. "Edgar, I do love you; I love all who are kind to me."

"You do not know what love is; you are incapable of its passion."

"Ah, you think so. Shall I tell you, Edgar—but, no, I am not so insane. 'Tis you who know not what love is. A man! a base, selfish man, you are incapable of sounding the depths of a woman's heart? Love! 'Tis true I have no love out of my profession; but, as an actress, I have; the delicious, dear, kind, appreciating public—the one in all, that, with its hundred hands, claps down the golden shower which gives me wealth and pleasures—the public is my constant sweetheart, my generous friend. But hear me, Edgar, would it comfort you to know that I am as weak and fond as yourself?"

"It would, Angeline."

"Then, with all the strength of my strong heart, Edgar Wenlock, I *have* loved!"

"And whom?"

"Don't ask too much."

"Dear Angeline, confide in me. I will forget your sneering levity and falseness. Who has won your love?"

"Won? My high-minded lover was too proud to 'win' my love; he gave me his pure and noble heart in exchange for my frail, bad one, and he profited little by the bargain. Now you look savage; of course you do. Well, if you could behold your rival now, perhaps the sight would cure you of jealousy. Yet I would I were in his arms."

Angeline turned away her head, and laughed hysterically.

"He is dead, then?" said Edgar, softly.

"Aye, my heart moulders with his under the sod of some forest or savannah in the far West. He was a Confederate soldier; he perished in the late horrible war."

"And his name?"

Angeline did not reply, but the tears welled up to the melting blue eyes, and the arched lip curved in proud sorrow.

"In which battle did he fall?"

"I cannot tell that; but I know he is dead."

"How did you learn the fact?"

"If he were living he would write to me. He is dead!"

Angeline folded her hands on her lap with a look of weary sorrow.

She started and rose, and laughed musically.

"Come, Edgar," she said, "we are no longer children; in childhood we have our fairy dreams, a little later our love dreams, alike bright and illusive; but it is vain to weep for unreal visions that flee the stern reality of life. There is my hand, Edgar; is it peace?"

The young lover fervently kissed the little palm, and then pulling from his breast a small morocco case, opened it, and produced a gold bracelet studded with sparkling diamonds, which he clasped around the moulded arm.

"Accept this little peace-offering, dear Angeline," he murmured.

The fair girl glanced at the brilliant gift carelessly, and then faintly smiled cold thanks.

"Oh! what *are* you talking about?" cried Lydia St. Clare, springing up from the piano and joining them. "You have been quarrelling, you both look so stupid and tragical. Come now, both of you. Fie! fie! unknit that threatening, unkind brow, Miss Lablonde; and you, master Ned; leave your 'abominable faces,' be good children for once. Georgy proposes we should go somewhere to-night; what say you to the opera?"

"Gracious goodness, Lyddy, don't mention the theatre!" exclaimed Angeline, pettishly, "the ring of the prompter's bell is as pleasant to my ears as a passing knell. Anywhere, anywhere out of the world, if one may escape the theatre!"

"Well, dear, suppose we go to a music hall? What do you say, George?"

Grant whistled some execrable popular tune, and shrugged his shoulders.

"Come, you tiresome boy, why don't you make a proposal?"

"Make a proposal? of my 'and and 'art?" exclaimed the gallant youth, dropping on one knee, and kissing her hand in a sentimental manner. "But look at poor Edgar, of Ravenswood, his tendencies are decidedly suicidal, if one may judge from his gloomy countenance," he continued, clapping Wenlock on the shoulder. "For pity's sake, old boy, don't look so pitifully weary and woe-begone."

"Pshaw! never was more jolly in my life! Where shall we go?"

"Yes, yes," cried Lydia, "without nonsense, do decide now."

"Ha! I'm entranced!" cried George, with a melo-dramatic start. "As before the eyes of a clairvoyant, a vision rises, a vision of beauty!—An earthly paradise illumined by bright twinkling lamps, and brighter twinkling eyes; there are sounds of stirring music and gushing laughter, a perfume of flowers, and other fragrant 'weeds,' a display of native beauties and beautiful natives, some with beards as the swells and—oysters —coruscations of fun and fireworks, a ball, and a balloon."

"Oh, capital, George, Cremorne!" Lydia exclaimed, clapping her hands with delight. "My dear children, could anything be more delicious?"

"Is it agreed, then, sweet princess with the golden locks?"

"As you please, George," replied Angeline, with indifference.

"Come, then, Ned, you and I will run and fetch old Puffy; as the showman's elephant came over in two ships, perhaps we may manage to convey our modern Falstaff in a couple of four-wheelers; the hansom will have none of him, their very springs groan at him as he passes. Come, then, my boy."

When the girls were left to themselves Angeline sauntered to the window.

She gazed abstractedly out upon the groups of passengers hurrying by.

Humming the "Mabel" waltz, Lydia drew to her side, and placed her arm round her waist.

"You are not yourself to-night, Angeline," she said, gently.

"What am I, then?"

"Something that you have never appeared to be till now. Good gracious, child, whatever makes you look so pensive?"

"Lyddy."

"Well, dear?"

"Do you put any faith in dreams?"

"Of course I do; but what kind of dreams do you mean?"

"Last night I had a vision; it was more than a mere dream."

"Never!"

"Yes, and it has made a powerful impression upon my mind."

"Pray tell me all about it."

"Well, then, I thought that I was once more at home—at the old, old home, Lyddy, where I was so happy and innocent —I thought that I was wandering down the long dim avenues. Edgar was with me. He was urging his love-suit very earnestly, and I was yielding, when——"

Angeline broke off suddenly, and uttered a shriek, as she recoiled from the window.

"Again!"

"Good Heavens, Lina, how you frighten me! My poor child, you are ill. What has startled you?"

"Look, look!" cried Angeline, eagerly pointing from the window. "He is gone now; but did you not see him?"

"La, dear, of course; the tall gentleman, wrapped in a cloak. He has just turned the corner of the street. Do you know him?"

"It is Arthur Aubrey!"

"Impossible! Why does he not come to you?"

"He scorns me!—shuns me! I cannot blame him!"

"My dear Angeline, you are nervous and excited. I feel quite sure that you are mistaken. Poor Mr. Aubrey has fallen. Remember him tenderly, but don't brood too long and deeply over the irrevocable past. Surely, the future before you is brilliant enough? Look onward, then; you can afford to do so with hope and joy."

"You are very kind to me, Lyddy," replied the fair girl, embracing her companion. "No," she added, drawing a deep sigh, "the past, as you say, is irrevocable! Even if he lives, I cannot be his. I will not think of the past! Oh, I am wretched!—what then? There is a skeleton in every man's house, a hidden regret in most women's hearts; but need one parade the skeleton in the banquet-hall? No, no. Come, Lyddy, let us think only of the bright to-day, and leave yesterday to forgetfulness. Make haste, dear, or we shall have our gallants chafing at our delay. Cremorne! Yes, I shall enjoy myself! Mr. Humphrey Puffy is such a devil, and George Grant is lively and good-natured."

"That he is, Lina; waltzes like an angel."

CHAPTER III.

THE HOME OF POVERTY—A HARD LANDLORD—THE RETURN
OF THE LOST ONE—NEWS OF THE ESCAPED CONVICT—A
MERRY PARTY.

OUR scene changes to a wretched, half-furnished room in a mean house, situated in one of the back streets in Lambeth.

The persons present are an old man, seated in an arm-chair, his leg bandaged, and resting upon a low stool. His face is pale, and pinched with want, his brow is furrowed deeply with lines of care.

His wife, a tidy, matronly-looking woman, leans timidly on his shoulder, while in one corner cowers a lovely child—a girl about two years of age—and, with her large, thoughtful eyes dilated, and swimming with silent tears, watches a low-browed, ruffianly fellow, who, leaning against the door, is addressing the aged couple in a loud, hectoring tone.

"It's all werry well, Mr. Beamish; there's lors in this yere country, I s'pose?"

"Aye, and some on 'em are hard ones," replied the old man, dolefully shaking his hoary head.

"Hard or soft, there's lors, I say, made for rich and poor; and them as is made for the poor is oncommon good and char'table. Now, I s'pose you calls yerself a honest man, don't yer?"

"No one never said as I ever acted otherwise than straight-for'ard and seamanlike, Mr. Grip," replied the old man, softly; "but old age and accidents——"

"Is both pervided for. There's the workus and the 'firmary for them as is old and useless like yerself and Mrs. B."

"But any one with independent spirit——"

"Sperit? Oh, my stars! A purty thing to talk about 'sperit' and 'independence' when yer livin' on a poor man as 'as nothin' to depend upon but a chandler's shop and unfurnished lodgin's. Yer a robbin' me and my fam'ly, Mr. Beamish; and him as robs is a robber, that's what he is. You owes me three weeks' rent; do yer, or don't yer?"

"Aye, aye! we'll—we'll go, we'll go," returned the old man, mildly; "as you say, the laws have provided a home for us, we'll avail ourselves on it, even though they sep'rates man and wife there; won't we, lass?"

The old woman made no reply, but burst into tears.

"I hopes so, and when?" said the landlord.

"As soon as you like, Mr. Grip."

"Well, seein' as it's late, I'll give yer till to-morrow; there's a party a comin' in as I've let the room to, they comes in early to-morrow, so you must take yerselves off accordin'. But, come, I say, Mr. Beamish, how about my rent? I ain't agoin' to be swindled, I can tell yer."

"There's the poor bits of goods."

"Goods! ho, werry fine; what's the wuth of these yere sticks as ain't scarce fit for firewood? There agin's another proof of yer fine 'independence;' you've been and pawned or sold half on 'em, knowin' as you owed me more'n you could ever pay."

"'Twas for bread, Mr. Grip; only for bread!'

"Werry fine! you're to snatch my bread out of my mouth and fam'ly's, and I'm to be call'd hard-hearted acos I won't see them starve as belongs to my werry self. Then there's that noisy little young 'un as larfs and crows about the passages, a disturbin' of my children, who is she? You're pet, I s'pose? A fine thing for you to keep 'pets' at other people's expense! Some drab's brat, as you chooses to adopt, like gentry, is to be fed with my fam'ly's wittles, is to live on my rent, not to say nothin' about encouragin' wice. There's a noble institootion t'other side o' the water, namely, Mill-bank Penitentiary, as is the fit and proper place for the edi-cation of sich young infanticides. Well, what sticks there is I takes, and I shall see if I can't recover the back rent from the parish; so be up betimes, and be off afore noon, Mr. Beamish."

"Oh, Mr. Grip," cried the old dame, brokenly, "do have mercy on us! The doctor says that with his broken leg my husband must be kept very quiet; to move him would be sheer murder—he would die."

"Oh, lor, no, marm; nothin' o' that sort. Besides, we all has our time, and sixty's a good age. I've got my fam'ly to look to; char'ty begins at home, marm, and, as a fam'ly woman and a mother, you orter know that fac'."

"My boy, Shem, will come home soon, I know he will, and he will have money in plenty to save us. A little while, only be patient a little while."

"Fudge! where's the use of deceivin' yerself? Now you knows as you're not like a young creetur, a hopin' agen hope, you orter be resigned to anythink at your time o' life; there's been no end of gales, and storms, and whirlpools, and sich like; on'y the other day a hemigrant ship was lost. You says as you haven't had no letter from him for months; he's been wrecked and drownded; it's a bad job, in course, but it can't be helped, and where's the good o' shuttin' yer eyes to the truth? But, there, old folks is that obstinate as to aggrewate the saints!"

"Oh, my dear, brave boy. Spare me that, at least, Mr. Grip," sobbed the old dame; "do not try to make me believe that he is dead. Oh, no. God is so good, and my boy has been so blameless and kind. Oh, do not break my heart."

"Ah, well; I likes honesty—there's a deal of artfulness in this world."

"Quiet, Martha; don't let this skunk see thy tears," muttered the old man, his faint blue eyes flashing. "My heart! if I could have back but ten years out of the three score!"

"There's on'y one chance as I can see of that fellow's being alive," said Mr. Grip, who seemed to enjoy the pain he was inflicting on the defenceless old couple; "the younger branches of these days are gettin' too wide awake to stick to infirm parents which is a burden to 'em. It ain't quite onpossible as he's given ye the go-by and gone off with some young woman to Australia or New Zealand, or some sich parts; if so, you'll never hear no more on him, depend on it."

"Harkye, shipmate!" cried the old seaman, raising himself in his chair with impulsive strength, while his wife flew to his side in great alarm. "Harkye, here! I owe ye three weeks' rent. Do I deny the debt? You threaten me. Do I resent your insults? You say you will seize all the cargo—good, it's yours. You talk about mooring my old hulk into the parish dock. I don't mutiny. I'm disabled, dismasted, and hauls down my flag; but, dam'me, if you dare to hoist-to a lying yarn about my boy Shem, I'll make ye repent it."

When greatly excited, old Beamish, who had served on board a man-of-war, resumed a mode of speech which he had long discontinued on ordinary occasions.

Mr. Grip was rather startled at this display of indignation on the part of his victim; but seeing the old man was much exhausted by the effort, he bawled out,

"You imperant, disgustin' old blackguard! Who is there will make me repent a distressin' for my own rightful rights, and turning you ungrateful, ondeservin' set of beggarly paupers into the streets?"

"One!" said the old man, quietly, and in a faint voice, for he was breathless with exhaustion, "One who hath said 'Vengeance is mine,' and who is mightiest to 'avenge the poor.'"

"You wicked old heathen. Haven't I shown you a mercy as I ort to be punished for, a lettin' you occupy a respectable house for three weeks arter you took to a reg'lar swindlin' system of sellin' goods as is forfeit?"

"Avast, you miserable swab!" cried the old man, once more rousing into passion, "if I were but twice your age, aye, or if I numbered only half your years, I'd smash every bolt and timber in your pirate hulk. I'd cut ye out by the board!"

"Oh, Shem, be quiet, dear; you'll kill yourself; you must not talk so; you are wrong to give way. Don't let such a mean fellow excite your anger," cried the old dame, clinging to her husband, who was vainly struggling to rise from his chair.

"This is the rewards of havin' charitable feelin's!" cried Mr. Grip, raising his eyes with the air of a penitent. "Well, I repents my evil weakness."

"Sheer off, ye pirate shark, sheer off. To-morrow I'll clear out of these dirty waters; to-night leave me alone, for I'm old and can't stand your attack. Clear away, you paltry lubber; brush, and be hanged to ye!"

"And ye orders me out of my own rooms?"

"Oh, do go, Mr. Grip; come in the morning. Poor Shem will listen to you then; but he's so ill, the dreadful accident in the river has quite destroyed him; he will die, and you will be guilty of his murder!"

"This yere snivellin's all werry affectin', marm, but I beg as you'll notice as your husband, marm, has threatened if I don't leave my own apartments, I'm to be——"

"Kicked down the gangway!"

These words were growled in a deep ringing voice by a fine hale youth, who had entered the room.

Mr. Grip started, and turned as if he had heard the roar of a lion.

"Why, bless my soul, if it ain't young Mr. Shem in property persona!"

The old dame gave a wild cry, and bounding forward, threw herself into the young sailor's arms.

"Shem, my own dear, brave son!" murmured the enraptured mother, clinging fondly and appealingly to his broad, heaving breast.

"Shem!" shrieked the old man, almost hysterically, "come here, lad, come here, boy; let thy old father grapple ye. Don't be cruel, Shem; don't 'ee vanish like the flying Dutchman. Ho, ho! It's the boy! it *is* our Shem! there's no doubt on't, the Loard love ye and bless ye. I cried out for twenty years of hard toil some years back; I've got nerve; I've got all my hearty prime again, aye, and thou'rt a finer lad e'en than thy father was at thy age, and that's no small word. I want no more, Shem, no more; I can fold my hands, and am ready to depart in peace."

"Not yet, dear father; another kiss, mother. My jib! this is hearty; but this cussed land shark, has he insulted ye?"

"Lor' no, Mr. Shem, I'm truly glad to see ye, sir. You've growed amazin' and are lookin' extremely well; just a leetle, leetle, leetle difference about the—well, we won't mention it. I shall see ye in the mornin', I respex fam'ly feelin's, bein', as you may say, a childed man myself. Good night, Mr. Shem, be happy!"

Mr. Grip sneaked out of the room, and having smartly closed the door, sprang nimbly down the stairs, and barricaded himself in the back kitchen.

"Hulloa! this isn't all a-taunto; what's in the wind, mother?"

"Nothing, darling; we've been very much tried lately with father's accident and my own illness——"

"Hulloa, who's this?—who's this?" shouted young Shem, as the child, with a joyous scream, leaped into his arms; "what little mermaid's this? I've a dim remembrance of a certain little Elfie, but this isn't that fairy; no, no, this is a fine young woman I don't know; who is she?"

"Elfie, your little Elfie, brover Shem! Elfie so glad, so glad. Oh, you dear brover Shem."

And the little one nestled her golden head upon his shoulder.

"Can't be, can't be! but never mind, she looks like a good little girl, don't she? so I think she might give 'brover Shem' just one kiss, only one. Ah! that's just like Elfie; well, I suppose it's she."

The child threw her arms tightly round his neck, and kissed him with rapturous affection.

"And now, mother, what's the matter? You seem all astrand here. Where's the old tool chest, and the pictures, and the old clock and the curtains? What does this mean? What storm has made you lighten the ship? And father, too, lying there like a wreck on a reef; what storm has driven ye on such a barren island?"

"Why, my dear, in the first place, father met with a sad accident at the new works on the river; a heavy beam fell and crushed his leg; at the same time I was ill, and, excepting for the little help we could get from the parish, we had nothing to depend on for support."

"How was that, mother? Didn't you draw on the benefit club to which father subscribed so many years?"

"That purser swab, the secretary, Shem," said old Beamish "'bezzled all the money, and got clear off to Ameriky."

"What, that pious, preaching, sea-lawyer fellow that could use his jawing-tackle like any ship's chaplain?"

"Allus the wust, Shem," cried the old man, shaking his head; "but don't 'ee talk any more 'bout past troubles. I thank heaven that I see ye once again; and now, my boy, as ye've filled my heart with gladness, perhaps ye can charge my pipe with 'baccer. There's no sort o' privation so cruel as bein' 'prived of a quid or a pipe."

Shem loaded his father's pipe.

"And now, dad, you'll excuse me awhile. I'll go to market and see what's to be had in the way of provisions. And, mother, do ye hand down the black bottle. If I run astarn of the land-skipper there'll be a collision, that's all."

"Oh! my dear Shem, let us have no disturbance. The man was very hard on us, but his claim was just; and now you are restored to us, my dear boy, we cannot feel ill-will against any mortal creature. We are too happy to be resentful."

"Hush! Martha, my lass, I hear a step on the stairs; it's Hogan."

"I'm glad of it," cried Shem, with animation. "How have you found him?"

"Wonderful! allers grumbling, as usual; but so kind to us, though he's out of luck himself, poor chap."

"And how's Kitty O'Roone?" asked Shem, his cheek reddening, and his eyes glancing down.

His mother smiled, and his father, taking his pipe from his mouth, burst out right heartily,

"Your Molly has never proved false, she declares,
Since the last time we parted at Wapping Old Stairs."

"But I've a good thought, Shem; stow yourself away in the cupboard, we'll have a trick of sky-larking with Master Hogan."

As Shem, stepping into the cupboard, closed the door, Hogan entered the room.

"Humph! you seem to be enjoying yerself, Mr. Beamish. I'm glad to see you keeps up your sperits under all existin' circumstances."

"Never say die while there's a shot in the locker, Hogan; and if provisions runs short, crying won't fill the hold with anythin' better than salt water, so—

"'Ne'er heed the wind without boys,
Starboard here larboard there,
Turn yer quid, take a swear,
Yo!—yo!—yo!'"

"Well done, I'm sure! I'm glad to find you in sich a sanginary mood, for my news is cold enough."

"Then you didn't succeed with the master of the workhouse, I fear, Mr. Hogan?"

"No, marm, my most forcible argyments wouldn't prevail. He says he can't by no means raise the weekly 'lowance; howsomever, you can go into the 'ouse whenever you likes, and he sent this loaf, and as I came along I bought a steak, and some wegetables; sorry as it won't run to more."

"God bless you, Mr. Hogan, you have been a true friend to us," said Mrs. Beamish, with a grateful smile, the tears springing to her eyes.

"Never mention it, marm. Breakin' up your bit of a home will prove a sore trial; but life is made of little else but of troubles and trials, and the on'y comfort is, marm, as none on us can live for ever, and so our troubles must come to an end sooner or later."

"And how do you get on yourself, Hogan, my hearty?"

"Oh! I've got a berth. 'Tain't werry lucrative, but it will serve for a time, and I don't look for anythin' extra in this world. Life's all a 'ardship."

As Hogan made this remark, he heaved a heavy sigh, and, drawing from his pocket a little black bottle, set it on the table.

"I've brought ye a drop of summat short, to warm our hearts a bit."

"Ha, ha! that's cheery," cried old Beamish; "bring some glasses, Martha."

His wife obeyed this order.

As Hogan rose to take one, Shem glided from the cupboard, and, snatching up the bottle, carried it off into a dark corner.

"If the wust comes to the wust, which it allers does in this wale of tears, I'll take care of little Elfie," continued Hogan, who had not seen Shem ; "and now, marm, in spite of my sad conwictions, we'll join in drinking good health and a happy return to poor Mr. Shem, who, maybe, is now a tossin' on the briny hocean ; but—hillo ! why, where's the bottle ?"

Mr. Hogan stared with great amazement on the table from which the bottle had so suddenly disappeared.

"That was a cruel trick of some inwisible conjuror," laughed old Beamish.

"Why, the place must be haunted !"

"Shall I raise the ghost ?"

Shem darted from the corner and seized the hand of the astonished Hogan, who was quite bewildered by the surprisal.

"The ghost is the ghost of Shem, and he comes from the 'vasty deep,' as the poet says, to thank you with all his heart for your kindness to his bereaved parents."

"Well, I never did ! Why, Master Shem, if you're a ghost, you certainly seems one of the best of good sperrits—hale and hearty. Lor' bless me ! ain't I pleased ? Shake hands agen. Ah, you deep dog ! Shem's a lucky name. Shem was in the ark ; there's no drowndin' of Shem. Well, my boy, you've come at a crisis, and, certain'y, for once, we've got the right man at the right hour."

"Sit ye down, sit ye down," cried old Beamish, "and fill the grog kid while the mother gets supper ready. We knew ye'd return to make us happy, boy——

"'For, d'ye see, there's a cherub sits smiling aloft,
To take care of the life of poor Jack.'"

The happy party ranged themselves round the fire, on which the good dame had piled a huge heap of fuel, whereon to place the hissing frying-pan, from which rose a savory incense.

Shem took Elfie in his arms, who soon fell asleep in his embrace.

"And now, my dear," said Mrs. Beamish, to her son, "you must tell us all your adventures, that we may know why we never got any tidings of you for such a long and weary while."

"I'll spin the whole yarn, mother, when——"

"When Kitty comes," Hogan interrupted, quietly, "and that will be soon, for I met her this morning, and she told me she would be here to-night."

Shem did not make any answer, but turned his face towards the cheerful blaze.

There was a long pause.

A grave look sat on every face, for deep happiness is always grave.

Shem broke the silence.

"Father, what became of that convict chap—the fellow you picked up on the river—he had escaped from Millbank prison —what became of him ?"

"Can't tell, lad ; but he was a sad scapegrace. We had our hands full about that time. Elfie's poor mother died before you went away. Well, p'r'aps it was wrong on our part, most likes it were so, but we never found heart to turn him away, till, at last, he got tired of our dull company, and left us of his own accord. We heard a queer account of him arterwards, but one day he came back and offered us quite a little fortune in return for what he was pleased to call our disinterested kindness."

"But you refused to accept it ?"

"In course, Shem. I says to him, says I, 'Mr. Robinson——'"

"Was his name Robinson ?"

"I has my doubts on't, but that's what he called himself. 'Mr. Robinson,' says I, 'while you were our guest we made no mention to the cur'ous carcumstances which led to your coming amongst us ; we axed you no questions. To speak straight for'ard and above board, no offence bein' meant, I'm rayther afeared, Mr. Robinson, as we shirked a onpleasant dooty when we hid you from justice, and cheated the law. Now, take my adwice, and do you cheat the law too, but by keepin' out of its clutches, and actin' in a seaman-like manner ; but as for your money, it's quite out of the question that we could accept a penny on't.'"

"And you never found out what his real name was, and what crime he had committed to bring him into prison ?"

"'Twarn't our business, Shem," returned the old man, laying down his pipe with a thoughtful air. "But, somehow, one couldn't help liking the chap ; he made much of little Elfie, and though by his talk he seemed to be without honest principles, he had a gay, good-humoured manner with him, which was taking, like, you know. Then he dressed himself up in an old suit of clothes I gave him, and sneaked out at dark, and he came home in another dress. He was rigged out like a parson, in a suit of seedy black. Some days passed, and a man, a strange-looking customer, called, and asked for him by the name of—What was the name, lass ?"

"Renshaw."

"My jib ! what a strange thing."

"What is, dear ?"

"Why, mother, I heard from a man I met in the train that brought me from Portsmouth that a convict had made his escape from Millbank Gaol by the most ingenious means, and that he had tried to get off in a vessel outward bound, but that the detectives being close at his heels, he was forced to double, and make his way back to London, as it is supposed. A reward has been offered for his apprehension. He is an awful rascal, convicted of forgery and embezzlement of enormous sums."

"But are you sure it's the same man ?"

"Aye, aye, there can be no doubt of it. I saw the poster on a wall in Portsmouth ; his name is Richard Renshaw, and his description exactly answers the man's you rescued."

"Humph ! I'm 'fraid, Shem, we've been guilty of a werry mischievous act. I hope they won't make us suffer for it."

At this moment there was a tap at the door.

"It's Kitty !" cried Mrs. Beamish, with a joyful laugh, as she rose and opened the door.

A pretty girl, with charming features, and fine dark eyes, glided into the room.

Seeing Shem, who had turned away his head, she drew back.

"Sure, dear, I'm sorry to disturb ye wid your company," she said, shrinking away from the door, Mrs. Beamish following her, "but I thought I'd jist call and ax if the father was betther, and it's a trifle of mate and bread, and some candles and soap, sure, and other sich ateables, I've tied up in the bundle, and jist a twist of Cavendish to plase the owld gintleman."

Mrs. Beamish thanked the girl for her kindness, and requested her to come in, saying that a young gentleman visitor was impatient for an introduction.

In an instant the quick bright eyes of the pretty Irish girl scanned the mother's beaming face, and guessing the reason of her joyous looks, gave a faint scream, and bounding into the room sank in her lover's arms.

"Arrah ! dear Shem, but behave now ; sure ye're outrageous, and in the eyes of all the company !" she murmured, disengaging herself from his warm embrace with a rosy blush. "Be aisy, dear, and let us sit round the fire and hear how you were kilt at say, and left yer father and mother poor mournin' orphans for so many months, ye bad bhoy ! Ah, Mistress Bamish, wasn't it meself now that tould ye he'd come back agen ? Wasn't I sure of it, for all Mr. Hogan could say ? Och, but I knew sich mischavous fellows were sure to come back to taze one when laste expected and not wanted at all, at all !"

With gladdened hearts the merry party once more formed a ring round the fire, and Shem told an exciting story of disasters by land and sea, and showed his audience a heavy purse of prize money which he had carried by his gallant conduct during a fire on board his vessel.

In celebration of the happy re-union old Beamish, with rather questionable taste, insisted upon entertaining the company with his favourite song, "The Death of Nelson !"

CHAPTER IV.

A SCENE AT CREMORNE GARDENS.

CREMORNE was densely thronged.

The chief attraction, which drew such crowds of revellers, was the glorious autumn night, for the broad, bright glowing harvest moon, and the glittering stars in their silver bril-

THE MURDER AT CREMORNE..—*See page* 14.

liancy, eclipsed the milder golden glories of the illuminated gardens.

Drinking from foaming glasses of sparkling champagne, and diverting themselves by a smart exchange of jest and banter, Angeline Lablonde, Lydia St. Clare, and their lovers, with Mr. Humphrey Puffy, of whom mention has been made in a previous chapter, and who is now, for the first time, personally introduced to our readers, rested themselves after a long, exciting waltz.

They were seated round a little marbled table in a gaily-painted alcove near the orchestra.

Mr. Humphrey Puffy, though still in his youth, was enormously fat, very prim, and with a smooth rosy cheek that, as yet, could not boast those coveted adornments of manhood—whiskers. He was dressed in the height of the prevailing fashion, and sported some costly jewellery.

"It's envy, mere envy!" he exclaimed, in reply to his companions' chaff. "The grapes are sour; a fine portly figure, such as I am blessed with, always commands admiration."

"I'm blessed if it don't!" laughed Wenlock.

"You are, indeed, for I may say of you, Master Ned, in the words of your favourite poet, 'Yon Cassius has a lean and hungry look; he thinks too much; such men are dangerous.'"

Edgar Wenlock started, and turned rather pale.

"Even the great Cæsar admired such men as me," Mr.

No. 2.

Puffy rattled on, "for he says, mark you, 'Let me have men about me that are fat, sleek-headed men, and such as sleep of nights,' which you don't, Ned, or why did I find you this morning at daybreak pacing about your room like a white bear in a den? I say, with Cæsar, 'Would he were fatter?'"

"Bravo, Puffy, you know how to defend yourself. If you are the whale Ned is not the swordfish; his wit is not keen enough to pierce your 'stout' heart. But, hark, they are playing the Guards' waltz! Shall we dance, Lyddy?"

"Again, George," continued Mr. Puffy, not to be put down, "does my portly form prevent my dancing with the best of you? When Ned waltzes he reminds me of an ugly picture of the dance of skeletons; he hops round like a starved magpie, whilst I am whirling like a humming-top, or a——"

"Tumbler's tub."

"Well, I appeal to the ladies. To whom is Miss Lablonde engaged for the next dance?"

"To the most acceptable of partners, Mr. Puffy," said Angeline, taking his arm with a merry smile and roguish look at Edgar.

"Let us once more fill the flowing bowl, and then to mingle in the mazy dance," cried George Grant, pouring the frothing champagne into the glasses. "Here's a bumper to those we love best."

"And that's—ourselves," muttered a tall, slim fellow, dressed in a suit of seedy black, who came lithely gliding round a tree that shaded the alcove.

The young gallants each raised his glass.

"A health to the lovely beloved!"

"Permit me, gentlemen, to join you in that capital and appropriate toast," said the stranger, suddenly stepping from the shade. Making a sweeping bow, he raised the wine to his lips and quaffed it at a draught.

"What barefaced impertinence!" cried the young ladies.

"What do you mean, you rascal?" panted Mr. Puffy.

Edgar Wenlock had risen, his cigar fell from his quivering fingers on to Angeline's misty draperies, his eyes seemed starting from their sockets, his lips parted, and he vainly struggled to speak.

The stranger fixed his bright cold eye upon him, and smiled blandly as in recognition.

Edgar sank down on the seat faintly murmuring—

"It is RENSHAW!"

"Who are you, sir? On what grounds do you dare intrude in this abominable way?" cried George.

"My name is—hem!—Felix Alfonso Fitz-Altamont St. Julian, and I have the honour of being acquainted with Mr. Edgar Wenlock, whom I congratulate on his hearty and cheerful looks. Gad! my boy, no wonder you look happy in such charming company."

"By Jove! the acme of impudence is reached at last!" cried George, clenching his fist and reddening with passion.

"Edgar, at once disown this beggarly imposter!" cried Angeline, her eyes sparkling with indignation.

"Yes, yes, my darling; but patience one moment," stammered Edgar. "Come, sir, you claim acquaintance with me. I think—I believe I remember your face."

"I hope I am not forgotten; we have cause enough to remember each other, my dear Edgar—our boyhood's frank friendship—mutual, I am sure. Our former——"

"Come—come this way, fellow; I will hear what you have to say. Confound you, sir, don't you see that your presence is distasteful to——"

"Not to the dear ladies, I trust most humbly."

"Curse ye—this way!" gasped Edgar, wildly, quite losing his presence of mind, and dragging the stranger by the arm.

"Softly, softly; surely I am at your service without this violence; and it's too cruel to sever me from such charming society without even so much as honouring me by an intro——"

"Come away!" growled Edgar, savagely.

The two men disappeared behind a clump of trees.

His face showing ghastly white in the flooding moonlight, his hair strewing in the fresh breeze, his hands tightly clenched, Edgar stood beside the stranger.

"Villain!" he gasped.

"Well, partner!" responded the man, with perfect coolness. "Slap bang, here we are again!"

"I thought you were dead or as good—caged for life."

"The wish was father to the thought, Neddy. I was caged for life; but liking neither the life nor the cage I broke loose, and here I am. La-la! la-la-la-la! My! that's better—pretty waltz! How they improve in music! And for me this gay scene has the charm of comparative novelty; for though I've been at large for some time, I have thought proper to lie close. How refreshing is this cool air! how well it becomes the touches of sweet harmony!"

"You wretch! What is it that you want with me?"

"One of your fragrant cigars, Neddy. I know you always smoke the best; and a light, please?"

Edgar's cigar-case protruded from his breast-pocket.

The man coolly took it, opened it, and having selected a cigar which he lighted at a lamp, returned the case with a bow.

"Ah, that's convenient. Now we can talk. Sit down, Neddy. A luscious weed! Waiter!"

"Yes——sir!"

"What do you stare at, fellah? A slight abrasion of my elbow?—yes, sir. Look at it, sir; shows the spotless fine linen, don't it, sir? Very well, sir, trim your cussed gooseberry bushes in this garden, or I'll spoil your trade, sir, by a letter to the *Times*. Well, don't run away. Aw, Moselle! you keep Moselle?"

"Yes, sir; any kind o' wine, sir; but —"

"No, Hock!—yes, I'm fond of Hock! Bring a bottle of Hock. And, waiter, some oysters with pepper—wine. Look sharp!"

"Come, I say, sir, is this gammon, sir, or is it a boner fide horder?"

Mr. St. Julien had thrown himself upon a seat.

"Bless you, Neddy, be kind enough to kick that menial. I shall esteem it a favour," he said, in a languid tone of entreaty.

"Bring what he tells you," said Edgar, faintly.

"Yes, sir; oysters, sir; and Hock, sir? Two bottles? Yes sir."

And the man darted away on his mission.

Edgar fetched his hat.

He looked round for a moment to see what had become of his partners.

They were swaying round at the platform among the rest of the dancers.

With some sense of relief, he hastened to rejoin the exquisite St. Julian.

He stood for a few moments somberly regarding him.

"You're taking my measure, Neddy," said the man, still placidly puffing at his cigar. "Egad, it's time some one did, for my style of dress is shockingly antiquated; but the fashions change so fast, it's hard to keep in season."

"I was wondering how you got admission in that garb."

"Bless you, dear boy, my distinguished appearance gains me an entrée everywhere. It's the duke in disguise, you know; but wishing to escape being lionised by the populace, I came incog., and, to manage the thing more privately, I made entrance quietly."

"How?"

"Simply, dear boy, by clambering the wall when no one was looking."

Edgar chafed about for a few moments, then walking before his tormentor, he began in a low threatening tone,

"Hear me, *Richard Renshaw!*"

"What? Who? Richard what? Any relation of Richard Turpin?"

"Rogue enough to be first-cousin to Jack Sheppard, or Thurtle, or Greenacre, or any other thief and murderer."

"Is he, indeed? Have nothing to do with him. Dangerous character, I should think. Who is he, dear boy?"

"Fool!"

"Ah, that's worse still, dear Neddy; cut him dead. Never go partners with a fool. A rogue may serve your turn; but a fool! have nothing to do with him."

"I shall kill you!"

"After supper, Neddy; you look as if you could eat me, and I'm in poor condition, too—off my feed. Cuss that bandy-legged son of a sea cook! has he gone to Whitstable to fetch my oysters? I—I famish."

"Once more, hear me, Renshaw——"

"Who—is—that—man?"

"An idiot, who has thrown himself into my power; a viper, whom I will crush as I do this leaf under my foot; a wretch, whom I will denounce to that law which he has eluded only for a moment to render his punishment tenfold severer when he is once more caught and prisoned, as he shall be!"

"Phew! how hard you are upon the poor fellow. Egad! I think I remember him—a fellow who was your colleague, your trusting, self-sacrificing helpmate in a certain pleasant piece of business, involving forgery, burglary, and other vagaries, and who possesses damning proofs of your complicity from first to last; a fellow who still cleaves, in spite of every wrong, to his faith in you, and who, if you don't prove the blackest of ingrates, will get you out of your last and dreariest scrape, and crown your happiness by giving you the hand of the angelic Angeline."

"And you dare—you dare to mention *her* name? You dare to threaten her?"

"Threaten a lady? Fie! And yet I must plead guilty; I

hold out a most diabolic menace—I threaten to marry her to the meanest rogue alive."

"You—but it's useless to ban the devil. What influence do you hold over Angeline ?"

"The same, Neddy, dear, that I hold over you. I am master of your secret, eh ?"

"What follows ?"

"Nothing unpleasant while you act square. Now, I have *her* secret too."

"It's a lie !"

"Right ; never believe anything upon mere report. Wait and watch—a good motto. But you said just now that, at any cost to yourself, you would betray me. Do you stick to that ?"

"No, I spoke that in passion."

"I thought so. Well, Neddy, then I'll give you the key to her secret in a very few words, which you have but to breathe in her ear, and see if they don't act like a love-philtre. She'll marry you right off on the strength of them."

"Ha !"

"Here's the prescription—'*a packet of white rose-leaves !*'"

"You are insane."

"Perhaps so ! but try it—apply the dose, and tell me the result."

"White rose-leaves ? Pshaw ! And is there no more ?"

"Well, they were *dried*, so you may say, by way of amendment. 'Withered white rose-leaves !' Ha, ha ! quite poetic !"

"Pish ! this is all bosh. But if I use this charm, how must I follow it up ?"

"When she begins to faint, roll up your eyes, sigh, and look sagacious ; but resist all her entreaties to tell what you don't know."

"I have no faith in your recipe. Yet, come, Dick, we'll be friends for once ; let us discuss these rose-leaves."

"No, we'll first discuss the oysters—the snail-footed waiter shows up at last. I die with hunger. The rascal deserves to be broken on the wheel—that is, after he has brought a little salmon, and a salad. Pay him, dear Neddy."

Edgar Wenlock complied with his demand.

He tipped the waiter, who bowed, and walked off, casting behind him a furtive look of suspicion at the two men.

"Elysium !" murmured the adventurer, gazing round upon the enchanting scene ; "and a feast ambrosial ! Sit down, Neddy, and pour out the nectar."

"Hear me, Renshaw," said Edgar, gloomily, as he sat down at the opposite end of the table. "We are to work together."

"Aye, my brave boy, and pull together, for we row in the same boat. We'll cleave to each other like the Siamese twins. Fill up a bumper to your fairest Angeline, and another to our dear selves. Your health, my boy !"

"You want money, Renshaw ?"

"Rather ; and, as the saying is, 'to be poor, and to seem poor'—you know the rest."

"Yes, you must get yourself up in better style than that. Here, then ! you will find in this pocket-book some banknotes, but I insist that you leave me for the present. When," he added, with a deep sigh, "when shall I see you again ?"

"Henceforth, dear Neddy, I shall be your shadow."

"There is an old German legend of a man who sold his shadow to the devil !" muttered Edgar, grinding his teeth.

"And a famous story it is too ; but, alack, dear Neddy, I am not to be so disposed of. That sable gentleman don't buy up what he already looks upon as his own property. We have long since struck that bargain, and have taken the receipt ; besides, if you remember, the shadowless man found, to his cost, that the appendage he parted with so recklessly was of more value than he had supposed while he held it in possession, and were I gone from you, my friend and partner, you would soon have cause to grieve at the bereavement. I mean to make your fortune, Neddy, and my own at the same time ; so just a parting bumper, and then au revoir, till to-morow."

"Where shall we meet ?"

"At the old drum, the 'Blind Beggars,' that spot endeared to memory by so many pleasant associations ; that cheerful rendezvous, where once upon a time, we——"

"Hush ! Oh, patience ! patience ! This is more than I can bear ! No more of the past : not a word, Renshaw ! You shall not torture me by these dark allusions to the wretched past ! I am shaken in nerve, enfeebled in brain, heart-broken. I am whirled on and on to a gulf, down which I must plunge inevitably !"

Edgar leaned his face upon his hands, and groaned.

"Try these oysters ; they are delectable ! What ! man, 'ne'er pull your hat across your brows.' Uprouse ye, my merry man ! The music calls you. Go, mingle in the mazy dance, and kick away care with your 'light fantastics !' Defy fortune, or woo her as the lion woos his bride ! She loves the brave face ; faint heart never yet won her favours. Ta, ta ! Go, forget me !——till to-morrow, at seven in the evening, at the old retreat."

"Good night !" gasped Wenlock.

He found Angeline seated alone, near the platform.

George and Mr. Puffy, with Lydia and another young lady, were dancing gaily.

"Angeline, you think—of course, you must think—my conduct strange ; but that fellow, the somewhat disreputable-looking person who accosted me just now, rendered me an important service, and, for my life, I cannot roughly cast off any one to whom I have once been indebted for an act of kindness. He is wild, profligate, and always in some scrape."

"La ! my dear child, do you imagine that *I* could wish to censure you in the matter ?" returned Angeline, with a low, half-scornful laugh. "What are your friends to me ? Though, certainly, it is slightly annoying to be intruded upon by such a character ; in public, too. Who is he ?"

"A—Well, he was once a fellow-clerk of mine ; he disgraced himself by rushing into a mad career of thoughtless extravagance. He wants me to use my influence to get him another berth. But, hang the fellow ! he is such a dangerous protegé ; nevertheless, he is good-hearted."

"And he has a fine face, though with sinister expression. It is very strange, Edgar, but he reminds me of one whom I shall never see again ! But away with such a shameful fancy ! Can such a pitiful wretch bear the least resemblance to *him* ? Never ! never ! Come, let's dance, Edgar."

Soon they were whirling round in the throng.

Among the groups who were looking on at the circling crowd of dancers was a tall, but well-proportioned gentleman, dressed in a grey suit, and wearing a short grey cloak freely flowing from his shoulders, and a beaver hat slouched over his brows.

His dark eyes pierced the broad shadow thrown from his hat upon his pale face by the lights that glittered round the orchestra.

His form was very noble and statuesque, his features perfect, his hair dark and richly clustered ; he had a pointed beard and thick moustache.

He seemed unconscious of all surroundings, fixing his gaze upon Angeline as she swayed round with infinite grace and fay-like agility.

The music ceased.

Edgar led his fair partner from the platform.

Arm in arm they wandered down an illuminated avenue.

Angeline's dress touched the stranger as she passed.

He stepped back under the deep black shadows of a spreading tree.

Angeline was laughing gaily ; her lovely blue eyes sparkled, and a stream of merry prattle flowed from her mobile lips.

Edgar clasped her arm tightly to his side, and gazed beamingly upon her beautiful and changeful face.

The stranger stepped quickly after the pair as they strolled down the leafy arcade.

His brow bent in a dark frown, and his cheek waned ashy pale.

"No ; you are right in that," said Angeline. "There is nothing that can make life endurable but forgetfulness. Well, then, let us forget, and, as for this storm in a tea-cup—now, dear Edgar, why should you be jealous because I am admired ? Why can't you say with the chivalrous bard—

"'Yet no fear of rival know I,
Neither touch of jealous-y,
For, the more make love to thee,
I the more shall pleased be.'"

And her low, sweet laugh thrilled through the silence.

"Ah, if you were always as kind as now, Angeline."

"Then you would be wearied of me.

> "'She who would her lover keep,
> Must not let his passions sleep;
> Frequent frowns do more beguile
> Than the still, consenting smile.'"

You see I can justify what you ungraciously call my fickleness by chapter and verse?"

As Angeline spoke this in a bantering tone she turned and recoiled with a wild shriek.

Edgar, whose arm encircled her waist, looked up to discover the cause of her alarm.

Before him stood a tall and stately man; his cloak thrown back discovered his left arm rested in a sling; from beneath the deep shadow of his slouched hat his fine dark eyes were fixed in stern reproach upon the girl.

Before Wenlock could utter a word the stranger turned, and, passing behind one of the statues that sentineled the path, disappeared.

The girl, recovering herself, clasped her hands and smote her forehead.

Then she tried to break away from Edgar's embrace, but he clasped her close.

"Let me go," she whispered in a tone of intense agitation; "he has come! he has come! it is he! Ah, there is no error now! Arthur, pity me, pardon me!"

She struggled to free herself from Edgar's clasp.

"Is this, then, he of whom you spoke as of one dead? Is this your cold-hearted suitor who left you so long to your loneliness and despair, and did not send you so much as one cheering letter? who now steals on you like a vile spy and rewards your constancy by a sneer, and then leaves you abruptly without a word? Oh, Angeline, I have sacrificed all—all for you; will you prefer this worthless fellow to me, your own, your fervent lover? Stay! stay!"

The girl leaned upon his arm, trembling violently.

"Angeline, my best, my dearest, you relent."

"Ah, God!" muttered the girl, sinking on her knees and burying her face in her hands.

"No, no, no! it must not be! I cannot, I dare not!" she exclaimed, wildly wringing her hands. "Edgar," she added, with a gasp, "you have rightly guessed, Arthur Aubrey stood there a moment past; but—but I must not speak with him; I love him, Edgar, love him madly! But no, it is too late now. Oh, that I could die! I shrank from the dreadful deed; I had not nerve for a single act that would have spared me so much mortal agony. I cherished his memory so fondly, so freely and fearlessly, for I could not dream that he was living. Give me your arm, Edgar, and let us begone; I will keep my senses if I can, but they seem passing away. All darkness! all horror!"

"My own, my dear Angeline."

"Oh, do not hold me, do not caress me; one endearing word, and I—I shall go mad," cried the girl, wildly. "Yes, I must, I will, it can do no harm! One word, one little word; sad as it was it was not all my fault. Arthur, beloved, come to me once more; I will even live and endure all that I have incurred, but let me hear you speak once—only once!"

Angeline sobbed bitterly.

"Nay, dearest, if he can treat you so insultingly, scorn him for the slight. You are terribly agitated; let us leave this place; rest upon me. Think of your own preservation, for you will kill yourself if you give way to this violent excitement; think of me."

"Of you? Let me go, Edgar; I will not be stayed, I will speak to him at any risk. You, you! I respect you as my trusted, my kindest friend, Edgar; but never, never more speak one word to me of love. Promise that to me; say you will not torment me?"

"When I cease to love you, Angeline, I shall cease to exist."

The girl took his hands in her own and clutched them entreatingly.

Her blue eyes tear-brimming, were fixed upon his with a look of unutterable anguish.

"You have cause enough to despise me, Edgar. Hate me! hate me!"

"Angeline, this is shocking! What can be the cause of this strange emotion? What have you done that I should hate you?"

"Edgar, tell me——"

"My love!"

"Tell me truly, by all that you account holy, do you really, really love me as you say?"

"Can you doubt, Angeline?"

"Ah, but I pity you!"

"Pity is the fostering parent of love!"

"Out of the very selfishness of my despair I pity you. Now I know what it is to feel as you do, constant but hopeless. They say that love dies when hope perishes; they speak of a girl as 'heartless,' as an 'arrant flirt,' but what shallow stuff is this! Every woman loves her heart's elect; in an hour of madness she may sacrifice her lover to base motives of vanity or ambition, but she cannot hush the whisper in her breast, it sounds the louder in the hollow, void heart! But how is it that I can talk so calmly when every nerve seems fired? I tremble, but I can now command myself, thank heaven! Stay here, Edgar, I'll rejoin you presently; I will seek him and speak with him and then I will return to you."

"No, no; indeed you must not."

"If you attempt to prevent me I will never see you again."

"But you will return at once?"

"Yes; if he will forgive me! Yet I dare not tell him," murmured the girl, abstractedly. "I ought not, why should I render his life one horror as mine has been? Stay here, Edgar; do not follow me."

"But you will remember, Angeline?"

"Remember? what must I remember?" returned the girl, with flashing eyes.

She was now calm and self-possessed.

"Only how dearly I love you! that you are mine!"

"Miserable villain!" the girl exclaimed, with an air of infinite scorn, "have I not humbled myself to entreaty? Have I not implored you never again to breathe one word of love to me?"

"Never, Angeline?"

"Never, never, Edgar! Still, I am your friend, your sister. I am changed now; I repent my pride and levity, I have not sufficiently respected your kindness and affection towards one who is worthless; but if you press your hopeless suit again I will avoid you henceforth."

"I will not lose you, Angeline!"

"I am lost! lost indeed!"

"Angeline, I have sacrificed all for you!"

"Sacrifice? can you talk of sacrifice?" exclaimed the girl, fiercely, "but there, there! a man! a mere selfish man! Leave me for ever; we must part on the spot, Edgar; your selfishness forbids all further communion between us; henceforward we will be as strangers."

Angeline broke away from him.

Edgar rushed after her and seized her arm.

"It must be told! Angeline, you must, you shall be my wife!"

"What, do you threaten me? Now you assume your true colours. Let me go, pitiful, mean——. But, no, I will not upbraid you; I can spare no hate for any one, I keep it all for my wretched self; yet if you dare, Edgar Wenlock, again to insult me by your presence I will appeal to some chivalrous champion to teach you propriety by the help of a horsewhip."

"Take care, Angeline," hissed the lover, shuddering with passion, "I will not yield my claim to any rival!"

"Your claim?"

"Angeline, you drive me mad! I know not what I say. I do not wish to threaten you, but I swear by my love itself that I will not lose you. I could menace you with——"

"Gentle shepherd! do you mean to beat me?"

"You are in my power!"

"You are certainly stronger than I, but if you do not let go my hand I can call for protection against a brutal ruffian."

"I have your secret, woman. You are a murderess, and I will not pardon you!"

"A—a—*murderess!* Whom have I murdered?" gasped the girl, a smile so ghastly spreading over her pale face that she seemed about to fall dead at the feet of her accuser.

"Me! Since I have known you, since I have been tortured at your caprice, my life has been one long agonizing death."

"Yet you give pretty strong proofs of your vitality," retorted Angeline, with a scornful laugh, as she struggled to free herself from his grasp. "I warn you, for the last time, to release me, or I will shriek my loudest for assistance."

"One word ere we part, then. Give one backward glance at the past—cast one thought upon the dark path which you have trodden."

"Surely, my path has not been one of roses."

"No, Angeline, the roses—the *white rose-leaves have long whithered*, but the odour remains!"

The girl stood like a beautiful statue, as pale and as motionless, transfixed to the spot.

A look of intense horror and dismay brooded for a moment in her large blue eyes, strained and burning with deadly fire.

Then she sank down upon the grass and fainted.

Edgar rushed to her side with a cry of remorse and pity, and lifted her fair and frail form in his arms.

"Just Heaven! what dreadful mystery is this? I have killed her! Angeline, dearest, brightest Angeline, look up! speak to me!"

But she still remained sunk in a deep swoon.

A man darted from beneath the dark shadows of the trees.

He pushed Edgar aside, and lifted the girl on his right arm, for his left was disabled, and slung in a scarf.

Confused and amazed at the effect of his rashly-spoken words, Edgar gazed on distractedly but could not preserve his presence of mind sufficiently to offer any resistance.

The stranger tore open the girl's boddice, and removed her hat.

He chafed her cold hands, and mingling his glossy raven locks with her golden tresses, whispered soothingly in her ear.

She opened her eyes, and reclosed them with a shudder.

"Arthur," she moaned, "save me! save me!"

The stranger turned a stern look upon Edgar, who quailed like a craven.

"Sir, I know you," he said, coldly, "and I shall call you to account for this dastardly act."

"Indeed, you wrong me; I am bewildered; I am guiltless of any violence. It was a sudden attack of faintness to which Miss Lablonde is subjected," stammered Edgar, with burning cheek. "Miss Lablonde is betrothed to me."

The stranger regarded Wenlock with a scornful glance.

"It may be so," he said, in the same cold tone; "but it will be my first care to acquaint Miss Lablonde with the character of her intended husband, which is well known to me."

"Do you dare, sir, to impeach my character?"

"I do. You are Edgar Wenlock."

"And what cause have I to blush for my name?"

"A hardened scoundrel is insensible to shame, perhaps, but will shrink from punishment."

"Punishment?"

"Aye, sir, the punishment which follows detected crimes."

"Crimes?"

"Fraud and forgery are accounted such, and of both you have been guilty."

Edgar tried in vain to speak; he could not utter a word in self-defence, but staggered back as if struck by lightning.

The next moment the group was surrounded by a crowd, amongst whom were George Grant, Mr. Puffy, and Lydia St. Clare.

"Good heavens! what has happened, Edgar?" asked George.

"Angeline, my dearest girl, what is the cause of this terrible scene? How pale you are," cried Lydia, bounding to the side of her friend, who had now recovered her senses, and was leaning faintly upon the stranger's arm; "and your dress is disordered, your hair unbound, your cheeks stiff and stained with tears. Gracious powers, my poor girl, what has occurred?"

But Angeline made no reply.

She tried to disengage herself from Aubrey's embrace.

He gently detained her.

"My own, I have been cruel. Oh, forgive me," he murmured, with tenderness, enhanced by the deep tones of his manly voice. "You will not leave me, Angeline, now that at last we are re-united? Dearest, do not judge me harshly for not writing to you. I have been a prisoner, wounded, as you see—defeated. Yet I heard of you even in my far prison, for your fame reached me in my despair and loneliness, and I fondly prepared for you what I hoped a glad surprise."

Angeline flew wildly from him, and threw herself in Lydia's arms.

"Arthur!" she murmured, in tones of such exquisite anguish that the byestanders looked from her to the noble and handsome stranger with a thrill of genuine sympathy.

"Oh, Lydia, dear, dear friend, away!—take me away! These people—this is shameful! I am ill; take me away, dear, take me away!"

Her head drooped upon her friend's shoulder.

"Do not leave me so, Angeline; let me accompany you. I must not, cannot leave you thus."

"No, indeed, no; I implore you, Arthur, leave me now. To-morrow—to——"

Once more she became unconscious.

There were in the crowd many coarse faces, but no expression of levity or contempt marked one of them; the wail of the lovely girl, as she sank down crushed under the torture of some mysterious stroke of affliction, was so touching that the most callous heart was moved with sympathy.

Arthur Aubrey stood bewildered; George came to his side and questioned him as to the cause of the strange scene which had been enacted, while Lydia and Mr. Puffy bore the fainted girl through the crowd, who stood back respectfully to make way for them.

The stranger, with some agitation, but yet with dignity and self-possession, gave him a brief and vague explanation, and then raising his hat, bade him good-night.

George Grant, not seeing Edgar Wenlock at hand, started off in search of him.

Not finding him, he went straight to the gate of the gardens, where Mr. Puffy awaited him.

"Why, Puffy, where is Edgar?"

"Have you not found him, then?"

"No; I made sure he had returned to you. But what has become of the girls?"

"Poor Angeline recovered sufficiently to insist upon being left to return home with Lydia alone."

"Then they are gone?"

"Yes; I expected every moment to see you and Ned, and intended that we should call a cab, and together give chase to the fair fugitives, and you have not found him."

"It is most extraordinary! Are we awake, or is this some nightmare?"

"It is certainly passing strange, George; I have sad misgivings that a very dark solution might be found to this riddle. What can be the nature of Ned's connection with that felonious-looking customer who accosted us so impudently? Who is this gentlemanly stranger? He looks like an American. I should surmise that he is an ex-Confederate officer; and, wonder of all wonders, why and whither has Ned vanished? Besides, did you hear Angeline's muttered exclamation—*murderess?*"

"Pshaw! what a farce!"

"A farce, Georgy? Let us hope that it may not prove a tragedy. But we'll be off at once, for I am deeply concerned for poor Angeline."

CHAPTER V.

DARK DEEDS.

THE moon had become overclouded, and the wind was freshening, as Edgar emerged from the gardens and bent his steps down a long dark lane, which, skirting the gardens, runs along the side of the river.

He looked at the sleeping waters which mirrored calmly the heavy, dark shadows of the clouds, and the dull, silver span of the shaded moonbeams, the short, twinkling streaks of the lamps on the distant bridges and the opposite banks.

It was a wild and rugged spot.

A line of weird, ragged elms waved along the brink of the river, and soughed dismally in the night wind.

His brain afire, his heart frozen, Edgar stood staring vacantly before him.

A hand was laid on his shoulder.

Turning, he confronted Renshaw.

The face of the escaped convict was flushed with drink, his eyes glittered with strange brilliancy, his voice was husky, yet his tone and his step were firm, and he seemed fully possessed of his faculties.

"*He is coming this way*," muttered Renshaw. "Like you, he seeks this lonely spot to ruminate on the strange events of this night."

"But what brings you hither?"

"To see the fire-works—always seen to best advantage from a distance. But, Neddy, he's coming, I say; what do you mean to do, my boy?"

"You cursed spy, you dogged my steps, then. You saw, you heard all?"

"I'm your mentor, Neddy, and must keep at your elbow to render you my loving assistance in every ugly dilemma, and I must own you have got yourself into a precious scrape."

"Do you know, then, what passed between me and Angeline? Do you know with what I was charged to the teeth by that cursed rowdy?"

"I know all, my boy, so you will be spared the pain of unpleasant explanations. Once more I ask you, Neddy, what is your little game?"

"I should like to cut his throat!" was the savage reply.

"Nothing more natural than such a wish, dear boy; but, unfortunately, some of our most natural wishes are those it is most dangerous to gratify," returned Renshaw, with a leer; "the alternative—not pleasant, is it?"

He lifted the end of his black neckerchief, and dropped his head on one side, making a clucking sound in his throat.

Having performed this expressive piece of pantomime, he continued, with a dark, clouding brow, and suppressed savagery in his voice,

"Yet, Neddy, something must be done; we must come to some understanding with this infernal meddler; our mutual safety requires that."

"But how is it possible?"

"Humph!"

"I fear I have lost Angeline; I deserve to lose her; but I was distracted!"

"Ned!"

"Well?"

"Are you sure you don't know the chap?"

"I know him thus far; I recognise in him Arthur Aubrey, one of whom Angeline has spoken. He was formerly her accepted lover; she supposed that he had perished in the late American war; but it seems that she was in error. Perhaps he had been taken prisoner, and had no means of sending her word of his position; but how he can know anything of me I cannot imagine."

"Aubrey! Arthur Aubrey, eh? Why, Ned, if you remember, when you and I worked the oracle together at old Mammonson's bank, we had dealings with a certain Valentine Aubrey, a Georgian planter."

"Right, right; and his nephew, Arthur Aubrey, corresponded for him."

"And made some unpleasant discoveries in—— Hist!"

"He is coming now—right, left; 'tis the true soldier's step."

"Aye, Neddy, and maybe he is armed—a 'colt' or a bowie knife is as common in the fist of an American as a silk umbrella in the gloved hand of a London swell. Harkye, Ned; back here, under this tree. Good, the shadows envelope us, and so, my boy, prepare yourself for the worst, he may 'draw' upon you. Take this."

"What is it? What do you mean, Renshaw?"

"Twenty million curses! can't you drop my name? This is a life preserver that I wrested from Pounce the detective; use it if there's need, but, for your neck's sake, don't be hasty. I'll steal away behind that boat and you must beard the prowling thief, and make him give up his proofs, or swear not to peach on ye. I'm by ye, Ned; we're two to one, and

rather than I'd be caged again I'd murder ever spy and trap in the four quarters of *terra firma*. Look out, he approaches!"

Edgar thrust the weapon into his breast, and advanced to meet Aubrey, who, with his eyes fixed on the ground, and his grey cloak fluttering in the keen breeze, was slowly advancing.

Wenlock braced his nerves for the encounter.

"Stay, sir!" he cried fiercely. "An hour ago you dared, in the presence of a young lady, my affianced, to charge me with certain crimes. I forget the exact nature of your absurd charge. Was it burglary or murder?"

"Neither," replied the American, cooly. "I believe you quite incapable of committing the crimes you mention."

"You are very gracious, sir. I'm proud that you have so good an opinion of me."

"I do not think you have sufficient nerve to commit either burglary or murder. I charge you simply with forging cheques on my uncle, and embezzling your master's money."

"Well, sir, you shall answer for this!"

"I can answer any reasonable question, Mr. Wenlock, and any conscientious jury in Great Britain; but what is your business with me now?"

"My business, sir? Do you suppose that I will allow you to slander me without seeking to vindicate myself?"

"This is neither the time nor place for vindication. If I have charged you falsely, you have a remedy. You can, if you dare, appeal to the law."

"If I dare?"

"But you dare not, Mr. Wenlock, unfortunately for you. The proofs in my possession are quite conclusive."

After a struggle to speak, Edgar clutched the American's cloak.

"*We are alone!*" he gasped, savagely.

"And I am partly disabled. I did you wrong, Mr. Wenlock, when I thought you were incapable of committing murder. I see that desperation will make even a coward brave enough to assassinate an unarmed and wounded man. Take your fingers from my left arm; my wound is painful and my right hand is heavy."

"You say you have proofs—proofs—"

"That are sufficient to consign you to gaol for many years, Mr. Wenlock."

"Where are they?"

"Out of your reach; and you will do well to keep yourself out of mine, for I am loosing patience."

The American caught him by the collar, and with terrific force hurled him backwards against the trees.

Staggering to his feet, his eyes glaring into fury, Edgar made a wild rush upon the American.

There was a crash.

The stranger tottered giddily for a moment to raise up his right arm, and then fell flat on his face.

Horror-stricken at what he had done, Edgar glanced downwards.

His feet were dappled with blood.

He uttered a fearful cry, and leaping back, dropped the life preserver from his trembling hand.

Renshaw rushed out from his ambush, and throwing himself on his knees by the side of the American, dragged the body over.

The fine face, now deathly white and rigid, glared ghastly in the moonlight, for the moon now emerged from the black margin of a dark cloud, and flooded the spot with silvery brilliance.

The brow was battered in thick red gore, and the lower lip had fallen; the limbs lay limp and pulseless.

"Phew! A case, Ned."

"Is he dead? Am I a murderer?" panted the conscience-stricken wretch, leaning heavy against the trunk of a tree.

"Aye, Ned, you're 'worth your weight' now, lad; why the devil did you not heed my warning?"

"A murderer!—tried—hanged!—blood—blood! What have I done?"

He dashed himself frantically against a tree.

"Humph! there are but two ways by which I can get out of this precious mess. I had no hand in it. I may fetch the crushers, and give him up," said Renshaw, reflectively ; "but, then, the weapon was mine ; he can swear anything. And if I escaped the gallows, which is doubtful, I should be forced to serve out the rest of my natural life in restraint and punishment ; that is certain."

Wenlock flew upon his companion with the fury of a tiger.

"Do you threaten to inform against me, cursed tempter ? Who but you put the instrument of death into my hand ? Nothing can save me now ; yet there is but one witness, and he is a felon."

Wenlock, however, found himself no match for the convict, who dashed him off, and, snatching up the life-preserver, awaited a renewal of attack.

"I am beside myself ; I meant you no harm," Edgar muttered feebly. "If you mean to betray me, say so at once ; I am helpless—at your mercy, Renshaw."

"Your excitement is quite excusable under the awkward circumstances, Neddy," returned the other, with a ghastly grin. "Only, for your own sake, be more rational. If you kill me you kill your best friend, and leave yourself no chance of escape."

"What is to be done ?"

"We must get rid of the body at once—the river ! But no, we shall be seen, there is nothing at hand to sink it ; the river may be dragged ! I have it, Ned ! While searching for a convenient spot where I might clamber over into the gardens and escape the imposition of paying toll at the ordinary entrance, I got over this fence and entered a brambly enclosure, and well-nigh broke my neck by slipping across the brink of a deep fissure in the earth, at the bottom of which is a sluggish pool of ditch-water. I thought at the time what an excellent place it would be for such a purpose as the present. He's a stranger in England ; he may not be missed, and he certainly will not be found. We can make our escape to the West—to the land of the free, and this little catastrophe may have no unpleasant results. So quick, lad, lend a hand to heave him over the pale."

The villains raised the body, and pushed it over the fence.

They clambered over, and dragged it along through the dense bushes and briars.

In the midst of the little dingle they found a mass of furze and briar.

"Careful now, Ned, or you will slip as I did before. How now, fool ? why do you pause ?"

Dropping his hold of the body, Renshaw turned towards his companion.

(*To be continued.*)

TALES OF THE INVISIBLE WORLD.

THE WRITINGS OF AN ESTATE FOUND THROUGH THE APPEARANCE OF AN APPARITION.

THE subjoined tale, which is one of thrilling substance, forms but the first of a Series of Intensely Exciting Ghost Stories, Sensational Sketches, and other Interesting Extracts we intend to publish weekly with the "JOLLY DOGS OF LONDON," and which will be selected from a Bundle of Very Rare and Choice Old Manuscripts which, at Great Cost, have lately come into our possession, the perusal of which have entranced us with pleasure and surprise.

Although we cannot, as the conductor of this work, cordially give credence to the sketch appended, or vouch for its accuracy, we know full well that a taste for the Supernatural and Marvellous has not yet died out in the hearts of either the old or young of Merrie England, and that even now in many a pleasant nook of our happy land there yet remains a cosey and a welcome corner for one who can still tell an absorbing Ghost Story round the merry crackling fire, or beneath a shady grove.

In this spirit, and without endorsing what follows, we introduce our readers to the following quaint and startling narrative.

The following story is told by the late Rev. Dr. Scott, a man whose learning and piety were eminent, and whose judgment was known to be so good as not to be easily imposed upon.

The doctor was sitting alone by the fire, either in his study or his parlour, in Broad Street, where he lived, and reading a book, his door being shut fast and locked. He was well assured there was nobody in the room but himself, when accidently raising his head a little, he was exceedingly surprised to see, sitting in an elbow chair, at the other side of the fire-place, an ancient, grave gentleman, in a black velvet gown, a long wig, and looking with a pleasing countenance towards him, and who spoke thus,

"Be not afraid, or surprised, for I will do you no hurt, but am come upon a matter of great importance to an injured family, yet, knowing you to be a man of integrity, I have pitched upon you to do an act of great charity, as well as justice, and I can depend upon you for a faithful performance."

The doctor was not at first composed enough to receive the introduction of the business with a due attention, but seemed rather inclined to get out of the room from him if he could, and once or twice made some attempt to knock for some of the family to come up, at which the apparition seemed somewhat displeased.

But it seemed he need not, for, as the doctor said, he had no power to go out of the room if he had been next to the door, or to knock for help if any had been at hand.

But here the apparition, seeing the doctor still in confusion, desired him again to compose himself, for he would not do him the least injury, or offer anything to make him uneasy, but desired he would give him leave to deliver the business he came about, which, when he had heard, he said, perhaps he would see less cause to be surprised, or apprehensive, than he did now.

By this time, and by the calm way of discourse above mentioned, the doctor had recovered himself so much, though not with any kind of composure, as to be able to speak.

"In the name of God," says the doctor, "what art thou ?"

"I desire you will not be frightened," says the apparition to him again ; "I am a stranger to you, and if I tell you my name you do not know it, but you may do the business without inquiring."

The doctor continued still discomposed and uneasy, and said nothing for some time.

The apparition spoke again to him not to be surprised, and received only for answer,

"In the name of God, what art thou ?"

Upon this the spectre seemed displeased, as if the doctor had not treated him with sufficient respect, and expostulated a little with him, telling him he could have terrified him into compliance, but that he chose to come calmly and quietly to him, and used some other discourses, so civil and obliging, that by this time he began to be a little more familiar, and at length the doctor asked,

"What is it you would have with me ?"

At this the apparition, as if gratified with the question, began his story thus :—

"I once lived in the county of ———, where I left a very good estate, which my grandson enjoys at this time ; but he is sued for the possession by my two nephews, the sons of my younger brother."

Here he gave him his own name, the name of his younger brother, and the names of his two nephews ; but I do not choose to publish the names in this relation, nor might it be proper for many reasons.

Here the doctor interrupted, and asked him how long the grandson had been in possession of the estate, which he told him was — years, intimating that he had been so long dead.

Then he went on, and told him that his nephews would be too hard for his grandson in the suit, and would oust him of the mansion-house and estate, so that he would be in danger of being entirely ruined, and his family reduced.

Still the doctor could not see into the matter, or what he could do to help or remedy the evil that threatened the family, and therefore he asked him some questions, for now they began to be a little better acquainted than at first.

Says the doctor,

"And what am I able to do in it if the law be against him?"

"Why," says the spectre, "it is not that the nephews have any right, but the grand deed of settlement, being the conveyance of the inheritance, is lost, and, for want of the deed, they will not be able to make out their title to the estate."

"Well," says the doctor, "and still what can I do in the case?"

"Why," says the spectre, "if you will go down to my grandson's house, and take such persons with you as you can trust, I will give you such instructions as that you shall find out the deed of settlement, which is concealed in a place where I put it with my own hands, and where you shall direct my grandson to take it out in your presence."

"But why, then, do you not direct your grandson himself to do this?" says the doctor.

"Ask me not about that," says the apparition; "there are divers reasons, which you may know hereafter; I can depend upon your honesty in it, in the meantime; and I will so dispose matters, that you shall have your expenses paid you, and be handsomely allowed for your trouble."

After this discourse, and several other expostulations (for the doctor was not easily prevailed upon to go, till the spectre seemed to look angrily, and even to threaten him for refusing), he did at last promise to go.

Having obtained this promise of him, he told him he might let his grandson know that he had formerly conversed with his grandfather, but not to say how lately, or in what manner; and ask to see the house; and that in such an upper room or loft he should find a great deal of old lumber piled up, and that in such particular corner there was a certain old chest, with an old broken lock upon it, and a key in it, which could neither be turned in the lock nor pulled out of it.

Here he gave him a particular description of the chest, and of the outside, and lock, and the cover, and also of the inside, which no man could come at, or find out, unless the whole chest was pulled in pieces.

"In that chest," says he, "and in that place, lies the grand deed, or charter of the estate, which conveys the inheritance, and without which the family will be ruined and turned out of doors."

After this discourse, and the doctor promising to go down into the country to dispatch this important commission, the apparition, putting on a very pleasant aspect, thanked him, and disappeared.

After some days, and within the time limited by the proposal of the spectre, the doctor went down accordingly into ————shire, and finding the gentleman's house very readily by the directions, knocked at the door, and asked if he was at home, and after being told he was, and the servants telling their master it was a clergyman, the gentleman came to the door, and very courteously invited him in.

After the doctor had been there some time he observed that the gentleman received him with unexpected civility, though a stranger, and without business. They entered into many friendly discourses, and the doctor pretended to have heard much of the family (as indeed he had), and of his grandfather; "from whom, sir," he said, "I perceive the estate more immediately descended to yourself."

"Aye," says the gentleman, and shook his head, "my father died young, and my grandfather has left things so confused that, for one principal writing, which is not yet come to hand, I have met with a great deal of trouble from a couple of cousins, my grandfather's brother's children, who have put me to a great charge about it. Upon this the doctor began to be a little inquisitive.

"I hope, sir," says the doctor, "you have got over all this?"

"No, truly," says the gentleman, "if I may be so free as to speak my mind, I think I shall never get quite over it, unless we can find the old deed, which, however, I hope we shall find, for I intend to make a general search after it."

"I wish, with all my heart, you may find it, sir," says the doctor.

"I doubt not but I shall," adds the gentleman, "for I had a dream concerning it last night."

"A dream about the writing?" says the doctor. "Then I hope it was that you shall find it."

"Why," says the gentleman, "I will tell you. I dreamed that a strange gentleman came to me, whom I had never seen in my life, and helped me to look for it. I do not know but you may be the man."

"I should be very glad to be the man, I assure you," says the doctor.

"Nay," says the gentleman, "if you should think proper, I am certain you may be the man to help me to look for it."

"Aye," says the doctor, "I may help you to look for it. Pray, when do you intend to make a search?"

"I had appointed to do it to-morrow," says the gentleman.

"But," says the doctor, "in what manner do you intend to search?"

"Why," replied the gentleman, "it is the opinion of us all that my grandfather was so very much concerned about preserving this writing, and had so great a jealousy that somebody about him would rob him of it if they could, that he hid it in some very secret place; but I am resolved I will find it, if I am obliged to pull half the house down."

"Truly," says the doctor, "he may have hid it in such a manner as to oblige you to pull the house down before you find it, and perhaps not even then, for I have known such things utterly lost, notwithstanding all the care imaginable used to preserve them."

"If it was made of anything fire could not destroy," says the gentleman, "I would burn the house down but I would find it."

"I suppose you have searched all the old gentleman's chests and trunks, and coffers, over and over?" says the doctor.

"Aye," says the gentleman, "and turned them all inside out, and there they all lie in a heap up in a great loft or garret with nothing in them; nay, we knocked three or four of them in pieces to search for private drawers, and I then burnt them for anger, though they were fine cypress chests, and cost a deal of money when they were in fashion."

"I am sorry you burnt them," says the doctor.

"Nay," says the gentleman, "I did not burn a scrap of them till they were all split to pieces; and it was not possible anything could be there."

This made the doctor a little easy, for he began to be surprised when he told him he had split some of them and burnt them.

"Well, sir," says the doctor, "if I can do you any service in your search I will come and see you again to-morrow, and attend you in your search with my good wishes."

"Nay," says the gentleman, "I do not design to part with you; but since you are so kind as to offer me your help, you shall stay all night with me, and be at the first of it."

The doctor had now gained his point so far as to make himself acquainted and desirable in the house, and to have a kind of intimacy, so that though he made as if he would go, he did not want much entreaty to make him stay, so he consented to lie in the house all night.

A little before night the gentleman asked him to take a walk in the park; but he put it off with a jest.

"I had rather, sir," said he, smiling, "you would let me see this fine old mansion-house that is to be demolished to-morrow; methinks I would fain see the house once before you pull it down."

"With all my heart," says the gentleman.

So he took him immediately up stairs, showed him the best apartments, and all his fine furniture and pictures, and coming to the head of the great staircase, where they came up, offered to go down again.

"But, sir," says the doctor, "may we not go a little higher?"

"There is nothing above," says the gentleman, "but garrets, an old loft full of rubbish, and a place to go out upon the turret and clock-house."

"But, sir, I should be glad to see it all now we are about it," says the doctor. "I should like to see the old lofty towers and turrets, the magnificence of our ancestors, though they are out of fashion now. Pray let me see all now we are about it."

"Why, it will tire you?" said the gentleman.

"No, no," says the doctor, "if it do not tire you who have seen it so often it will not tire me, I assure you. Pray let us go up."

So away goes the gentleman and the doctor after him.

After they had rambled over the wild part of an old house, which I need not describe, he passed by a great room, the door of which was opened, and in it a great deal of old lumber.

"Pray, what place is this?" says the doctor, looking in at the door, but not offering to go in.

"Oh, that is the room," says the gentleman, "that I told you of, where all the old rubbish lies—the chests, the coffers, and the trunks. Look you there; see how they are piled one upon the other."

With this the doctor goes in and looks about him. He had not been in the room two minutes before he found everything just as the spectre at London had described, went directly to the pile he had been told of, and cast his eye upon the chest, with the old rusty lock upon it, and the key in it, which would neither turn round nor come out.

"Upon my word, sir," says the doctor, "you have taken pains enough if you have rummaged all these drawers, and chests, and coffers, and everything that may have been in them."

"Indeed, sir," says the gentleman, "I have emptied every one of them myself, and looked over all the old musty writings, one by one, with some help, indeed, but they every one passed through my own hands and under my own eyes."

(To be continued.)

THE JOLLY DOGS OF LONDON.

WENLOCK'S ALARM AT RENSHAW'S APPEARANCE.—*See No.* 10.

CHAPTER V—*(continued)*.

' Overcome by horror at his situation, the assassin had fallen to the ground senseless.

"Humph! perhaps it is well. I can leave him here and make my lucky," muttered the convict; "but first I will ransack the pockets of this luckless foreigner; perhaps I may find something that may feather my wings for flight, and recompense me for this night's work."

The broken moonbeams filtered down through the dense dark foliage of the high trees upon a packet of letters and bank notes, which the convict was shuffling in his trembling hands.

* * * * * *

Edgar Wenlock feebly unclosed his eyes.

He gazed upwards to behold the broad moon struggling amid the dark towering clouds, to hear the dismal ripple of the waters rushing under the gunwale of a boat, across the thwarts of which he was lying passively. Renshaw was tugging at the oars; a large bundle lay beside him, and he did not seem to notice that his companion showed signs of returning consciousness.

They were now in the middle of the dark river.

No. 3.

Renshaw drew in the oars.

The boat drifted.

He rose, and bending over Wenlock, passed his arms under his shoulders, and dragged him to the side.

The boat rocked fearfully.

Edgar leaped up, and caught him by the throat.

"Ha! treacherous villain! Do you mean to murder me?"

"I—I thought you were dead, Neddy," muttered the other, staggering back; "but lie still, or you'll force me to try which scull is the hardest."

So saying he raised the oar.

"Lie still! you are mine, now, Ned, and henceforth we sink or swim together!"

CHAPTER VI.

RICHARD RENSHAW PLAYS A HIGH GAME FOR A HEAVY STAKE.

RICHARD RENSHAW stood before the door of a tall, dingy house just as the pale golden sunbeams of early morning began to shine with a watery glare upon the bleak, dead streets.

NOTICE.—*With No.* 1 *was presented No.* 2 *and a large Engraving representing the Jolly Dog under various phases. Another Engraving is in course of preparation, and will be presented with an early Number.*

He had come home by dark and devious ways, through low and filthy neighbourhoods.

On his way he had met few passengers ; a solitary policeman, or a labourer starting early to his daily labour.

All was profoundly still.

He dropped upon the step the heavy bundle he carried in his hands.

His face was livid white, his eyes red and sunken, his lips parched and quivering.

With palsied fingers he drew the latch-key from his pocket.

Several moments elapsed before he could effect an entrance into that silent house.

The lock was out of order.

After every vain attempt to fit the ill-made key into the clumsy and disordered lock, he cast a hurried glance up and down the street, muttering an imprecation.

At last, losing his temper, he dashed the key violently down upon the step.

Greatly alarmed at his own act of indiscretion, he looked around him quickly to see if any one had been disturbed by the noise.

All was quiet.

He glanced up the side of the house.

The dirty blinds, or rags which served as curtains, remained unstirred.

Finally he took out a pen-knife, and, inserting the blade between the lock and the door-post, thrust the lock back into its case.

The door waved open with a creaking whine.

He entered the passage, and closed the door softly.

Then, listening breathlessly at the parlour-door, he waited some moments.

No one had been aroused by the slight noise he had made in entering.

The Dutch clock within kept up its ceaseless "tick-tack," and the deep breathing of the sleepers within was the only other sound he heard.

He quietly slipped off his shoes, and, holding them in his left hand while he carried the bundle under his arm, he softly crept up the dark, dusty staircases.

At the landing of each flight he paused to listen.

Nothing but the sounds of clocks ticking and of people breathing deeply in their sleep broke the silence.

He reached the garret in which he lodged ; as he quietly stepped in, a clock in a room below struck four.

He threw down the bundle, after locking himself in, and then flung himself on his hard truckle bed.

He lay for some time quite motionless, and seemingly lost in gloomy thought.

As at length he wearily raised his hand to his head, he gave a sudden and violent start, and leaped up with a ghastly look.

Something red had passed close to his eyes as he raised his arm to his head.

He stared aghast at his sleeve and wristband.

They were stained crimson with blood.

He eagerly scanned the pillow and the coverlet.

There was no tell-tale stain upon them, for the blood on his clothes was dried.

He rose from the bed shudderingly.

He opened the window as if to purify the room of some taint in the air.

For a moment he glanced out over the forest of smokeless chimnies and down upon the dirty stone dens of yards at the back of the densely-packed houses.

Cocks were crowing, and a flight of pigeons wheeled past his window.

They seemed to make a wide circle, as if to avoid approaching the house polluted by the presence of an accomplice in the dread crime of murder ; and a frightened mouse fled from beneath the bed, and scampered not towards his hole in the dark corner as was his wont, but towards the door ; these little tokens, in themselves insignificant, had a terrible significance for that lone watcher as he sat in his squalid garret eyeing the pale yellow sheen of the rising day with a feeling of intense relief at beholding the returning light.

As he thought of the horrible events of the past night, the anguish of the beautiful girl, the frenzied passion of her slighted lover, the dark, rugged, elm-bordered lane, the quick quarrel, and the sudden, but fatal blow, the hiding of the corpse, the dreary passage of the river, the abject fear and impotent raving of the horror-stricken murderer, he hid his face in his hands, and quailed with horror.

" It was not my deed ; if my hands are stained it is not with blood of my shedding," he muttered. " True I put the fatal weapon into the murderer's hands ; but only that he might —that—well, at the worst, I did not anticipate the dread result of my act. No, no ; I am not the murderer ; yet if I had betrayed him, if I had gripped him by the throat and dragged him to justice, what would have been the good to myself ? I should have at once been fastened on by my gaolers and should have been hurried back to the cell, and the whip and the chain—for life ! Besides, his secret is a secret still to all but himself and me ; his guilt unsuspected, he is held guiltless ; mine proved, I am known to be guilty. His word is better than mine. I elude justice. I defy it as the wolf turns at bay on the hunter. I have suffered enough for my sins. I will not be hanged for a crime of which I am innocent. Oh, conscience ! quiet, quiet ! Why should you tear my heart when I see so many silken rogues ? Merchants and tradesmen, who are but licensed swindlers ; task-masters, who coin gold from the heart's blood of their operatives ; men of genius, who prostitute their rich gifts in the course of vice and licentiousness. Yet these are respectable citizens—they go down to the grave in peace and are honoured with fine elegies. I am a villain ; my heart will not be silent, it is ever reproaching me ; yet I am but one small luckless villain among a thousand big and lucky ones. The hangman shall hang me. I will not hang myself. Though the hunter tracks me down at last, I will play him many a fox-trick before he catch me. This American is dead. I did not kill him ; but I will profit by his murder ; out of evil cometh good, and *my good* is good to *me*. If the king is dead long live the king ! Arthur Aubrey is no more ; I will be Arthur Aubrey !"

He rose and began to light the fire.

" Yes, that foul job over, I shall breathe more freely. ' A little water' does very well, but a little fire is better !"

When the flitting blaze began to shoot up through the coals and wood, Renshaw placed a kettle on the fire, and seating himself before the hearth, ruminated long and profoundly.

He rose again and drew the bundle to the side of his chair.

Then from his pockets he took a pocket-book, a heavy purse, a gold watch and chain, a ring, and a locket, a bunch of keys, and a small paper packet ; these he placed on the table at his side.

He then pulled out another pocket-book, old and soiled, his own, which he placed on the mantle-piece.

Taking up his coat, he looked at it for a moment with paling cheek.

He then cut off the blood-stained sleeve, and ripping it into shreds with his pocket knife, burnt the pieces one by one.

This done, he demolished the rest of the garment and burnt it in the same manner.

This done, he drew from the bundle various articles of wearing apparel.

First a furred cloak, which he examined carefully.

" It has not reached that," he gasped.

He threw the garment aside.

He next drew out a suit of clothes, which he also carefully examined.

There was a slight stain of blood on the waistcoat.

He laid this aside, and threw the other clothes on to the bed.

He next examined a long silken sash which was tinged in one place with blood.

" I must not burn this," he said, inwardly, " his wounded arm was bandaged in this, and the blood spots on the waistcoat tally with this stain. I'll spare the waistcoat too, for my disguise would not be complete without it.''

Upon further reflection, however, he thought he would make some attempt to wash out the stain on the waistcoat.

He laid it in the hand-basin and poured scalding hot water from the kettle upon it, and rubbed out the mark.

He shuddered as he saw the pinky tinge suffuse the water.

He then threw the water from the window, and carefully wiped out the smear at the bottom of the basin with a rag which he afterwards burned.

He gave a sigh of relief, and once more walked to the window.

" I was a fool after all for not throwing the body into the Thames," he muttered, half aloud, " I must see to it."

He now seated himself at the table, and drew an inkstand and writing case towards him.

" Stay ! I have some foreign note paper, it will do better," he thought, opening the case and producing some sheets of paper of fine texture, which he carefully spread before him.

He took from Aubrey's pocket-book a number of letters and papers which he read attentively. Selecting one, he placed it by the side of the paper as a guide to the style of writing in which he was to forge the letter he proposed to write.

After several unsatisfactory attempts he accomplished the work, and neatly folding it, he slipped it into an envelope which he thus addressed :—

" MISS LABLONDE,
"5, Eden Square,
" New Stucco Town, N."

Again he thoughtfully perused the letters and papers.

" It will be playing a high game ! But, then, it is for a heavy stake, and any peril will not be so very much increased by the assumption of his character, for the poor devil seems to have been a sort of Lara or Childe Harold, to judge from his letters. Where shall I post this billet-doux ? Somewhere near the London Docks. It will give a sort of corroboration to my expressed determination of leaving this 'tight little island' for ever. Humph ! that's decided. But now comes the most delicate part of the business ; to carry out properly my little 'role' in this melo-drama, my 'get up' must be perfect. Let me see, I have here a packet of photographs. Then these are the Confederate celebrities, Lee, Stonewall Jackson, and the rest ; and here are more uniforms ; faith ! quite a parade. And these—ha, these are his friends, and each has the autograph of the original attached ; these may prove invaluable by-and-bye, at least, I shall know my friends. Stay, here is his own portrait—*my own* portrait, I should say. Let me see what sort of figure I shall cut as the romantic patriot and refugee."

Renshaw set the swing glass on the table and then bringing a box from the cupboard, took out a number of wigs of various shades, white, grey, red, black, and brown, with false whiskers and moustachios to match.

The small packet which was mentioned in the list of articles which he had laid on the table contained a lock of black hair which he had cut from Aubrey's head.

He shuddered as the rich glossy curl writhed round his fingers.

Applying it to one cut from his own head he found that the two locks were identical in colour.

" I shall not want a wig then," said he, with a grim smile. " It is strange that this man resembles me so closely ; they say I was a twin-child, and my brother died. I will try this cavalier and this imperial. So."

He put on the moustache and pointed beard.

He started at the exact counterpart he now appeared to the figure in the photograph beside him.

" That will do," he said, contemplating himself with satisfaction.

He dressed himself in the clothes of the unfortunate American, attached the watch to his waistcoat button, put the rings on his fingers, placed the pocket-book, purse, and keys, into his pocket, then packing all his own property in a small carpet-bag, he threw the cloak across his arm, and quietly creeping down stairs stole out into the street.

The clock struck eight as he reached a wide and busy thoroughfare.

He called a cab and bade the man drive to St. Katherine's Docks.

CHAPTER VII.

EDGAR WENLOCK AT RENSHAW'S LODGINGS.

ABOUT half an hour after the departure of Richard Renshaw from his lodgings, Edgar Wenlock, pale and agitated, arrived at the house.

He knocked loudly at the door.

No one answered his summons.

He waited a long while, beating his foot impatiently on the step ; still no one came.

Stepping backwards he glanced at the house.

The blinds were still closely drawn.

" He said he should go straight home to his lodgings. He told me so last night after—— Ugh ! not even in thought ! I will sear it out of my brain with seething hot iron, but I'll forget it ! Down, down, down !"

He knocks loudly at the door.

The kitchen window was pushed up, and a dirty-faced boy thrust out his ugly head and lifted his squinting eyes towards the early and imperious visitor knocking so fiercely.

" Vell, I *am* blowed ! is it a fire, or a murder, or vhat is it ?"

" A murd——. No, no, my boy, no," muttered Edgar Wenlock, gripping hold of the iron railings.

" Vhat's the row, my covey, is yer ill ? 'cos, if yer is, this ain't the doctor's ; lives down t'other street along agen the chandler's, with a blood-red lamp over the door. What *is* the row ? Been and goned and cut somebody's throat, or on'y pisoned yerself and want to find a hexekitor ; you can app'int me. But, I say, vhat's up ?"

" No, boy, I want——"

" Oh, you're a 'tective, and wants some of our lodgers, p'raps ? Well, this 'ere's a respectible 'ouse, and father don't screen nobody ; says as I eats too much, and's agoin' to send even me to the 'formatory. You shall have him, sir ; who's yer man ? There's Black Bob here, and Hedge-penny Jack, and little Tidy as smashed the Brummy benders."

A fierce, growling oath sounded from within the room, and, with a crash, the boy was hurled backwards from the window.

A hideous-looking rough now peered out.

" What's yer bisness, guv'nor ?" he asked.

" Oh, nothing more than that I want to speak with one of your lodgers."

" One on 'em ? Oh, lors ! do yer s'pose I can afford to keep this yere great house without makin' the most of my rooms ? There's about a dozen in each crib ; which do yer want ?"

" He has a small room to himself."

" P'raps so ; but what's his name, guv'nor ?"

" Richard Rensh——"

" Wrench ! there's no ' Wrenches ' here, nor no ' wenches ' neither. Have you got a warrant ?"

" A warrant, what for ?"

" Oh, I sees ; you're a trac' distrib'ter. Clear out, it's no go ; we're all the right sort here, and never listens to no sich fallaral, 'special' at these early times in the mornin'."

" The man's name is Robinson."

" Oh, Robinson ! vell then, if yer knock loud enough, yer may wake him, if so be as he's at home at all. Ah ! he lodges in the second back attic ; knock six, but look out if yer knocks more nor less, and brings down some other party, 'cos some of my folks isn't over nice, and yer may get yer 'ead punched, that's all."

The window slammed down.

Edgar Wenlock gave six distinct knocks at the door.

No one came.

Again he knocked impatiently.

After awhile a shambling step was heard in the passage.

The door was half opened and a woman peered out.

She was a dirty, wretched-looking creature, but half-dressed and more than half asleep.

" I'm sure you're a nice 'un, ain't yer ?" she said, yawning. " What do yer want a disturbin' respectable married women out of their beds at these unheard on hours in the mornin' ?"

" It's nine o' clock, ma'am."

" Is't now ? Werry fine for sich a Lord Much-and-Mighty as hain't got to do his dirty work at night, I spo'se, but can afford to go to his feather-bed when the fowls roostes. Who do yer wan't ?"

"Does Mr.—hem—Mr. Robinson live here ?" asked a voice close by Edgar's ear.

He started convulsively, as if he had felt a policeman's sudden grasp laid on his shoulder.

Turning quickly he beheld a thin, keen-eyed, white-faced fellow, dressed in a shabby suit of black, standing by his elbow.

"Ho, ho ! this is 'most too good, here's another wisitor. I s'pose Mr. What's-his-name, Esquire, is a goin' to hold a lev-*ee*."

"My good woman, my business is urgent," said Edgar, quickly. "I am sorry to have disturbed you, I'm sure. You won't refuse to accept this trifle for the trouble I've given you ?"

He held out a half-sovereign.

"Won't I ?" returned the lady, rather ungraciously, yet snatching it with eagerness. "P'raps you wants to give me a little more trouble ? Most likes it's smash, and you wants to get me in a line."

She bit the coin.

"But s'welp me ! no, it's a good 'un ! Oh, sir, I begs yer honour's most partickler humble pardon ; Mr.—who did ye say, sir ?"

"Robinson."

"Oh, yes ; the young man as lives in the fourth—no, the fifth, back attic. This way, gents, if yer please ; I'll lead yer hup myself. But, no, Bob might take it crusty ; he never likes no interferin' in other people's little games. Right up, sir—up top ; turn on the left, and knock at all the doors till yer comes to the right 'un. But mind the stairs ; they're awful rickety. The parish inspector comes and looks at 'em now and agin, but when he's relieved his mind vith a grunt away he goes for a twelvemonth, and there won't be nothin' done till the house crushes down on us, and then there'll be a blowin' up in the newspapers, and arter that it'll settle down quiet agin, same as ever. Take care, sir !"

Edgar Wenlock rushed up the stairs, the other visitor following close at his heels.

A savage ruffian, with one of his eyes blackened, and a hideous scar on his upper lip, stepped out of the room.

He clutched the woman's wrist.

She opened her hand, and showed him the gold coin.

"Ah ! then he's a gilt cove. Here's a go ! Oh ! I'll ease my nob of some of his shiners. He's over-weighted, it seems," growled the fellow.

The woman clung to the ruffian's arm, for with cat-like step he began to mount the stairs.

"No, no, Bob, you shan't," she whispered hoarsely. "The feller acted square, and came down well. He's paid his footin', and must go free."

The ruffian replied with an awful oath, and tried to shake her off.

"Hulloa, there ! lie down, Bob, will yer ?" cried the landlord, looking over the rail of the stairs which descended into the earth to the kitchen below. "Bet's right ; the cove has paid his footin', and if you tries it on, my kiddy, I'll just call in the crushers, and give you over."

Black Bob shook his fist at the landlord, and growling another foul oath, blundered back into his den.

As soon as he had shut the door, a woman's screams were heard.

Bob was punishing Bet for her interference.

No one interposed to save the poor woman from his brutal violence—why should they ? People ought to mind their own business, and it is the worst policy to interfere in family rows.

"Take care of number one !" It was the sum-total of the morality of the tenants of this den of sin and misery.

Meanwhile, Renshaw's visitors were knocking at the door of his vacant garret.

Getting no answer, they opened the door, which was not fastened, and entered the room.

"He is not here," said Edgar, in a chagrined tone, as he glanced round the room.

"I thought as much," rejoined the other. "Was your business very particular, sir ?"

"No, not very," said Edgar ; "still, I am vexed at not finding him."

"Ha ! he slept here last night, or, rather, this morning," said the man. "It was this morning that he returned."

"How do you know that ?" Wenlock asked, sharply.

"Oh, it's plain enough ; the coverlet is not turned back—he lay on the outside of the bed. And see, he has raked out the fire ; and the window is open. Haugh ! what a smell of fire ! He's been burning something."

"I smell nothing. You're mistaken," gasped Wenlock.

"*Me* mistaken ? Catch me mistaken."

"We're all liable to error."

"Liable to all sorts of things," returned the man, quietly.

He drew a chair towards the grate and seated himself.

"Do you know Robinson ?" he asked, carelessly, taking up the poker, and playing with it by tossing it from hand to hand.

"Yes, a little."

"*As* Robinson ?"

"What do you mean ? How else should I know him ?"

"Ha, all I mean is, you are not a friend ? You only know him in the way of business ?"

"Only in business."

"Some of his business is in a queer line. He's downy, downy, is Rensh— Robinson, I mean, a man of great talents ; he deserves to prosper ; a useful man, a man I respect for many clever things he has done in his time. But, confound it all, sir, I should like to know what he has been burning."

"Paper, I should think."

"I have burnt papers before now. It is not paper," said the man, decisively.

He stooped over the grate, and then, raking the ashes with his fingers, pulled out a piece of singed cloth.

"Humph !" he ejaculated, looking at it with a suspicious stare.

In an instant Wenlock had snatched it from his hand, and thrown it out of window.

"What do you mean, sir ?" cried the astonished man, jumping on to his feet, and looking at the excited face of the other visitor with a frightened air.

"What do *you* mean ? What right have you to pry into Rensh——into his affairs ?"

"What, must I not pick up a piece of tinder from the hearth without being bullied in this fashion ?"

"No. But why do you indulge this mean inquisitiveness ?"

"Well, when such a poor scamp as Robinson burns the only coat he has to his back, it is time his friends should begin to feel anxious about his sanity."

"You have hit the right nail there, sir," replied Edgar. "My friend Robinson has burnt his old clothes because he does not know what else to do with them ; he is too proud to sell them now that he has a better suit to wear."

"Has he ? I'm glad on't."

"Yes, sir ; I have been able to put him in the way of doing good for himself."

"Ha ! that's more than he'll ever do for any one else."

"And you perceive that he wishes to destroy all relics of the indigence into which he had fallen now that he has bettered his circumstances."

"Bettered his circumstances, has he ? Phew ! Then it strikes me that I may as well make my bow at once, for I expect that since he has more profitable business to attend to my poor little affair will not be likely to meet with much attention ; besides, as I see no signs of anything like a box, a bag or bundle, I am inclined to think he has bundled off himself, Mr.—, but I don't know your name. What is it ?"

"Pray let me know to whom I am to introduce myself. What is yours ?"

"Mine ? Oh, I have none ; I am 'a youth to fortune and to fame unknown.' "

"But as I am neither fame nor fortune, perhaps you will not object to confide in me."

"My name ? Well, it's—Smith. And yours ?"

"Jones."

"Ah ! now we understand each other, Mr. Jones."

" Perfectly, Mr. Smith."

" Well, I think we might as well wait for the Nelson lions as wait for Master Robinson. What a pity we have not a Brown to complete the firm. Odd now, Brown is the name of that intelligent officer ; the detective-inspector is named Brown ; but if we have him in the firm at all it must only be as a sleeping partner."

" I dont care a hang for the detective."

" Well, if you don't care a 'hang,' as you say, there is nothing to fear from him ; but I'm off."

" And I too."

" So the fellow has bettered his circumstances ; all the better. I knew that he was cursedly hard up, and so I thought it would be a charity to put even a bit of bread in his mouth."

" Honest bread, of course ?"

" Why, Mr. Jones, you see Robinson has a good digestion, and when a man is hungry he will eat anything."

" But Robinson is not obliged now to 'eat anything,' as you elegantly put it ; however, as I'm of your opinion that he has left the place for good——"

" For the good of the place, rather."

" I shall take my departure."

" There's nothing else to take, it seems."

" Mr. Robinson no doubt anticipated your visit, and arranged accordingly."

" There was no need to do that as you were to be the first comer."

" If I was the first to arrive I will be the last to remain."

" Oh ! by no means ! I yield precedence to you, sir," said the man, with a dry smile, advancing to the door ; " but come, enough of this banter. I like you very well, Mr. Jones, you are a precious clever fellow, and I should like to be on better terms with you."

Wenlock glared upon the man ; but passed him and stepped out on to the landing.

Mr. Smith followed him close ; but before leaving the room he contrived to stoop and pick up *a piece of crumpled paper.*

They parted in the street with many ironic compliments, and Edgar Wenlock hastened to his office in the city.

CHAPTER VIII.

THE COUNTERFEIT LETTER.

" GRACIOUS, my dear Angeline," cried Lydia St. Clare, setting down the breakfast tray, " I was just coming up to you. Why, dear, did you leave your bed when you are so ill?"

" There is but one bed which can give me relief, Lyddy," replied Angeline, sinking faintly in a chair. " The green deep bed where is found rest for all heart sickness."

Lydia kneeled at the side of her friend, and threw her arms about her neck.

" I did not dream, my poor Angeline, that you could be a girl of such acute sensibility. It is plain that you love this stranger fervently, then why not marry him ? He is jealous—angry with you, perhaps ; but what of that ? He who has crossed the wide ocean to find you, will he lose you so lightly ? Not at all probable. Oh ! the agony we make for ourselves without cause. When you are—as you surely will be, it's on the cards, and in the tea-cups—Mrs. Aubrey, and he bores you with his husband impudence or indifference, you will be so mad with yourself for having ever tortured yourself in this needless, sentimental way. Depend on it there are no rods that sting so sharp as those we make for ourselves. Cheer up, Lina, all's well that ends well."

" 'It can never end well that must end so fatally.' "

" What, still in the tragic vein ? If you could look so touchingly sad and speak as pathetically behind the foot-lights as you do behind the scenes, you would make your fortune."

" Mr. Bluster, the manager, is coming to-day about my new engagement, is he not ?"

" Yes, dear ; but you shall not see him in the state you

are ; go back to bed like a good child, and I will sit by your side and read you the new comedy."

" No, I cannot afford to lose more time ; I have not played this season. The public soon forgets its favourites, and I want action—action ! In action there is forgetfulness."

" But you have all to remember and nothing to forget. Look, back on your triumphs—look forward to your wedded bliss; for I vow myself, henceforth, as determined as the most inveterate match-maker, to bring about your union with Arthur Aubrey, if I have to plead on my knees to that cold, stern stranger, who walks with a tragedian's strut and wears such a vinegar aspect. Courage, my dear Lina ! presently we shall be singing and laughing with Manvers, with Leoni, with Mr. Falstaff, Puffy, George Grant—that ruffian, Wenlock, of course is excluded—with Quavers and young Peronette, and the rest of your adorers."

" Are they coming, Lyddy ?"

" Of course, dear."

" I will not see one of them !"

" Don't be perverse, or I shall shake you. Their society and sympathy will cheer you, my poor child."

" I will see no one to-day but the manager, unless ——."

Rat-tat !

" My poor Angeline ! how ill—how nervous you must be to start and shriek at every knock as if it were a pistol-shot. 'Tis only the postman, and I will venture the prophecy that he brings you good news. The stranger relents ! Ah ! that too fortunate good-for-nothing, the viscount, would give his coronet to stand in that fellow's boots."

A servant maid entered the room.

" A letter for Miss Lablonde," she said, handing the little note to Angeline.

" Annie, when Mr. Bluster calls, say that Miss Lablonde is ill."

" Yes, Miss Lydia."

" No, I tell you I will see him ! You may go, Annie."

A sickly pallor overspreading her cheek, and her fingers violently trembling, she opened the little note, and read these words :—

" For ever ! The worst is known to me, Angeline, beloved. For ever, then, we must part. Our love-dream can never be realised. I could not support the torture of a last interview. I am gone, dear Angeline, for ever ; but I leave with you all the fervent love of my heart, all the happiness and peace of my existence. A thousand adieus,

" Your over devoted
" ARTHUR."

The fair girl raised her hands to her sunny brow, and clutched it tightly as if to crush the agony that was racking her brain.

She then rose, and clasping her writhing fingers together, and lifting her tear-streaming eyes, murmured in a voice of terrible calmness,

" Be it so ! It is well ; that moan is moaned ! I *will* be happy, happy in a memory that is dearer to me than any boon the brightest future could bring me ! Arthur, dear, farewell !—farewell ! You know the worst ? Ah ! the worst has not yet come !"

Bursting into bitter weeping, Angeline stole from the room.

As she did not reappear for a considerable time, Lydia, who had been shedding sympathetic tears, and moaning disconsolately, suddenly rose with a feeling of alarm.

She crept to the door of Angeline's bed-room.

It was ajar, and she pushed it softly open.

Looking in, she perceived the unhappy girl kneeling by the bedside, her face buried in the pillow.

" She is praying," whispered Lydia, as with a feeling of awe and anxiety she drew to her friend's side.

She wound her arms affectionately about the poor girl's waist, and gently raised her.

The golden tresses fell idly on her supporting shoulder ; the beautiful face was deathly calm and pale.

" She has fainted. It seems as if her nature cannot support the burden of her blighted life, but sinks beneath it at every weary step. She will be very ill—perhaps she will die. My own kind sister, my dear Angeline, I thought you proud and arrogant at times, but I do not, will not think that guilt ever had a home in your generous, noble heart, and whatever your secret may be, whatever you have been to others, you have been all that is good and kind to me, and I will cleave to you come what may."

The kind-hearted ballet-girl lifted her companion on to the bed, and then ringing for the maid, sent her to fetch a doctor.

Meanwhile she tended the patient with tenderest solicitude, and was rewarded at length by seeing the fringed lids gently unclose, and the soft bosom heave with returning life.

CHAPTER IX.

RENSHAW PERSONATES ARTHUR AUBREY.

HAVING breakfasted, and further fortified himself with Dutch courage at a tavern on the way, Renshaw went straight to the house where the unfortunate man whom he personated had lived.

With some slight misgivings he knocked at the door, bracing himself up for the ordeal through which he must pass, and summoning all his native pluck and acuteness for the essay.

The door was opened by a fine, tall, dark girl, dressed in black silk, who pulled out her gold watch as he entered.

"So you have returned at last, *Arthur!*" she said. "We fully expected you home to supper last night, but were not sorry you did not come, for we had that tiresome fellow, Jehoram Jackson, here last night, and he called again this morning. I suppose he wants more money; but he said nothing to mamma. La! Arthur, why do you stand there in the passage, staring at me so strangely? How pale and altered you seem!"

Here was a dilemma. Who was this young lady who addressed him so familiarly? Was she his *wife*, his *sister*, a *relative*, or *friend?* Who was she?

"*She is not in my portrait-gallery*," he half muttered. "Yes, my dear," he said, mastering his confusion, "I was detained last evening, I—— By the way, I must write a note before the next post to my friend Captain Armand."

This was a random shot and a most unlucky one. He had found among the letters a recent one from a Virginian gentleman of that name, and thought it would be safe to hazard the remark.

"How absurd to be sure! Do you mean to make a letter-box of the chimney, and send it by that route to his residence in the next room to your own? One would think you had been drinking, Arthur, you look and talk so queerly. But go and release poor Cato. Why did you lock him up in your room when you went out last night? As I was passing your window I saw his black face peeping out. He was asking so piteously to be let out that I had a great mind to burst open your door."

"Ah, the nigger rascal! I'll—I'll let him out directly. I must send him on a message—I must. Well, I'll let him out at once."

The young lady burst into a merry laugh.

"On a message? You are beside yourself!"

But Mr. Arthur Aubrey stayed to hear no more; he rushed desperately up the stairs.

He tried the first door he came to.

It opened, disclosing a large pleasant room.

An old lady was seated by the fire-side reading.

"A thousand pardons! I mistook the room," said he, drawing back.

"Oh, nephew, is it you? Come in, my dear," said the old lady, turning towards him with a smile.

"Humph! It's *my aunt!* Phew! what a precious lot of relations I have. Yes, I remember the face, I scratched it down in No. 4."

"And how did you find poor M. Georges?" asked the lady. "Is he better?"

"Not much, my dear aunt," replied Mr. Aubrey, who remembered that he had found in one of the letters an account of the heavy losses sustained by a gentleman of this name

through a failure in business. "Poor Madame is looking very poorly."

"What! You never mean to say that you saw his wife?"

"Aw—yes, yes, aunt; she was at home."

"Never! What, then, they are reconciled at last?"

"At last—yes, aunt, at last."

"Wonderful! Have you told Bertha?"

"Not yet, I thought I would reserve the news till I could find leisure to tell her the whole story. I've some important letters to write; I must step to my room for a few moments."

"And your arm, Arthur? Tsa! It has been bleeding again. Well, Dr. Probe will be here by-and-bye; you must have it attended to."

"Aye, aye, aunt; but I'll let Cato out of my room."

"Do; if you meant staying out all night, why did you lock him up?"

"I—I'll let him out at once."

"The poor faithful fellow deserves better treatment; since you have been in London you have neglected him, Arthur. He used to be with you constantly, and he pines sadly, and he is getting thin and his coat looks quite loose and ragged."

"I'll get him a new one," Mr. Aubrey exclaimed, desperately, as he rushed from the room.

He found himself in a passage, at the end of which was a door.

From within was heard a scratching of canine feet and piteous whining.

"Oh! then Cato's a *black dog* and not a black *man*," thought Mr. Aubrey, as he applied the key to his door and entered.

A splendid bloodhound crouched backwards as he entered.

The brute eyed him suspiciously, and set up a fierce growl.

The window was open.

Quick as thought the adventurer sprang upon the animal, and with a strong effort, and despite his fierce struggling and savage yelping, dragged him by the collar to the window and pushed him out.

"Curse the dog!" he muttered, "I will not be betrayed by a speechless witness."

Wiping the sweat from his brow he looked out of the window. It was not very high-placed from the ground.

The dog was not much hurt.

Limping along, and sniffing the ground as he trotted painfully, he turned the corner of the street and disappeared.

Renshaw—Mr. Aubrey then proceeded to take a survey of the apartment.

He opened drawers and boxes, and ransacked cupboards. He found amongst other things a sword and an officer's accoutrements, with the captain's commission, which Aubrey had borne through the war.

He also found a well-stocked cash box, a case containing a pair of splendid revolvers, and a large book filled with entries, in fact, a journal of poor Aubrey's experiences.

The adventurer stood thoughtfully turning the leaves of the diary.

"Humph!" he murmured, "if I can only get away from my 'aunt' and my 'cousin'—I suppose the dark girl is the old lady's daughter?—all will go well enough; at all events, it is no small feat to have done so much as I have achieved already. I will carry off the cash and credentials, and remove them to a safe place, either at an hotel or at a quiet lodging. Yes, that must be done first."

He looked about the room in search of a hand-bag, and selecting one from several that lay in the corner of the room, he proceeded to pack in a very deliberate manner.

The uniform, sash, and commission papers, the cash-box, the diary, the pistols, with a few articles of clothing, made up the items of his first haul.

He opened the door, and, affecting a martial step, bounded down.

"Adieu for the present, aunt," he said, looking in at her door.

"What an erratic fellow you are, Arthur," said the old lady, looking up from her book with a smile; "I thought we might count upon keeping you at home, at least, to-day."

"I assure you, aunt, I am much vexed that business compels me to leave you, perhaps till to-morrow, for I may be detained for the night. I am going to see the skipper of 'The

Wyandotte about the letters I expect from our friends at home."

"I hope they may contain good tidings," said the old lady, sighing. "Well, I shall not tell Bertha about M. Georges' affair; I shall leave you to give the story in all its details. I hope it will not bring that woman here. I suppose you will take Cato with you?"

"Yes, aunt; the rascal has already made off through the door; he is impatient for a run after his long imprisonment. Good morning, aunt; make my excuses to Bertha."

Renshaw breathed freely when he had reached the street.

"The game is more difficult than I thought it would prove," he reflected, "So Aubrey was not such an anchorite, after all. Ah! God; what a thrill of horror courses through me! I must not think of that. At least, the prize was worth the venture; it was well won. I have it safe—safe! I will draw a cheque for a heavy sum to-morrow, and then—well, then I shall see how far the game is worth the candle."

He suddenly stopped in his walk with a gasp of terror.

A fearful recollection shot through his brain.

"The blood-hound! he is gone! Whither has he gone? The beast will track his master to—to his——Oh, cursed folly! I should have poisoned him! I must be mad! That shall be my first care. As soon as night falls I will go back to the place; I will see what can be done to make all safe. If all is well I will be gone—I will bid 'my native land, good-night!' The deed was not of my doing; in the new world I shall begin a new life. By this time Angeline has got the forged letter. She dares not stir against me; the shadow of the beam is in her path as well as mine, and she will think twice ere she takes a forward step. Oh, let me hurry on; every stone I tread upon is like the shuddering scaffold-drop, when the bolt is being drawn. Edgar Wenlock—I must see him once before I go, but if he attempts to balk me, ha! then I shall not hang for nothing."

CHAPTER X.
EDGAR WENLOCK MEETS WITH AN UNWELCOME ACQUAINTANCE.

"I CAN make every allowance for your natural feelings of passion and anguish, Ned, but your violence to poor Angeline is quite inexcusable," said George Grant, in a serious tone, to Wenlock, as they were returning home from business. "So unmanly was your conduct that, hang me, if I can help telling you flatly that you have immeasurably fallen in my estimation. Say the girl is a heartless flirt—what then? A strong man, you were dealing with a frail woman; you should not have forgotten that. But enough of this unpleasant affair, Ned; I will not allude to it again. Only, tell me how you came to quarrel so fearfully?"

"Did you not see? Did you not see the cursed Yankee rowdy——"

"Pish! you are still playing the ruffian; the fellow was gentlemanly and temperate. It appears that he was the poor girl's first lover; she thought that he had fallen in battle, and was overjoyed to see him restored to her; her conduct was quite reasonable. Upon my life, Ned, I see no excuse for your brutal conduct, and if you are offended with me for speaking thus bluntly I must regretfully abide by the consequences, and we must henceforth be strangers."

"No, George, not so," whispered the poor wretch, clinging nervously to his arm; "I want no enemies. I am my own bitter foe; no reproof from you can equal the reproach of my own tortured conscience. I had no controul over my vile temper. I have lost her, and I deserve to lose her. I would do anything to prove my sincere regret. I hate, despise, abhor myself!"

"There, there, old boy, no more about it; you are looking wretched. Where shall we go? What shall we do to drive away all recollection of this stupid and ugly affair? Let us have an hour in the theatre, the music hall, or the billiard room. Let's make a stand against the blue devils, for I feel dull too. Where shall we go?"

"Nowhere to-night, George; I have a visit to pay to a friend who expects me at ten o'clock."

"Ah, a private affair?"

"Well, yes it is."

"What the deuce have you done to yourself, Ned?" cried Grant, suddenly halting in his walk, and catching hold of the rim of his companions waistcoat, and pulling it open. "*The front of your shirt is spotted with blood!*"

(*To be continued.*)

TALES OF THE INVISIBLE WORLD.

THE WRITINGS OF AN ESTATE FOUND THROUGH THE APPEARANCE OF AN APPARITION.

Continued from page 16.

"Well, sir," says the doctor, "I see you have been in earnest, and I find the thing is of great consequence to you. I have a strange fancy come into my head this very moment: will you gratify my curiosity with only opening and emptying one small chest or coffer that I have cast my eye upon? There may be nothing in it; for you are satisfied, I believe, that I was never here before; but I have a strange notion that there are in it some private places which you have not found. Perhaps there may be nothing in them when they are found."

The gentleman looks on the chest, smiling.

"I remember opening it very well; and," turning to his servant, "Will," says he, "do not you remember that chest?"

"Yes, sir," says Will, "very well. I remember you were so weary, you sat down upon the chest when everything was out of it, and said you were ready to faint."

"Well, sir," says the doctor, "it is only a fancy of mine, and perhaps there may be nothing in it."

Upon this the gentleman immediately caused the coffer to be dragged out and opened. When the papers were all out, the doctor turned his face another way, as if he would look among the papers; but taking little or no notice of the chest, stooped down, and as if supporting himself with his cane, chops it into the chest, but snatched it out again hastily, as if it had been a mistake.

"Sir," said he, aloud, "can you not send for a hammer and chisel?"

"Yes, sir," says the gentleman. "Go, Will, fetch a hammer and chisel; and in case he should fail to find one, I myself will go with him."

The doctor had not long been left alone by the squire and his servant Will when he sat down and began to entertain various wild fancies that flitted through his excited brain.

"What a chance is here," he said, "for any one of evil disposition to appropriate all he finds amidst this heap of rubbish, and so become the rightful heir."

While thus he thought, and while, indeed, the cold perspiration flowed from his pallid brow, he heard a strange and mysterious rustling among the heaps of lumber by which he was surrounded.

"What if I am but the silly victim of some strange delusion," he muttered, half aloud. "How long the gentleman and Will, his servant, are away! What if all my movements are watched by some unknown villain!"

Thus he thought, and, as he sat trembling in expectation of again beholding the apparition, and wishing for the speedy return of his host and servant, a rough and heavy hand was rudely laid upon his shoulder!

He turned.

To his horror he beheld, standing beside him, a tall, dark, villanous-looking man, in a black mask, dagger in hand.

"In the name of heaven, who and what are you?" the doctor tremblingly gasped.

"Speak not above your breath on peril of your life," was the hoarsely-whispered answer.

"In mercy speak to me," the doctor faintly enquired. "What have I done? Where am I? What want ye with me?"

"What brings *you* intruding here?"

"I was bade to come hither."

"Ha! by whom? I fear me thou art an enemy. Speak I say! Who sent thee hither?"

"A creature of the dead."

"Of the dead?"

"Aye, truly. In a vision that appeared to me———"

"Be brief; what of that vision?"

"It bade me come hither and discover certain documents that are now hidden—parchments that shall prove priceless in establishing the squire of this hall in rightful possession of his vast estates."

The man in the mask for a moment spoke not, but seemed to tremble.

"A ghost, say you?" he said at last.

"Truly, a ghost."

"With grey hair, pleasant features, and attired in black velvet garments?"

"The same."

"Spoke he aught of anything beside the recovery of the deeds?"

"It did not."

"Were his clothes disordered, as of one who had a deadly struggle?" the stranger asked, with a great effort.

"They were not."

"Saw you no mark upon his breast?"

"Mark," whispered the old doctor, his curiosity now thoroughly aroused, "mark, say you? What mark?"

"A blood-stained gash in his breast."

"There was, now I come to think of it, a small mark of the colour you describe. It looked to me like a small piece of ribbond."

"Pointed he to it?"

"He did; and now I remember it, whenever he so pointed to the mark, he sighed, and turned paler and paler."

"And is this all?"

"It is."

"'Tis well that I so believe it," was the calm response of the dark, mysterious stranger, "or else———"

"Else, say you? What, pray?"

"Why *this*," said he, holding the long dagger over the old man's heart, while his eyes flashed deadly fire through the eyelet holes of his black mask.

The doctor trembled with fear.

"And he bade you come hither in search of these lost deeds that the squire below may possess them?"

"Yea."

"And that the rightful owners might be reduced to beggary," the masked man said.

"Nay, I know not that; I came an unwilling agent of his bidding. The squire I know not; that he *is* the rightful heir I do believe."

"And you found not the deeds?"

"I have not."

"And the apparition pointed out to you the secret hiding-place?"

"He did."

"Secret then must it be indeed," the stranger said, "for, know you stranger, *I* have been in this mansion for weeks in search of the same title deeds."

"You?"

"Yes, I; and though you know me not, I have watched all your movements since you have been in this house."

"Impossible!"

"Nay; speak not so, for I have heard all your words, and know all your thoughts and intentions."

"Who and what art thou?" again asked the doctor, half aloud, in surprise and wonder.

"It matters nought to thee. List to what I say."

"I will."

"I have to propose two things to you."

"Two things?"

"Yea; and upon your acceptance or rejection depends *your* life," the unknown said, in a fierce, determined tone.

The old doctor trembled.

The man in the mask again went on.

"You know where these parchments are to be found?"

"I *think* I do; at least, I imagine so."

"And you would have given them up to the squire?"

"Yes; because I consider that it is but just and lawful."

"But you must not."

"Must not?"

"No; you *shall* not."

"Are those your propositions?"

"They are. You must discover these deeds, and give them up to me. If you refuse, you die; if you consent, wealth shall be yours. To your task on the instant!"

Thus forced to obey the unknown ruffian's orders, the doctor moved towards the old chest we have already described, and carefully examined it in every part.

Inside and outside were looked at in every conceivable way, yet still was he baffled.

While he looked into the old chest, he thought he perceived at the bottom what seemed to be a brass button that shone in the lamp light.

The old doctor could not reach it even by stooping.

He therefore got into the large, deep, old chest, and trod upon the small piece of brilliant brass.

In an instant the lid of the chest fell down with a loud crash, and was fastened by two strong spring locks!

At the same moment a small drawer at the bottom and on the outside of the chest flew open as if by magic.

The masked villain, for a moment, was so surprised at the sudden disappearance of the doctor in the chest, that he took no heed of the drawer and what it contained; but when he beheld the treasures it concealed, he hastily clutched them.

Among other things was a bundle of old and dusty parchments.

"Ha, ha! It is, it is! Here are the title deeds! They are mine! they are mine!"

So saying, and just as he extinguished the lamp, in order more effectually to escape, the sounds of footsteps were heard.

It was the squire and his servant Will!

Come along, Will, come along," said the impatient squire, "we have been a long while away. I fear me our strange guest will become impatient."

A distant rumbling noise was heard above them, as they ascended to the old lumber-room.

"What was that?" the squire asked, turning hastily around to his servant. "What was that?"

"I doesna know, sur," William answered, at the same time turning deadly pale, and seeming half inclined to return.

"Why, you seemed frightened, Will."

"Me, sir? lor bless yer soul, sur, I bean't afeered o' nowght."

"Then why don't you hasten forward?"

"Well, thee knaws, maister, I bean't afeerd o' nothing; but atween you and me, that old place is haunted."

"Haunted?"

"Yes, sur; and I'm sure on't, or I be———"

"What makes you think so?" the squire asked, interrupting.

"Why, sur, I'll tell thee. I wor coming past the old lumber-room t'other night, when I hearn all kind o' noises; so jest as I passes, I pokes my head in to see what were amiss loike, and the first thing, thee knaws———"

"Well, what?"

"I gets such a crack across my sconce as made my eyes twinkle agen."

"Oh, you were dreaming, Will."

"Nay, sur, it so please you, I was na dreamin', for I got a lump on my head still as big as ony walnut, and as to my nose, why, that were swoled as big as ony cabbage, sur; so I made sure ever since as how the lumber-room were haunted."

The squire smiled and went up stairs.

"Have you got the hammer, Will?"

"Aye, sur, two on 'em; chisels, crowbars and all enough to knock the old Hall to pieces, if that be."

They both entered the old chamber at one and the same time, but Master William retreated a step or two, as if momentarily expecting to be confronted by some deadly apparition.

He was mistaken.

No ghostly spectre hit him on the nose this time.

He boldly followed his master.

"But where is the stranger?" the squire asked, after peering about the apartment for some time without discovering the doctor anywhere. "Why, he has vanished!"

"Vanished, sur?" gasped Master Will.

"Aye, he must have done so, for he is not here."

"That is jest like them ghosts," said Will, holding up his lantern, and peering about.

Just at that moment a loud rumbling noise was heard in the chest.

As quick as thought Master William put down the lamp, and, very valiantly took to his heels down stairs again as fast as he could go.

The squire, however, was bold and brave.

(*To be continued.*)

NOTICE! NOTICE!!—With our next Number will be presented a Supplement, gratis, containing the Opening Chapters of a New Ghost Story, entitled "The Dead Man's Visit."

THE JOLLY DOGS OF LONDON.

THE JOLLY DOGS AT THE DERBY.

No. 4.

AFTER THE DERBY—THE JOLLY DOG ALONE.

CHAPTER X.—(continued.)

Edgar Wenlock could not repress a cry of horror.

He hastily buttoned close the waistcoat, which had come open.

"I—I wounded myself."

"On the breast? A wound on the breast?"

"A wound in the heart, too, George," said the other, shaking his head, as he turned livid pale.

"You never mean to say that you attempted——"

"Suicide? No, though in my agony of soul I felt strongly tempted to destroy myself last night. But this was accident, purely an accident. I had a penknife in my hand, and I stumbled, and struck myself against the blade. But come, let us turn into this tap; they sell good liquor here, and just a brimmer of brandy will set me to-rights, for the events of last night have terribly shaken my nerves. You said something about billiards. Yes, we'll have a game or two. I can spare an hour, and there is a table here; come in."

They entered the bar and called for cigars and brandy.

The place was tastefully decorated and brilliantly lighted, and the company gathered in the compartment in which they were standing consisted of a respectable class of men—city clerks, and the like.

The company were carrying on a general conversation, the subject of which was a report which one of them had been reading from the evening paper.

"It does seem very strange, and very horrible that in this age of social improvement, such fearful crimes should be of such frequent occurrence," said one of the gentlemen, seriously. "No sooner has the sensation caused by one horrid murder subsided, than some deed yet more fearful is perpetrated. Where did this tragedy take place?"

"Across the water. They have not taken the murderer yet."

"Drink, Ned. By Jove, it distresses me to see you look so confoundedly haggard and ill."

"Yes, yes!—hush!"

"On the scent—Inspector Brown, eh? A clever man that; an intelligent officer, and no mistake. Look at that Hornsey affair. No one would ever have thought he could have cleared up that last mystery."

"Oh, he'll catch the villain, no doubt."

"Of course, of course!"

"But what could have been the wretch's motive?"

"Don't you hear? He had quarrelled with the girl on account of her having met a former sweetheart whom she preferred to him."

"Well, and what instrument did he use in his bloody work?"

"The doctors are of opinion that death was caused by a blow from some heavy, blunt instrument—such as a bludgeon, or a life-preserver."

"Ned, you must get home. You are very unwell. Come, my poor boy, I'll call a cab, and we'll get home at once."

"Wait, wait! Listen!"

"The body of the deceased was dragged across the path, and thrown into a deep dry ditch, where it was found next morning by some labouring men who happened to be passing the spot."

"Poor girl; and it seems she was respectably connected."

"Yes, and the man suspected is a clerk in some merchant's office."

"He has absconded?"

"Yes; after having murdered his sweetheart, it is not very likely he would return quietly to his daily employment."

"Then—then the victim was a _woman?_" asked Wenlock, in a hollow voice.

"Yes, sir. You have not seen the evening paper, I presume? A man has killed his sweetheart in some lonely fields, on the Surrey side. Brown is after him, and I expect in to-morrow's paper we shall read of his capture."

"Are you sure it was a woman?"

"Of course! Here's the paper; you can read the report for yourself."

"A-ah! Thanks! By-and-bye I will read it."

A tall, keen-eyed, sallow-faced man, dressed very shabbily, glided into the compartment.

"Three of rum, please."

The girl drew the quantum of spirits and looked at him enquiringly, as he had not put down the money.

"This gentleman is very good-natured; _he_ pays, my dear," said the man, pointing with his thumb to Edgar Wenlock.

The clerk started with a wild stare.

He flung down a shilling.

The girl gave him the change.

"Your very good health, Mr. Jones," said the man, leering, and tossing off the rum at a draught.

"Who is this, Ned; another cad?" asked George Grant, in a stern whisper. "Please to tell me if you have many more such eligible acquaintances?"

"A friend of his, George—of the man who intruded on us at Cremorne; I'll tell you all about it presently. Excuse me one moment."

The man stood at the door beckoning.

Wenlock rushed after him.

They passed out into the street.

"Who are you? what do you want?" he asked, fiercely.

"You remember me, don't you?"

"I saw you this morning at ——. You call yourself Smith?"

"Well, yes; I call myself Smith."

"What do you want?"

"I want to show you a little article I have for sale."

"I want nothing."

"Nothing in the way of cravats, now? A choice article, last you your life, with a knot that's really lovely. I've something in the way of a strong cravat, if you like. You shall have it—for nothing!" and the fellow pulled out a piece of looped cord.

"What have you to sell?"

"A small quantity of superfine broad-cloth."

"What? I want none of your wares."

"Sorry for that. You shall have it at a bargain. Five pounds the price."

"I don't want it."

"Sorry for that, Mr. Jones. Well, there's no harm done; I thought to give you the preference, but I can find another customer. Inspector Brown will buy it at once."

"Let me see it."

The man pulled from his pocket a shred of cloth, which seemed to have been singed in the fire.

"Examine the texture; observe the pretty crimson tinge on the nap."

"You beast! Give it me."

"For five pounds."

Edgar opened his pocket-book, placed a note in the fellow's hand, and snatched the costly piece of rag.

"Have you more?"

"No, unfortunately; but I have another little treasure for sale—an autograph—a scrap of writing from the hand of one who is likely to make a name in the world; but for that I shall find another purchaser. If ever you _do_ want anything in the way of a cravat or a night-cap, say. I've a friend named Calcraft who will supply you with both at the lowest possible prices. Good evening, Mr. Jones; hope for your continued patronage."

The man leered, and, with a profound bow, walked off.

Wenlock was about to re-enter the public-house when George Grant came out.

There was a look of grave displeasure on his face.

"You will think this second rencontre with a disreputable character very strange, George," said Wenlock, in a feeble tone, "but if you will listen patiently I will give you a satisfactory explanation."

"It is quite unnecessary," returned Grant, coldly.

"Well, if you will defer it, I shall be glad, for I am in no mood for conversation to-night. I shall leave you now."

"As you please; I shall return home at once."

"And when I have—have finished what I have in hand, I will hasten back."

"Good night."

"Good night, George."

They parted, and Wenlock rushed on wildly.

'Let them go! What are they to me? Friends! I can have

none ; I have cut myself off from all society, for, with a bloody hand, I have severed the bonds of nature. I am isolated ! I draw breath in this living world only on sufferance. The mask will melt from my face, which will stand out from the crowd blood-boltered. It will be accounted a pious act to take my forfeit life. I shall be killed like a wolf, but shall be passed through the sickening phases of mental torture, in the dock, in the condemned cell, in the press-yard, before they rid me with the final *coup de grace* on the scaffold ! Yet I may escape ! If the waves could speak—if the stones could find utterance—how many a dark crime would be brought to light whose perpetrator has died in the odour of sanctity ! Murders ! Ah ! they are common. For one that is discovered there are a hundred that are never found out. I'll go to *it*—I will drag it from its hiding-place and it shall drop into the deep waters. I will sink it with stones ; it shall never rise to confront me. I shall die easier when I know that they can never look upon my work. If I had struck a second blow there would have been no witness. That villain Renshaw must beware how he tampers with me, for I am desperate, and desperation makes me dangerous !"

CHAPTER XI.

RENSHAW SEARCHES FOR THE BODY OF AUBREY—WENLOCK'S ALARM AT RENSHAW'S APPEARANCE.

"THE cursed dog has been here !" gasped Renshaw ; "these are his foot-prints."

He was standing beneath the weird, rugged elms in the dark lane on the river's bank, where the crime had been committed.

"There are no footsteps of men, and all seems quiet, but the hound may be lying in ambush. I wish the moon would rise ; I am sweltered with a cold sweat, and tremble like a child in the dark. I can scarcely manage the thing alone ; I wish I had brought Wenlock. Pshaw ! he is such a craven that it's as well as it is. That confounded bloodhound, I will be prepared for him."

He drew out a broad-bladed, murderous-looking knife, and gripped it tightly.

"I'll stop his growling with six inches of this if he attacks me. I wish it were over."

He climbed the rail and stepped through the bushes and under the shadow of some gloomy firs.

He still wore the dress of the unfortunate Aubrey.

He drew his cloak tightly about him to prevent it coming in contact with the trees, and, grasping the knife firmly in his hand, he crept on.

He listened intently for a few moments.

There was on one side of an opening in the thicket a mound of stones, fallen boughs, and drifted sere leaves.

He got on to the top of this hillock.

Peering through the trees he could trace out the windings of the rough and narrow lane, and could see the broad river surging heavily along, with the lines of lamps glimmering on the other side.

The distant roar of vehicles and the subdued and mingled voices of men travelled across the unruffled space of water, and enhanced the silence which reigned immediately around him.

There was no sign of any intruder.

He came down from the mound, and, stooping low, pulled a dark lantern from under his cloak and cautiously turned on the light.

The bright beams streamed along the miry ground.

He uttered a cry and sprang back.

A foot-print !

"Some one has been here !" he muttered, shudderingly. "Perhaps"—a qualm of wild joy for an instant glowed at his heart, but it died out and left him chilled and trembling —"perhaps he was not dead. Oh ! if he lives ! No, he is there ; here are the blood spots scattered about — not wet crimson now, but ruddy and smeared. But these steps."

He walked on, carefully examining the ground.

The footprints swerved aside and disappeared among the thickets ; they did not lead to the deep ditch down which the victim's body had been thrown.

"It may be that some one has entered the enclosure, and yet has not discovered the rift in the earth where he lies. What's this ? A glove ! and one of his too ! Ah, could I have been such a fool ? Is this a proof that nothing has been discovered, or is it only a bait to some trap the detectives have laid ? It is plain, at least, that the dog is not here now. Well, if I am caught in the toils, at least I will not be drawn out of them alive, for I'm armed for my own destruction with lead and steel. Hark ! some noise ! A bough breaking before the wind, perhaps. Again !—no, it was fancy. If I excite myself in this fool's fashion, I shall fill the air with thunders ; it's crying wolf, and soon I shan't be able to distinguish real from fancied danger. Yes, this way."

He stooped beneath some low trees, and as he forced through the thick, low-placed branches, a thorny bough recoiled, and struck him such a violent blow on the forehead that when, half-stunned, he raised his hand to his forehead, he found that it was bathed in blood.

Muttering a curse, he dashed on.

He stood on the brink of the crevice.

He looked about him : the bushes were trampled, and the branches of the trees were pushed aside and broken.

But this might have been done by himself and Wenlock when they were dragging the body to its rude and hidden grave.

"The rats may have got to *it*," muttered Renshaw, as he knelt down, placing the lantern by his side ; "it will be horrible. I doubt now whether I had not better leave it where it is."

A quick step echoed through the little dell, and the scattering of sere leaves was plainly heard.

In an instant Renshaw had started up.

Wrapping his mantle close about him, and holding the pistol in his hand, he stood listening aghast.

The form of the pretended Aubrey might well have been mistaken for the ghost of the awful owner of that name.

His face was ghastly, while his brow, bathed in blood, and the glare of the lantern, itself hid by a bush, shone with an apparently sourceless, weird halo around him.

The step grew nearer.

The adventurer seemed paralyzed, and stood rooted to the spot.

A figure glided from behind the trees close to the spot.

It was Edgar Wenlock, who, with a yell of horror, bounded forth, and sinking on his knees, extended his hands, trembling like a storm-shaken reed towards his accomplice.*

"It is true, then," he hissed, "that the dead rise, that their spectres haunt the murderer ! Oh, this is not mockery !—it is Aubrey. The face, the wound, the blood ! Speak, speak ! What shall I do for rest—an hour's reprieve, a moment's oblivion ? Oh, pardon, pity ; my punishment is more than I can bear ! My God, my God !"

He leaped up, and with clenched teeth, staring eyes, and starting hair, he tottered forward.

The expression of his face, distorted in its agony of mortal dread, was so terrible that Renshaw could not summons his voice to break the horrid spell.

He stepped forward ; but Wenlock recoiled with a maniacal shriek, twisting his hands in his hair, and glaring frightfully.

Suddenly he turned, and, with a pealing yell, bounded off towards the river.

Then Renshaw, suddenly recovering his presence of mind, cried out in a loud fierce whisper,

"Wenlock, dolt, fool, it is I—Renshaw. Stay, you infernal coward !—you are rushing to the gallows ! stay ! Look at me— a mere disguise ! The wretch is gone ! he will rave out his secret in the streets. Ah ! this fearful excitement will betray me !"

He sped wildly in pursuit of the flying wretch.

* In our last Number a typographical error occurred in the line under the engraving. Instead of " See No. 10," it should have been " See No. 4." The matter to which the engraving refers is given above.

The gloomy lane was still quiet.

Wenlock had reached the river's banks.

He seemed to have lost his senses, to be suddenly struck with madness.

Renshaw pounced on him just as he was about to fling himself from the bank into the dark gliding waters.

He turned and struggled violently.

His hand passed across Renshaw's bleeding brow, and when he felt his fingers wet with the red clinging moisture, he uttered an idiotic shriek, and bursting into a frantic laugh, sank down on his knees, his head drooped, and then all was darkness; the hour of oblivion was vouchsafed him by the haunting furies of remorse, as if, like the old tormenters in the dark ages of fanatacism, they wished their victim to recruit his strength in order that they might rack him with renewed tortures.

A second time Renshaw rowed his accomplice—insensible and lying heaped on the gratings of the boat—across the wide rushing river.

A second time the villain brooded over him with a dark and anxious frown, and with a half-resolve to cast him deep down into the silent stream.

CHAPTER XII.

THE BLOODHOUND ON A TRAIL OF BLOOD.

ABOUT two hours before Renshaw had reached the scene of the assault on Arthur Aubrey, two rough-looking fellows in coal-grimed blouses, and wearing sou'-westers, were shambling along the banks of the Thames, between Chelsea and Cremorne.

They were smoking short pipes and talking in gruff, low tones.

"I'm blowed, Jemmy, but there's a fine dog for ye," cried one of them, suddenly, as he pointed with his pipe at a huge hound that came trotting along from the distance, sniffing the ground, and evidently following up some trail with eager sagacity.

It was a large bloodhound, strong, and broad-chested, with pendulous lips, large, drooping ears.. He was of a deep tan colour marked with a black spot over either eye. He had a large brass collar round his neck, and trailed a short steel chain.

"Some swell cove's been and lost him," rejoined the other. "I say, Bill, here's a chance for somebody. There won't be no small reward offered for that ere creetur, oh no! I wotes we capture him, and if s'pose as we don't find no owner, we can sell him to the fancy for a little fortun'."

"All right, Jemmy, you stands o' that side o' the road whiles as I takes my persition on this side. We'll both make a grab at him simulta'nous, and then we can muzzle him with the chain, and drag him off like a small calf."

"That's the idear, Bill. Here goes. Look out, he's a comin'. Don't pertend to take no kinder notice till he gits within reach, least for fear as he should turn about and make his lucky. My heyes, hain't he jest a pictur'?"

The huge hound came swaying along, his noble head close to the ground.

He seemed so intent upon the trail he was following, that he paid very little heed to the two men.

As he passed between them they both made a rush to seize him by the collar.

He crouched with a deep growl.

The heads of his would-be captors came in sharp contact, and they rolled over on either side of him.

One of them lay half stunned, the other stumbled on to his knees.

The hound, with an awful snarl, made a fierce snap at the latter's unmentionables.

The man was fain to take to his heels, leaving a precious portion of his nether vestments as a trophy in the hound's jaws.

The dog then began deliberately to fix his fangs in the neck-cloth of the other and procumbent foe.

The man roared mightily, and striking out with his huge fists, managed to get on to his legs, which he used to his best advantage by fleeing past, with the dog following close behind him, furiously baying.

Then, having fairly put his enemy to flight, the huge brute, still growling savagely, sniffed about for some time, and when he had recovered the scent, trotted off in a straight direction, swaying his head as before, and apparently quite forgetting the little interruption he had met with.

The men followed at a respectful distance.

A policeman appeared on the scene.

"Hi-hi, there! Bobby! Stop thief!—stop him!—stop thief!" roared one of the men.

Now, the policeman had newly joined the force, and was as eager to secure his first 'case' as a young lawyer to obtain his first brief.

"Who? Where? What?" panted the policeman. "Have you lost anything?"

"Yes, I *has* lost summut," groaned the man, applying his hand to the wounded part.

"Hey! how much have ye lost?"

"I leaves that to the surgeons. Anyways, he's got his supper, the cannibal! Why don't yer cut arter him?"

"Where is he? I'll apprehend my nab in a jiffey."

"Try yer luck, then, and we'll all go whacks in the reward."

"What is it—the dog?"

"Yes, or the lion, or whatever f'rocious beast it is as is let go unmuzzled, agen all hacts of Parlimint, to the endangerin' of the lives and limbs, and all other parts of the British subjec's. Jist you catch him, Bobby, if you can."

"Hi, dog! here, fellow! good dog! come *here*, s-sir!"

If the policeman had issued the favourite mandate of his cloth, and bade the brute "move on," it is possible he would have been obeyed; as it was, the noble animal set the representative of the law at passive defiance, by continuing on his way, quite regardless of his threats or coaxing.

The valiant policeman gave chase.

The brute turned snarling; a spark of dangerous fire glinted red in his deep-set eyes, and his hanging lips wrinkled back, showing a fearful array of sharp, snowy fangs.

"Ah! would ye?" roared the policeman, shaking his truncheon.

He would, and did.

With a fierce grip of his canines, he snapped the staff of office from the policeman's hand, and, shocking to relate, carried the sacred symbol of constitutional authority some dozen yards, and then dropped it in a puddle.

Unbounded was the policeman's wrath at this lawless outrage, and with a shout he followed hard upon the audacious culprit.

The bloodhound seemed little inclined for a fray, for, though on ordinary occasions he loved fighting "better than his food," he was now absorbed in another pursuit than that of glory, and seemed anxious to avoid every let and hindrance.

The policeman picked up his truncheon from the dust, or, rather, the puddle, and shaking it with dread meaning, swore he would make the beast pay dearly for the insult.

"You'll have him up, I s'pose?" said one of the coalies, grinning.

"No, but I'll have his master in the dock before I'm a day older. The dog is trained to insult the authorities—trained, sir; and I've no doubt his master is a Fenian."

The blood-hound did not stay to vindicate his master's loyalty, but ran on till he reached the foot of Battersea Bridge.

Here he stopped, puzzled and at fault.

Sedulously trying for the scent, he straggled about, and then, finding himself still baffled, he lifted his noble head, and vented his dissatisfaction in a piteous howl.

The policeman and his colleagues came rushing up.

Their sudden appearance decided the animal in the course to be taken, for he could not escape without crossing the bridge.

So he darted ahead, and was soon in another county.

The conscientious policeman did not consider himself justified in leaving his beat.

The two coalies did not venture to tackle him again un-supported by the strong arm of the law, so he trudged on, sniffing as he went, but from time to time raising his head, and repeating his piteous howl of disappointment.

At length he reached the corner of a long, dirty lane, run-ning parallel with the river.

Here he stopped once more, and after testing the ground, gave a deep, joyous bark, and ran quickly but cautiously down the miry lane.

On one side was a row of stables for the dray horses that worked on the wharves by the river.

On the other side was a low, long wall, and at the distance of a rood down the lane there stood an old, tumble-down wooden structure that had no further claim to be called a house than that it was provided with a door and a few partly glazed loop-holes, that could not be legally dignified as windows.

The dog ran past this house and then returned, and, raising himself on his hind legs, pawed at the door, while he made the whole neighbourhood ring with his deep, thunderous baying.

The door was opened by a dirty-faced urchin, who gave a cry of dismay as the huge animal bounded into the dark and narrow passage.

The next moment the youngster lay yelling lustily on the floor, and the bloodhound was scampering recklessly up the winding stair.

CHAPTER XIII.

THE ABDUCTION OF ELFIE EARL.

KITTY O'ROONE, dressed in her Sunday best, was sitting in old Beamish's room with little Elfie Earl in her arms.

The old man occupied his arm-chair by the fire-side, his wounded leg resting upon a chair; he was smoking his long pipe, and looking benignly happy.

His wife leaned on the mantle by his side.

Shem was brushing his best coat prior to making a start.

He and his sweetheart were going to see the illuminations in celebration of the birthday of one of the royal family.

"Arrah, Shem, have done wid your botheration, I say she shall go," and Kitty spoke decisively.

She tied on little Elfie's hat, kissed her, and set her down.

"Come, Shem, it will be a mighty grand trate for the little darlint."

"Aye, Kitty, but yet I'm half afraid——"

"Is it *half* afraid you'll be, Shem? Faix, then, my honey, I'll lend ye half my courage, and shift with what's left, trusting the saints to look afther their little stray cherub. She'll not come to harm at all."

"What do you say, mother?"

"Why not take her, my dear? Bless me, she is not an infant, and you can take care of her, I suppose."

"Aye, Shem, take her along," cried old Beamish, smiling through his cloud, "she'll be right enough. Lor love ye, boy, I mind how, in the old king's days, the mother and I went to see the fireworks on his majesty's birthday, and you sat on my head, over-looking the mob, and crowing, as blithe as a saucy mid at the mast-head. You couldn't ha' been more than two years old, eh, Martha?"

"Eighteen months, dear."

"Aye, lass, it's you that keeps the log. I wish I could go wi' ye; I've lost none o' my taste for sight-seeing. But get under weigh before the streets are thronged."

Shem took the laughing child on to his sturdy shoulders, and, with Kitty holding his arm, started off towards the West End, where the illumination was to be seen in its grandest display.

The sky was dark, the air clear and frosty.

It was capital weather for the brilliant display of mellow, glittering lamplets, and flaming jets of blazing gas.

The grand effect of the bright haze of light that filled the streets now faded off into the blackness of the sky; the beauty of the sparkling combinations and starry galaxies of lights; the softening, richening tone imparted by the green, crimson and opal-coloured lamps that were scattered at intervals amid

the blinding glory of the gas, like jewels floating in a fiery sea; the striking effect of the vivid light upon the upturned shadeless faces of the interminable streams of people flocking from all quarters, and consolidating in a dense mass; the surging murmur of ten thousand voices! Altogether it was a spectacle to be remembered.

Elfie clapped her tiny hands and crowed with delight and bewilderment.

"What a love of a little one!" exclaimed a man who was walking behind Shem.

He patted the child's hand caressingly.

Little Elfie drew it away with instinctive aversion.

Shem Beamish turned his head.

The man smiled.

"Lovely child, sir, that little girl; an honour to you, I'm sure," he said, in a suave tone.

Shem glanced at him rather doubtfully, for, though he was tolerably well-dressed and seemed respectable, a soft, in-sidious smile lurked on his lip, and a sinister expression in his deep-set eyes.

"Your child is truly be-utiful!"

Kitty blushed hotly, and Shem looked rather shame-faced.

"Well, my hearty," he said, "it happens that little Elfie is not exactly ours, seein' as I—that is Kate——. Why, of course, dam'me, I'm not twenty-one, and Elfie is four years old!"

"No offence, I humbly hope, my dear friend, but the extra-ordinary loveliness of—how did you call her? Something pretty, I know."

"Elfie Earl."

"*Very* pretty! A sister, I presume?"

"No, not exactly so, neither, mate," said Shem.

"I'm a family man myself," rejoined the stranger, drawing a deep sigh; "I have lately lost a dear little one about the same age as Elfie."

"Sure, dear, don't look so rough now at the poor man," whispered Kitty to Shem, "he has a feeling heart, good luck to him."

"This is a grand sight, is it not, sir?" asked the stranger, looking about him with an air of admiration.

"Aye! it is, hearty."

"And how much little Elfie seems to enjoy it!"

"Sure, she does—bless her precious heart."

"Ah, ma'am, at her age it is so natural to be pleased with this kind of thing. To her mind all is perfect and beautiful in this pretty scene. She does not reflect that the money wasted upon this useless and childless exhibition of flaring bank notes, as one may say, would bring the light of gladness to many a starving family," said the stranger, sentimentally.

"Sure no, the pet, it's little bother she gives herself at all about the expense, and she don't know as we do, worse luck for ourselves, that this is all nothing but bits o' wire, and globes of glass, and rusty pipes, and nasty gas, and smeared paint and canvas. Perhaps she thinks that all the thousands of stars have come down from the sky (which look black and empty enough, like a big house when everybody is out) to dance in grand parade about her, and to pay this dull world a visit. Sure it is a sad thing to be wise!"

"But sadder still to be ignorant. Please Providence, I shall take care to well educate my own children. Oh, what a crush!"

A crowd of people thronging from a narrow thoroughfare now bore against them.

Shem and his sweetheart, by some means, got parted in the crowd.

The gentleman was very courteous to Kitty, and it was by his gallant exertions in her behalf that she escaped being hurt.

When they had been borne by the living stream far out into the ocean of a wide square, where the waves of this particular confluence dispersed and mingled with those of other streams, pouring in from all directions, Shem appeared, looking about him in search of them.

Little Elfie, still perched upon his shoulders, clapped her hands and pointed them out to him.

Far from being frightened in the rough scramble, she had crowed with delight,

Beamish began to feel more favourably disposed towards the stranger, seeing that he was so kind and attentive to his sweetheart.

"Come, my hearty, as Kate is so flushed and tired, and I am hot and thirsty, and you must be the same, suppose we slip into some quiet caboose just to freshen our hawse a bit?"

They got out of the crowd, and passing up a quiet street, found themselves in solitude.

As they were turning a corner, a handsome, well-dressed man passed them.

His eyes were fixed moodily on the ground. It was Wenlock.

"Good evening, Mr. Jones, he said, with a peculiar look at this personage, who started nervously.

"Ha, you, Smith?"

"Yes, *good* evening, Mr. Jones," and he passed on.

"Sure, sir, the young gentleman you spoke to looked very ill and sad," Kitty remarked.

"Ah, yes, poor fellow," returned the gentleman, gravely shaking his head, "a sad affair—something preying on his mind. This is a life of trial and trouble!—but here is the leetle place I spoke of. Oh, I thought so ; we shall have it all to ourselves. Come in'; don't shrink back, miss, I'm the father of a family, and this is an exceptional occasion ; come in, come in."

They entered the compartment, and Kitty taking the child from Shem's arms, shyly seated herself on a bench in the corner.

The gentleman called for two glasses of rum hot, and a glass of wine for the lady.

Soon they were chattering very confidentially.

With shrewd tact the gentleman elicited the most important details of little Elfie's history.

Elfie sat on his knee, and biting her tiny finger, gazed up into his face with a half-frightened look.

The gentleman called for some biscuits.

He had placed Elfie on the seat beside him.

He took his glass from the counter, and sipped it.

He emptied a powder from a small packet into the glass.

Then dipping a biscuit into the liquor he gave it to her, and she began to nibble it with her tiny white teeth.

After some time a number of flashily-dressed young fellows entered the public-house.

One of these spoke to the gentleman, and took a seat by his side.

"Ah! Shem, when first he spoke to us you looked as black as a thunder-cloud. What do you say now?"

"He seems to be a nice fatherly man. See, poor little Elfie has fallen fast asleep in his arms."

Several men now stood between their new acquaintance and themselves.

Being, as it seemed, quite unregarded, lover-like, they fell into a long and nonsensical chat, and, for the time, quite forgot poor Elfie's existence.

Suddenly, however, they were aroused by finding that the crowd of fine-dressed fellows had left them.

They turned to see if the gentleman were still chatting with his friend.

He had vanished with the child!

Shem rushed out frantically, telling Kitty to await his return.

She waited two weary hours, and he only came back to tell her that his search had been fruitless.

CHAPTER XIV.

HOW ELFIE EARL EXCITED GENERAL ADMIRATION, RE-CEIVED A COSTLY PRESENT, AND WAS CONSIGNED TO THE CARE OF THE GIPSIES.

AT the instant that Shem Beamish started off in search of Elfie's abductor, that pleasant gentleman was hailing a cab from the rank a few streets distant from the tavern.

"Where to, sir?" said the cabman, looking with softening glance upon the sleeping child's cherub face, from which the shawl in which she was wrapped had been wafted aside by the wind. "What a lovely little 'un—like waxwork."

"Aye; her's is the 'fatal dowry'—beauty!" murmured Mr. Smith, half-abstractedly ; "but it's cold. Keep out of the crowded thoroughfares, cabman, it will save time, for the illuminations have made the streets almost impassable, and drive me to the corner of Drury Lane."

"Right, sir," returned the cabman, as he clapped to the door.

He mounted the box, and "tchek'd" to his jaded hack, and the cab rolled off.

The cabman, as directed, avoided the open, crowded thoroughfares, and drove on his tortuous course through deserted by-ways where all was as quiet as in a city of tombs.

The passenger kept his eyes fixed on the lovely features of the slumbering child, and he seemed to be lost in a deep reverie.

"Elfie Earl," he said, inwardly, of course. "I wish I had questioned the simpleton and his sweetheart more closely. I might even have left the child still in their charge, have procured myself an invitation to their home, have learned every circumstance respecting the mother, have obtained the clothes, and the handkerchief he spoke of. Perhaps there were other proofs of identity. And then I could have done what I have done too prematurely. No matter, she is mine now ; I will watch her carefully. The voice in my heart tells me that she is, indeed, Mabel's child. And they call her 'Earl,' as if it were a simple surname and not a noble title! And Mabel died thus! If I had seen this little one in the arms of the prosperous, smiling mother, I think I should have slacked the scorching fire of my jealous vengeance in the blood of both. But she, the peerless Mable! Deserted, self-murdered, and her child an orphaned outcast! Oh, world! world! world! If *I* had been the prime mover in this tragedy, there would have been something evilly human in it. But *he*, for whom she jilted me, broke my wild, fervent heart ; he, whom she loved so richly ; he, the proud, stony-hearted, brainless fool, and blundering villain! To cast such a rare flower upon the foul river of this cursed city to drift away and perish upon the miry shore, to nip in the bud such a sweet offspring as this! Oh, it was inhuman! Devils! Who says there are no devils? Here was a fiend manifest. A demon in a mortal coil. Ah, that there were now on earth some holy one to exorcise such hideous potent devils!. Oh, Mabel! Mabel!"

Leaning his head over the dimpled cheek of the lorn child he burst in a passion of tears, and kissed the half-closed, balmy rose-lips with reverent tenderness.

"And I--so hunted, so poverty-stricken!" he went on, gnashing his teeth and speaking half aloud. "What can I do? Well, at least, I can wring a little more gold from the gripe of that cowardly hound, Wenlock ; but not much, for he is on the brink of ruin. I will use the poor means I have to the best advantage, and after this storm I shall calm down and can resume my acquired craft and intensity of purpose. Here's the theatre. I'll not let the driver see what road I take."

He pulled the check-string, and got out of the cab.

He found himself at the box-entrance of the theatre.

A rank of handsome equipages was drawn up before the door of the theatre.

As he passed, a tall and gentle-looking lady, of graceful mien and patrician features, in evening dress and bearing a costly bouquet, was handed from her brougham by a handsome but cold and haughty-looking gentleman.

Little Elfie's new guardian paused to make way for the noble pair, who were about to enter the theatre.

Absorbed in his own painful thoughts, he looked only upon the child's face, and did not scrutinise them till the utterance of a name caused him to quickly lift his glance.

"Oh, Basil," said the lady, "was ever such an angel of a child?"

The gentleman turned with a cold smile, and then his black brows met and a tinge of scarlet rose to his cheek.

"Such rare loveliness challenges admiration," he said, stiffly.

"Forgive me!" rejoined the lady, in a sweet tone, as she kissed the little one. "You must think my exclamation very rude, but who could pass such a pretty little fay without notice? May I ask—is she your daughter?"

"Yes, she is my child," was the reply, muttered in a low, hoarse tone.

The gentleman looked steadily upon the haggard, pale, and glaring face of the speaker.

"I am impulsive," she said, smiling. "Let me claim your indulgence; I must leave this little one some slight token by which she may learn to remember how her infant beauty attracted the admiration even of strangers."

The lady quickly unfastened a little gold chain and locket from her breast, and placed it about the child's neck.

"The little darling!—how deeply she sleeps!"

"Aye, madam, we have come far—she is very tired."

"And she is your daughter? Oh, you are happy!" returned the lady; and with a parting smile, she swept gracefully up the steps of the theatre.

Two sallow, close-shaved, shabbily-dressed fellows—"supers" belonging to the theatre, and on their way to the stage door, were witnesses of this little incident.

"Gad, my dear boy," said one of them, "how I do admire the spontaneous gush of generous sympathy!"

"As the tippler said to the tapster who treated him with a glass of gin."

"Barbarian!"

"Well, 'twas a lovely chyild."

"And the lady! Marry! a fairer, kyinder cr-rectear breathes not beneath the skyies!"

"Her accent was somewhat foreign. I wonder who she is?"

"Cudgel thy brains no more, but when thou art asked again, say, the Countess of Lindenwold."

"And her chaperon—is he the earl?"

"E'en so, my lord; a very Sir Oracle—a proud, arro   t, imperious patrician."

"How know you that?"

"My brother is a retainer in his household."

Little Elfie's captor passed on, and turning down a dark, narrow court, entered a vile neighbourhood, the haunt of thieves and criminals of the lowest class, and known by the cant name of Cat's Bay.

"He does not know his own child! Nature does not tug at *his* heart-strings with complaining cries. He is deaf as the adder to the voice of the charmer," muttered the man, bitterly. "He is given to the devil, this Earl of Lindenwold. The devil of caste, pride, and heartless self-worship—well, my own wrongs and Mabel's are now concentred, and I will wreak bitter vengeance on the miscreant. I pride in my degradation, I hug my penury, I peer in my rags. A blow dealt by the grimed hand of a base plebeian will fall heavy on this choice piece of 'delf.' I'll warrant I'll break his 'repose of caste.' I'll bespatter his tawdry escutcheon with mire. Mabel was his *wife*—I am convinced of that; Elfie is his child, and I, who was once his rival, am now his deadly enemy. It remains to be seen whether I am to be dreaded or despised."

Still muttering passionately, the man stopped at the door of a large, lumbering, filthy house.

He knocked at the door.

After a long delay he was admitted by a short, burly, ragged old fellow, carrying a shaded candle.

This person eyed his guest curiously.

"You, Mr. Darrell?" said this man, with a leer. "Glad to see ye."

"Show me at once to some of your hiding-cribs. Any place that's retired; I want no meddlers."

"Ho! I see. Well, then, the *loft* will do."

"Is it furnished?"

"Not werry elegant; howsomever, there's a bed in it."

"Ha! Any one sleep there?"

"No; not since Renshaw broke the jug, and was stowed away in that garret for nigh a month."

"Well, go ahead, Mitchell."

The old fellow conducted his guest to a low, dirty garret, with a small but heavily barred door, and a sloping roof.

On the walls were a crooked looking-glass, some old penny prints, a crow-bar, or jemmy, and a lantern.

There was a heavy trunk in one corner, and in a recess a truckle-bed.

Every pane in the skylight which lighted this den was broken; some of the squares were stuffed with fluttering rags, but for the most part they were open to the sky.

"Nice and airy," grinned Mitchell.

"And devilish noisy," grumbled the other as the rotten flooring creaked loud beneath his tread.

"Oh, but safe enough, for all that, Mr. Darrell, for you see it perched up on this here gable, jest like a pigeon-house on a dead wall. Quite removed from all t'other parts of the house; and as for noises, no one notices them, though sometimes in winter when the winds blow they are most 'stronary onearthly; but no one never comes near this sanctuary, I warrant ye."

"Why not?"

"They calls it the condemned cell."

"How did it get that name?"

"In consequence of a cove as hid here some while ago, as was fearful worrited by the traps. They was dead on his track, so he give them the slip for good; he took the jump."

"What, from the window?"

"No, from the door.";

"Well, what harm came to him?"

"Ho, I ought to have mentioned that afore he took this jump he had tied a noose round his neck, fixing t'other end of the rope to a nail in the beam."

"Ha! and that's why you call it the 'condemned cell'—a pleasant reason, to be sure."

"And there's another reason. They says as he haunts this crib. So it's never used except by them as is hard driven to escape the crushers; they're generally coves as comes it 'capital.' They're awful bad customers to deal with. I don't encourage 'em no ways. On'y a man will pay down stiff to keep his neck put of the halter, and his relations generally backs him for fam'ly reasons."

"Well, the place will serve my turn. I shan't want it long. Bring the light."

Darrell carried the child to the bed, and laid her softly down.

She seemed sunk in a trance rather than a sleep.

"Oh cry! What a sweet little kid! Who is she?"

"Mitchell, you once were noted for a good habit of yours."

"What's that?"

"You used to mind your own business, and never pestered your customers with inquisitive questions."

"That's all the more reason as you should indulge me in this case. The ducky little diamond; she's a regular cherub. I really should like to know who she is."

"And I should be very sorry to tell you a lie, as I'm conscientious; and I couldn't tell you the truth."

"Nabbed her?"

"Entrusted to my charge."

"Really! Well, well, don't look black; not my affair, in course not. I'm dumb, hem! See and say nothing. I learned that when a child, and have allers kep' to the dooty he taught me. Never divulged a secret in my life."

"You shall never divulge mine, my friend, for I never divulge them myself."

"She seems deep asleep."

"Yes, she won't wake just yet; but now I am going below. Who have you got in the kitchen?"

"On'y some tramps, Romanies, and hedge drapers on the way to Dingledown fair."

"What gang are they?"

"Black Isaac's their king."

"Good; I know the rascal."

"Come down, then."

Darrell hesitated.

"What's in that box?"

"See for yourself."

Darrell lifted the lid.

The chest contained nothing but an *old rope with a loop and slip knot, and a rusty clasp-knife.*

(*To be continued.*)

TALES OF THE INVISIBLE WORLD.

THE WRITINGS OF AN ESTATE FOUND THROUGH THE APPEARANCE OF AN APPARITION.

(*Continued from page 24.*)

It was of the utmost consequence to him that he should discover all that was possible about the missing title deeds ; and, therefore, hammer and chisel in hand, he commenced operations on the chest, saying,

"I care not if the whole room was crammed with ghosts, I'll see into the affair. The stranger's appearance much struck me, and if he be not flesh and blood, he might yet have been some restless spirit that came to advise me."

Much to his astonishment the squire found the chest locked, but soon with the aid of a hammer and stout chisel he re-opened it again.

He looked into it, and was greatly surprised to see the doctor lying at the bottom, more dead than alive.

With much difficulty the squire extricated him from his tomb, and after some little time learned from his guest all that had happened.

"This is a very strange and mysterious affair," the squire said, looking in blank astonishment at the pale and trembling stranger.

Together they searched the whole room from top to bottom, but except a few stray pieces of old parchment that the robber had left behind him, nothing was discovered.

"Could you tell your grandfather's handwriting if you saw it?" the doctor asked, as he knelt on the floor poring over a scrap of parchment he had found in the drawer.

"I could."

"Is this like it?"

"It is. What does that slip of parchment speak of? What is it?"

"It is a small portion of that very will you are in search of."

"Ha!"

"Yes, and in his haste the villain who abused me has left it behind."

"What does it say?"

"Why, it fully proves as far as it goes that your father was the true and rightful inheritor of this Hall and the surrounding estates."

"Has it the signature? If so, my cause shall triumph in the courts of justice!"

"It has *not* got the signature; so much the worse for you. The villain has escaped with it."

"Then, alas! all is lost," said the squire, turning pale, and heaving a deep and bitter sigh. "My wife, children, all, all are cast upon the world friendless and in beggary. All is lost; nought is left to me but to destroy myself!"

And the squire, with tears rolling down his manly cheeks, knelt on the floor beside the doctor and pored over the remnant of parchment, trembling violently with agitation.

At that moment, while a death-like silence reigned in that lonely chamber, a rustling sound was heard among the piles of old lumber that were heaped in a corner of the room.

The squire and the doctor simultaneously raised their heads.

Their eyes became greatly distended at what they saw.

There, in a strange halo of white and shadowy vapour, stood—

The spectre!

For a moment neither the squire nor doctor spoke, but after a few seconds the latter whispered half aloud,

"'Tis he!"

After a solemn pause the spectre said,

"I *am* he! The same who appeared to thee in London!"

"I did your bidding," the doctor feebly answered.

"You did. Had you *not* done so, you had not been now alive! The ruffian would have murdered you, but for my protection."

Turning to the squire, who looked as if transfixed to the earth, he said,

"Fear not. He who has stolen from you my long-lost will is now speeding on his way to London, and rejoicing in his villany. Follow him; and rely upon my guidance and protection. For the present, farewell."

With these words the spectre vanished.

The squire and his new friend found themselves in total darkness. Rising to his feet with an oath the squire dashed from the lumber-room, and went immediately to his stables followed by his excited guest.

"Saddle me in haste the best horses I possess," he said. "Say not a word to your mistress of my intended journey. I go to London; and shall not be more than a week away. Where is Will?"

"He be in bed, sir," said the groom, with a broad grin; "he ran by the stables not long ago as if the very devil were after him, sir, and swore he saw more than twenty ghosts."

"Let him sleep, then," said the squire, moodily. "This is no time for faint hearts or faltering hands. Have *you* heard any strange noise to-night, Jem?" he asked the groom, who was hastily saddling two splendid riding horses.

"Yes sir, I have ; but can't account for it."

"What kind of noise was it, Jem?"

"Like a horse, sir, galloping in great haste away on the London road."

"How long ago."

"About half an hour, sir. Just as Will ran past me by the stable door."

The squire exchanged significant looks with the doctor.

"Have you put pistols in my holsters, Jem?"

"Yes, sir."

"You are provided with weapons, doctor, I believe?"

"Yes ; I also have two good serviceable pistols."

"Then we will away," said the squire. "You are not afraid to see the end of this strange adventure, I hope, doctor?"

"Not in the least ; on the contrary I am desirous of chastising the rascal who maltreated me, and will see the end of this very mysterious affair, if it costs my life."

"My hand, sir," said the squire, clasping and shaking his friend's outstretched hand.

"Thee be not going alone, sir, be thee?" said Jem.

"Are you not afraid to encounter highwaymen and cut-throats?" asked the squire, with a smile.

"Not I, sir. Where thee gooes, *I* can goo ; and if it so pleases thee, master, let me come too."

"Please yourself, Jem. Mount a good horse. You might as well ride the doctor's, as he is going to London ; but mind you well arm yourself, for there is no knowing what may or may not happen ere any of us return."

Jem, the groom, was delighted at the prospect of following his master, and many minutes had not passed ere he was galloping behind the squire and his strange guest, the London doctor.

The three horsemen had not long been on their way before they reached a toll-gate.

The squire's horse was already in a foam from furious riding, but the doctor, in his sombre black attire, sat his horse so calmly and quietly that Jem, the groom, often said to himself,

"He seems fastened to his horse, *he* does. He rides for all the world like a ghost. Who the devil *is* he, I wonder?"

"Has any one passed through the gate within the past hour?" the squire asked of the toll-gatherer.

"Yes, squire; yes, truly, there hev."

"Horsemen or a carriage—which?"

"A single horseman, squire."

"What kind of person was he?"

"Rather tall—slightly drunk I thinks, and wore a mask."

"A mask, say you?"

"Yes, squire."

"And did he pay the toll?"

"Not a farthing, squire. He was a vagabond whoever he was."

"Why then did you not refuse him passage and arrest him?"

"Nay, squire. I opened the gate, and as soon as I had done so, the rogue rushed past me, and, with a savage oath, he struck me athwart the shoulders with his heavy riding whip."

"Which way did he go then?"

"Straight on, squire. He took the main coach-road, and as he spurred up his horse, I heard him shout, 'Ho, for London town! ho, for merry London!'"

(*To be continued.*)

THE JOLLY DOGS OF LONDON.

ELFIE VISITS THE DERBY IN CHARACTER.

CHAPTER XIV—(continued.)

"What is it?"

"A cur'osity, worth no end o' money; a kinder relic, you see."

"A relic of what?"

"Why, of Nathaniel Calder."

"Not the murderer?"

"That werry person."

"I remember the case; killed his sweetheart?"

"Yes, and then dissected her. That box held her mangled body; you may see the stains in it, and that rope hung the rascal."

"Horrible! the associations connected with this pretty spot must be pleasant to poor beggars lurking here from justice."

"Good for 'em, bless ye.".

"How so?"

"Keeps 'em constant in mind of their danger, and makes 'em cautious."

"Oh, when once a man loses his balance and slips over the narrow verge how rapid, how deep his fall!" muttered Darrell.

No. 5.

"That's a tex' for a parson."

"A sentence for a sinner!"

"Rayther squeamish to-night, eh, Mr. Darrell? It's the cold weather, p'raps; it's werry searchin'."

"Come on, you fool, take me to those tramps and gipsies; I want to speak with Black Isaac the Gipsy King. Have you a key?"

"To this door?"

"Yes."

"Here it is; I keeps it on the bunch, but seldom uses it."

Darrell took the key.

He stooped over the child.

He muttered something unintelligible to Mitchell in a low, wild tone.

Then the men stepped from the room.

Mitchell held the light.

Darrell locked the door.

The former leading the way the latter followed him down the creaking staircase.

When they had reached the hall the sounds of loud laughter and rough jesting broke on their ears.

NOTICE.—*With this Number is given away a Supplement containing the opening Chapters of a new Ghost Story.*

They descended into tartarean regions.

At the end of a long stone passage a ruddy light streamed from a half-open door of the kitchen.

They directed their steps towards this chamber.

Entering they found themselves in a large, white-washed room with an immense grate and roaring fire.

The place was lighted with gas, and furnished with long tables and benches.

It was crowded with a motley gang of thieves, tramps, gipsies, cheap Jacks, low pugilists, tumblers, street musicians, orange girls, and show people.

At one table a considerable number of sallow-faced, black-eyed, curly-locked, half-wild and garnish-looking fellows were gathered.

These were gipsies.

In the arm chair at the head of the table sat Black Isaac the monarch of the tribe.

He was a tall and well-made fellow, with fine, wild, restless eyes; they shone with clear black light, if one may use such an expression; he had a flowing black beard, a high forehead, and rich clustering black locks, and his appearance altogether was quite regal and imposing.

He wore a long, loose grey coat, a red velveteen waistcoat, a heavy gold watch chain, a number of valuable rings.

Upon the table lay a large beaver hat and a cudgel.

At the moment that Mitchell and Darrell entered the kitchen the king of the gipsies, glass in hand, was trolling out in a deep bass voice some rollicking song which elicited from the hearer's shouts of laughter and applause.

The song concluded, Darrell advanced towards the gipsy king, who rose and extended his hand.

"Welcome, my ben cove," said the monarch, with a smile; "join us at the festive board, and take the seat of honour."

Darrell seated himself at the right side of Black Isaac.

Several of the gang nodded and smiled in recognition.

"And how wears the world?"

"I don't know," returned Darrell, tossing off a glass of spirits which the gipsy king pushed towards him.

"Don't know? Are ye out of the world?"

"Yes; I'm living incog. and in expectance."

"And what do you expect? A turn of fortune's wheel? Hang it, my pal, why not pull the spokes yourself?"

"I have tried, but the wheel's too stiff on the axle."

"Wants oiling."

"Yes."

"Ah, I see; can't you get the grease?"

"No."

The gipsy king laughed, and then trolled out,

"Money, money, funny, funny,
It should be man's bread and honey.
Some can make it like the bees,
Some can take it at their ease,
Some must want it or must seize,
Never starve for honey, money!"

"Not if I can help it!"

"Don't," laughed the gipsy. "Base is the slave who pays —let me add, baser the slave who starves! Honesty and respectability have little in common, as this world now goes; while roguery and respectability are by no means irreconcilable. He is but a fool who cannot play the rogue without running amuck of Father Antic the law."

"From what book did you learn that philosophy?"

"From the horn-book of Dame Experience," returned the gipsy. "But come, my friend, let us see if we cannot find some charm for raising the wind. What say to accompany me on my intended tour through the country?"

"In what capacity do you travel?"

"Horsemonger, book-maker, travelling jeweller, quack, and cheap Jack."

Darrell laughed and declined the offer.

Then drawing the gipsy king apart from the rest he entered into a long and earnest conversation with him, carried on in an under tone.

At last he rose, and, followed by the gipsy, left the room.

The two men mounted the dusty and rickety staircase, and Darrell opened the door of the room in which the child was confined.

They entered together, and Darrell held the light over the child.

"She is indeed a beauty," said the gipsy, drawing a deep breath. "It seems, too, she is the heroine of a sad story; but these romances of life, like those of fiction, sometimes begin darkly and end brightly. Well, my ben cove, as a medico and mountebank, I am unequalled in my profession as an unmitigated liar and cheat; but with friends it is different. I have given you my word that I will protect this pretty doll, and I will be true to my promise."

"It will suffice; I feel that I can trust you."

"You may. She shall be adopted in the tribe, and made free of all Romany. As you say, she will be safer in our hands than in those of any of the prying, questioning Busné. Your pardon, Master Darrell, I must explain: we gipsies call all those who are not of our race Busné. But I must bear her off at once."

"But she will not be exposed to the hardships of the gipsy life?"

"Trust me for that. She is a sapling that must be fostered under shelter. Well, there is one of my tribe who rents a cottage near Epsom. He gets his living by caning chairs, making baskets, and the like. His wife, though of gipsy birth, has lived in service, and is a kind and trustworthy woman; to her charge we will commit this fair changeling, and that to-morrow."

"I leave her, then, to your care for the present," said Darrell. "I shall meet you in the morning. And now, as I have a little business on hand that cannot be waived, I will say good-night."

The men shook hands.

"Ben Darkman's, my ben cove," said the gipsy, heartily; "meet me here to-morrow."

CHAPTER XV.

HOW SHEM BEAMISH JOINED THE CREW OF JOLLY DOGS.

SHEM BEAMISH was wearily plodding the streets of a London suburb through the dusk of an autumn evening.

A look of chagrin and depression sat on his homely but pleasant face; his hands were thrust deep into the pockets of his pilot coat, and his eyes were fixed gloomily on the ground.

All day long he had been engaged in a fruitless search for the stolen child; but though he had enquired at all the station-houses, the workhouses, and at many of the taverns within a wide area, he could gain no tidings either of the poor little one or of her mysterious abductor.

"Shiver my timbers, I'll not give up the chase yet!" he cried half aloud, stamping his foot on the pavement. "Though outsailed, I may run down the pirate shark who has taken our pretty prize in tow, and, if I do come athwart hawse with the smooth-tongued, lawyer-like lubber, I'll spoil his fine jawing-tackle, I'll warrant; but—hillo! what's that? The pale-faced muttering chap, that hailed the pirate scamp on the night he stole our pet! I'll speak to him."

It was Edgar Wenlock who passed.

He was walking rapidly, and, before Shem could reach him, passed quickly down a narrow street.

Shem followed at a distance.

Midway down the street a projecting lamp glowed in the purple dusk, and was emblazoned with the sign of a large and brilliantly lighted tavern, "The Harp and Crown."

Edgar Wenlock entered the house.

Shem posted himself on the opposite side of the way and gazed rather sheepishly at the gilded, blazing windows.

A card, printed in gaudy colours, and displayed in the window, attracted his notice.

He crossed the street, and found that it bore this inscription:—

"THE JOLLY DOGS

"PHILHARMONIC SOCIETY.

"Harmony Wednesdays and Saturdays.

"Subscription—Five Shillings a Quarter."

"My jib!" muttered Shem, as he nervously passed his fingers through his crisp, dark hair. "'Jolly Dogs,' eh? Well, now, that sounds hearty like. Five shillings a quarter—ah! that's for the new dog-tax, I suppose. Well, a seaman just home can spare a dollar. I'll see how I like the crew, and, if it's all a-taunto, blow me if I don't enter on the ship's books and be a 'Jolly Dog' myself!"

With this resolve he entered the crowded bar.

He looked round for Wenlock, but he was not there.

Probably he had gone into the smoking room, behind the green-baize door, from whence came the tinkle of a piano and the cheery sound of laughing voices.

Shem gently pushed his way to the bar, on which he leaned his sturdy arm and stared naively at one of the dapper barmen, who was rushing about, drying glasses, and drawing beer and spirits.

"Ahoy, my hearty! heave to, I want to speak to ye," said Shem, beckoning the man.

"Yes, sir; what d'ye want, sir?"

"You're the ship's steward, arn't ye?"

The man shook his head, smiled, and rubbed away ferociously at the shining tumblers.

"Don't understand ye."

"There's a super-cargo of Jolly Dogs aboard. What sort o' mess is it?"

"Mess? Do you think we cook bow-wows, then? Just home from China, I s'pose?"

"Dam'me! these London swabs beat all for discarnment!" muttered Shem. "I don't know how you can tell that, my cheery; but I won't deny it, and at Hong Kong they roast a puppy as we should a sheep's head here, and 'tain't a bad dish neither. Good for you you don't cruise in them waters, eh? Well, excuse sea manners, a bit of a sky lark is all Jack's way; but, I say, hearty, can't I join this ship's company?"

"Yes, if you're proposed and accepted in the usual form."

"Oh, aye! I fall to your meaning; must be entered on the books? That's all right, and above board. Who's the captain?"

"The famous Harry Rattleton is the chairman; but there's one condition, can you sing?"

"Like a bird!"

This answer did not proceed from honest Shem, but from a dandified, cockney-faced little gent, who clapped him on the shoulder.

Shem started and smiled broadly.

"Are you a Jolly Dog?"

"Yes, my 'earty, I am!"

"Blow me if I didn't think so. Well, give us a grip, my cherub, and tell me, how's it to be managed? I want to join the crew."

"You must be perposed, I'll interdooce ye; but fust, I must know yer name."

"Aye, aye; let's exchange signals, I'm Shem Beamish, second mate of the merchant barque, 'Christabelle.' What's yours?"

"Aw, James Gimp, there's my cawd; I've been one of the Jolly Dowgs for two seasons."

"A two-year old, eh? Thought you was but a puppy. Ha! ha! well, you shore-going fellows have some queer customs. Is that chap, Jones, one of the crew?"

"Jones? Don't know him."

"Oh, I saw him enter this caboose; tall, fair, trim-built chap, but looks as pale and melancholy as Billy Taylor's ghost."

"You don't mean Wenlock?"

"Perhaps so, the pirate called him 'Jones;' perhaps they're all of a gang and carry false colours. But don't look flabbergasted, I mean no offence, Mr. Gimp. When shall we go aboard?"

"Oh, at vonce, if you please; I'll interdooce you at once to some great celebrities: there's Mr. Pharamond Fitz-Hubert, author and publisher; little mad Charley Vert, the 'sensation' writer; there's the Bethnal Big 'Un that beat the Conky Pet in three rounds; and there's Dandy Jack the bookmaker, and a score of Jolly Dogs besides. But, come along, I've the privilege, as a member, of interdoocing a friend for the even-

ing, and can get the Bethnal Big 'Un to second me in per-posin' you to be one of the members."

Mr. Gimp twirled his massy gold watch chain, shouldered his gold-mounted walking cane, and passed through the green baize door, followed by Shem Beamish.

The young sailor looked round with a feeling of mingled awe and delight at the branching gas-lights, red satined walls, long mahogany tables, and padded benches, and at the gay assembly of 'Jolly Dogs' dressed in the showiest style of the prevailing fashions.

They were ranged along the tables drinking and smoking, while Mr. Harry Rattleton, a fine young dog, the chairman, and a favoured few, were seated at a sort of low platform, on which was a table bearing two books, writing materials, and a number of glasses of steaming hot brandy and water, not to mention pipes, cigars, and various etceteras.

On one side of the platform was a grand piano, on which a pale, dissolute-looking young fellow was strumming some wild chords.

Mr. Gimp conducted Shem to a seat at the end of the table, and desired him to place himself beside the Bethnal Big 'Un, to whom he introduced him in a patronizing manner.

"I'm von of the priv'leged, reg'lar Corinthian; ain't that right, Big 'Un?"

"That is right," returned the athlete, sententiously, at the same time taking a furtive glance at Shem.

The prize-fighter's broad, bruised, meaningless face assumed a frank and pleased expression as he gazed on the manly countenance of the fearless tar.

He gave him a hearty grip.

"I likes yer looks, guv'nor," said he; "wet up."

Shem took a draught of the brandy and water.

"Your health, my hearty," returned Shem, in his bluff tone. "This seems a pleasant berth and a jolly crew."

"Seafairin'?" asked the Big 'Un, stopping his pipe with his finger.

"Aye, born to the sea," returned Shem, the honest light in his brown eyes beaming pleasantly.

"Thought as much. I say, who's yer patron? Who inter-dooces yer? Is it Jemmy Gimp?"

"Aye; I'm a stranger."

"Well, s'pose I puts ye up to the ropes?"

"Avast! the ropes! Do ye think I want to be taught by a landswab? as if I didn't know 'em all from the jib-stay to the gaff halliards, and we don't call 'em ropes aboard."

"Ah! you don't take; s'pose I gives yer a hint as to who's who, I think I can trust ye?"

"I hope so, cheery."

"You see that flash cove yonder? that's Pharamond Fitz-Hubert, author and the likes."

"Oh!"

"Keep yer eyes open, he's werry downey, he is."

The Big 'Un shook his head with profound gravity.

"Avast! I'm not much of a book scholar. So that's a live author, is it? Very insignificant, considering. There's another of 'em, arn't there?"

"Yes; mad Charley Vert."

"Aye! what sort o' customer is he?"

"Well, you're a match for that chap; but lors, he's un-fort'nit, and he dreams, bless yer. Thinks as he's goin' to do summut surprisin'; but he arn't got the stuff in him, won't accommodate hisself to what's required on him; arn't game, wants 'cuteness; but you needn't be afeared on him, on'y don't be too kind to him 'cos he'll never do no good for hisself. Then there's Jemmy Gimp, he's all right; awful fool, stoopidly good-natur'd. Tell him as you're a Navy captain, and call him a 'Corinthian,' and you'll find him jannock to any amount. Jemmy's a prize, he is; he's had a legacy lef' him, and he don't want for friends as kindly helps him to spend it."

"And who's that red-whiskered, sharp-eyed chap, with the spotted neckerchief and horse-shoe pin?"

"Oh, that's Dandy Jack, the tout and betting man. Mind him, anyways."

"Thank ye, for your advice. Now I know my soundings I can steer clear of rocks and shoals. There's one question more

I'll ask ye : Who's that handsome chap standing beside the skipper ?"

"You means Wenlock. Oh, he's a clerk at a banker's. Smart chap ; there's some queer rumours about him though ; they say he was in the same plant with poor Gentleman Dick that got lagged for forgery."

"Gentleman Dick ?"

"Yes ; his name was Dick Renshaw."

"Phew !"

"Know him ?"

"Heard of him. How did this chap get off then if he was the other's accomplice ?"

"He had friends, and old Dick was a stunner. They couldn't get a word out on him all as they could promise and threaten ; and there was nobody else but Dick as could give evidence strong enough to convict Ned Wenlock. Dick was a wild hawk ; but true as a Trojan. Poor Dick, many's the time we've been out on the spree together, and now he's breaking stones in Millbank jug ! Sich is life !"

"Belay, hearty ; let's fill up the grog-kid. What are ye drinking ?"

"Brandy hot."

Shem ordered and paid for the liquor.

"In course you're fly to it, that what I tells ye is told in friendly feeling?" said the prize-fighter. "Musn't go no further ; but I likes the look on ye, you're a fine bit o' mahogany—14 stun odd, I should think? Can you use your mawlies ?"

"In my own defence."

"Ah, well said. Now, if you'd like a scientific treat, you'd better take a card for my benefit—on'y a half-crown—game set-to 'twixt yer humble and Boss Hammers ; comes off nex' week at the 'Fightin' Cocks.' All the 'Fancy' 'll be present, and the Great Brass sings in character. Take a ticket ?"

"With all my heart, messmate ; wish ye success and a good haul o' prize money."

At this moment the chairman struck the table sharply with a little wooden mallet.

Rat, tat !

"Order, gents, please ! it is time to commence the evening's proceedings."

"Order—chair !" chorused the assembly.

Mr. Harry Rattleton rose, and was received with enthusiastic cheers.

Silence being at last obtained, the chairman thus addressed the company :—

"Brother pups and Jolly Dogs, it is not my intention to retard the genial pleasures of this evening's entertainment by a long and prosy harangue."

"Hear, hear !"

"But this evening I intend, without further preamble, to break into harmony with a song of my own composing (loud cheers). According to the rules of our society, I have endeavoured to suit my rhymes to the prevailing taste of modern 'Jolly Dogs,' and I appeal in the usual way to any 'six magnificent bricks' (cheers) whether it is or is not up to the present standard of such compositions (hear, hear)."

MULBERRINA.

"I've lost my heart to a bright young belle,
   Indeed you should ha' seen her ;
She ran away with the howling swell,
   And her name was Mulberrina.
She sported a pair of shiny boots,
   And a dainty knickerbocker
Was fairer far than 'Tilda Toots,
   In fact, right up to the knocker."

"Brayvo ! Have you seen her lately ?"
"Order, please."
Rat-tat !
"Chorus, Jolly Dogs."

"Oh, Mulberrina !
   How much we do esteem her !
   She's belle of the ball,
   And the music-hall,
   And ain't she jest a screamer !

"She has yellow curly hair, and a crinoline
   As wide as Etna's crater,
With a gingham umbrella and a sewing machine,
   And a neat perambulator.
She slyly winks, and pouts her lip,
   As by her side you pace, sir ;
Her darling feet so deftly trip
   Beneath a dome of lace, sir.

Chorus.
"Oh, Mulberriner !
   Isn't she a screamer ! &c.

"She's one of a lot of nice young gals,
   So pretty and provoking,
Whose shocking ways and mo-rals
   Are subjects for such joking.
Of course she's false—of course she's 'fast ;'
   She drinks like any drayman ;
She'll fleece and fool you first and last,
   As bold as an old highwayman."

"What, then, Jolly Dogs? we can but say——"
"She's sweeter than a lollypop !"
"You should on'y see her 'air."
"Order, gents, and chorus altogether."

"Oh, Mulberrina !
   Isn't she a screamer ! &c.

"Now, on my word I loved that gal !
   I stood no end of oysters ;
She eat ten dozen, shells and all,
   Got drunk, and fought the costers.
She prigged my purse, my watch—Ah, well !
   Though much I did esteem her !
She's just a match for the 'howling' swell,
   For, isn't she a 'screamer ?'

Chorus.
"Oh, Mulberrina !
   How much we all esteem her !
   Long live sich gals
   At the music-halls,
   We only wants a screamer !"

Tumultuous applause followed this exquisite ballad.

Fresh packs of Jolly Dogs came pouring in till the room was crowded almost to suffocation.

Mr. Gimp now approached Shem Beamish, and whispered him to follow to the platform.

Shem readily obeyed, and was formally introduced to the chairman, by whom he was received with great condescension. He was proposed and accepted, and, his name being duly entered in the books, one sterling, manly fellow, at least, enrolled in the society of Jolly Dogs.

The ceremony of inauguration over, Shem's first act was to accost Wenlock.

"Good evening, Mr. Jones," he said, quietly, "I think I have had the honour of meeting you once before ?"

"Jones ? met me ? No ! Where ?" gasped Wenlock, turning livid pale.

"I was in company with a Mr. Smith," said Shem, carelessly.

"Hush !" muttered Wenlock, gripping the young sailor's wrist, and glaring wildly upon his honest face ; "you mistake ; my name is not Jones ; we have never met before."

"I know your name, sir, is Wenlock," said Shem, with a slight frown. "If you do hoist false signals, it's no consarn of mine ; I don't want to overhaul your ship's papers ; only maybe you can tell me where'away that pirate shark, who calls himself Smith, is cruising. I'm in chase of that vagabond."

"In chase ?" gasped Wenlock. "Why, what has he done ?"

"Many a black, bad deed, that I'll be sworn," returned Shem. "His last and worst was to steal away our poor little foundling, Elfie Earl."

"I know him only by sight—met him in mixed company —can't assist you, indeed," returned Wenlock, impatiently ; "however, let's choose a fitter time for explanation ; yonder come some friends of mine, I must leave you."

Wenlock smiled feebly and turned away to salute George Grant and two or three others who entered at the moment.

Shem looked rather dubiously upon the group, returned to

his former place, and re-seated himself between Mr. Gimp and the Big 'Un.

"Going to the Derby, Mr. Beamish?" asked Gimp.

The seaman smiled.

"Why, shipmate, since I've become a Jolly Dog I must not shirk the muster; every Jolly Dog is bound to go to the Derby. When will it be run?"

"Ve'n'sday veek. Have you much coin on? I back Redan against the field," said Mr. Gimp.

"Well, hearty, I wish you may overhaul a prize. For my own part I don't understand the creatures—never saw a race in my life, and never rode a horse except old Blind Bess, that used to tug the lighters on the Regent's Canal."

"Never saw a race?" exclaimed Dandy Jack, joining in the conversation. "Ah! a sea-faring gent, I perceive. Well, yours is a class I *do* pity."

"Avast heaving, messmate!" grunted Shem, glancing with ill-concealed disdain upon the vulgar face and flashy dress of the "tipster." "Jack is better off than you shore-going chaps, after all. At least he steers clear of many temptations. Dam'me, there's none at sea to cheat but the purser, and to do that's a vartue. Then for the women—bless their sweet peepers!—except on a day's leave ashore, or when they come alongside in the bumboats, we see nothing of 'em. Wine's not Jack's treat, and a glass of grog's all according to regulations. And as for a race! what is there in the short gallop of some score of spider-legged animals, bred so fine that there's no bottom in 'em, and ridden by ugly, merciless, little monkeys in harlequin jackets, to compare with a spanking chase over the angry, bouncing seas, between splendid craft, every stitch set, and worked by a manly crew of skilful mariners? Bah! I *do* pity all poor land lubber swabs!"

Those of the company who were near enough to hear this speech of the jolly tar laughed heartily at its enthusiasm.

Dandy Jack growled half wrathfully, but Pharamond Fitz-Hubert turned with a gracious smile, and nodded encouragingly.

Pharamond was a tall, good-looking fellow, straight as a dart, dressed in good taste, and with military precision and neatness.

His voice was deep-toned, and somewhat pompous, and his manner quietly assumptive, but not without dignity.

"I agree with you, sir," he said, "that a chase at sea is very exciting to those on board the vessels; but take a regatta, for instance, and you will find that to the ordinary on-looker it's a dull affair. You confess that you've never seen the Derby run; I trust you will make one of the party of 'Jolly Dogs' who are going to Epsom from this place, all of whom are members of our honourable society?"

To this proposition Shem readily consented, and having remained some time longer to hear the songs and music, he left the "Harp" with Mr. Gimp and the "Big 'Un."

Among the last to leave were Wenlock's party; but that guilty and care-worn youth did not accompany his friends home, but parting from them at the door of the public-house, went off with Dandy Jack and Harry Rattleton.

"We shall have a glorious spree on the race day," said Rattleton, laughing. "All the 'crème' of our set are going, and, that the charm of female society may not be wanting, I shall take Amy and Madeline."

"Gad's my life! that's well said, Harry," cried Dandy Jack, rubbing his hands. "I've made a goodish book this time. George Grant is very sweet upon the favourite, only Grant is such a cautious beggar. Little Gimp's cock-a-hoop on Redan; there's no hedging about Jemmy. But, Ned, what makes you look so glum?—You've a straight tip on. What then? You'll land all right; take the word of an old turfite."

"I *must* win!" cried Wenlock, fiercely.

"Hiegho, Neddy, I can't but think of your old fellow clerk, Renshaw, he *was* a Jolly Dog! Fun? He'd all the animal spirits of a school boy let loose to play, and all the wit of a Yorick at a court banquet. Poor Dick! I'll warrant he's a favourite even in the jug. Well, we shall miss him on the Derby-day."

Wenlock turned aside his head, and made no reply.

"It may be very culpable on my part to pity such a rogue,

but I can't help it," continued Harry, "he was such a pleasant scamp. Well, I must be off, for here our paths diverge. Don't forget, you fellows, subscriptions for the Derby jaunt must be paid up next Wednesday."

"All right, my tulip; we're gentlemen, and behave as sich. And mind ye, lad; remember my tip, if you're offered 16 to 1 on the Toxopholite, take it, that's all."

"Good-night, Harry!"

"Good-night, Jolly Dogs!"

CHAPTER XVI.

INTRODUCES A JOLLY DOG TO THE "LUMMY COVE."

"*Come under the lamp, Ned; the course is clear—there's no one down!*"

Dandy Jack uttered these words in a low whisper to his companion, as soon as Harry Rattleton had disappeared round the corner of the street.

Wenlock obeyed mechanically.

The pair stood beneath a glimmering lamp.

The clerk placed his hand in his breast.

"Is it all right, Ned?"

"Yes."

"Glorious! How much?"

"A thousand!"

"A check?"

"No; hard cash!"

"Bravo, Neddy!"

"Jack, you won't deceive me? you will act square in this case, at least?" asked the wretched young man, in a tone of almost maudlin entreaty, as he grasped his companion's arm and lifted a haggard glance to his face.

"Deceive ye, my tulip? I've always been jannock, haven't I?"

"Always, Jack, always; but you don't know—you cannot dream what suffering this act has cost me."

"And yet you're not quite a novice," sneered the tout; "after a time or two you'll get use to it. Dam'me, Ned, a man must have money now-a-days! What is your paltry salary? not enough to keep a Quaker, let alone a 'Jolly Dog.' What is the use of life if one can't enjoy it?—and how can one enjoy life without the ready? The wealth in this precious old hulk of a country is so unequally distributed that one *must* sometimes go a leetle out of the rigid road of rectitude to supply one's wants. Where's the harm? Life's all a scramble, where some get the kicks and others the ha'pence; some both —it's all in the day's work. Better pick oakum for a year or so, than scratch the foolscap at a miserable pittance for your whole lifetime! Honesty!—pshaw! Where do you find your 'honest' man, old Diogenes? Better be a rogue than a fool, and you can only be one or the other as the world goes."

"Hush!" cried Wenlock, in a hoarse tone, "do you not believe in conscience?"

"No; and shouldn't like to entertain such an uncomfortable faith. Pish! all bosh, Neddy! Conscience! whoever heard of a man with a conscience that ever did good for himself?"

"And you never felt remorse?"

"Often, Neddy, over and over again!"

"Ha!"

"Yes; when I've been fool enough to let a good chance of besting my fellow sharpers slip through my fingers."

"But honour!"

"There you're right, Ned; a certain amount of honour among——well, of course we hunt in couples, and it's never good policy to betray a partner; our interest is mutual. Oh, you may trust me."

"And the stake, do you think it's safe?"

"Safe as the bank; though that's not saying much; but have you arranged things well for putting back what you've borrowed?"

"Yes; if our horse does not kick the pot over, all will be well."

"And we can retire on our laurels, my jolly Corinthian."

"But if the worst should happen—if—Ah! I sicken at the

thought!—and this is manly English sport! Well, well, all I would say, Jack, is—we must be prepared for the worst!"

"Aye; you must stick at nothing, then; then we must play the trump card to win or lose."

"You mean—the safe—my assistant. If we can get the tin, we must——"

"Take a tour on the continent, or a run across the Atlantic. Well, it's best to look the devil in the face. You mentioned your *assistant*—you haven't seen him yet?"

"No, Jack, who is he?"

"The knowing ones call him the 'Lummy Cove.' Suppose we hunt him up at once?"

"It is so late."

"Never mind that; I know where to find him. Will you go?"

"Yes; it will be better. If we are let in for it when the event comes off, not an hour must be lost. Yes; I will see the man to-night."

They quickened their pace, and progressed in the direction of one of the East end suburbs, still conversing as they went.

"Neddy, I want to ask you a question about your chum, George Grant?"

"Don't you like him?"

"Humph! 'twouldn't be natural."

"Why not?"

"Because he hates me."

"Does he?"

"Well, at least, he pretends to despise me."

"Ah! but he's not horsey; George is no sporting man."

"But do you think, now——"

"What?"

"What's his worth? Is he up to nothing but the vulgar pursuits of legitimate hard labour, and that kind of thing? Not 'fast,' is he?"

"Fast! There's not a jollier dog in London. He is up to everything, knows everybody, every artistic or dramatic celebrity at least—painters, authors, actors, actresses—and then he is most accomplished, quite a Crighton; for, besides being a ripe scholar, he sings, dances, boxes, bats, bowls, rows, swims, and is considered a crack shot in the volunteer regiment in which he holds a command. Oh! George is 'fast' enough; but being strong of body and light of heart, he looks upon amusement as a thing both needful and lawful. George catches pleasure as she flies; but he is moderate, and therefore wise—as well as merry."

"You speak warmly of the fellow."

"And with reason; he has been a true friend to me, though I am rather out of his books lately."

"Then it would not be easy to get him in a line?"

"There is no power on earth that could induce George Grant to tell a lie or commit a base action!"

"Humph! you seem sincere for once."

"I am; I respect George. I used to like him, but, somehow, I begin to hate him for his good qualities."

"And Puffy—what of him?"

"He is not so sterling as George; there's more deviltry, more levity in him; less self-controul, less strength of purpose; but still he is a gentleman and a man of honour, though a 'Jolly Dog.'"

"Then they are not the men for our money. Gentleman! Pish! Don Quixote was the last gentleman unless there may be found some solitary specimen in Hanwell or Colney Hatch."

"You are hard upon the world!"

"The world has been hard upon me."

"Well, I don't see that you have much cause for grumbling."

"Not professionally, I admit; these are piping times for 'touts' and 'tipsters.'"

"Let's stash this nonsense! Where are we now, we are in queer quarters?"

"Yes; keep your trap shut and look to your pockets. 'Slushington Row'—yes, this is the turning."

Passing under a low archway they entered a paved court surrounded on all sides by tall but black and filthy dwellings.

All the denizens of this retreat seemed to be still up and stirring, for lights shone in most of the windows, and the tainted air rang with mingling shouts, screams and drunken laughter.

Dandy Jack descended by some steps into a sort of area, and knocked at a low-browed, heavy door.

A slatternly, dissipated woman opened to the summons.

"Who do yer want now?" she asked, in a shrill, drink-harshened voice.

"The guv'nor, Sal, if he's at home."

"Well, p'r'aps he is at home to *you*," returned the woman, leering; "but I say, now—come, who's this 'ere t'other cove?"

"A friend, Sal; it's all right, my dear."

"Well, you don't come in till *he* lets yer," rejoined the woman.

She turned her head, still keeping fast hold to the door, and bawled into the house,

"Hulloa, Bill, come here! Here's a couple of fine fellers wants yer. Don't know one on 'em—better bring yer bludgeon."

A growled oath sounded from within, and a burly, ferocious-looking ruffian came forth with a heavy stick in his hand.

"Well, Bill, how goes it? It's on'y me and the friend I spoke of," said the tout.

"Come in, can't ye?" growled the ruffian.

"Only waiting for the invite, Bill."

"Come in, come in, yer cussed fool! I were thinkin' about yer—expected yer days ago."

"Busy time, my rum 'un," replied the tout. "Step carefully; mind the step, Mr.—hem—Walker."

Closely followed by Wenlock, the betting man blundered down a narrow, dark passage, and entered a spacious, but ill-furnished kitchen, in which, despite the warmth of the weather, a mighty fire was blazing.

The air was impregnated with a villanous compound of foul smells, amongst which the reek of fried onions was predominant.

The host closed the door, locked it, and took out the key.

Wenlock started at finding himself thus encaged in the burglar's den.

He instinctively thrust his hand into his breast, and clutched the pocket-book, which contained one thousand pounds, which the "Jolly Dog" had robbed from his master.

"Sit yer down," said the robber, scanning Wenlock with a keen scrutiny. "Make yerselves at home."

He went to the door, and opening it with a burst of choice oaths, commanded the woman, who was lurking in the passage, to "clear out of it," she not being "wanted."

"Ho! so this is the gent of the plant, is it?" said the burglar, with a grin.

"Yes, this is Mr. Walker."

The robber laid his finger on the side of his broken nose, and winking his eye repeated the name with much unction.

"Walker!"

"Yes, Bill; I've brought the gent *as* promised," said Dandy Jack, a little huskily.

"Vell, you've not done the honours arter all; but I'll interdooce myself. I'm the 'Lummy Cove.'"

"And now let's to business, Bill," said the betting man. "This gent has a heavy tip on the Derby, and if there's any mistake, why he must, he will be obliged to speak to his guv'nor's swag-box; but he's not a professional, and wants your assistance."

"You knows my terms, Jack; we go halves, mind that."

"But I must be considered."

"No doubt, by the gent, he'll come down well; he looks generous. Of course, I must have my share without deductions?"

"Well, well, we won't split about that," returned Dandy Jack; "but let us at once come to arrangements."

"Is it an easy plant?"

"Easy as lying; this gentleman can manage to let you in before the office closes, and will show you where to hide yourself; it is his regular duty to go round the premises to examine the safes and locks, and to turn off the gas when the day's business is over. There is not the least danger, Bill."

"We'll do it clean," returned the burglar, chuckling. "And how much do ye think there is in the safe?"

"Some thousands in hard cash, besides the bonds and flimsies."

"Ah! but the notes arn't worth much," said Bill, shaking his head. "Allers dangerous they are, but for all that the crack seems worth the venture. Well, then, this little business is settled, and where am I to meet my pardner?"

Wenlock winced at the coarse familiarity of the man's tone, but answered,

"I'll settle that with my friend here. If ill-luck should befall on the race day I will send you word by him."

"Ah! that's right, guv'nor," returned the burglar. "But what sort of safe is it?"

"A Brahma."

"Ah, then I shall want a 'citizen' or an 'auctioneer;' but, there, I've a splendid set of tools. I think I shall take a brace of bull-dogs."

"Bull-dogs?"

"Pistols, he means."

"In course—barkers."

"No, I insist that you shall take no offensive weapons."

"Well, then, I'll take a de-fensive one. Just a life-preserver; ever seen anything like that afore?"

And the burglar, as he spoke, held a short, loaded staff towards his visitor.

Wenlock quailed with a mortal shudder; he tried to speak, but could only mumble something incoherently.

Dandy Jack caught the expression on his companion's face, mistook its cause and import, and said with a sneer,

"You may depend upon the Lummy Cove; he'll manage all quietly, safely, and in a masterly manner."

"True for you, old sporting bung," cried the burglar, slapping him on the shoulder. "Never was lagged in any lay, 'cept when a pal played booty and buffed on me, and Mr. Walker's too much of a gentleman to do that. We understand each other."

The ruffian gave a significant wink as he said this, and then turned away towards a cupboard which he opened.

"This is my magazine," he said, with a grin. "Have a peep at the interesting collection of instruments; here's one, a centre-bit—we calls him 'Samson,' because of his being able to unhinge the gates of Temple Bar, if s'pose they were closed agen him; and here's a pick-lock; but you don't look interested. I'll explain the natur' and use of these new patents on a more favourable opportunity, for you'll want an hour's trainin' jest to get your hand in for the plant."

"Right, my covey, but it's getting late, or, rather, it's growing early, and we must be off homeward. I shall see you in the morning, and then we can come to the clinch."

"One word afore you starts," said the burglar, touching the betting man's arm, and motioning him to withdraw a few steps.

"What is it, Bill?"

The burglar dropped his voice to a whisper.

"You knows that Romany cull, Black Isaac, don't ye?"

"Yes; the horse-dealer, the king of the gipsies?"

"Jes' so; he has trapped a pretty little gal; the kid belongs to some swell people. Know anything about her?"

"No, 'pon my life."

"Ah, well, I thought you might be fly to the little game. I've a certain reason for wishing to know something about her."

"Is she with Black Isaac now?"

"No; he's given her over in charge to that tumbler chap as calls hisself Mounseer Hercules; he lives near Sutton. You remember the cove?"

"Very well; had engagements at music-halls, but fell and hurt himself. He has been down on his luck lately; goes about performing at fairs and race-courses; has a son, a very clever lad—young Paul."

"That's the identical. Well, I'll have a word with you about this affair by-and-bye; meanwhiles, gents both, I must say Or revwoir."

The burglar leered and bowed them out with mock politeness.

Wenlock parted from his companion when they had reached the West End, and took the direction for his own lodging.

Late as it was, numerous vehicles rattled past him as he walked thoughtfully onwards.

As he was passing along a genteel but retired street a hansom came dashing at a rattling pace round the corner, and drew up before the door of a neat and pleasant-looking villa.

A gentleman leaped out from the vehicle.

He was tall and graceful, his dress rich and of the most fashionable style, his luxuriant hair was parted in the centre, and he had a long silky pointed black beard, and a pair of finely-curled moustaches.

"Renshaw!" cried Wenlock, suddenly halting in his pace.

"Neddy!" cried the adventurer, buoyantly, "glad to meet ye; nothing could be more fortunate. Let me dismiss cabby, and then I am at your service."

The fare being paid, the driver touched his hat and drove off.

"My dear boy, let me implore you to avoid committing such an infernally dangerous indiscretion."

"What indiscretion?"

"You called me Renshaw!"

"Ah! Aubrey, then," gasped Wenlock.

"Right; don't forget it. Renshaw is no more! I am henceforth Arthur Aubrey. But come into my kennel, brother pup; I think you will say that your Jolly Dog is well housed."

The adventurer opened the gate, crossed the trim, bright path, ascended the drift-white steps, and opened the glazed door with a latch-key.

Wenlock found himself in a charming little hall, adorned with stags' heads and pictures, and carpeted with fur rugs.

A spruce page-boy in a smart livery now appeared, with a lamp in his hand.

"Any cards, Tom?" asked the adventurer.

"Yes, sir; several gentlemen have called, and the postman brought letters and newspapers."

"Good! This way, Ned. Light the gas, Tom, and bring up some supper."

"Yes, sir."

The page threw open the door of a back room, and lighted the gas chandelier.

The sudden burst of bright, mellow light showed a scene of luxury and comfort—couches, arm-chairs, book-cases, flowers, and glowing pictures.

The adventurer threw himself wearily upon a sofa, and motioned Wenlock to seat himself.

"Well, Ned, what do you think of this?" he asked, glancing round with a smile of satisfaction.

"Wonderful!"

"Am not I a diplomatist?" laughed the adventurer. "I have manœuvred to perfection; I have got rid of my aunt— a very nice woman, and my cousin, a fine, dark-eyed girl— must introduce you. I have got rid of them, Ned; for awhile, at least; they are off to the Isle of Wight, and have left me monarch of all I survey. I have bamboozled all my friends and comrades into the belief that I am the veritable Simon Pure, the true Arthur Aubrey. I am courted, lionised, fêted, wherever I go; I am received in the best society, have talked of guns and drums and wounds to the oldest veterans, have fought my battles o'er again, have read up the 'late war,' and know the particulars of every campaign, the details of every battle and skirmish from the Secession to the 'chawing up' of the Confederacy, have turned the heads of all the belles and fired with envy the hearts of all the beaux in Belgravia. Oh, Ned, Ned! if I had been Perkin Warbeck or Lambert Simnel, my descendants would now be wearing the British crown!"

"Your success is certainly almost incredible," returned Wenlock; "but—the—the body?"

"Ah! that is the only thought that maddens and alarms me," said Renshaw, turning pale, and speaking in a low serious tone. "The corpse is gone!—gone! But—s-sh!—the boy is coming!"

(To be continued.)

TALES OF THE INVISIBLE WORLD.

THE WRITINGS OF AN ESTATE FOUND THROUGH THE APPEARANCE OF AN APPARITION.

(Concluded from page 32.)

(Concluded from page 32.)

"It *must* be the man we seek," said the squire to the doctor. "I have not the slightest doubt of it."

"Then onward let us go ; we may overtake the villain yet."

"I fear not," said the doctor, "if he once gets into that huge town, we might as well look for a needle in a bundle of hay. It will be impossible to arrest him."

"I care not so much to secure him, doctor, as I do to arrest the progress of the suit in court, for if this be my grandfather's will which he has stolen, he has no doubt been engaged by my enemies to discover and steal it."

"Exactly so."

"And once having it in their possession, it might be altered, and prove the stumbling-block to all my hopes and fortune, except—"

"Except what ?"

"Simply this ; they cannot produce it in court in its mutilated state. He has secured the best part of it truly ; but I have a fragment, and, until it is presented as a whole, in courts of law it will prove useless to my enemies, vengeful as they are."

"And equally as useless to you," said the doctor, "for you are in the same position as they in regard to it."

"True," said the squire ; "I am ; but yet I have hopes that we may overtake the villain ere he reaches London ; in truth, I feel almost certain that the good apparition of my grandfather will aid me in this adventure, if only out of revenge for his cruel murder."

"The villain hinted at that horrible deed," the doctor said.

"Ha! then I have no doubt now that he *has* secured the old will, and that he has been employed to watch the Hall for a long time past. This accounts for the many hobgoblin ghost stories which have, for some time past, been the terror of the servants' hall."

As the squire rode along he looked both to the right and left of the road as if in search of something.

The night was dark, and the clouds were lowering.

All at once the squire stopped, and pointed to a mile-stone.

"That is the spot," he said, sadly.

"What spot ?" the doctor asked.

"Where my grandfather was murdered."

"Indeed !"

"His body was found lying against that mile-stone at midnight. He had been shot by some one unknown, and the bullet had passed through him. He bled intensely internally, but little blood was seen upon his garments. When we first discovered him, we thought he was asleep ; but there was a small red mark upon his white linen which at a distance looked like a piece of crimson ribbon."

"Ribbon !" said the doctor, half aloud, and then thought of the strange conversation which had transpired between himself and the villanous, black-looking rascal in the lumber-room.

He did not interrupt the squire, however, who continued.

"With our lanterns, we went a little further along the road in search of his horse, and had not gone many yards ere one of the party stumbled over the body of the animal, which lay in the middle of the road with its throat cut. The night was such a one as this," said the squire, with a sigh. "I shall not, I cannot ever forget it !"

He had just spoken thus far when a cry from Jem the groom arrested the attention of the two gentlemen.

His horse had shied and stumbled over something in the darkness, and threw its rider upon the ground.

The doctor and squire rushed to the spot, and discovered a dead horse lying in the road, nearly opposite the fatal milestone.

It had broken some bloodvessel, and a pool of gore lay smoking near the animal's nostrils.

"What means this ?" the squire asked. "Is this a judgment?"

"It is !" said some phantom voice that died upon the breeze.

The squire and doctor looked at each other in blank astonishment.

"The same voice," said one, half aloud.

"The spectre," the other replied.

While, for a moment, their thoughts were confused, the same voice said,

"It *is* a judgment. It is only completed in part as yet ; it remains with my grandson to do the rest—to London !—to London !" said the voice aloud, and gradually died away.

Obedient to the spectre-voice the squire and his friend turned their horses' heads towards London, and galloped quickly away, followed by Jem the groom, who was loudly growling at his own misfortune.

"It is the same mare which was stolen from my stables about a month ago. I have no doubt the villain has been secreted about the Hall for months past. I should not have cared for the mare so much, but it bore the name of my grandfather's half-sister, who left England, and was never afterwards heard of. She was shipwrecked."

"Shipwrecked ?" said the doctor, quickly. "What was her Christian name ?"

"Matilda."

"Matilda ? Why that was my mother's name," the doctor said, quickly. "She was shipwrecked on the American coast but was saved, and was afterwards married. What was her name ?"

"As I have said, she was my grandfather's half-sister, and was named Shelton—Matilda Shelton—and to keep her name familiar among his sons, my grandfather always named some favourite valuable mare in memory of her."

"Strange," said the doctor, "that I am a relation, and that we should have become known to each other in so remarkable and mysterious a manner."

The squire and doctor shook hands, and were greatly surprised at their discovered relationship ; but so intent were each upon overtaking the fleeing villain, if possible, before he entered London that for several miles they spoke not, but rode on in deep silence.

At last they came to two roads, both of which led to London, and they knew not which to select.

While they stood debating as to the route a white and shadowy horse and rider passed them without noise or warning, and with snow white garments floating in the wind, the grim rider pointed his lean hand towards the right hand road, which they instinctively followed.

Long during that stormy night they rode amid flashing lightning and pealing thunders, but still onwards they seemed to fly, and always with the spectre horseman far in advance waving his hands wildly in triumph.

At last the distant glimmering of numberless lamps was seen.

With clattering hoofs they dashed into town, but all of a sudden their horses started as if startled by some ghastly and appalling apparition.

They were then before the door of a humble-looking inn. All were a-bed, and deep silence reigned.

They dismounted, and would have knocked, but the door was mysteriously opened for them.

A figure in white beckoned them through the passage !

They followed in fear and trembling to a chamber on the first floor, and this door, like the other, was opened by unseen hands.

In a halo of unearthly, deathly, ghastly light lay the robber on the floor in a pool of blood.

The terrors of that night had well-nigh killed him, but another hired villain had wounded him in a quarrel, and there he lay dying with the precious parchments partly forced into his gaping wound.

The squire eagerly removed them, and blood gushed forth in streams !

With a heartrending groan he died.

A loud unearthly laugh then rang through the apartment.

The doctor and squire looked up from the gory corpse in alarm, and——

There stood the spectre in grim triumph.

"I am avenged !" he said, "and the deeds are yours. I am avenged !" he cried, and vanished.

TALES OF THE INVISIBLE WORLD.

A MARVELLOUS STORY.

CHAPTER I.

THE MARRIAGE FEAST—THE STRANGE GUEST—THE DISAPPEAR-
ANCE.

THERE are indeed more things in heaven and on earth than are
dreamt of in most persons' philosophy. The strange events, full
of horror and despair, as they are, which, after a painful struggle
with a feeling which has prompted the one person who alone
could record them, to carry them with him to the grave, will
sufficiently prove the assertion.

That the immaterial world, upon the confines of which humanity
is hovering, has at times, through the medium of some of its in-

no seeming eye upon him but that of Heaven—with every sound
that should remind him of the great world to which he belongs
hushed, and then ask him—or, rather, let his own heart ask him,
if he will scoff at the supernatural. If he can he is something
more or less than man.

* * * * * * *

A marriage feast is spread in a large but superbly decorated
room of an old mansion; lamps are lighted in an ancient hall;
the clash of pleasant music fills the air with joyous sounds; the
guests are met; smiles are upon every countenance; gladness
in every heart, excepting two. Yes, excepting two; and, strange
to say, those two were the very persons for whom, and on whose

ST. LEON WITNESSES THE EFFECTS OF THE ELIXIR ON JASPER.

habitants, mingled strangely and fearfully with the human
creatures who live, and talk, and have their being on the surface
of this globe, is too well-established a fact now for scepticism to
touch. We have seen instances of Heaven's providence overtaking
the guilty, and not by mortal means; we have seen the current of
a higher destiny protecting the innocent; and we have too many
well-recorded narratives of persons, still denizens of this world,
who have looked upon the beings of another, to doubt that there
may be circumstances under which the disembodied spirits that
hover in the regions of air may make themselves visible to
mortal eyes.

And, although it may be repugnant to our notions of divine
intelligence to imagine that these beings of immortality visit us
for other than good purposes, yet the weakness of human nature
converts that into a terror and a source of maddening excitement,
which else would be received as a warning of some ill to come, or
as a means of holy preparation for that world which lies beyond
the grave.

Let the boldest scoffer of the supernatural that ever lived be
asked to lay his hand upon his heart, and, in the name of Heaven,
declare his disbelief in, and his contempt for, the spirits of another
world, and we may believe that he does truly give no credence to
the existence of such beings; but how few there are who will go
so far in an expression of such belief!

In the hour of careless enjoyment, when the brain is in a state
of jovial excitement, and the spirits are full of pleasurable feelings,
the dim spectre may be scoffed at; but let the individual stand, in
the hour of solemn midnight, in some place of tombs—alone—with

account, so much bustle and excitement had taken place. They
were the bride and the bridegroom.

We will not wrong the gentle and the beautiful girl who was on
that day led to the altar by one who had ardently sought her love,
by saying that lightly had she given her consent to be his, and
now repented of her choice. Oh! no; her heart was all affection
—all sincerity; but, on the face of the bridegroom had appeared
a cloud of care, which had each moment deepened, until no one
could fail to perceive deep traces of mental agony stealing over
him, until, by the time he should have taken his place, with such
smiles as should have become him on such a festal occasion, he
looked as if the saddening weight of an additional fifty years was
added to his age.

The bride had noted this with anxious eyes, and no wonder then
that the tears stood in her eyes, and she trembled to see him, to
whom she was now attached for life, in so fearful a condition.
Twice she asked him what was the cause of such evident agony of
spirit, and twice he answered,

"Nothing—nothing!"

But the tone in which the answer was given was heart-rending
in the extreme; and now, as the beautiful Linda hung upon her
husband's arm—the husband of an hour—at the door of the
banquet hall, in her father's house, she again looked imploringly
in his face and said,

"Oh, St. Leon! St. Leon! Tell me, I implore you, what has
occurred. You are not the same person that you were. I—I
should not have known you. Is this all a horrible dream, or can
it be that I still behold in you the object of my love? St. Leon,

answer me! oh, answer me, as you hope for mercy here and hereafter."

St. Leon, for such was her lover and her husband's name, shook like one in an ague. A fearful spasm crossed his face, and, instead of entering the hall, which was rapidly filling with the wedding guests, he stepped aside into a small ante-room where were burning several lights, in massive silver candelabra, and he sunk into a chair with a deep groan.

Linda had followed him, and now she clasped her hands in agony as she exclaimed,

"It is illness!—it is illness! and you have been battling against it because you would not alarm me. Oh, it was cruel of you, St. Leon—dear St. Leon!—but I will instantly summon assistance——"

"Hold—hold, Linda!—not—not yet! Close the door. The music jars upon my ears—I—shall be better yet."

"You are then ill?"

"Not as you fancy. It is a sickness of the soul."

Linda trembled as she repeated his words in wonder and amazement.

"Hush, hush," he said, as he laid a trembling hand upon her wrist; "saw you not at the altar's foot—an—unbidden guest?"

"I saw your eyes fixed upon a stranger whom no one knew."

"But I knew him! God of heaven, I knew him!"

The door of the small apartment in which they were, and which Linda, agreeably to the request of St. Leon, had closed, was now opened suddenly, and a tall, gaunt, cadaverous-looking figure presented itself, saying,

"The banquet waits, St. Leon. The banquet waits."

A half shriek burst from the lips of St. Leon, as he beheld this man, and then, stretching forth his hands, as if he feared he should come closer to him, he cried, in agonised accents,

"Away, away! What seek ye of me? Away, away, I say! Hence, horrible being, or phantom, I know not which you are. Away, I say—away!"

"Not yet," said the figure. "St. Leon, the change is at hand."

St. Leon shook from head to foot, as he muttered,

"No, no, no! That was a dream!"

"It was not," said the figure. "Do you hear that crash of music? They are drinking the bridegroom's health."

"Oh, horror!"

"You or I must respond to the toast. That you know well. St. Leon, have you forgotten that this is September the 20th, 1750?"

St. Leon let his head drop on his hands, and groaned deeply.

"Lady," said the strange figure, "will you leave us?"

"No, no!" cried Linda. "This is my husband. Heaven has now united us, and man shall not part us. Help, help!"

She flew to a bell-rope as she spoke, and made an attempt to ring the bell to which it communicated, but the rope came down at a touch, and fell to the floor.

"Maiden," said the stranger, "it is useless to contend with destiny. St. Leon, follow me."

"Oh, no, no, no!" shrieked the bridegroom. "No, no! oh, God, no!"

"St. Leon," said the mysterious stranger again, in the same cold accents, "follow me."

"Help!" shrieked Linda.

"Hush!" said the stranger, and he waved his arm. When she tried to speak again, she felt half choked, and that she could not utter a sound above a whisper.

She sunk, trembling, on a settle that was in the room, and then again the stranger said,

"St. Leon, follow me."

Wringing his hands like one in a state of the most frantic grief, St. Leon rose, but it was only to totter forward a few paces, and to fall in an attitude of abject supplication at the stranger's feet.

"Mercy!" he said, "mercy! Tell me this is some trick, some juggle, to make me ashamed of what occurred ten years ago, and I will bless you. Oh, have mercy upon me!"

"What is done," said the stranger, "may not be undone. You have sought on this very date to drown remembrance of what you never could forget in the joy and the novelty of such a scene as this; but you are mistaken. Once again, I say, St. Leon, follow me!"

"No, no! help me, Heaven!—mercy—mercy!"

"What ho! St. Leon—Linda—St. Leon!" cried several voices from the hall, which was just across a corridor. "St. Leon, the banquet waits. Linda—Linda, where are you?"

The sound of footsteps came rapidly towards the ante-room. The tall, mysterious stranger seemed to hesitate a moment, and then he strode into the room, and with one sweep of his hand he overthrew the lights. All was darkness; and an old clock, that had been for years above the principal gateway of the hall, struck twelve. Linda felt her senses leaving her, a film spread itself over her eyes, she thought she heard a shriek, and she thought she saw a flash of light, and the forms of several of the wedding guests; and then all to her was chaos.

*   *   *   *   *   *

There was a strange, benumbed sensation about the heart of the beautiful Linda, as she now slowly recovered from the swoon she had fallen into. An universal tremor shook her for a moment, and then she opened her eyes as she began to hear the murmer of voices around her.

"Linda—Linda! My own—my beautiful Linda!" said a voice in the kindest accents, a voice which she knew full well. "Oh, look upon me, dearest Linda; speak to me—tell me that you live, and that this seeming trance of death has passed away, never—never to return."

The voice was rich and melodious; an arm—it was that of the speaker—supported her; and now, as she looked up, she saw a face close to hers, upon which fell the glare of many lights, showing its handsome features to the greatest advantage, and the agitation which alarm for her safety likewise had depicted on it.

"St. Leon!" she gasped, "St. Leon!"

"Yes, dearest," said he who supported her, "I am St. Leon. Do you not know me, beautiful Linda, as him to whom you have so recently plighted your marriage vows, and whom you have made the happiest of men by so doing, dearest Linda?"

"Good God!" she said as a convulsive shudder shook her frame, "Good God! how wonderfully changed!"

"She has not quite recovered yet," said Sir Marmaduke Beaufoy, her father. "I much wonder what can have produced this sudden and unlooked for illness."

"Oh, she will be quite well soon," said St. Leon, as he pressed her gentle hand in his.

"Oh! tell me, St. Leon," said Linda, as she looked up beseechingly in his face, "tell me what has happened. Conceal nothing from me, I charge you. You were strangely altered, and now, as if by magic, you have returned to the likeness of your former self."

"Why, girl, are you mad?" passionately exclaimed her father.

"No, father, no! I am not mad; but there was a dreadful scene enacted in this room, in which St. Leon bore a part. I am not mad now, but I fear I shall be. Oh, father! father! implore him to tell you why, a short time since, he looked so pale and wan—so aged? why he implored for mercy of one who seemed to have a dreadful power over him? why the lights here were dashed to the floor? why he now is restored to his former appearance? Ask him all that—I wait, and tremble for an answer."

Sir Marmaduke Beaufoy was not the most clear-headed man in the world, and he was rather a matter-of-fact personage, and one whom too many matters of fact at once were extremely likely to confuse; so no wonder that he felt quite in a maze of bewilderment after this speech of Linda's, and knew not what reply to make. St. Leon, however, spared him the pain and difficulty of shaping any answer, by saying,

"Probably I can throw more light upon the matter than any one. You know, honoured sir, and you all, most welcome and respected guests, that my sweet Linda lingered some short space with me on our route to the banquet hall. You all had passed into it, when she complained of slight indisposition, and requested that I would bring her, for a moment, into this apartment, that she might recover the flurry of her spirits before she made her appearance at the banquet. I, of course, complied, and led her to this settee, on which she sunk in an apparent state of great physical exhaustion. I strove, however, to cheer her as best I might; but, to my great grief and alarm, she fainted here in my arms as you found her."

Linda never took her eyes off the face of the speaker while these words were uttered, and when St. Leon had done talking she shuddered for a moment, and murmured some words, but in too low a tone for any one to hear.

"My dear," said Sir Marmaduke, "you see it is all nothing but agitation of spirits, in consequence of this auspicious occasion."

"Why do you look so sad, Linda?" said her brother, Robert Beaufoy, who now stepped forward. "Don't you now remember what St. Leon has said?"

"Not one word," said Linda.

"Indeed? That is very strange."

"Not at all," said St. Leon. "Excuse me, my dear Robert, for contradicting you; but it is far from unusual for these kind of swoons to obliterate from the memory all trace of what circumstances immediately preceded them."

"That is stranger still," said Robert.

"And yet so true," remarked St. Leon. "Come, now, my Linda—lean on me, dearest. We will not allow this little incident to disturb the banquet. Come, dearest, come. To the hall—to the hall."

Linda looked as pale as a marble statue, but she rose, and said nothing. She did lean on the arm of her husband; but Heaven only knows what a whirl of strange conflicting thoughts and sensations filled her brain.

The banquet hall had been completely now deserted, for the guests, as many of them as could, were in the small ante-room, whither they had hurried upon the first alarm of something being amiss having reached them, and those who could not obtain an entrance there had lingered in the corridor. When the bride and the bridegroom walking abreast, with whom was Sir Marmaduke Beaufoy, entered the banquet hall, they were surprised to see but one person there. That person was the mysterious stranger who had been present at the ceremony, and with whom St. Leon had had so strange an interview in the ante-room. The moment Linda saw him, she cried,

"There, there! Oh, father, question that man. Speak to him—oh, speak to him! St. Leon, can you now tell me it was all a vain and delusive dream?"

"What was all a dream?" said St. Leon.

"Oh, do not torture me by this pretended ignorance. There is the man—the man to whom you knelt for mercy!"

The guests looked amazed and stupefied, as well they might, and Robert Beaufoy, stepping forward, said,

"Seeing that this person was a stranger to us all, I asked him in the chapel who he was, and he told me he was a particular and intimate friend of St. Leon's; upon which I bade him stay and welcome, and said no more."

"A friend of mine!" said St. Leon; "I never saw him before in all my life."

"Good God!" said Linda.

"Then I will question him upon the presumption of intruding himself upon us," said Sir Marmaduke; and he walked up to the stranger, to whom he said, "Pray, sir, may I enquire who you are?"

"Yes," was the reply, in a deep tone; "my name is St. Leon."

"Oh, a madman!" cried several; "a lunatic, who may be dangerous. We had better have him removed at once."

"Decidedly mad!" said St. Leon; "turn him from the house—turn him from the house immediately!"

"Hold!" said the tall stranger, in a melancholy voice; "I am not mad. Linda, God bless you! pray for me, dearest—farewell! farewell! But let no one touch this feast! The curse of one who is agonised beyond mortal knowledge shall light on all who touch this repast. In ten years from this date I shall return; and, oh, Linda! Linda! let me entreat you to forsake that man who hangs upon you now. He is not your husband. Oh, shun him—shun him as you would a pestilence. I say shun him, Linda. You are young, and you are beautiful. You are on the threshold of an existence which should be one, to such as you, of unalloyed sweets; but bitter indeed will be the cup of your destiny if you continue to look with eyes of affection upon that dreadful being by your side; I cannot—dare not call him man. He is not the lover who won your gentle heart. Farewell—a long, a sad farewell. On this day ten years hence we shall meet again, Linda; till then, farewell."

The mysterious stranger sighed deeply, and smote his breast as he moved slowly towards the door.

"What strange freaks," said St. Leon, "the diseased imagination takes. The poor fellow is most decidedly mad."

"Yes," said Sir Marmaduke, "and, unless he leaves this place instantly, I will take some means which may be disagreeable to him of telling him, sir, that, mad or not mad, it is not safe for him to intrude himself here an uninvited guest."

The tall stranger turned a mournful but not an angry glance upon Sir Marmaduke Beaufoy, and he said,—

"Sir, folly speaks from your mouth, and consequently what you say is to me innoxious. I am going of my own free will and consent. Linda, have you not one kindly word——"

"I do not know you," said Linda; and yet as she spoke there arose in her heart a strange kindly feeling towards that now melancholy-looking man, who at first in the small ante-room had awakened no sensations but those of terror in her mind.

"You hear," said St. Leon; "she does not know you. Why do you linger here? The lady does not know you."

"Nobody knows you," said Sir Marmaduke. "You have confirmed my previous opinion, that you are quite mad, by calling me a fool. I am the representative of one of the most ancient families in this kingdom, and to call me a fool is enough to prove anybody mad. Nobody ever presumed to say so much."

"Nobody was candid enough," said the stranger, and he walked slowly and deliberately from the banquet hall.

His manner had until now been quiet even unto melancholy. He had seemed to be deeply depressed, but now, when he reached the door, he suddenly turned, and in a loud, impressive voice he cried,—

"Let this banquet remain till I return, Linda; let it not be touched. Close the doors of this hall, and leave all that you now look upon untouched till I return; and, more than all, let me charge you, as you value life, happiness, and the approbation of Heaven, not to retire to night until you shall see in the eastern sky the first grey tints of morning."

"Begone!" cried St. Leon, furiously, as these words fell from the stranger's lips,—"begone!"

"I have given my warning," said the stranger; "see how he quails under it. Linda, remember that which I have said. Forsake the banquet, but keep up the dance if you will—the song and the jest, but let it be till morning."

He passed across the corridor and down the grand staircase which led to the lower part of the vast building, where the preparations for the ball that was to ensue after the banquet were made. No one liked to interfere with him to stop him. St. Leon, it is true, half drew his sword from its scabbard, and looked ferocious, but in a few moments he managed to subdue his passion, and to present the same smiling aspect he had always done.

"Dear Linda," he said, as he looked fondly in the face of his bride, "dear Linda, why for one moment can you permit the ravings of a madman to cause you uneasiness?"

Linda trembled as she replied,—

"An unknown fear oppresses me. I am very unhappy. Heaven only knows what crisis of my fate is at hand; but I am much oppressed."

"To the banquet, dearest, to the banquet! You will soon rid yourself of these uneasy thoughts. Let us take our seats at the banquet, and we shall soon forget this little incident, which has cast a temporary gloom over our joyous proceedings. Come, dear Linda, let me see you smile again, as oft I have seen you smile while listening to the words in which I have delighted to paint my love."

Linda did not smile: each moment seemed to add something to the vague feeling of uneasiness which was filling her mind with terror; she trembled, and her cheeks turned pale, while ever and anon she cast her eyes towards the door through which the mysterious stranger had passed, as if she hoped and longed to see him re-enter.

St. Leon bit his lips, and those of the guests who observed him closely could see that now and then he knit his brows, and an awful aspect of passion came across his face—an aspect such as they had never observed before; and not a few of them entertained lively fears for the future happiness of the beautiful girl who was about being committed to the care of such a man.

"Yes, of course," said Sir Marmaduke, "to the banquet, good friends—to the banquet. All is ready. But one cup of wine has been quaffed, and that was to the health of the bride. And now, my friends—How now, Linda! what is this?"

Linda had suddenly thrown herself at her father's feet, and had clasped one of his hands in both hers.

"Father, dear, dear father," she said "listen to me. I will not rise from this humble posture until you have promised to grant me that which I shall now request of you."

"God bless me!" said Sir Marmaduke. "I—I—really, now——"

"Nay, do not refuse me, dear father. I have no mother; I have not been cheered, as well you know, by a mother's smile for years now past; but you have, by an unvarying kindness I can never forget, filled to me the place of both father and mother. Never came there a harsh word from your lips to your motherless girl. Father, father, you will not now refuse to me the boon which I kneel to you to implore you to grant."

"But, my dear Linda, what is it?"

"You promise me that you will grant it, father?"

"Why—why, without knowing——"

"Oh, it is an easy boon; it is one which will cost but a word of assent. Say that you will grant it to me, father. Swear solemnly, by your hopes of heaven, you will grant me this one request."

"Nay," interposed St. Leon, "this is too bad, Linda; if your request be a proper one, wherefore should you exact an oath?"

"Sir," said Sir Marmaduke, who on the whole was rather flattered that his beautiful child should pay him so very handsome a compliment as he considered she had done, by what had fallen from her lips before so many people,—"sir, don't you interfere, if you please."

"Idiot!" muttered St. Leon, as he turned aside.

"Rise, Linda, my dear," added Sir Marmaduke. "I must confess that even to my judgment your conduct is somewhat extraordinary; but, as you truly say, I have been an excellent father to you. That point is settled, and therefore I will promise to grant your request, whatever it may be."

"You will swear, father?"

"No, no; but I will promise on my honour."

Sir Marmaduke laid his hand upon his heart, and made a sort of circular bow to all the guests as he uttered these words, as if he bade them take notice that when he mentioned his honour, it was something that required particular notice from everybody.

"I am content," said Linda, as now she rose and flung her arms around her father's neck, "I am content. Dear father, I wish that this banquet hall should be closed for ten years just as it is. Extinguish the lights, and place your seal upon its doors for ten years."

St. Leon had assumed an attitude of the most eager listening while Linda propounded her request, but when he heard it a great weight seemed to be lifted off his heart, and he drew himself up and smiled as he fetched a long breath of relief.

"Shut—up—the hall?" said the father.

"Yes, father, yes."

"And the banquet—the wines—the—the made dishes—the—the rare confections—the family plate—the—the everything——"

"Yes, yes."

"Bless my soul!"

"You have passed your word, father; the honour of our house demands a fulfilment of it. You will keep your word?"

"Why—oh, yes; I suppose I must. My good friends, I will order a fresh table to be spread below in the reception hall. The cellars of the mansion are stocked with wine, and the kitchens are full of provender. Since it is Linda's wish that this apartment should be closed for ten years, let it be so. I have given her my word, and that is amply sufficient, surely."

The guests looked at each other with surprise, as well indeed they might, when this most extraordinary whim was propounded to them. They scarcely knew which to think was the maddest of the two, the old baronet, or his daughter. If she, they considered, were insane or romantic enough to shut up the hall for such a period merely because a mysterious and melancholy man, whom nobody knew, had started the idea, they at least had hoped that Sir Marmaduke would have had worldly wisdom enough to have hindered the execution of what nobody could denominate anything else but a mad freak.

However, the baronet locked the door, and, at Linda's desire, he handed the key to her.

"How late it gets," said St. Leon, "did you not hear the turret clock strike one?"

"Yes, yes," said Linda; "let us now to the ball-room."

CHAPTER II.

THE DANCE—THE MORNING LIGHT—THE DEEP BAY WINDOW—
DISAPPEARANCE OF THE BRIDEGROOM.

THE hall in which preparations had been made for dancing was much larger than that in which the banquet had been spread, which was now locked up for so long a period of time. It was hung with garlands of flowers and brilliantly lighted, while unseen musicians played the most bewitching melodies from those masters of the art of music, from whom modern composers filch with all the unblushing impudence of sparrows in a wheat field.

The whole floor was chalked in fanciful devices, in different coloured crayons, and the vast apartment, at first sight, presented a picture of great beauty and taste.

Into this hall streamed all the guests, and each minute was adding to the arrivals, so that, vast in its proportions as it was, there was every likelihood that it would soon be filled.

Linda seemed to have recovered some portion of her spirits now. Occasionally she smiled, which seemed to satisfy St. Leon and her father that all was right, and that the shutting up of the hall had satisfied her; but there were some present who were keener observers, and probably who knew her better than either her father or her lover, and they shook their heads as they came to the conclusion that this seeming serenity of Linda was not of the right stamp.

She conversed freely with St. Leon, but it was in a bewildered kind of tone; and she danced with him several dances; while refreshments for the guests who had been disappointed of the banquet were being profusely laid at the far end of the dancing-hall, so that every one could go and help himself or herself, as they might fell disposed, during the pauses of the dance.

It was not exactly etiquette for the bride to dance all the evening with the bridegroom, although St. Leon seemed to wish to monopolise her hand for that time, and kept so close to her that no one could for nearly an hour get an opportunity of asking her hand for a dance.

There was one, however, who report had said was a disappointed lover, and who appeared thoroughly determined on dancing, if it was but for the last time, with her. He made his way through the throng, at the conclusion of a dance, towards her, and with great courtesy he said,

"May I request the honour of your hand for the next dance?"

"I regret," interposed St. Leon, "that she is engaged for the next dance."

"Then the next dance after that," said the persevering guest.

"Yes," said Linda, "I am free for that."

"I am greatly honoured," said the guest.

"Oh," said St. Leon, "I will waive my right then this next dance, to take it after, if you please."

This arrangement Linda consented to, and when she and the new partner she thus had had taken their places, she said, with an endeavour to speak carelessly, but with an evident agitation in her manner,

"Can you tell me, Courtney, at what hour the day breaks?"

"What a strange question, Linda,"

"You must not call me Linda now."

"Pardon me, I cannot shape my lips to name you by your new designation of the Lady St. Leon."

"Heed not that, but answer my question."

The dance at this moment commenced, and as they were situated they were compelled at once to take part in it; so that there was no opportunity, for some minutes, for Courtney to answer the question which Linda had asked of him. When, however, during the progress of the figure, they had again a moment's pause, Linda anxiously repeated the question, and to which her partner replied,

"Oh, Linda, in watching the casement of the room in which you slept, and in dreaming of the possibility only that you might one day be mine, I have too often noted when, at different seasons, the slant beams of the morning sun first rested on the tree tops, not to be able to answer you."

"A truce to this language," said Linda. "But that I know you honourable and in high esteem with my father, your present mood would be insulting. If you will answer me my question do so at once; for see, we shall in another minute be involved in the dance."

"Then, Linda, the sun will rise this morning at a quarter past four precisely,"

"Thanks, thanks."

"And can you not dance the next dance with me?"

"No, no. You know I am engaged to my—husband."

Courtney made a despairing gesture, and then was compelled to lead Linda to St. Leon. As he did so some one whom they passed remarked,

"It is two o'clock," and Linda murmured,

"Two hours and a quarter yet."

"What on earth," thought Courtney, "can she want to know when the sun rises, and so particularly, for?"

St. Leon smiled when she came back to him, and bowed and thanked Courtney in the most bland manner. When he had an opportunity of speaking to Linda, he said,

"Dearest Linda, I forgot to mention that I should be forced to be up and out early this morning."

Linda was silent; so with some slight amount of vexation in his face, St. Leon resumed,

"And you see the time is flying fast now. I presume you do not intend to dance again to-night?"

"Yes; yet awhile I shall dance. You cannot think how passionately fond I am of dancing."

"Yes; but consider, it is two o'clock."

"Hark! how inviting the music sounds. Come, we are wanted in the measure; or, if you do not feel disposed to dance, Courtney will gladly take your place. You cannot feel jealous of him now."

(*To be continued in No. 6 of* THE JOLLY DOGS OF LONDON.)

THE JOLLY DOGS OF LONDON.

THE STABBING MATCH.

CHAPTER XVI.—(*continued.*)

The page entered at the moment, and brought in the supper.

It was a delicate repast, no luxury in season was wanting, and the wine was of the choicest quality.

Having despatched the supper, this brace of miscreants sat for some time smoking their fragrant cigars in silence, each occupied with his own thoughts.

"This will not last! It cannot last!" cried Wenlock, leaping up nervously. "We shall be betrayed! Some little accident will arise, some slight clue will be discovered which will lead to our detection and our ruin."

"Hush! hush! It is not safe to talk thus even with closed doors," rejoined Renshaw, in an anxious whisper.

"But surely you will not act so insanely as to keep up this perilous game to the risk of your neck? Why not draw as much of your usurped wealth as you can lay your hands on, and escape."

"I have thought of that," said Renshaw, gloomily; "but it can't be done yet. The least mistake may destroy us; one false move will lead to a sure result. Out of my very desperation I am firm and fearless. I must play out the game!"

"Dick, I must have five thousand pounds."

"Well, you will win more on the Derby."

No. 6.

"I doubt, I doubt."

"What horse have you backed?"

"Redan."

"Humph! you should have laid on the first favourite."

"You must advance me the sum."

"Impossible! I dare not draw so much. There are reasons, cogent reasons, Ned, why I must keep quiet yet; but have you given up all thoughts of carrying fortune by storm."

"No; I have seen the man—the man who is to assist me," muttered Wenlock.

"I have seen him to-night, and if all's lost in the event, the thing will have to be done."

"Who is your assistant?"

"Why, the filthy cad; his fellow rascals call him the Lummy Cove."

"Ha, the very man!"

"And now, Dick, as it is growing light, and I don't care to go to bed for so short a time as is allowed me for repose, let us speak on a subject I have nearest at heart—let us talk of one whom I fear I have lost for ever."

"Of whom?"

"Angeline!"

"You want to know the secret of the *white rose leaves?*"

"Yes."

"Well, I will see that there are no eavesdroppers about. I'll send the servants to bed, and then, my boy, I will tell you *a part* of the strange story."

Renshaw rose, rang for the page, told the servants to retire, and when he had fully ascertained that all was safe, and that he could speak freely, he seated himself, and for more than an hour he enchained the attention of his confederate by a wild and tragic story.

Lest the interest of our romance should be impaired by a premature revelation of Angeline's cruel secret, we suppress for the present the particulars of the conversation of this brace of desperate villains, and will proceed to give an account of the Jolly Dogs' trip to Epsom on the Derby Day.

CHAPTER XVII.

THE DRIVE TO EPSOM.

A dashing four-in-hand, crowded by a large party of the Jolly Dogs, drew up before the door of a gay-looking little house in Pimlico.

Among the company were several young fellows, to whom we have been already personally introduced: Harry Rattleton, Edgar Wenlock, Humphrey Puffy, George Grant, Pharamond Fitz-Hubert, Charly Vert, Shem Beamish, Jemmy Gimp, and Dandy Jack, who took the ribbons.

The whole party were gaily dressed for the occasion, and sported coats of various light colours—dun, lavender, or pale primrose; some white hats and veils of royal blue, green, violet, and other gaudy hues; and carried in their daintily gloved hands bouquets and race-glasses.

Harry Rattleton leaped down from the box.

There was no need to knock at the door, for a pair of glowing beauties, who had been watching from the window, rushed out upon the steps to meet their gallants.

Amy and Madeline were lovely girls, one as bright and fair as summer noon, the other as dark as summer night. They were extravagantly dressed in the very newest and gayest mode, wearing Fanchon bonnets of white fancy straw, trimmed with small ivy leaves, and glistening with crystal beads; dresses of light mousseline de laine, and tight-fitting boddices of the same material, while light shawls of rich material, and brilliant colours and design, were cast loosely and gracefully about their finely-moulded shoulders.

The president of the "Jolly Dogs" gallantly handed the ladies into the drag, and then remounted the box.

The bugler gave a shrill, loud blast, and Dandy Jack, shaking the reins, drove on.

The road over Vauxhall Bridge was crowded with vehicles of every variety, burdened with passengers of every class and every character,—

Barouches, drags, wagonettes, Hansoms, omnibuses, dog-carts, Broughams, landaus, chaises, vans, carts, and "boards of trade;" nobles, gentry, swells, merchants, tradesmen, gentlemen of the press, artists, actors, sporting-men, costers, cads, tag-rag and bobtail!

Whisking, jolting, bumping, swinging, rattling, rolling along in an endless, roaring stream of buoyant life, the tide flowed strongly ever onwards, through the crowded, buzzing streets, past the closed shops and under the tiers of windows, which sparkled with constellations of bright smiling eyes!

Here and there mounted policemen stemmed the dense tide, bawling their scarce regarded mandates with a vain assumption of authority.

The wretched little street ragamuffins, "to be found every-where," as the grim advertisements hath it, tumbled, whooping and yelling, amid the horses' feet and close beside or before the whirling wheels, their hungry eyes aglare for "coppers," and their skinny, half-bare limbs whisking over and over in the dust-clouds.

Cheers, chaff, songs, volleys of oaths, outbursts of ringing laughter, occasional shrieks, shouts of remonstrance, swearing, or command, sudden blasts of the war-denouncing trumpet, the shrill tootle of penny whistles, the rump-a-tump-twum of the Ethiopian banjo, the rattle of the Baltimore bones, and the continuous, panting screech, "k'rect card, gents; card o' the day!"

The morning sky is overcast, the sun's face being veiled by billowy clouds that surge like a cold grey sea overhead, while the wind blows keen and chill; but soon the day's lord exerts his genial power and pours a brightening flood of his warm, dazzling rays through the envious cloud-curtain, and far and wide the rich green fields glare forth, spangling, as if they had been sown, as Dandy Jack remarked, with "sov's and shillings," for we are now on the outposts of this British Babel, and are breasting the fresh, sharp breeze through the open country.

The "Swan," at Stockwell.

Dandy Jack pulled up, and the party refreshed themselves with "shandy gaff," and then once more wedged into the rank and file of vehicles and rattled merrily on.

Another halt at the "Bells," at Tooting; a third at the "Cock," at Sutton, and then pouring, roaring, cheering, the mighty tide plunges into the rugged lane that leads on to the course, the trampling hoofs and fervid wheels flying, dashing on through soaring clouds of fine dust, which render the gaudy, fluttering veils a desirable protection.

Emerging at last from its narrow channel, the living tide discharges itself upon the open Downs.

Dandy Jack waves his whip, Jemmy Gimp gives a triumphant flourish on the horn, the Jolly Dogs jump down from their seats on to the crisp, trampled sward, while Pharamond Fitz-Hubert and Harry Rattleton gallantly hand the ladies from the drag.

Amy, the fair-haired, throws a languishing glance into the eyes of Pharamond, who has written sonnets in her praise in the Weekly Penny Buster, and for whom she has a predilection; then, sweet maid, she coyly downcasts her eyes, while on her soft fair cheek rests the rich rose blush—permanently.

All this while she is leaning on the arm of Harry Rattleton, who adores her.

"Are you tired, my dear?" asked Harry, tenderly.

Sweetly the coral lips ripple forth a gentle answer.

"Yes, ducky; and, I say, 'Arry, when are we going to have something to heat? I'm so 'ungry, dear, I could heat a hox."

Hampers were unpacked, and a snow-white cloth being spread upon the sward, the gallants and the two fair ladies sat down to regale themselves al fresco with a luncheon of cold chicken, pigeon pies, ham, lamb and lobster, with champagne, sherry, Bass's bitter beer, and Guinness's stout.

During this arcadian banquet the party of voyagers were entertained by a band of nigger minstrels, conducted by that illustrious musician Mr. Punch, who led them round and round in a merry circle, thrashing themselves and each other with their tambourines, banjos, and other instruments of music, and blending their chording voices in a lively chorus,

"Oh, we all feel gay
When Johnny comes marching home!"

They were an unusually smart set of fellows, had good voices, and, it deserves to be recorded, they toned down much of the coarseness of their silly ramp songs. A shower of coin rewarded their pains.

Harry Rattleton rose glass in hand, and thus addressed his party,

"Bumpers round, Jolly Dogs! Hurrah for the Derby Day! England's great carnival! Europe's grand event! Spring's prime holiday! Let not black care sit behind the horseman. Let those who make the straight tip and are landed safe be moderate in their exultation; let those who are 'sold' when some dark horse kicks the pot over, grin and bear their adverse fortune manfully. Nothing should dash the spirits of a Jolly Dog! Call Ned Wenlock to order; he wears a phiz like that sorry pup of the nursery, who 'must be hanged to-morrow.' Fill up; here's the blue ribbon to the best horse, and the best jock to ride him!"

"Hurrah!"

"Do you remember, Humphrey," laughed George Grant, "when you and I and Ned rode the handicap on Blackheath?"

"Oh, what a falling off was there," groaned Mr. Puffy.

"At least you were master of the situation," rejoined Grant, in the same tone of banter. "*We* were thrown by our fiery steeds, but *you* threw your horse. He went down with a crash as if Atlas had shifted the globe on to his back."

"No wonder Puffy has laid on the Redan," said Harry Rattleton.

"Chaff! miserable chaff! Winnow it as you will, you won't find one grain of wit in it," cried Mr. Puffy, his broad face beaming with mirth. "Like Pharoah's lean kine you would devour me for being in better condition than yourselves. Body of Banting! I scorn your puny shafts; they are but——"

"Needles thrown at a whale."

"Lilliputian arrows aimed at Gulliver."

"Gnat stings to an alligator."

"Pshaw! listen to the band."

"Gad, my sportive pups, talking of 'bands,' what a drum-major old Humphrey would make!"

"True, Jack; and what a pioneer to an army."

"How so, Mr. Pharamond?"

"Why, my boy, in crossing a river, for instance, if it kept close in your wake a whole regiment might pass dry-shod."

"Out on ye, starvelings, I'll no longer sit in the seat of the scornful. Hark! the bell rings; I'll just take a turn round the course."

"The bobbies will bless ye. They are clearing the course; go and assist them."

"Pah! you wasps."

And Mr. Puffy rose and sauntered towards the grand stand.

The party now broke up, some following Mr. Puffy, others straying off in twos and threes.

Dandy Jack and Edgar Wenlock slipped away unobserved.

Harry Rattleton and the ladies remained by the carriage.

"Dear 'Arry, you will keep your promise, won't you, now?" said Amy.

"Yes, if I win."

"What promise was that?" asked Madeline, sharply.

"A promise he made to *me*. Mind your own business," returned Amy.

"Well I'm sure," cried the dark beauty, tossing her head and curling her lip, "I hope, miss, that Harry will not forget his engagements with me."

"Oh, how happy could I be with either!" mumbled poor Harry, shrugging his shoulders.

"Or with neither," said Amy.

"Better still."

"Or with the favoured one," said Madeline, her black eyes flashing. "I see I'm not in the fashion."

"The fashion, my love?"

"Ay, the fashion! It is but fashion; a man keeps his carriage, his servant, his leman, for fashion."

"His lemon!" rejoined Harry, drawing in the fresh breeze through his clenched teeth.

"Miss Madeline is allers readin' a parcel of nonsensical pero'dicals and novels," said Amy the fair, "and she uses sich queer words. What's a leman?"

"A wretched ——," gasped Madeline, striking her forehead. "No, but I'm *not* romantic."

She laughed hysterically.

"But what do you mean, Madeline, not in the fashion? Why, my black diamond, your last dress——"

"Dress! *she* thinks of dress! I think of you, of myself. My life——"

"Massy tresses of silken sable that rival the raven's wing, as mad Charlie Vert would say. What is the matter with your hair? Haven't you paid for it?"

"No; it should be dyed—the cursed gold colour, that's the colour of the age. Now, if my 'raven tresses' were red like hers——"

"Phew! here's a storm in a teacup! You girls have been quarreling again. Oh, dear! oh, dear! I swear, by all that's expedient, if you keep up this stupid feud I'll leave you both."

"Leave *me*, Harry, leave me for this—but there, what can I expect from you?"

"You a——"

"A Mormon and she a——"

"Fust engineer in a milliner's shop!"

"You make me mad."

"Poor paltry guv'ness; I wonders you—with your edication—— !"

"Hold hard!" cried the gallant Harry, interposing between the ladies; for Madeline was about to throw herself upon her rival.

"Leave her bide," screamed Amy. "Let her come on—if my 'air is the prettiest and most fashionable. Much! This comes of learnin' the pianer and parley vous Francais. Oh! werry refined!"

Madeline dropped her head on the young roué's shoulder."

"Oh, Harry!—you know—you know how I—I loved you," she sobbed bitterly; "and why do you so deeply degrade me? Why do you——Oh, oh!" And she brust into a passion of weeping.

"My God!" cried Mr. Rattleton, stamping his foot with vivacious vexation. "Love me! Don't be a fool then! You know," he added, in a fierce whisper, "you know, my dearest, prettiest, truest Madeline, that I——that you are all the world to me; but here, on this day, to make me a butt—a laughing-stock—to subject yourself to the insolent triumph of—her; why, love! you hate me! Your selfish——"

"No, no, dear, no; I'll bear it, I will—I will indeed," murmured the girl, excitedly. "Kill me if you like, I know I'm to blame!"

"There—there; no, you're *not* to blame, darling Madeline. Hush! believe in me, trust me,—there, there; that's right—and only trust me! I'm in a fix—you see I am! I've gone wrong! Wait, if you had been more patient——"

"Yes; yes."

"That's well! Now you're a dear, good girl; now you're reasonable—and you won't quarrel with——well you won't quarrel with her?"

"I'll not, Harry. There, it's over now."

Madeline dried her eyes.

Harry tenderly handed her into the carriage.

In less than ten minutes she and Amy were embracing each other with all the fondness of affectionate sisters.

Drawing a long breath, and bending his arched brows, the modern Macheath moved away some paces from his mistresses.

"Vell, 'Arry, I must say you are jest a enviable feller!" said Jemmy Gimp, with a grin; "the deah gals——"

"Blast the 'gals!'" exclaimed the Jolly Dog, with more vehemence than gallantry.

CHAPTER XVIII.

THE COURSE.

DING, dong! ding, dong! The race-bell was ringing sonorously forth its intimation to all stragglers to leave the smooth turf of the course on which the fated steeds were to run their fierce race for so many thousands of golden sovereigns; and ranks of policemen tramped steadily and peremptorily along, hurrying the crowd before them, and sweeping the masses right and left like grass before the mower's scythe.

Meanwhile, Mr. Puffy, George Grant, and the two literary gentlemen strolled through the dense, vast multitudes that spread for miles across the Downs.

As they passed along, a fair girl seated in an open barouche, and dressed in snowy white, shielding her eyes from the sun-blaze, with a parasol of delicate white silk, embroidered with butterflies, smiled and nodded at the party.

George Grant sprang to the side of the carriage, leaving his companions to saunter on.

"My dear Lyddy," said George, taking the girl's hand, and pressing it to his lips, "this is quite a surprise, I thought you were not going to the Derby; but where is Angeline?"

"Why, she—there, George, she did not come."

"And who is your chaperon?"

"Young Leoni. The dear fellow, how hard he tries to amuse me, and to make me believe that his happiness is completed by my presence when all the while he is inwardly chafing, because that foolish girl disappointed him."

"Why did she so? What could have prevented her from coming?"

"Indeed, George, I don't think I ought. I'm sure I ought not to tell you; but, then, you have always been so kind to me," said Lydia, blushing.

George also reddened a little, and the clasped hands pressed closer.

"I mean we are such old friends, Geordie, and I'm sure you won't betray my confidence. The truth is, that I am quite alarmed about poor Lina. You know that for some time after that terrible and mysterious affair at Cremorne the poor child was wretchedly ill. Well, after a few weeks she began to improve, and appeared to be moderately cheerful, though I could see that she was still silently grieving about that ridiculous, heartless—there, if I lived in his own country, in America, I'd get some strong-minded lady-lecturer on the right of women to give him a sound horsewhipping. Oh! I wish I were Aurora Floyd for his sake. I haven't patience with such fellows!"

"You allude to the gentleman we met at Cremorne, Mr. Aubrey, who claimed Angeline as his fiancée?"

"A pretty swain for a lover, certainly! Not to write a line to the poor girl for two years, and then to start up like the accusing spirit of Alonzo; but even Alonzo carried off his Imogene. But this oaf, although Angeline adores (but now I'm getting too confidential) to bounce off and slam the door in the face of such a paragon as our Lina! Ah! let him go back to America, and marry a Tomahawk squaw, the best partner such a block-headed, stone-hearted creature deserves; and now I've spoken my mind, Geordie."

"But, Liddy, yet you haven't told me why Angeline is not here?"

"But I will. Listen, then. Last evening, after you left us, young Leoni came, and he pleaded so earnestly to Angeline to go with him to the Derby, and I seconded his appeal so importunately, that at last she yielded. Well, we were preparing for the start, Angeline was already full-dressed, and I declare she never looked more beautiful, when a man, a stranger, called. Angeline descended to the parlour to see him, and then, without returning to give me any explanation, sent me word that she was forced to quit London for a few days, and went off with the stranger."

George Grant looked grave and thoughtful.

"All this is very strange," Lydia continued. "But, of course, Angeline is mistress of her own actions; perhaps the man might be a messenger from Arthur Aubrey; but even in that case——"

"Might it not have been Aubrey, himself?" asked George, quickly.

"Oh! no. I ascertained that it was not he; but please, Geordie, let us drop this subject. I am anxious only for poor Lina's happiness, and wish she would trust me fully, for I love and respect her more than any other creature in the world, and, indeed, I have good cause so to do. But here's Mr. Puffy; what a pity he is not one of the jockeys; that would be fun!—not for the horse though."

The lively girl extended her hand to Humphrey, who kissed her glove with great gallantry; the young Italian Leoni returned at the moment with a bouquet of flowers.

"What a charming bouquet! Oh, thanks, thanks!" said Lydia with a sunny smile, which reflected itself in the steadfast eyes of George, watching her with deep emotion.

"And if you had seen the little peri from whom I obtained it, Miss St. Clare! By the simplicity of Venus's doves! there never wandered out of paradise such a sweet, pure, graceful——"

"Fie, fie! do you know I shall tell all this to Lina?"

"A fair gitana?" asked George, laughing.

"No, no; a little Saxon cherub," replied Leoni; "she is in charge of an acrobat, a sturdy, good-tempered looking fellow, though I rated him soundly for bringing the little one forth to be coarsely stared at in such a rough, mixed multitude; he seemed to be ashamed of it, and said he would hasten home with her."

"A child, then?"

"Yes, not more than five years old, I should conjecture, but a real wonder of loveliness."

"Where is she, then?"

"By yonder booth. Her beauty attracts a crowd of admirers."

"I'll go and have a peep at her, for, though I'm no gusher, I dearly love children," said George. "I'll return, Lyddy, when the first race is run; so adieu, so long."

With this he lifted his hat and went off in the direction Leoni had indicated.

Meanwhile Mr. Puffy and his literary friends continued their stroll round the course.

The scene was extremely varied and picturesque. Here a band of nigger minstrels tuning their instruments; there a party of Jolly Dogs seated at luncheon on the sward; yonder a group of tired policemen reclining in the shade, and, scattered broadcast, knots of touts, tipsters, welchers, and their dupes. Three-card men, tramps, gipsies, conjurors, pigeon-flyers, and roughs; swells, ladies, liveried servants, lame, halt and blind beggars; fat, rubicund farmers; lean, pale-faced artizans. And then the medley of extraordinary noises; the rattle of sticks hurled at the Aunt Sallies, or at the poised cocoa-nuts, dolls, or toys; the patter of the thimble-rigger and card-sharp; the popping of rifle-caps for nuts and trinkets; the shrill, nasal "hoy squoy" of the immortal Punch; the cry of the "K'rect card" sellers, and still, through all the hurly-burly, the dirge-like ding-dong of the race-bell.

"My heyes, Bill, here's a prize for the Agricult'ral," cried a sly blackguard, as Mr. Puffy came sailing along, his loose white coat and long mauve veil fluttering in the breeze.

"Try yer weight, sir? Noo patent model weighing machine; on'y a sixpence, sir."

"Sixpence, Jim, you've riz yer charge. Don't be done, sir; he charges on'y von penny."

"Hold yer row, Boosy; this yere gent's six times the weight of any or'nary mortial, and, bein' a gemman, pays accordin'."

"What is your weight, Mr. Puffy?" asked Pharamond.

"This impudent scamp shall know to his cost," grunted Mr. Puffy, seating himself in the scale.

Crash! The machine fell to pieces, and poor Mr. Puffy was rolled to the ground.

"Was yer insured, Jim?" roared a bystander.

"No," grumbled the fellow, scratching his head, and staring stupidly at the mighty form of poor Puffy, who was being raised by his companions, "but if I'd a know'd what kinder customers I were to have, I'd a tested the strength of my machine vith von of those Sydenham antediluv'ans."

A few yards from the scene of this mishap the Jolly Dogs were arrested by a stout form—no less a personage than the gallant Bethnal Big 'Un.

The illustrious "pug" stood at the door of a booth which was surmounted by the following inscription:—

"THE BETHNAL BIG 'UN.
"Member of the Pugilistic Association.
"All the pets of the Fancy.
"Game set-to every ten minutes!"

"Come in! come in!" cried the fighting-man, extending his hand, encased in a boxing-glove, to Mr. Puffy; "you're just in time. I'm now a goin' to take it out of the Tottenham Tickler. A novice he is, and a clever lad, do assure ye. He'll fight for the championship one fine day, and see if he don't make a drawn fight on it; and won't that be a honour?"

"Pah! brutal!"

"Brutal? Vouldn't hurt a fly, bless you!—got too much science. Knows how to keep out of reach and save his backer's money. All right, Bos, these 'ere gents is my guests —don't take their money. Admit 'em to the inner ring, and put 'em among the harmy officers and other Corinthians."

The Jolly Dogs found themselves penned close in a stifling den, amid a crush of savage curs of the most mongrel breed.

They were witnesses of a game display of the fistic art.

Two lazy-looking roughs, in dirty shirts and ragged breeches, capered round each other for a few moments, occasionally letting drive at each other's heads, mostly missing their mark, and striking their seconds "bursters" on the dial-case, which proof of their "science" was received by their "patrons" with great approval.

"Is there any gent would like to put on the gloves, and go

in for a round with the Tickler? Now, gents, on'y got to throw in your castors."

Mr. Puffy declined putting on the gloves, but volunteered to try a round without them.

This offer, however, was declined on the plea that Mr. Puffey was over weight, and so, greatly edified by the manly exhibition they had witnessed, the Jolly Dogs left the booth.

Strolling onwards towards Tattenham Corner, they pushed their way through a selfish, jostling, hawkish crowd of betting men, some of whom were high in oath, others hotly wrangling about their stakes, while in almost every face there rested a hard and degrading expression of low cunning and grasping avarice.

"Well," said Charlie Vert, "I may be very blind, but certainly I am not prejudiced in this case. I looked for 'sport'— I expected to find every one discussing the various merits of the horses, descanting on their points, their breed and ancestry, the skill of the jocks, and so on; but not one tenth part of this assemblage seems to care a straw for anything but the 'odds'—the hard, hard cash. There's nothing more of what one would really understand by 'sport' in this crack race than there is in the shuffling of cards in a common hell. The charioteers of old Greece and Rome struggled chiefly for fame——"

"And a wreath of parsley," rejoined Pharamond. "Fame! If you wouldn't be laughed at, my boy, never use that obsolete word. The modern expression is 'notoriety.'"

"Come, Jolly Dogs, it's on the stroke of two," said Humphrey, to his companions; "the horses are already taking their trial spin along the course. Let us return to the Grand Stand; perhaps we shall meet George on the way."

They were now standing on the rising ground that overlooks the Banstead Downs.

Their gaze rested lingeringly upon the calm, fresh, and lovely country, slumbering in the sun glow.

Behind them lay a sea of weak, sinful, passion-fraught humanity—wealth, poverty, dissipation, despair, beauty, deformity, love, hate, gay prodigality, and grim avarice.

Before them spread the balmy landscape—yellow spangled, waving meads; nodding, vivid copses; the deep, pure, blue sky; the white clouds, from which the viewless larks poured down their rippling pæans of innocent gladness. But, then, the passionless face of nature would have worn the same summer smile had the struggle about to take place been a bloody fight between stern men for the dominion of this fair and prosperous kingdom, instead of a May-day contest between fleet steeds for the blue ribbon of the turf.

The three Jolly Dogs turned their faces towards the Grand Stand and began to quickly retrace their steps.

Among the many gay equipages they passed was one, a large barouche, so full of richly-dressed ladies that it resembled a basket of gorgeous-hued flowers.

There was but one gentleman in this party, and he stood beside the carriage, pouring out glasses of sparkling champagne for his fair and merry companions.

A group of ragged, dirty-faced, hungry-eyed tramps, male and female, crouched on the ground at the distance of a few paces, looking on with mute envy and dislike.

As our Jolly Dogs passed, the gentleman crumpled a piece of paper, wherewith he lighted his fragrant Manilla.

He threw it aside, and the breeze wafted it, still flaring, to the feet of Mr. Puffey, who, being in want of a light, picked it up.

A written word which caught his eye caused him to open the paper.

He frowned as he read the contents, and then handed it to Mr. Vert.

"Here, Charlie," said he, with a stern smile, "here's something will serve you for a motto to some chapter in your sensational romance."

The paper contained the following words :—

DEAR HUSBAND,—We are starving! Return, oh, return to us! If not for the sake of your wretched wife, for the sake of our dear little ones. The accursed passion for gambling, I know, has ruined you, but do, pray, return home at once. Your pet, Nellie, is dy——.

The rest was singed and burnt away.

Charlie made no remark, though he felt his cheek turn cold.

The poor devil of a penny-a-liner scarcely deserved to be called a Jolly Dog; he was rather a friendless, homeless, timid tyke, who had been buffeted about in the rough world into which he had been driven out too early in his puppyhood, before his teeth were sharp enough to snap again when he was attacked by stronger, jollier and rougher animals; so he had lost his "gameness."

This little incident dashed his spirits for the remainder of the holiday.

"What the deuce has become of Geordie?" asked Pharamond, looking around, "the horses are about to start."

"Perhaps he has returned to the drag," rejoined Mr. Puffy; "at any rate there's no time to waste in seeking him. Now, then, you chap, let us mount your stand."

"Don't think as it'll stand your mount, yer honour," said the sly rogue who kept the ricketty platform, already overcrowded by spectators.

But Mr. Puffy was not to be deterred by the chaff of the cads, the screams of the women, or the growls of the men; he leaped on to the platform, which literally groaned beneath his ponderous weight.

But where was George Grant all this time?

Let us retire a little from the crowd, and we shall find him seated behind yonder show-booth, quite oblivious of the race in which, to say sooth, he did not take much interest.

We refer our readers to the artist's capital sketch [See No. 5] where George is portrayed sitting on the drum with a little fairy girl on his knee, while the manly, good-looking tumbler and the performer on the Pandean reeds look on with beaming faces.

"And her name is Elfie?" said George, kissing the little one. "And you say she has no brothers or sisters?"

"Oh, yes," returned the child, in a sweet, clear tone, "brover Shem."

"Shem, eh? That's odd. And so you have a brother Shem?"

"No, no, capt'in," rejoined the tumbler, gently disengaging the child from George's embrace; "that's all a fancy of hers. Some kind folks had the care on her for awhile, and the son of these people was very fond of the little 'un, and she of him; she used to call him her 'brover Shem.'"

"Yes, and he went away, oh, so long; and father Shem and mother used to cry and say he would come back tomorrow, and to-morrow, and so many to-morrows!" persisted the little girl; "and father Shem was very ill, and people came and took away the clock and the chairs, and sometimes we had nothing to eat, but Kitty brought us nice things and gave father Shem money pieces, and then, after, oh, such a long, long time, brover Shem came back, and we had such fun! and brover Shem and Kitty took Elfie to see the pretty lights shining all over the streets, and——"

Here the child broke off suddenly.

She looked about her as if bewildered, and then burst into sobbing.

"I want to go home! Where is my brover Shem? Why does he not come to Elfie?"

"We are very kind to her, indeed we are, sir," said the tumbler, his cheek reddening, and his voice growing husky.

"You would be more kind if you kept her at home," returned George, rather sternly; "this is no place for such a delicate little creature, and in that flimsy dress, too. Shame!"

"Why, sir, you see, sir," stammered the man, hugging the little one tightly to his broad breast, "she is such a picture! We have been very unfortunate; the wife was very sick, and I—I once had a great name, sir; you may have heard on me, p'raps may have seen me perform at the music-halls and theatres. I were known, sir, as Mounseer Hercule, the daring vaulter, but one unlucky night I fell from the trapeze and broke my leg; if 'thadn't a been for my son Paul we should a starved."

"And what is he?"

"Well, sir, he's a hacrobat, too; it runs in the fam'ly."

"Then why didn't you bring him here instead of Elfie?"

"Couldn't, sir; he's got another hengagement at a music-hall; ain't that true, Joe?"

The drummer, to whom this appeal was made, nodded assentingly.

"Joe's short-spoken, but it's a fac', sir. Well, my wife bein' ill, and Paul's money not bein' much, I got reg'lar desprit, and says I, 'I knows a trick wuth two of this 'ere chair-mendin,' says I—I mends chairs and makes baskets in a or'nary way, sir—'I'll take this lovely child to the Derby, and the people 'll give her no end o' tin for the sake of her beauty.' My wife she says, 'no,' 'but,' says I, 'she's too young to be anyways perwerted in heart or mind by what she sees and 'ears; I'll take her.' So we togged her out in some of my wife's old finery—she were a ballet-girl onst, sir, *she* were; and a better dancer or a better wife, as the saying is—but that's not to the pint you'll tell me. Well, we begged some flowers, and made 'em up in buckets; and I must say, that they went off well, and we've taken a tidy sum of money—ain't it right, Joe?"

The saturnine drummer once more grunted assent.

"And so, sir, don't you go for to think that we ain't kind to the little un, 'cos rayther than you should think that, I'd chuck this 'ere 'andful of coin over this 'ere booth and not sile my fingers with it, and Joe'd sacrifice his share as well, wouldn't ye, my pal?"

Another grunt of hearty assent.

"Well, well," said George, much mollified by the man's evident sincerity, "there's another race to-morrow; but don't bring her out, she's too frail, too young to stand the fatigue and excitement."

"Oh, shan't be here to-morrow, sir—goin' to a picnic, ain't we Joe?"

"Stop, my friend! What does that shout mean? Blessed if I haven't lost the sight of the first race. Well, it does not much matter. Now, here's a half-sov. for yourself, and a sov. for Elfie. You won't expose her thus again, will you, your hand on it?"

The tumbler gave him a hearty grip, and said with a grateful smile,

"God bless ye, sir; my word, and I'm no liar. Home I takes her at once; we've done enough for to-day, ain't we Joe?"

Joe again assented in his taciturn manner, and George rewarded his compliance by tossing him a half-crown; then once more snatching a kiss from the sweet fresh lips of the pretty child, he darted away to join his companions.

On the course he encountered Jemmy Gimp and Shem Beamish.

"Ahoy, there, Mr. Grant," cried the young sailor, "where have ye been cruising, sir? Though we kept a bright look out, we could sight you nowhere. You haven't lost the sight, have ye?"

"But I have though," returned George, smiling; "but pray tell me, is not your name Shem?"

"Aye, aye, sir!"

"*Brover* Shem," said George, with a peculiar smile.

"Why, yes," gasped Shem; "but, dam'me, sir, 'scuse sea-manners, who told you I was 'brover' Shem?"

"The sweetest elfin little creature—"

"Our Elfie!" shouted the sailor.

"How strange! Her name *was* Elfie."

"Hold taut! *Her* name? Whose name? What, when, where away?"

"A little girl, Mr. Beamish, tricked out as a dancer; met her with some tumbler chaps, yonder—"

Shem was off like a shot.

In an out and round about, along the course, across the Down, through the lanes, right away towards the village, everywhere Shem Beamish sought the lost foundling; but, alas! M. Hercule was a man of his word, and had borne off his little prize.

Shem's chagrin and despair were beyond word-painting.

———

CHAPTER XIX.

THE DERBY STAKES.

MILES of anxious faces; on either side of the swerving course a living wall.

The stands crowded densely; the betting ring thronged; the royal box filled with princely company; the vehicles alive with standing spectators; the hills covered with the dense multitude as with a mantle.

A sudden hush!

The bell has ceased tolling the knell of many bright hopes and good resolutions.

The course is clear for the racers, and the slant sunbeams glint along the smooth-shaven turf.

Opposite the Grand Stand, and close against the barricade, stand Edgar Wenlock and his tempter.

A smile of satisfaction sits on the face of the book-maker, while Wenlock's countenance is haggard with horrid suspense.

The fine-bred sleek horses, mounted by the pigmy jocks in their rich, silken jackets of many hues, flit swiftly and easily past on their trial spin.

Wenlock leans his arm on the rail, and buries his face in his hands.

"Dreaming?" asked Dandy Jack, touching him on the shoulder.

Wenlock started.

"Yes," he muttered, hoarsely.

"Of success, I hope?"

"No, no; the—the crowd!" gasped Wenlock.

His veil fluttered round his face.

He suppressed a shriek as he tore it away.

Dreaming! He was dreaming of another vulgar, heartless, cruel crowd gathered round the scaffold; the flaunting gauze sweeping about his face, like the filmy mesh of the spider web, it seemed to his excited imagination like the ghastly white night-cap drawn down over his doomed head.

"Look, look, Neddy; there he goes! Gad zooks! observe his pacing; that's Redan!"

"Will he win?"

"Moral safe."

"But this beautiful light chestnut; it's Lord Lyon, is it not?"

"A slug, sir, a caterpillar; he'll be nowhere."

A long, long pause!

A deep, breathless hush.

"They're off!"

The cry rings along for miles.

A carnate flash of faces turned towards the starting point.

A few moments of deadly agony.

"They're coming, they're coming! They're round the corner—all in a ruck! Now, now! Rustic for ever! No, no, the colt has it, the colt!—the Bribery colt! Now, the blue and white hoops! The Cannon's the gun! No—now——"

Swifter than the lightning's flash they sweep by.

Red and yellow; then the black satin and scarlet cap; afterwards a rainbow of varied colours.

"Custance! Bribery—the colt wins! 22 to 1 on the colt! No—neck to neck! The Grand Stand! The winning-post!"

"Hurrah! the favourite wins—Lord Lyon has it!"

Up runs the fatal signal, 4, 17, 9.

Wenlock reels amid the deafening thunders which proclaim his ruin.

"*Where are we now, guv'nor?*" growls a deep voice at his ear.

The Jolly Dog's assistant stands at his side.

Wenlock glares at him half stupidly.

"To-night?" asks the Lummy Cove, with a beastly leer.

"No, no, to-morrow," groans Wenlock. "I'll meet you to-morrow."

"All right, guv'nor; keep up you sperrits. Havn't got a quid to spare? Awful dry work this. I'm down on my luck —lost a small fortun'."

"Here—here!"

The burglar grasped a handful of coin, and, grinning and touching his hat, turned on his heel and disappeared in the throng.

"Come, Neddy, it's all over," said Dandy Jack, plucking his companion's arm. "It's a devilish mishap—the favourite wins—awful bad for the book-makers. Lor' knows I'm let in for it ; but where's the good o' whining over spilt milk ?"

With these he dragged the half-stunned wretch from the crowd.

"After all, Neddy, just as well first as last. You would have had to come it, I'm sure of that—success would have driven you ahead. Besides, putting back borrowed tin is not so easy as it seems ; and then what an easy lay ! One haul out of the swag-box will set you to rights, and then for the new world, and let bygones be bygones. Have a glass o' brandy ?"

Wenlock staggered on till he came to the drag where the rest of the Jolly Dogs were gathering.

"Lost, Neddy, eh ?" said Rattleton.

"Yes, yes."

"Well, luck's all. I've got on pretty well. How much did you lose ?"

"A ten pound note or so."

"Come, that's nothing to make such a wry face about—better luck next time. By the bye, a chaise drove by just now, and the driver was the very double of old Dick Renshaw."

"Indeed, but of course it could not be he."

"No, certainly ; besides, this gentleman was driving his chaise, his servant by his side. I should take him to be an American by the cut of his jib ; but his features were the exact counterpart of poor old Dick's."

"Very strange."

"George, George ! yonder, look yonder !" cried Lydia from the barouche, to Grant, who stood leaning on the panel ; "do you observe that gentleman driving that fine spirited grey ? do you not recognise him ?"

"Why, yes ; it is no other than Mr. Aubrey."

"Yes, there can be no doubt of it, for, see, he carries his left arm in a sling. Oh, George, will you do me a great favour ?"

"Surely, dear Lyddy, I'm ever at your service."

"Go to him, George ; bring him hither. I *must* speak with him."

"But, my dear girl——"

"Go this instant, sir, or I will never speak with you again."

"But permit me, with all the deference in the world, dear Lyddy, just to point out to you——"

"Pshaw ! so much for your gallantry !"

"Well, if you insist——"

"I *do* insist ; go at once. Surely there can be no impropriety in my craving a few words with an old friend of Lina's ? Go, there's a dear boy. Do, now."

Further opposition was, of course, out of the question, so, with somewhat of an ill grace, George went off on his errand.

Presently he returned with the favoured gentleman, who gracefully raised his veiled hat.

George Grant withdrew a few paces.

Lydia raised her eyes in womanly curiosity to the fine face of her friend's romantic-looking lover, and then lowered them, richly blushing.

"Sir," she said, her voice slightly quivering, "pray pardon my seemingly unwarrantable boldness in seeking this interview——"

"Pardon, my dear young lady ? I am but too grateful for the honour done me ; and Miss Lablonde—Angeline ?" he stammered, with apparently genuine solicitude.

"Mr. Aubrey, I am sorry to tell you that she has been very, very ill."

The gentleman clasped his delicately-gloved hands, and expressed his concern with an eloquent look of mute agony.

"He's not such a bear, after all," thought the warm-hearted Lydia, "but I won't spare him. Yes, indeed, she has been dangerously ill, and if I may presume to tell you plainly what I think, your conduct towards her has been shamefully harsh and unfeeling."

"From your lips, my dear young lady, even reproach falls——"

"Tush ! I detest meaningless compliments and inane flattery," cried Lydia, sharply. "Enough. I thought, sir—I hoped that you entertained feelings of tenderness and respect towards my dear friend, Angeline ; but I find that you are thoroughly heartless, and, I fear, quite unworthy of her attachment."

"You are severe."

"I am just ; though, indeed, I own I have no right to take upon myself the part of censurer ; but, then, I dearly love my kind, good, Lina, and my deep anxiety for her happiness makes me bold to speak."

"But, surely, you cannot blame me. Rather, do not I deserve credit for having ceased to pay attentions to Miss Lablonde, which are distasteful to her ?"

"Your jealous suspicions are altogether unworthy, unmanly."

"Good God !" cried poor Mr. Aubrey, with pardonable vivacity, "when it is well known that Miss Lablonde has withdrawn from me her cherished favour, and has bestowed it upon another ; when she has discarded me—when——"

"Oh dear ! oh dear ! this is nonsense. I know I ought to be ashamed of myself, for addressing you at all on this subject. Poor Lina would never forgive me for having thus spoken ; but I am a matter-of-fact person, and I know that much misery is ofttimes saved in such cases by a timely eclaircissement, and, relying upon the purity of my motive, I feel encouraged to overstep the rigid line of conventional reserve, so pray do not misapprehend when I assure you that, having sounded all the depths of Lina's generous heart, I can say, with knowledge and truth, that she has ever been, true to you."

"Ah, if I could believe it !"

"Shame that you should doubt it ! Well, well, I have spoken—forgive me if too presumingly."

"I will see Angeline."

"Oh, yes !" cried the kind-hearted ballet-girl, with animation, "but I rely upon your honour not in any way to compromise me. I am so glad to have had this opportunity of speaking my mind to you, but poor Lina would die of vexation if she knew what has passed between us."

"I will respect a confidence which does me so much honour. I will venture to pay a visit to Miss Lablonde, and will leave my fate in her hands."

"Pray do so ; and till then, Mr. Aubrey, I bid you adieu."

Mr. Aubrey pressed the plump little hand extended to him, raised his hat, and with a martial stride moved away.

"He is very handsome," thought Lydia ; "but there is a sinister expression in his countenance which displease me ; altogether I am disappointed in him. At first sight I thought him so different from what he now appears. How one may be deceived by first impressions ! I wish I had not gone so far !"

The eventful day was drawing to a close, the last race had been run and the mighty multitudes were thronging from the Downs.

George Grant returned home in the same carriage with Lydia and the young musician ; the rest of the Jolly Dogs, who had bedecked themselves with dolls, painted feathers, artificial noses, and coloured wigs and beards, and had armed themselves with pea-shooters and flour-bags for the "sportive" fray, remounted the drag.

Dandy Jack once more took the ribbons ; once more Mr. Gimp played the most distracting tunes on his cracked cornopean, and with a loud "huzza," once more the four-in-hand rattled along the dusty road, with the mighty stream of vehicles. Soon all was pell-mell, havoc, and confusion, stinging showers of peas, blinding clouds of flour, discordant clangour of all manner of music, shouts, shrieks, chaff, catastrophes, concussions, rolling, rattling, roaring, while the dosy fields and hedgerows whirl wildly past ; but what need to repeat the oft-told tale, or to describe what has so often been the theme of the most skilled pens—the return from the Derby—the mad carnival of all the JOLLY DOGS OF LONDON !

(To be continued.)

St. Leon now found that he was either compelled to allow Linda to dance with her former lover, or himself to take her hand in the new measure which had just commenced. He adopted the latter course in preference, and although it was with evident disinclination that he did so, he advanced and went through the dance.

About the middle of the hall in which the ball had taken place was a bay window, which projected several feet from the wall. Across it was a massive curtain of silk drapery, which was now drawn, and completely hid the window from observation, as well as adding much to the ornamental appearance of the room.

This window looked directly to the east, as Linda well knew, and now as, in the whirl of the dance, she passed it, she could not refrain from casting an anxious glance towards it, and wishing that the light of morning would show itself through even the folds of the massive drapery which hung before it.

St. Leon, with evident uneasiness, watched her looks, and when they paused for a few moments, he said,

" Linda, you seem to regard that window with some uneasiness."

" Not with uneasiness," she said; " it looks towards the east."

The sudden start which St. Leon gave alarmed her, and she glanced in his face. It was of a death-like paleness.

" You are unwell," she said. " Let me call my father."

" No, no; call no one," he replied; " but tell me, on your sacred word, why it is you feel interested in that window because it looks towards the east?"

" It is from the east," said Linda, " that we can see the first rays of the morning sun."

A visible convulsion shook the frame of St. Leon, and it was some moments before he moved his lips to reply; but by then it had become their turn to join again in the dance, and all conversation for several minutes was necessarily put an end to.

What were the thoughts and sensations of St. Leon during that period could only be guessed by the fluctuations of his countenance. He was flushed and pale by turns, and when he could again address a few words to Linda, he said,

" The dance fatigues me. I have not been in robust health of late; I shall retire now."

" As you please," said Linda.

" And—and you?"

" Can continue the dance. The bride will have no lack of partners because the bridegroom deserts her."

" Now, Linda, this is wilfulness, or are you jesting?"

" Jesting, say you? How could you suppose me jesting? Is it three o'clock?"

" Linda—Linda—I tell you that by the earliest dawn I must leave here a short time to visit a friend."

" Who?"

" Oh, his name—his name is Fercilu."

" A strange name."

" Very. So we will now, while the dance is proceeding, and we shall not be missed, retire to the nuptial chamber, dearest Linda. How beautiful you look to-night, though rather paler than you were wont to be, sweet one. Lean upon my arm. Oh! what a happy, happy destiny is mine, to be allied to so much excellence and beauty! How sweetly our lives will pass away. We shall be all the world to each other, and very, very happy. Let me see you smile again, dear Linda. This way lies the door. I will remain here a short time, if it so please you, and then, when unobserved, step out to come to you."

Linda did not make the least effort to interrupt St. Leon in his speech, nor did she advance nearer to the door, but when he had concluded she said,

" I am not weary."

" Not weary, dearest? Certainly I did not mean to say that you were; but do you intend gracing this scene by your sweet presence, dearest Linda, until you are really weary?"

" Yes."

The affirmative was uttered rather abruptly, and St. Leon gave a slight start, as he bit his lip to keep down his rising angry feelings.

" Linda," he said, " I had hoped you loved me."

" Is it," she remarked, " so poor a boon to ask of you that you should remain some time longer here to allow me to mingle in the dance, that you cannot grant it without doubt of my affection?"

" No, no; but as I tell you, I have to leave early."

" Hark! is not that a glorious burst of music? Heard ye ever the like? Come, St. Leon, to the dance again! to the dance!"

St. Leon's face grew as pale as death, and he held Linda by the arm, as he said in a low, anxious whisper,

" Linda, tell me at once if you have made up your mind to remain here till—till—till——"

" Sunrise?" said Linda.

" Yes, yes."

" I have."

Deep vexation sat upon the countenance of St. Leon; he was evidently making great efforts to subdue an exhibition of it; and after a time he turned again to Linda, saying,

" Did I hear you right when I fancied you declared your intention of remaining here till daybreak?"

" You did."

" But you are surely joking, dear Linda? You do not mean to do so. I am sure that when I tell you that nothing so disagrees with my constitution as the morning air, you will retract such a resolution."

Linda cast her eyes on the floor as she said,

" In these halls you will be unconscious of the influence of the morning air."

" Shall I?" responded St. Leon, with a shudder. " Already the near approach of morning sensibly affects me."

" Indeed!"

She looked up at him and she saw that the paleness of his countenance now by far transcended what it had been before. She felt some little pang of alarm; but the words of the stranger recurred to her in the advice not to retire until the morning's light should appear, and she felt so strong an inclination to obey the injunction, that even thoughts of St. Leon's indisposition could not move her.

It was very strange, but her affection for St. Leon, which had been most abundant, was now nearly gone, and her heart yearned towards the mysterious stranger whom she had at first regarded with so much terror and aversion. She asked herself again and again what could have produced this most remarkable change in her feelings and why it was that she felt as laws for the governance of her conduct whatever the stranger chose to say.

" You pity me," added St. Leon, " and you will retire earlier than the morning light, dear Linda?"

" Is it well to refuse me the pleasure of the dance for another hour? Hark! that is three o'clock."

A muttered malediction came from the lips of St. Leon, and taking her hand, while his eyes seemed to flash with an unnatural brilliancy, he said,

" Well, Linda, be it so. To the dance then, if you will, but remember that I have an early engagement. To the dance, Linda—to the dance."

He led her into the midst of the gay throng, and from that moment none seemed to enter with more spirit and animation into the gay scene than St. Leon.

He laughed, talked, and danced, and jested with the greatest spirit, but still his face wore the marble hue of death, and it became the general remark in the hall of how terrible he looked, although he seemed in such a full flush of animal spirits that it was quite impossible they could be assumed.

He retained Linda's hand in the dance despite all remonstrances, and now the hour of four had struck and the hall was getting a little thinned of its guests, and many wondered to see the bride and bridegroom yet among the dancers.

The wild hilarity of St. Leon did not forsake him; on the contrary, he laughed, talked, and jested with greater gusto than before, but Linda observed that each time he passed the bay window, which looked to the east, he cast an anxious look towards it and a strange expression came across his face.

What he intended to do, or why he seemed to dread the dawning of the morning, she could not possibly imagine, but now she felt to the full as much prompted by intense curiosity as by any other feeling, to watch narrowly what might occur.

" In a quarter of an hour," she repeated to herself, " the sun's beams will illumine the eastern sky. At a quarter past four Courtney told me the day would first show itself."

It now could not want above a few minutes of that time, and St. Leon here whispered to Linda,

" You are my wife, Linda. The words have been spoken which made you mine, and no earthly power can separate us. I must leave you now."

" Leave me?"

" Yes; do not express an affected surprise at what I told you of before you became—became——"

He paused, and his frame shook with a visible emotion; he seemed quite unable to speak.

Terror completely choked his utterance, or some other feeling of which none but he knew.

" God of heaven!" exclaimed Linda, " Are you dying, St. Leon?"

" No, no. Make no—no—remark. The bay window—the bay window—get me a cup of wine—yourself."

As he spoke he dashed into the deep hollow of the window.

There was a faint ray of light from the east just glimmering with a sickly lustre through one of the panes of coloured glass of which it was for the most part composed.

Linda was now thoroughly alarmed.

She felt certain that some strange and terrible catastrophe was at hand, but what it was she could have no sort of perception.

(Continued from Supplement given away with No. 5.)

THE JOLLY DOGS OF LONDON.

GEORGE GRANT FLOORS THE BETHNAL BIG 'UN.—*See No.* 8.

CHAPTER XX.

AFTER THE DERBY.

WHILE the rest of our party of Jolly Dogs betook themselves to their favourite resort, the "Harp and Crown," intent upon "making a night of it," Harry Rattleton and his two mistresses, with Dandy Jack and Edgar Wenlock, visited a certain divan near the Haymarket.

In the mirrored, gilded, and luxuriantly appointed supperrooms they found a large company of gay fellows, and pretty but dissipated-looking girls, who were apparently at the height of enjoyment.

Harry Rattleton himself was in exuberant spirits; he had been successful in his betting transactions, and, as he had

staked heavily, and was in need of cash, his exultation at his good luck was extreme.

Amy the fair, and Madeline of the raven tresses, seated themselves at a marbled table.

They exchanged dagger-looks, and had evidently been quarrelling.

Harry, however, was not sober, and was so elated that he failed to notice the little disagreement between his fair companions, lavished his caresses upon the simpering Amy, while Madeline, dark as Medea, sat at the end of the damask couch watching the pair with the gloomy fire of wounded pride, and mortal jealousy glowering her black rolling eyes.

Dandy Jack and Edgar Wenlock, half-reclining on the opposite seat, were so absorbed in their muttered conversation that they left the luxuries before them untasted, and their brimming glasses untouched.

Amy exerted all her powers of fascination to enthral her lover, and from time to time cast a look of vulgar, insolent triumph at her rival.

"I don't believe one word of it," cried Harry, laughing; "you are all alike—Dalilahs who would sell your own sons to the Philistines for a handful of silver. Why do you smile on me so sweetly to-night? Why are your smiles to be bought? Because they can be sold—sold to the highest bidder. I'll warrant, now, if some shrivelled old dotard with a crutch and a coronet were to offer to make you a lady——"

"*Me* a lady! and leave you, 'Arry? Never! Not to be queen of the whole world. Strike me dead, if I would! *I* ain't no lady, I'm not sufficient educated to 'spire to things above me. I leaves that to *others*, ducky. On'y, *humble as I ham*, I tries to be *sweet-tempered*, and I loves you for your own sake, and never worrits ye with jealous fits, and angry airs and angry graces, even when you wrings my 'art, which, as the saying is—'there's no true love without jealousy.' Well, *some* people's airs is most ridic'lous. Thank Lor's *I* ain't 'ighminded, but alwis tries to be the same, don't I, darling?"

"Now, hang me, Amy, if you're not right there," cried Harry, speaking more and more huskily. "You do yourself but justice. Why the devil should a man be pestered with a lot of womanish namby-pambyism, be lectured and wept over like a naughty boy? No—hic!—I shay—I *do* shay you're a good girl, Amy. Kissh me for that."

Amy leaned her head on his shoulder, smiled fondly, and pulled his whiskers caressingly.

"And you've alwis been so liberal, so generous to me. Oh! there, it's no use for me to try to tell ye how grateful I feels."

"You're a good girl. To-morrow—hic!—you shall have what I promised ye—two hund——"

"Hush! dear; not so loud. Don't let that *cr-reature* hear you."

"Oh! never mind her. Well, well, I shop—'pon my soul, you gals ought to agree better; I shall have to part ye. Now, look ye here, I shay, jesh for a treat, lishten to reason. Why can't ye be——"

"But what about to-morrow, dear?"

"Well, I'm a man of honoursh. You shall have the hund'd p-pounds (but, I shay, my precious angel, don't drink sho much champagne) you shall have—yesh—the two hundred poundsh; but I shay, Ned, and come you, Jacksh, be shoshi-able. Fill up, Sholly Dogs! Hurrah for Lord Lyon! and here goesh for a—hic!—shong—

> "It ish not a bowl but a bottle I want,
> A bottle of—hic!—wine, and the friendsh of heart,
> Of nectar the poetsh in garretsh may rant,
> Can fanshy the pleashures—hic!—of drinking impart.

"The day after the Derby! Let fanshy paint that pictshur; but chorus, cheerful pups—

> "'Of drinking the pleasuresh—
> Of drinking the pleash——'

"Shomehow, my memorysh not half sho good as it wash. How'd 'count for that, Sholly Dogs?"

"The air off the Epsom Downs, my boy, has made ye feel a little 'fresh,' that's all," laughed Dandy Jack.

"Ah! sho s'posh; but never mind, we'll have a sholly good shong for all that—

> "'By the gaily shircling glash,
> We can tell, we can—we—k——hic!'

"'Pon my shoul, if I wash another f'ler, I should shay I wash drunksh."

Dandy Jack laughed heartily at this sally, and Wenlock feebly smiled.

Harry Rattleton had staggered from his former position and had seated himself in a settee at a little distance from the table.

The glass drooped in his hand, his rich, glossy curls strayed over his brow, his eyes glittered with drunken brilliancy, and his voice was thick and hoarse.

Meantime the gentle ladies were left to entertain each other.

They drew closer together and kept up a rapid conversation in low, fierce whispers.

"Ned Wenlock," said Harry, with drunken solemnity, laying his hand on his friend's shoulder, "you are not desherving of the name of a Sholly Dog if you look sho awful groggy. You have losht shome money—hic—on the race, 'bout how mush?"

"Oh, I told ye, Harry; no more than ten or twelve pounds."

"Did'sh ever know the time when Harry Rattleton washn't jannock with his friendsh? Fif-fifteen poundsh, did ye say? Heresh two tennersh; pay me when I'm hardsh up, and thatsh no' giving ye mush grace neither. Take it."

"But, Harry, though much moved by your kindness, I really can't accept——"

"Want to quarrel with me? Take it, I shay; do you hear?"

"Only till the morning, Harry."

Dandy Jack's keen grey eyes twinkled, and, as a spider fastens upon his prey, the tout book-maker seized the young profligate's arm, and forcing him down upon the couch, whispered in his ear,

"Hark ye, my lad, I'll put you up to a wrinkle. The Ascot will be run in a week or so; I'll give you the 'tip.' Keep it dark," and putting his hands round his mouth he whispered something in his drunken ear.

Harry started and winked with profound sagacity. How well Nature can burlesque herself!

"You don't shay sho? Humph! ah! I'm on, right on. I lay a hundred to one on——"

"'Ware, my boy! such a secret's worth a Jew's eye," muttered the tout, with well-affected agitation. "But have ye any of the ready *now*, just to put down, you know, just to clinch the bet, eh? You have? I'll lay it out well for you. Ten, fifteen, fifteen and ten—that's ten and ten, you see—making twenty——"

"All right. Hang the reckoning!"

"No, no, my boy; business is business, fair and square. What's this, another ten? Well, as we said just now, ten and five are fifteen; fifteen, we said, and five you give me now——"

"Thatsh ten, and five are fif-fifteen."

"Yes, fifteen. Count it yourself, and make a note of it."

"Here, wheresh my note-case. Well, chalk it up on the bellowsh, itsh all right."

"No, no, Harry, let us have your own sign manual."

"Can't, my boy, I've played that d———d penny-whistle till my fingers are sho shore, I can't hold the pen—hic."

"Well, Ned shall be witness. It's fifteen, eh, Ned?"

"Yes," assented the other, with a ghastly smile.

"You trust Ned?"

"Trusht him? with everything—'shept Amy, ha! ha!

> "'We're a crew of Jolly Dogs
> Never can get crosh——'

"Oh, it'sh all right. But whosh thish gent, dreshed like one of the Corshican brothers, who entersh the place ash if he were the sergeant of a crack regiment coming on p'rade?"

The new comer to whom he alluded was no other than Mr. Aubrey.

Upon recognising the partner of his guilt, Wenlock rose, and looked at him inquiringly, as if to ask whether or not he should greet him.

But Mr. Aubrey advanced and cordially shook hands.

"My dear Wenlock, I'm right glad to see ye; and how did you fare at Epsom, to-day? Come off pretty well?"

"Rather unfortunate, Aubrey; but I never put on much."

"Well, I've been lucky."

"Mr. Hedgepenny, Mr. Aubrey," said Wenlock. "Mr. Aubrey, this is my distinguished friend, Mr. Harry Rattleton, president of our club—the 'Jolly Dogs.'"

"Proud, sir, I'm sure, to meet with so illustrious a personage," said the elegant Mr. Aubrey, bowing profoundly.

"Mishter Aubrey, you're a trump, shir—hic. Tell ye what, I'll give ye the 'tip' for the Ascot; lay your money on——"

"S-sh!" cried Dandy Jack.

"What do ye mean? Ish there to be reserve between friendsh?"

"Between twin brothers, where the tip is concerned."

"All bosh; honour and c-confidensh——"

"Are out of the question."

"Out of the question?—hic—and between——"

"Touts, authors, artists, and publishers."

"That's hot."

"It's the rule, Mr. Aubrey, and a very good rule too," said the swindling book-maker, with a leer.

"Mr. Aubrey, you shay, sir, your n-namesh Aubrey?"

"Yes, sir; Arthur Aubrey, of Old Virginia, Ex-confederate States."

"'Pon my shoul, thought I knew ye, sheen ye b'fore; why, you're—yesh—you *are*—Gentleman Dick!"

And Harry emphasised this assertion with a sounding slap on Aubrey's shoulder.

"Yesh—Dick Renshaw!"

"Indeed, sir, you are mistaken."

"Oh, no offensh; Dick was a d——d good f'la—beg pardon, never shwear when I'm shober—not that—hic—I'm drunk now, not leasht in th' world."

"I assure you, sir, you are in error; I don't know such a person."

"Don't know old Dick? Besht fella out; made leetle mishtake though; got lagged for forgery and—hic—and 'besslement; convict, now, in Millbank Prison."

"Really, sir."

"Fact, do asshure ye; prince of Jolly Dogs—my predeshessor—form'lly preshident of our s'ciety; I can never hope to be what Dick wash."

"You amaze me!" stammered Renshaw, not a little taken aback, especially as Wenlock had sunk half dead upon the couch, while Dandy Jack was staring with keen scrutiny. "I really——"

But further deprecation was rendered unnecessary by a sudden and violent *fracas* between the respectable ladies—Mr. Harry Rattleton's—— friends.

"I can, I won't, I shan't stand no more on it!" shrieked the fair lady in the tones of a Billingsgate virago. "Come to me, 'Arry; this wretch Mad'line has been a calling a—everythink vile. Take that," &c.

And Amy snatched up a glass of wine, and dashed it in her rival's face.

"Will you suffer me to be treated thus, Harry?" wailed Madeline, wildly, as she dashed the wine drops from her face.

"Harken at her, 'Arry; she's been a insultin' me this last hour," cried Amy, "and all acos you admires my fair hair and blue heyes; she says—Oh, the rip!" &c. &c.

"Spare me this, Harry; you know, I was not *bought*," murmured Madeline.

"Down, ye quarrelsome hell-cat!" cried Rattleton, pushing her roughly off.

A moment!—the deed was done in a moment!—a pealing shriek chilled the blood in the veins of every bystander.

Madeline had snatched a table-knife, and had plunged deep into the breast of her vulgar rival, and the dainty *mousseline de laine* was limp and sopped with warm and crimson blood.

It required the united strength of the three strong men to prevent the maddened girl from adding the crime of suicide to that of assassination.

As for Harry Rattleton, the Jolly, drunken Dog, stood pale and petrified, an image of horror.

———

CHAPTER XXI.

PAUL.

OUR scene changes to the meanly-furnished parlour of a quaint old cottage in the neighbourhood of Sutton.

The walls are hung round with baskets, and in the several corners there are piles of chairs to be mended, stacks of canes, and bundles of withes and rushes.

Over the mantle of the old-fashioned brick fire-place is hung the portrait of a pair of acrobats, a man and a very little boy, in their performing costume, beneath which is the inscription—

"Mons. Achille Hercule and his clever son."

M. Hercule himself, the tenant of this cabin, is squatting upon a mat in the middle of the floor, his fingers busily weaving the slit canes, with which he is bottoming a chair.

He smokes a short pipe and hums some popular melody, and though working briskly from time to time, looks up with a comical grimace at little Elfie Earl, who is playing bo-peep over his shoulder, and puts her into a fit of silvery, childish laughter.

Madame Hercule, a finely-formed, but delicate-looking woman, on whose faded cheek the traces of beauty still linger, sits knitting by the open door, through which the balmy evening breeze wafts in the fragrance of the hawthorne and the May blossom.

Madame is very dark, has a pair of brilliant black eyes, and a wealth of black hair; her features are small, refined, and pretty; her mouth is arched, and her teeth are white and even.

Her dress, though consisting of the poorest materials, is nevertheless extremely becoming, and fits her rounded form to perfection.

Madame is decidedly French, though her husband's style has rather a "Brummagem" ring about it, and, for himself, good fellow, there is no mistaking his nationality, or doubting the fact that he was born within sound of Bow Bells.

Marie Tardant had been in her youth a stage dancer, whom the gallant Achille had met during one of his travelling engagements and married within a fortnight from their first meeting, for Achille was a gallant and impulsive fellow, and in his youthful prime had been a lion among the ladies, for his figure was noble and symmetrical, while his face, though not cast in a classic mould, was far from ill-featured, and his frank, simple, good-humoured expression was very attractive.

Marie had lived in England from an early age, and spoke English well, though with a slight accent, in itself extremely pleasing.

For a long time the couple sat at work without speaking, their ears drinking in the sweet fresh music that rippled from the laughing lips of the child at play, when suddenly Marie raised her great, round black eyes from her work.

"Achille!"

"What is it, m'amour?"

Achille was "well up" in French terms of endearment.

"I was thinking, Achille, of our little enfant trouvée; the good rector called to-day with his two daughters; they at once fell in love with our little Elfie and wanted to steal her."

"But, ma chère Marie, consider, we are bound by our promise to the gipsy king."

"Ah, bah! I am gipsy, too; my father was Bohemian," said Marie, smiling. "I will manage him, never fear; I will remind him that Elfie will not leave the village, and that we shall see her every day, and you remember he said she was to be bien elevée, well educated, you know; learn to read, and dance, and speak French. Viens ici, petite (come here, little one)."

Elfie sprang to her side.

The woman took her on to her knee, parted the gold threads from her brow, and kissed her.

"Ecoutes, donc! Listen, now; what is my name?"

"Marie."

"Mar—ie! little a—rogue!" she laughed, embracing the child. "Cependant, I tell you true, Achille; she has a good accent, and will soon speak French well. If she goes to live in the family of the rector she will receive a good education."

"But, mon ange, I don't like the idea of parting with her."

"Nor I, Achille; but if it is for her good?"

"Well, we'll consult Paul, and we'll see what old Joe says about it," returned her husband.

Here the subject dropped, and the worthy couple continued their work till the long twilight had faded out, and the bright full moon arose in her silver glory.

It was Saturday night, a time always looked forward to with joyous expectance by the parents, as, on that night, Paul, whose engagement was in London, returned to spend the Sunday at home.

Little Elfie had asked permission to set up till Paul came home, but long before the moon had mounted the mid-sky she had dropped to sleep on the door-step.

Marie gently raised her, and bore her into the cottage.

She laid the child softly down upon the bed, and then busied herself in preparing the supper.

Achille had knocked off work, and, having cleared away the litter he had made, took a wash at the pump without, and slipped on his coat.

Lighting his pipe he sauntered to the garden gate, and, leaning upon it, glanced down the moon-lit lane to see if his son was coming.

Marie stole out of the cottage and came to his side.

The village clock struck twelve.

The gallant Achille wound his arm around his wife's waist, and for a long time they stood star-gazing, and chatting in a very lover-like manner.

They recalled many sweet old memories, talked of past sorrows almost with exultation.

Their path had been a rugged one, but it had been gilded by the sunshine of their wedded love, and they had kept fast hold of each other's hand, and, aided by the mutual support, had surmounted many an obstacle which it would have quelled them to encounter singly.

The May moon still shone bright, and the dewy breeze still came laden from field and orchard, with the honied perfumes of the fair, rich Spring.

They had not noticed the lapse of time till they were startled by the clock booming one.

"The boy is late," said Marie, anxiously.

"There's a benefit to-night; this is a busy time."

"He will be so tired."

"Yes; I wish he would come"

"Ah, mon dieu!" murmured Marie, clinging to her husband's arm with paling cheek and fainting voice.

"What is it, Marie?"

"That cruel trapeze! And he is so fearless."

"There lies his safety; nothing can daunt my Paul."

"You had courage too, husband, but it did not avail to save you from that terrible accident."

"All the fault of the cursed carpenters. But I wish the boy would come."

The wish was gratified at the same moment that it was expressed, for young Paul vaulted the stile at the bottom of the lane, light as a chamois, and then came plodding rather wearily along.

The moon-beams fell full upon him as he advanced, displaying his superb figure, his rich clustering curls, and his pale but handsome face. He appeared to be about fourteen years of age.

Marie tenderly embraced her son and bade him welcome in her own pleasant language.

Achille shook the boy heartily by the hand and led him into the cottage.

Paul threw himself wearily into a chair, and dropped his bundle by his side.

"And where is Elfie, maman?"

"Asleep, dear, on the bed; don't wake her."

Paul raised his hand wearily to his head.

"You are exhausted and ill, my poor boy," murmured Marie.

"Not at all, maman," replied Paul, "only I had hard work to-night; the fellow who usually fixes the ropes got drunk, and I had to trust to a strange hand to do it. He did not understand the business, and once, when I was on the highest swing, holding on by my leg, about to take the grand summersault for the longest flying leap, I felt the——"

Marie uttered a slight shriek and buried her face in her apron.

Warned by a look from his father, Paul suddenly stopped, and broke into a merry, boyish laugh.

"Dear maman, it's nothing, only that it spoils the 'act.'

Sometimes I drop down for mere wantonness, and, like poor puss, I always come on to my feet."

"Achille, we are living upon our child's life-blood!" she cried, passionately.

"Pshaw! Paul flies like the eagle and perches as safely; besides, the trapeze act is getting stale, we'll find something easier for him soon," returned Achille, though his own lip quivered as he glanced at his beautiful boy, and shuddered at the thought of what might happen.

Paul rose, and, walking over to the corner in which the little girl was slumbering, kissed her softly.

"Dear little Elfie," he whispered, "I've brought you a bed-fellow."

So saying, he untied his bundle, and, throwing aside the spangled dress he performed in, unfolded from its envelope of tissue paper a large, flaxen-haired, showily-dressed wax doll, which he laid by Elfie's side.

"Elfie's face is as white as dolly's," he said, "but warm and soft, and the colour comes and goes like the pink shades in the clouds at sunset—now, don't it, maman? Oh, what a little love she is! When I get to be a man she shall be my wife and your daughter, shan't she, maman? But I won't be an acrobat then."

"Silly boy; don't talk such nonsense."

"Nonsense, maman? Elfie will want some one to protect her when you are old, you know, and who loves her so much as I?"

"Ah, no one can."

"Come, my son, let's have some supper. Bless my heart, I'm as 'ungry as a wolf."

"But you musn't gobble up our little Red Riding Hood for all that, father, though she looks so dear that one could eat her, as the nurses say. Sit down, father, I'll wheel round your chair."

"Hulloa! left-handed are ye?" cried Achille, with a start.

"I've been hanging by my right arm till it's quite nerve-less," said Paul; "but it's often so, but it gets all to-rights before morning, and to-morrow's Sunday, so I shall have a long rest."

"Oh, dear! oh, dear! Achille, the child shall *not* expose himself to risk and exhaustion for us. I declare he shall throw up his engagement; I would rather see him working at the plough or scaring birds off the corn than live in such a constant state of agitation for his safety."

"Well, my dear, something must be done. I'll ask Joe about it."

They sat down to supper.

"Paul, my child, you eat nothing," said the mother, anxiously.

"Had a snack in town, maman," returned the boy, making a brave effort at an onslaught on the pie before him.

"Take a drink, Paul. And over the beer-jug. What, still left-handed?"

"Yes, I'll rest the other arm. But, I say, father, there's been sad work in London after the Derby. Two or three suicides, and a woman at some café in the Haymarket has stabbed another woman in a fit of jealousy"

"How shocking! Is the poor thing dead?"

"I believe not, maman, though mortally wounded it is feared."

"Where did you hear this?"

"I heard it—yes, maman, that is, I heard——"

The boy broke down, his cheek was ghastly white, and his lips turned blue.

"My child, how pale you look!" murmured Marie.

"It's nothing, maman. Lend me those scissors, there?"

"What do you want?"

"The button on the wrist of my shirt hurts me a little."

He took the scissors and began to cut away his wristbands.

"Oh, Heavens! Something dreadful has happened, I am sure!" cried his mother.

"Why where you so late, dear, what detained you?"

"I—I—fell!" gasped the poor boy, dizzily. "The doctors would not let me go. I ran off from them. My arm!—cut the wristband, maman! Quick! quick!"

He uttered a piercing shriek.

His arm had swollen fearfully, and the tight wristband was cutting into the livid flesh.

Before his parents could rush to his side he dropped senseless on the ground, fainting with long suppressed agony !

CHAPTER XXII.

A DREAM AND STRANGE VISITORS.

FOR many days poor little Paul lay upon a bed of suffering, but the stout-hearted boy endured the pain with Spartan fortitude, troubling himself only because his accident, and the consequent illness, prevented him from working for his parents, whom he dearly loved.

His mother attended him with great devotion, and under her care, and that of a kind and skilful surgeon, he began rapidly to recover his strength.

His arm, which had been severely fractured, was bandaged and set by the surgeon, who declared that on no account must the boy be allowed to resume his former occupation.

Poor Hercule and his wife kept this decision of the surgeon's a secret from the boy, who was restless and impatient to be once more up and doing.

During poor Paul's illness, little Elfie Earl had displayed an amount of sense and affection that greatly surprised her guardians ; young as she was she seemed to understand the patient's position, and would sit by his side watching him with melting eyes and keeping herself quite still for hours, while she attended upon Marie, when she acted as nurse, like an experienced little hand-maiden.

"Maman," said Paul, one day, raising himself on the pillow and addressing his mother, who sat working at the bedside, "I've been sleeping, and I dreamed such a strange dream about little Elfie."

"My dear, I think you dream too much of her," said Marie, with a droll smile ! "you think of nothing else, day or night."

"Are you jealous, maman?" said Paul, clasping his mother's hand, a wan smile resting on his pale face.

Marie bent over her son and kissed his lips.

"Just a little," she said. "But what was your dream?"

"I dreamed that I and Elfie were dwelling together in such a pretty cottage, with latticed windows and a porch of trained roses. I thought the country all about the house was very beautiful, that we were poor, maman, but yet so happy. Well, after a time there came to our cottage a strange and evil-looking man—I knew at once that he was a wizard, a magician—"

"Some fairy has been whispering in your ear."

"It was Elfie, then, maman, for she sat by my side all the while I was asleep."

"Well, dear, and the wizard or magician?"

"He asked me for Elfie. I told him she was present ; but when he approached her she shrank from him with fear ; but he smiled and spoke gently to her, and she became more bold. I could not understand half their conversation ; but I thought Elfie gave him her handkerchief, and he went away. Soon after he had gone, a splendid carriage drove up to our door, and a party of noble gentlemen and ladies carried her away from me. Elfie would not go till they suffered her to take me with her ; but I was not allowed to ride in the carriage, no, maman ; and after we reached a grand house, Elfie's new home, though I was often her companion, and went with her to see many grand sights and meet much fine company, I felt myself lonely and despised, for Elfie was everywhere courted and caressed, while I was snubbed and kept at a distance. It was a strange dream. What did it mean, maman?"

"You are too young to know its meaning," returned Marie, biting her lip. "They may say what they will," she thought, "and it's easy to deny what one can't understand—the ignorant always do so ; but there are warnings received in sleep that it is unwise to disregard."

"Why do you frown, maman?" asked Paul, smiling. "You don't like my dream ; well, there is one mistake we made, maman, for Elfie could never have whispered it in my ear. I don't think she would leave us for all the fine people in the world."

"At her age, not willingly, perhaps ; but time works changes," said Marie. "Now, tell me, Paul, do you like your present calling?"

"As a gymnast?—yes, much, maman."

"And would not like to change it?"

"Well, perhaps one is never contented with anything ; is it not so, maman?"

"As a rule, dear ; but there are exceptions ; you are quite contented with your little pet, for instance?"

"Oh, yes, indeed."

"And with me?"

Paul put his arms round his mother's neck and kissed her affectionately.

"Well, then, let me ask you, once more, do you expect to remain in your present profession all your life?"

"Of course, maman ; what else am I to do that will pay me so well? I have not learned a trade ; if I were to leave the stage, now, what should we all do? No, maman, you need not fear ; this is but a slight accident, nothing serious will happen to me, I shall soon be well enough to return to business."

"You must not think of that for a long time, mon enfant," returned the mother, smiling sadly.

As she spoke, a knocking was heard at the door, and on opening it Marie confronted a withered old hag, dressed in dirty fluttering rags and leaning upon a crutch.

The wretched old creature mumbled through her toothless gums a whining petition for a morsel of bread.

Marie kindly invited the old crone to enter the cottage and rest herself awhile, and placed some bread and meat before her and then gave her some money, which she clutched at greedily.

Little Elfie, who had been playing in the garden, came in with a hoop in her hand.

Upon seeing the beggar-woman, she crept close to Marie's side and nestled there, her large eyes staring at the woman with a look of fright and aversion.

Marie, too, could scarcely repress a shudder as she looked upon the wrinkled, weather-stained, and malignant-looking old woman, who was devouring her repast as greedily as if she had tasted nothing for a week.

"You have come far?" asked Marie, suppressing a qualm of aversion.

"Yes, my dear ma'am, yes, yes ; many a weary mile I have plodded, and the roads are hard, and the peoples' hearts harder than the roads. This is the first crust I've touched to-day."

Marie looked surprised.

The woman's tones, though faint and mumbling, were coherent, and her keen black eyes seemed to have lost but little of their youthful brightness, and sent a wandering, heedful glance round the room.

Suddenly they fixed a steadfast look on the face of the child.

"That's a lovely little thing, ma'am," she said, with a hideous grimace, "but she does not resemble you ; you are so dark and she so fair."

Marie made no further answer than by an equivocal smile.

"Well, children are great cares, but they're great blessings too—at least, some say so. Ho, ho! mine was a blessing!"

The old crone shook her head and broke into a chuckling laugh, which ended in a husky cough.

"You have had children, then?" asked Marie, with a strange qualm rising in her throat, as she contemplated the woman's fierce and abhorrent countenance.

"Yes, ma'am, I had sons and daughters. They are all dead but one ; the youngest is alive."

"And she does not shelter you?"

"Why, no, ma'am, I refuse to be a burden to her," returned the hag, with a peculiar whine, peculiarly odious ; "but I'm thinking, ma'am, that you would like to know the future destiny of this pretty little thing. I'm of gipsy blood, ma'am, though for many years I lived in service."

"Pshaw! do you think I put any confidence in your pretensions of prophecy? Do you think I am so weak and misguided as to suppose that the Eternal would trust the secrets of his future providence to such as you and I?"

"Ma'am, you may or may not believe me, but I know that child is born to a strange destiny."

"So are we all, if all were known," sighed Marie.

"I have seen better days, as I told you," said the old woman, "but still I am of gipsy blood, and hold the gift of my outcast race, and can see into futurity. Come here, my darling."

And she held out her hand towards Elfie, but the child shrank from her trembling.

"She is not your child!" said the crone, with a chuckling laugh.

"Why do you think so?" asked Marie, taking Elfie up in her arms and clasping her close.

"That does not deceive me!" laughed the old woman.

"Deceive you? Why should I deceive you?" said Marie, while her cheek blushed rosily.

The old woman made no reply, but seemed lost in thought; suddenly she recommenced, in a croaking voice,

"I had a mansion once, a retinue of lovers, courtiers, and dependents, a carriage, jewels of price, siks, satins, and laces, and, what is hardest of all to realise, I had beauty—a fine figure, flashing black eyes, and showers of silken black ringlets. Ho, ho! look at me now, ma'am!"

"You make me shudder," said Marie. "What has brought you to this?"

"My own mad passions, man's falseness, and the curse of a rotten social system!" cried the old woman, fiercely. "You see how grey my hair is? I am not so old as I look. What I miss most is my voice—mumble, mumble, it makes me feel old to harken to myself. And then, I am so weak, so racked with pain—but my spirit is as untameable as ever!"

The crone's eyes glared with eldrich fire as she thus spoke.

"You must forget or repent the past life," said Marie, "and think of the life to come. At your time of life——"

"I thank ye, I thank ye, ma'am; what you say is right," returned the beggar woman, her voice sinking once more into a feeble whine, and all the strength and fire dying out from her glazing eyes. "I must think of the end! It is welcome, ma'am; if I had been younger I should have been less willing to wait for it."

Marie did not speak; she was awed and vexed by the woman's strange manner, and being anxious to get rid of her did not encourage her by any remark to resume the conversation.

"That child's destiny resembles mine," said the crone, suddenly.

"God forbid," murmured Marie, clutching the little one close to her breast.

"She is poor; she will be rich, and then poor again, as I am."

"You judge so from her beauty," said Marie; "but I trust sweet little Elfie will prove as wise and good as she is beautiful."

"Wisdom and beauty are seldom united," said the old woman, maliciously sneering. "But I see, you would have me gone."

A suggestive pause.

"Well, my dear, I'll go," returned the strange and weird woman, tottering towards the door. "Thank ye for all your kindness; guard the little one well. Remember my words; what I have told you is true. Let my case warn ye. Some day I may be of service to ye, but it must be in my own way. You are poor, I see that; well, you must not expect money from me, not money, my dear, anything but money. I've none, not one half-penny more than I owe to your charity, and that will be spent before morning. Good-bye."

She was gone, and had half closed the door.

"Mon dieu!" cried Marie, speaking aloud, in her surprise, "what a strange being! I could almost believe that Paul's dream has come true, only his wizard has turned out a witch, and I can hardly fancy that such an ugly god-mother could change into a beautiful fairy."

"Shake the snows of twenty hard winters out of my hair, and I should do that," cried the croaking voice of the old beldame, who peered back through the half-open door. "But good bye, my dear, and never forget my warning."

Marie hurried to the door; but without turning her head, the old crone had passed through the little wicket of the garden, and disappeared down the lane.

CHAPTER XXIII.

THE ABDUCTION LF ELFIE EARL.

SOME hours after the departure of this mysterious creature, and towards the close of the evening, which had turned out very stormy, Marie was sitting by the side of her son, who had fallen into a gentle sleep, when she was startled by the sound of mens' voices without, and a sharp knock at the door.

In some trepidation she arose, and admitted three men.

Two of them she knew, one being Darrel, who had once or twice visited the cottage; the other, Black Isaac, the gipsy king; but the third was a stranger, a tall, cadaverous-looking man, well-dressed, and wrapped in a heavy, furred cloak.

"Is your husband at home, madame?" asked Darrel.

"No, sir; but I expect his return every instant," replied Marie.

She walked to the window, which commanded a view of the windings of the road.

She recoiled with an amazed look.

Crouching along the laurel-hedge she distinctly discerned the crippled form of the mysterious beggar woman.

She quickly opened the window and looked out.

The shadow form had vanished!

Under pretence of seeking her husband, she hurried to the front door.

She walked out into the garden; she looked from side to side, and, leaning over the gate, glanced up and down the lane.

No one was to be seen.

With a feeling of discomfort and terror, she returned to the door.

"Am I not right?" muttered a voice—Darrel's.

"Aye, right enough; the child is the image of her mother," returned the man unknown to Marie.

She entered to find little Elfie sitting shyly upon Darrel's knee.

Black Isaac and the stranger were standing by looking on with interest.

They exchanged rapid glances when Marie came in.

"And how does the child reconcile herself to her new home?" asked Darrel.

"Indeed, sir, she seems happy enough," returned Marie. "We are so fond of her."

"I fear we shall have to remove her from your care, however, madame," said the stranger.

"Oh, I trust not," rejoined Marie, earnestly. "She is well cared for, and we should miss her so much."

"We have no doubt, madame, of your care and kindness, but there are reasons why she must be removed to other guardians whose duty it is to take charge of her."

"And, pray, sir, are they her parents or relatives or friends?" asked Marie, quickly.

"You have no right to ask these questions," said Black Isaac, with a frown. "If you remember rightly it was part of our compact that you should act directly according to my request, and seek no knowledge of the child's parentage."

"That is true," returned Marie, quietly. "I am anxious only for her sake."

"You may rest assured that nothing but good is intended towards the child," said Darrel.

"It cannot be otherwise, I trust," rejoined the woman, "for who could harm such an innocent little creature? But here is my husband."

Achille entered and looked with some surprise at his guests.

"Good evening, my boy," said Black Isaac, gripping Achille's hand. "You will think we have come to take you by storm, and so we are. We have come to carry off your pretty prize."

"You don't say so!—you can't mean it if you do say it!" gasped poor Achille, in great consternation. "Why, my son Paul would break his heart to lose his little playmate. Hang it, now, she's got use to us. She's all right here. Why remove her?"

"For reasons of our own, my boy. You know the terms of our agreement—you were to ask no questions, and to make no revelations. The child was to be trusted under your care for a year, and you to be paid so much the whole of that time for your pains and—discretion, whether the child were taken away before the term expired or otherwise. Is not that right?"

"Why, yes; but still I say it can't be done!" returned Achille, impetuously.

"Why not?"

"Why not? I tell ye why not. My boy, Paul, would break his heart at the mere thought of such a thing."

"Better break his heart than his neck," rejoined the gipsy, grimly. "That trapeze business will be the death of him."

"He has already had a narrow escape," said the poor tumbler, wringing his hands. "He had a fall and fractured his arm. But what are we to do? And now, when he is so ill, to vex him by taking all the sunshine out of our home. Let the little one stay with us a month, or a week even."

"You're an odd fish," laughed the gipsy king. "Don't you understand you'll be the better off, for you will have no further expense with the child, and the money shall be paid down in a lump according to agreement."

"Curse the money!"

"Well, the child must be given up."

"Oh! I'll ask Joe about it," cried Achille, stamping his foot, impatiently.

"Hulloa! Ask whom?" cried Black Isaac, savagely, catching the tumbler by the arm. "To whom have you been blabbing my secrets?"

"I?—blabbing? Not I. Certainly Joe knows everything, allers does—'cute chap, see through a brick wall; but as for him splitting on any matter, why one might almost say as he's dumb, leastwise he never puts two words together once in a season. He blab?—he split? the idea's ridic'lous."

"Humph! Well, I did think I could trust you, Master Hercule; but it does not much matter, the child goes with us to-night, so, madame, have the goodness to prepare her for the start."

Marie hesitated.

The child's face began to wear an expression of alarm, and she clung closely to her kind protectress.

"Come, look sharp, there's good people, for we must be off," cried Black Isaac, testily.

"Yes, it is time we were returning," added the stranger. "Pray, madame, make haste."

Darrel, who had kept his eyes upon the last speaker, suddenly stepped forward.

"No," he said, "the night is dark, and it threatens rain; we can leave her here till the morning."

"Better not," grumbled Black Isaac.

"But I say it shall be so," returned Darrel, with firmness.

"And who gave you a voice in the matter, sir?" said the stranger, contemptuously.

"One who has confided the child to my keeping," replied Darrel, in an even, serious tone, "and I will not suffer any one to take the charge out of my hands. The little one is delicate, and shall not be removed to night; that is settled. Madame shall bring her to some place of rendezvous to-morrow where we can decide upon future arrangements."

"Upon my word, sir," cried the stranger, briskly, "you take upon yourself——"

"A task which I mean to perform myself; unaided, if need be, so let us have no more words in the matter."

"Darrel, with all due deference to the world, allow me politely to hint that you are playing the fool most infernally," whispered Black Isaac. "Don't you know that without him we can't stir a step?"

"Then we'll remain where we are," was the dogged reply.

"Well, well, as you please. I said I'd not oppose ye, that I would help you in this affair in acquittal of a good turn you once did for me, but, 'pon my life, if you have any sense or prudence, you won't act——"

"In any other way than I'm now doing."

"But your reason?"

"Look at the child."

"Well?"

"She looks pale and frightened already."

"Pah! young children are always scared when they see a stranger."

"But hark at the beating of the rain and the whistling of the wind; is there need to drag the little fledgling out of her warm nest, in such a rough night?"

"As you will," returned the gipsy, with a shrug. "But there's many a slip 'twixt the cup and the lip."

"You must let her stay with us, at least till the morning, Mr. Darrel," said Marie, sorrowfully caressing the child; "surely you would not take her out in such bad weather and such a late hour?"

"And hang me if you shall either!" cried Achille, "'Tain't human! Let it be to-morrow."

"I will come myself and fetch her away," said Darrel.

"And I with you," rejoined the stranger.

"We will arrange about that," returned Darrel, coldly. "Let us be off now."

"Stay, gentlemen; I'll get the lantern and light ye down the lane—the way is rugged and the night's as dark as a wolf's throat," said Achille.

Lighting the lantern, he preceded them to the door, which he opened carefully, for the wind shook the house to its foundation.

The three visitors bowed their adieux to the little Frenchwoman, and passed out into the darkness and the lashing rain.

When they were gone, Marie took the child upon her lap, seated herself before the hearth, and gazed pensively upon the blazing fire, listening with deep depression to the mournful gusts of wind and rain as she pondered over the strange events of the day.

A vague feeling of restlessness and foreboding possessed her spirit, and she gave an anxious look towards the door, to see if her husband were returning.

The moments ticked heavily by.

The wind still roared around her little dwelling like a lion for its prey, and the swift darting rain-drops pattered against the window.

He had been gone but ten minutes, yet what a "weary while" it had seemed. At last a step.

He returns—she knows the light tread, and rises to open the door.

The flame of the candle flutters in the strong draft and is almost extinguished.

Achille enters and closes the door.

He then fastens the shutters and draws his chair close to the glowing fireside.

"I wish Joe was here," he muttered dolefully.

"I suppose we must give her up to these people?" asked Marie.

"Of course; as Joe sometimes says—and it's his longest speech—'Wot's the use of struggling'?'"

"Perhaps it is as well as it is," murmured Marie.

"Well, you know, I don't see that, now; but, ma chere, I know you are always right."

"Sometimes," said Marie, smiling; "but I hope these men have no design to harm the poor little child."

"Oh no, Marie; though Darrel has been in prison and Black Isaac is not a puritan, I think neither of them would link themselves in a plot against an orphan, outcast child."

"And who is the stranger that came with them?"

"I don't know him, Marie; he looks like a lawyer."

"Yes, I thought so too. Perhaps the child is a lost heiress. Ah! if so——"

"If so, what?" asked the tumbler.

"Our Paul is but a boy, but love sometimes takes root early."

"And he's fond of Elfie, is he not? Well, who knows what may happen?" returned Achille, rubbing his hands. "I always predicted that boy was born to good fortune; and as for the heiress, Paul's a match for a royal princess; there's nothing like him!"

(*To be continued.*)

Agony took possession of her heart and brain, and, as the heavy hangings that hid the bay window fell between it and the hall, again hiding effectually St. Leon from her observation, she turned to the guests, and in a loud voice of shrieking alarm, she said,

"Help, help! St. Leon is dying! Help, help! oh! help!"

The effect of these words, rising as they did above every other sound, was quite prodigious.

The guests who still remained from fondness of the dance, seemed for a moment transfixed in the different attitudes they happened to be in at the time.

It looked as if some enchanter had waved his hand over that throng, and, by his wondrous power, commanded each to pause where he was, and in the precise position in which he was.

If, however, the sudden exclamation of Linda had produced this strange effect, it was reserved for her again to dispel it, for at the first sound of her voice now, as she again cried,

"Oh, help him! help him!—he is here! Bring him wine—he is dying!"

There was a general movement towards the bay window, while several snatched goblets of wine from the side tables to bring to the relief of him who was proclaimed to be so ill.

The space of time comprehended in a minute and a half could not have elapsed before Linda, perceiving that she had thoroughly succeeded in awakening attention to the position of St. Leon, turned herself to throw aside the massive drapery which concealed him.

A dozen hands assisted her, and the curtains were drawn widely asunder.

The window was vacant! St. Leon was not to be seen!

CHAPTER III.

THE TWO STUDENTS OF ALCHEMY AND THE BLACK ARTS—THE STRANGE PROPOSAL AND THE AGREEMENT—THE ODD VISITOR.

JUST ten years previous, counting from the day on which these strange occurrences we have recorded in the preceding chapters took place at Sir Marmaduke Beaufoy's, two young men were seated in a small, turret-like chamber, which was in a castellated mansion, situated on the banks of a small stream, some dozen miles or so from London.

This mansion was of great extent, and no doubt had, from its position, been originally built for defensive purposes.

The stream, so close to which it was placed, had been partially diverted from its regular channel, so that it very nearly flowed round three sides of the building, while the fourth was protected by a high and dangerous wall, which had a slight incline outwards, that rendered it ten times more difficult to scale than if it had been exactly perpendicular.

But if this large castellated mansion had been originally constructed with an eye to its position in a military point of view, the advent of more peaceful times had, as people say, altered all that, and the various proprietors of it had made such alterations as tended more towards comfort than defence.

For nearly thirty years, however, it had been deserted, in consequence of the evil repute it fell into by a deed of blood which had been committed within its walls.

It had been put up to let by its proprietor, but the few persons who had chosen, in consequence of its romantic position, to fancy they should like it as a habitation, had made but short stays in it, until at last it was entirely neglected for some years.

One boisterous evening, however, in November, two young men had arrived in the neighbourhood, and seeking out the person in whose custody the keys of the deserted mansion were, they produced a brief note from its proprietor, which merely contained the words,

"Allow the bearer to reside at the moat-house."

This note was signed by the name of the proprietor, and as the privilege of residing at the moat did not, to the man who had charge of the keys, at all appear a desirable one, he never for a moment questioned the genuineness of the document, but gave up the keys accordingly.

These young men at once took possession of the old place, but the only apartment they seemed to occupy was a small turret chamber, which jutted out oddly from the western wall of the building.

In this turret chamber a light continually burned, night and day, and it was no small amusement to the children of the neighbouring hamlet to watch the strange and different colours which from time to time this light would assume.

Sometimes it would be a clear and brilliant white, then it would change to a green, and then again to a crimson, perhaps so intense that it would be impossible the eyes of any one could stand the steady glare of it.

The elder inhabitants of the little village would shake their heads at these odd phenomena, and declare, that in their belief, what was going on in the turret chamber of the moat-house must have a great deal more to do with a certain place down below, which they would rather not mention, than with either this world or the heaven above it.

But the young strangers lived unobtrusively. They only now and then came to the village to purchase the common necessaries of existence, of which they commonly bought as much as would last them for a month or more, and as they never made the least scruple about the price, but paid freely for whatever they purchased in current coin, they were treated with civility and attention before their faces, whatever might be the opinions entertained of them behind their backs.

Sometimes, too, strange sounds as well as strange lights would come from the turret chamber, and once so loud an explosion ensued that the whole of the inhabitants of the village thought that the house must be blown to pieces.

As they looked toward the turret chamber, from which the explosion had evidently ensued, they saw that a huge stone was loosened from the sill of the window, and it fell with a heavy plunge into the moat below; but nothing else occurred contingent upon such a state of things, and after watching the turret for about an hour, and all seeming much as before, the circumstance was allowed to pass over in silence.

We do not mean to say that no attempts were at any time made to discover what the two young men were about in the turret. One person, whose curiosity could not be restrained, in the village, asked them one day, but the look of intense surprise which he got in reply rather staggered him, and he was glad to walk away with his curiosity ungratified.

But let us peep into the turret-chamber, which in the neighbourhood caused such a world of inquiry and trouble.

The room was a much larger one than the appearance from the outside would at all have warranted any one in supposing it. It was of an octagonal shape, and the window occupied one of the sides of the octagon. The roof was lofty and of a dome shape.

To describe the contents of that most singular apartment would not only occupy too much of our space, but would involve us in a technical description of matters which would scarcely be interesting to the general reader. Suffice it to say, that in the middle of the room was a stove, and that the chimney belonging to it had been carried out at one of the walls, but to so trifling an extent as regarded its projection, that any one from without might look a hundred times at the turret without perceiving it at all.

Around this stove, and on the walls, the floor, and in many cases suspended from the roof, were articles of use, or fancied use, in alchemical researches, for at that period science had not made progress enough to detect the possible from what was merely probable.

There still existed a strong belief in the supposed fact that the discovering of the mode of transmuting all metals into gold was attainable, and many clung to the belief, too, that the *elixir vitæ*, or draught of long life, or rather immortality, would yet crown the labours of some fortunate alchemist.

How these things had all been brought to the moat house, no one knew; although one of the villagers, who, from a partiality to taking hares from other people's grounds, was frequently out at night, asserted that at times he had seen carts arrive at the moat house about midnight, and be unloaded of their multifarious contents, and then go away again, without going at all nearer the village than was absolutely necessary, from the shape of the high road which led to the moat house.

This account was paid but little attention to. Indeed, by the party who stated it, it was not much talked of; because, along with it, it carried the evidence that he was out at such an hour, or else he could not have become aware of what was going on, when honest people are generally supposed to be in their beds.

It is evening, however, on that day ten years past which we have introduced to our readers, and the two young men were in the turret-chamber of the moat house.

The sun was setting, and long shadows were being cast by the trees in the neighbourhood over the stream that winds so far round the ancient edifice. A cool wind, too, was sweeping over the meadows, and occasionally came in in puffs at the open window of the turret.

One of the young men was hanging, with great interest depicted on his countenance, over a crucible which was on the fire, and from which ever and anon there came a strange hissing noise, and a few sparks, which would shoot upwards to a considerable height, ere they became extinguished.

The other was sitting upon a low chair, with one of those high backs which go far above the head of whoever may be sitting in the chair. His attitude was desponding, and there was a hue of ill health upon his cheeks, as if close confinement in that place had been far from doing him any good, and he had suffered much from

(*Continued from page* 48.)

THE JOLLY DOGS OF LONDON.

THE JOLLY DOGS AT THE PIC-NIC PARTY.

CHAPTER XXIII.—(continued.)

"He had a strange dream though, an unpleasant one, and it seems to be partly accomplished. Do you put faith in dreams?"

"To be sure; on the day before our wedding, I dreamed I had found a priceless jewel, and that I placed it at my heart, and felt as proud as an emperor. Didn't that dream come true?"

"One ought to love you a little, Achille," returned Marie, with a quiet smile, as she pressed his hand, "if it's only for your nonsense. But I do not feel happy about poor Elfie; I do not like the prospect before us."

"The clouds will clear away, as they have done before, and the sun will shine out again; even despair never can last long; hope will spring up with the moss on a dungeon wall. Never say die, that is m'amie, du courage! all will end well, and Paul will marry the princess."

"Hark! he calls us."

Marie rose, and, accompanied by her husband, went into Paul's little chamber.

Elfie was left reclining on the hearth, and watching the glowing embers in the grate, her great blue eyes dilating with childish thought.

"Maman, I heard all that passed between you and the

visitors. Maman, do you love me ?" said Paul, with eagerness.

"I know what you would say, dear ; you mean that we must not part with the little foundling ?"

"Yes, maman ; pray do not let them take her from us. I am sure she will be safer and happier with us ; don't let her be snatched away."

"Marie, we *must* speak to Joe about it !" cried Achille, peevishly ; "I can't bear the thought of losing our little treasure."

A pealing shriek—then the slamming of the door.

"The child !" cried Marie.

She rushed into the little parlour.

Elfie was gone !

"The infernal villains have returned and have stolen her away !" cried Achille, aghast. "Yet—I'm bewildered ; I saw them go off in the train. Could they have got back so quickly ?"

"No—no ! it is not they, they had no hand in it !" cried Marie ; "it is the woman !"

"Woman ? What woman ?"

"The witch who came here this evening ; but run, husband, the fearful old creature cannot have gone far, she is so old, so crippled. After her ! she will murder the child !"

For an instant the tumbler stood petrified with astonishment ; then he snatched down a fowling-piece that hung over the mantel.

"Achille, what would you do ? Don't take the gun with you."

"I will, though, Marie ; and, by the living thunder, I'll use it too, if I catch the villains !" cried Achille, darting from the door.

Marie followed him.

It was pitch dark, and the rain fell in torrents.

Paul made an attempt to get out of bed to aid his parents in the search for the stolen child ; but the pain in his wounded arm was so acute, and he was still so faint and weak from the shock his system had received, that he could only crawl to the door, where he staggered, and was obliged to lean for support against the door-post, listening to the wailing and weeping of the night storm.

———

CHAPTER XXIV.

JOE'S REVELATIONS TO ACHILLE.

A BRIGHT and spring-like morning succeeded to the night of terror.

The moisture still clung to the herbage ; but it twinkled like a delicate robe of jewels ; the wind had veered to a milder quarter, and wafted its load of perfume from woods of May-blossom and the bowers of lilac into the open door of the cottage where Marie and her husband were sitting, weary, and mud-stained, for they had but just returned from a long and fruitless search for the lost child.

"And Darrel will be here soon ; how shall we face him ?" moaned Achille. "The black crows fly in flocks, and troubles never come singly. Oh, lor ! it never rains but it pours, and last night it poured with a vengeance."

"You must not despond," said his wife, faintly smiling. "Refresh yourself a little, and then start again in pursuit. I will meet Darrel ; we shall find Elfie yet. I'm convinced that the wretched beggar-woman I told you of has stolen the child for some unknown motive. You must make inquiries at all the police-stations and workhouses ; be sure you will find her."

But Achille shook his head and replied only by a groan.

However, he seated himself at the table and took a cup of coffee. He had no appetite, and looked terribly haggard and woe-begone.

He quickly rose from his breakfast, and sluiced his burning brow at the little pump in the garden. He brushed the mud from his coat and boots, and prepared himself to set off once more, when a step was heard on the gravel.

"Who's there ?" cried Achille, excitedly, as he thrust his head out of the window.

"Joe !" was the curt answer.

Then came a joyous cry.

The burly, sullen-looking fellow thrust open the door, and appeared in the room with Elfie crowing in his arms.

The worthy couple rushed to him, and while Marie snatched the little girl from his arms and smothered her with rapturous kisses, Achille seized his friend's hand and shook it up and down with great cordiality.

"And where did ye find her, Joe ?"

"In the sun," returned Joe.

"That is her home, I should think," laughed Achille, playing with the child's shining ringlets ; "she seems to have brought away some of the sunbeams."

"And where is the sun ?" asked Marie, smiling.

"O'er Banstead way."

"And in whose company was she ?"

"An old rip's—child-stealer."

"Didn't I tell you so, husband ?"

"And where is the wretch ?"

"Locked up."

"You gave her in charge ?"

"Yes."

"But how did you chance to meet her ?"

"Went in for a pot and a pipe."

"Well ?"

"Sat smoking in the bar."

"Yes—go on."

"Old faggot comes in with child."

A long pause.

"What then ?"

"Axed for a go of gin."

"Never mind the gin."

"She liked it, though."

"What followed ?"

"Two more glasses of the same."

"Yes, and you——"

"I'd a glass o' short."

"With her ?"

"No."

"And I suppose, then, Joe, you recognized the child ?"

"Yes."

"And the child knew you ?"

"Jes' so."

"And you claimed her ?"

"Yes."

"Well, what occurred then ?"

"A jolly row !"

"Tell us all about it."

"Woman swore it was her young un'—I snatched the child away from her—old gal threw a pewter pot at me—bobbies called in—old rip tried to stab the child—I got this cut on the wrist—bobbies walked her off to the station—I walked myself off with the little 'un."

"Good heavens ! what could have been the old woman's motive to act so ?"

"Anythink for mischief. Women is creeturs without motives."

"But I can't imagine—"

"Don't try, marm ; where's the use o' strugglin' ?"

"Perhaps it was for her clothes ?"

"No."

"But the wretched old creature was so poor ?"

"No."

"Not poor ?"

"No."

"How can that be ? She said she had not tasted food for a day."

"Werry likes."

"But if she had money surely she would have something to eat ?"

"Lives on gin."

"Well, this is a caution. How much money had she, Joe ?"

"Ten quid in gold, and three fip-pund notes."

"In her pockets ?"

"Sowed up in her bussum."

"What an extraordinary creature."

"Yes."

"Must be mad."

"Mischeevous.".

"And will she be brought up ?"

"Afore the beak."

"And you're to prosecute ?"

"S'pose so."

"And shall we have to appear ?"

"Yes."

"Well, thank heaven, the child's restored !"

"Amen to you, marm !"

"Joe, we can never requite ye."

"Yes."

"How, lad ?"

"I'm hungry and dry."

"Dry enough !"

"Yes."

"Sit down to breakfast."

"I'll take a snack."

"Do you know, Achille, I believe the wretched creature's wild story is partly true, and that she was once rich," said Marie.

"Yes—she were."

"A reg'lar lady, eh, Joe ?"

"Spiled."

"How ?"

"Drink and eddication."

"Ho !"

Breakfast over, Achille took Joe's arm, and drew him aside.

Marie busied herself in her domestic affairs.

The two men seated themselves by the open window, and lighted their pipes.

For some time they smoked in silence.

"Joe," said Achille, after a long pause, "I want to consult you on a delicate affair."

"Humph !"

"It's about Elfie."

"Ha !"

"You are aware——"

"As little pitchers has long ears———"

"I'll send her off to play."

"So do."

Achille dismissed the little one, bidding her take a run in the garden, but warning her to keep within the gate.

The child rose, and gravely obeyed his order.

"You know under what circumstances she were at first confided to us ?"

"No."

"You do, Joe."

"Not d'zactly."

"But I told ye."

"Tell me agin."

"Listen, then——"

"Go on."

"Well, she was brought here by Black Isaac, the king o' the gips."

"I knows it."

"In course. Now, once upon a time, before Marie married me, she was dancing through the country."

"That's rum."

"What is ?"

"Through the country ; purty good step for a ' pas seul.' "

"You know what I mean, Joe. She were travelling with a company from town to town, doing the provinces—now you have it !"

"I take."

"And she met this same Black Isaac at a fair. She had not a reg'lar engagement at a theatre then, and were forced to play where she could."

"Well ?"

"She fell ill, and Black Isaac finding she b'longed to the gipsy tribe by the brand on her arm, and by some letters she had about her, had her took care on, was werry kind to her. Isaac's not a bad sort, and true as steel to his tribe. Marie was adopted in the band, and pays gipsy taxes to his majisty's exchequer. It were some of the tribe as taught me my purty trade o' basket-making and chair-mending."

"Pah !"

"Well, Joe, anything for a honest crust."

"Come to the pint."

"You cares more for yer 'pint' than yer crust, I believe," grinned Achille.

"Ah ! now yer rollin' about. Why can't ye stick to yer tack ?"

"All right, my pal."

"Well, one day, or rather night."

"Which were it ?"

"Well, about dusk."

"That's better ; be k'rect."

"Black Isaac comes to my crib, with Darrel, and brings the little gal."

"Darrel ?"

"Yes."

"You never told me the cove's name afore."

"I promised to keep it a secret."

"Well, it's all the same."

"What is ?"

"Whether you promised or not."

"What do ye mean ?"

"That you never could keep a secret."

"Not from you, Joe ; no needs."

"Well, go on."

"It seems, from what little Elfie tells me herself, and just from puttin' this and that together, ye know, that this Darrel kidnapped the child from some people as brought her up, and his reason for so doin' was that she was the moral picture of a certain fine gal as jilted him, and led to his bein' got into trouble."

"I knows the circumstances ; he were tutor to some young haristocrat ; guv'ness gal in the 'ouse ; man and master both made love at vonce ; in course, master accepted, man got the sack. Nat'ral !"

"That's more than I knew before."

"Go on."

"How did you come to know Darrel ?"

"Ha !"

"Tell me, Joe."

"It's a secret."

"Never mind, you can trust me with a secret."

"You trustes me too much."

"Then can't I trust ye ?"

"Yes, 'cos I don't trust you. Go on."

"You're a rum character."

"Jes' so."

"Well, Joe, to proceed. I rayther fancy that I've got a clue to the mystery. The fac's is about these. The aristocrat had a child by his fine guv'ness ; p'r'aps he'd married her, p'r'aps not ; guv'ness gets sent adrift, dies or goes to the bad, child falls into the hands of the Beamishes—that's the name of the old people——"

"Hold hard !"

"What are ye cryin' on now, Joe ?"

"Beamish—Shem Beamish ?"

"Yes, in course, it is Shem."

"Lives over Lambeth way ?"

"Well, now, I should think so, accordin' to the child's description ; she talks about the river, and the bridges, and the steamers ; must be over Lambeth way."

"An old couple with one son ?"

"Blow me, you're as good as a London D'rect'ry !"

"I knows 'em. Beamish, eh ?"

"Why, you seems to know everybody, Joe. Did you take the last census ?"

"Humph ! ha ! Go on, Herc'les."

"Interestin', ain't it ?"

"Yes."

"Well, where was I ?"

"At the Beamishes."

"Ah, werry true. They has possession o' the child ; Darrel sees her, and, for some motive or t'other, carries her off ; that I do know, for a fac'."

"What nex' ?"

"He takes her to Black Isaac, who trustes her to our care ; but what I want to get at is, who's this t'other chap, the third party, as came with Darrel and the gip? Wife says she overheard him say that the child were the image of its mother, so he must be somebody as knew the poor creature."

"What's he like?"

"Why, Joe, looks well enough for a lawyer!"

"Ha! what age?"

"Hard to say. Looks as if he'd died about forty years ago and then been galwanised into a kinder mummyfied existence!"

"Then he's very white-faced?"

"Yes."

"Stoops a little."

"Yes."

"Ha!"

"Do you know *him*?"

"Yes."

Achille stared his ineffable wonder.

"How did ye fust come to know *him*, Joe; tell us that?"

"In the same way as I come to know the rest o' the parties you mentioned."

"It's as good as a riddle!"

"Better!"

"How so?"

"'Cos the answer ain't in print."

"Hark ye, Joe; if you don't tell me the secret of all this, I'll disown yer friendship and never apply to ye for advice any more."

"Well, now I think I'll wenture to trust yer thus far. You've sifted yer evidence werry cleverly, Herc'les, and you ain't far from the mark. How I came to know all these parties is simple—fust you say there were a certain haristocrat as married a guv'ness."

"What were he—a lord, or a knight, or a esquire?"

"A hearl!"

"Why, lors, and the child calls herself Earl."

"Elfie Earl."

"Right."

"And your little pet's the daughter of a nobleman!"

"My! what luck for Paul! He's over head and ears in love with her! But, go-a-head! The hearl married the guv'ness, that jilted the tutor!"

"Yes; and this lawyer was the steward of this hearl that married the guv'ness, that jilted the tutor!"

"And who's Beamish?"

"He was the skipper to a yacht that belonged to the hearl."

"As married the guv'ness as jilted the tutor, as lived in the 'ouse that Jack built! My eye! there's confidence. I see then—a sort o' Old King Cole business—he bein' the king, and the steward the lawyer; and the sailor being his fiddlers three. But, then, I say, Joe, 'scuse me, but who the devil are you?"

"Afore I drew the carawans and learned drumming, I was coachman to this hearl——"

"Of what?"

"Never yer mind—you'll know some day."

"Then you, and Darrel, and this lawyer chap, and Elfie's poor mother, were once all in the sarvice of this Earl of Somewheres?"

"You've hit it."

"But I say, Joe; one little thing wexes me, do tell me that."

"What is it?"

"Do you think, now, that the hearl really married Elfie's mother?"

"Yes; I know he did."

"How can ye be sure; come now, Joe?"

"I saw the wedding; *I was the Bridesman!*"

"To a hearl, and a guv'ness! what a honour! Shake hands, Joe; I feels ennobled by yer comp'ny."

"Well, 'nough said, what's o'clock?"

"Most eleven."

"When do you expect Darrel?"

"I expects he'll be here in a few minutes."

"Humph!"

"Shall I give up the child to him?

"Yes; of course you won't let him know that you have heard anything about her history?"

"You may trust me for that."

"Then look ye, Herc'les, I'll dog his steps and see where he goes to; they'll go to London by the train, most likes; I'll go too."

"Capital! you ought to be a detective."

A strange smile swept over Joe's face, and he uttered a low chuckling laugh.

"I say, Joe, I ain't known ye long, though I feels as if we'd been friends from our cradles; you ain't allers a drummin', when there's no fairs on, how do ye do for a living?"

"Pretty well, thank ye," returned Joe, coolly; "but I'll step off now."

"But that old witch, Joe, I wonder who *she* is? Can ye tell that?"

"Perhaps; I'm not sure yet."

"Well, my wife often laughs when I says 'I'll ask Joe about it,' but, arter this, you might crib the title of a book I saw t'other day, and stick it over yer door—'Enquire within upon everything.'"

"Well, good-bye, for awhile, Herc'les; I'll track these fellows through their journey, and then I'll come and tell ye the result; but keep dark, or you'll spile all."

Shortly after he took leave of the pair, and quitting the cottage, plodded thoughtfully down the lane.

A gloating smile played on his hard features, and from time to time he vented his satisfaction in a low guttural laugh.

Suddenly he stopped.

He was arrested in his walk by the sound of approaching footsteps.

He stepped aside.

Two men were advancing from the distance.

They seemed so absorbed in a conversation, which they were carrying on in an under tone, that they did not see him.

He, however, recognised them at once.

He agilely sprang over a stile and threw himself down upon a flowery bank.

For an hour he lay listlessly reclining, apparently half asleep, but in reality keenly heedful of every passing step.

At last the sound of voices from the other side of the hedge was heard.

He raised himself on his hands and knees.

He peered through the waving bush.

Darrel and Black Isaac passed by the former, carrying little Elfie in his arms.

When they had got to some distance Joe scrambled through the hedge, and, assuming a shambling gait, and an abstracted air, paced after them, threading the various windings of the lane, emerged at length close upon their heels on the racecourse.

The huge, empty stand, the deserted course, looked bleak and bare when contrasted with the scene presented on the Derby Day.

At last they reached the station.

They took first-class tickets to London, and got into an empty carriage.

Joe took a third-class ticket, and got into the train, keeping as near to them as he could.

They reached London.

Joe jumped upon the platform before the train stopped.

Darrel and his companion bore Elfie to a brougham, which stood awaiting their arrival.

They got in with her.

The driver whipped his horses, and the carriage moved off.

Joe rushed up to a cab standing first in the rank.

"Cabby, you see that brougham? Take me up and follow that carriage for one mile or fifty; don't lose sight of it, and don't let the riders know you're watching them."

"Blow me, this is cool. I say, my comical kiddy, what's yer little game now?"

Joe produced a card from a case, which he handed the man.

The man whistled.

"In course, sir; that's a hoss of another colour. What kinder case is it, sir? crim'nal?"

"Mind your own business, and that's to follow that brougham ; and, I say, cabby, don't be offended with my sharpness ; I want ye to take the task with a good will, and you shall be paid accordin'."

CHAPTER XXV.

A MERRY MILL BETWEEN TWO JOLLY DOGS.

ONCE more we join the crew of Jolly Dogs, assembled in the smoking-room of their favourite haunt — the "Harp and Crown."

Harry Rattleton occupies his place of honour ; but his haggard features and abstracted air proclaim that his thoughts are far away ; he answers questions with an air of inattention, his calls to order are less vigorous and imperative than usual, his gaiety is forced, and his whole demeanour bespeaks him as ill at rest.

Edgar Wenlock and Dandy Jack are absent—on a dark business, as the sequel will show ; but in their place at least one remarkable guest is present—the daring Renshaw, who has boldly presented himself, in his assumed character, to his old companions, who fail to recognise him, though many have a vague idea of having met him before, and more than one comment is made upon his striking resemblance to Gentleman Dick.

He is the lion of the evening ; he sings, jests, laughs, tells anecdotes of American life—all purely imaginary, and some carefully "adapted," as the phrase is, but none the less amusing.

Every one was enraptured with the new member—for he had enrolled himself among the Jolly Dogs—and voted him quite an acquisition.

The only one who watched him closely, or with anything like a feeling of distrust, was George Grant.

There was something in the manner of the gay stranger displeasing to the generous, but shrewd and straightforward fellow, which perplexed and astonished him.

Could this really be the noble Arthur Aubrey, the elected of one of so finely-toned a mind as Angeline's, the tender, gallant, high-souled lover and warrior ?

Yet why should he doubt the fact ? Had he not seen him at Cremorne?—the same face, dress, manners, martial step. Had he not seen his papers ? Surely, surely, love must be blind indeed ! What cared this laughing, light-hearted, extravagant fellow for the beautiful girl who loved him with such intense passion ? Nothing, simply nothing !

The conversation turned upon a late—not "mill" but "mull" between two pugilistic celebrities.

The Bethnal Big 'Un was profuse of his anathemas upon the recreant "pugs," and declared himself willing to match himself against any man for £200 and the belt.

George Grant expressed his contempt of the "manly art" as practised in this country, and Pharamond expatiated on George's skill with his "mawlies."

"And is it true, sir ?" asked Humphrey Puffy, "that in America, men, when they quarrel, have recourse to the revolver, the bowie, to gouging, and other disgraceful practices, or is it a slander, sir ?"

"I speak only of my *own* country, of the ex-Confederacy States," returned the elegant Aubrey ; " there, men carry revolvers in their pockets to ensure civility and to repress rowdyism. One man will be inclined to insult another when he feels that the quarrel involves a mortal consequence to one or both of the antagonists. At home, sir, we value honor more than life, and hold it a shame to brook an insult. In England, you see men put themselves in leading strings, and fly like children to their nurse for protection. By their nurse, I mean, of course, that praiseworthy protector of the public peace, the—"

"Bobby."

"Exactly so—Mr—hem—Mr. Bethnal."

"Bethnal's the name of the neighb'rhood where I puts up," grumbled the pugilist.

"In London, sir ?" asked Aubrey.

"Yes, in course. I could a sworn I'd seen you there in disguise," grunted the prize-fighter.

This sally caused a general laugh.

"Your pardon, sir, I never was in that quarter to my knowledge, yet it is at the fashionable end of the town, I suppose ?"

Renewed laughter.

"Oh ! but I've been told that the aristocracy are great patrons of the prize-ring, that even officers of the army attend the great fights."

"If they goes to see a manly exhibition of fortitood and courage, they had a treat last time," grumbled the Big 'Un ; " but, there, I means to retrieve the honour of the ring; catch me throwin' up the sponge till I'm knocked clean out of time. I'll tell yer what, Jolly Dogs, I'm ready to match myself rough and ready at catch-weight with any fellow alive for ten pound aside, money down."

"With a professional or a non-professional ?"

"Don't I tell yer—any one."

"Here's a rare opportunity, gentlemen, to win a capful of honour ! Does any Jolly Dog accept this gallant challenge ?"

"Why don't yer accept it yerself ?"

"No, comrade, I'm ready to meet you with the rifle, the revolver, the small-sword, the poignard ; but my delicate constitution would not stand your 'fibbing' five minutes. Besides, I'm not a Britisher."

"All the better for you."

"But, perhaps, my friend, Mr. Grant, would not mind gratifying me, as a stranger, with an exhibition of his skill in the fistic art ?"

"Pshaw ! a fine sight I should present to-morrow with a couple of blackened, blinded eyes, and a swollen cheek, plastered with a raw steak and swathed with a clout."

"And yet I don't see why a bruiser should not be as proud of his broken nose as a soldier of his sabre-scars and gunshot wounds ; it all comes in the way of honour," chuckled Aubrey.

Renshaw was a dauntless fellow ; there was too much of the devil in him for his own safety ; he had evidently got his knife in George Grant, but he handled it as skilfully as the most expert surgeon. He had not forgotten his rough reception by George on the fatal night at Cremorne.

"Absurd !" said George, his cheek flushing.

"Ah, I perceive, you practice only in the gloves."

"Dash my wig ! I should like to have a round or two with ye, in the gloves, Mr. Grant," said the Big 'Un, grinning.

"At any time, I shall be at your service," returned Grant.

"You're allers down on us poor pugs," grumbled the Big 'Un.

"You're not good-tempered to-night."

"No, I feels wicious along this last disgraceful exhibition. I should like some fellow to give me a chance of redeemin' the honour of the ring in a little set-to."

"It's almost a pity that you should lack an opportunity of showing your pluck," said Aubrey.

"Pluck ?" cried George, hotly, "no one I hope dares to impugn my courage !"

"George, I would never have thought you such an ass !" whispered Humphrey Puffy. "Keep cool ; don't give the Yankee rowdy the chance of goading you into making a fool of yourself."

"Courage, my dear sir; who dares impugn any Englishman's courage?" cried Aubrey, smiling blandly. "No, no discredit, of course, and certainly a black eye is a sad disfigurement, and painful besides."

"Pain ? Who thinks of pain ? Pshaw ! I *am* a fool !" muttered George, who was getting flushed and excited in spite of his common sense.

"Of course, were it an affair of honour it would be another case," continued the remorseless Aubrey. "Were it a gentlemanlike encounter with pistols, for instance——"

"God forbid, sir !" cried George, fervently. "In my country's service, I believe, I hope, I should fight as well as another ; but I would not have the blood of my bitterest foe on my head—no, not for all the laurels of Cæsar !"

"And if you were attacked ?"

"That is not the question. Self-defence is man's natural right; but I allude to deliberate duelling."

"Well, Mr. Grant, you give no small proof of your moral heroism in advocating such peace-at-any-price doctrines," said Aubrey, with a slight sneer, as he squeezed down the lemon at the bottom of his glass, and then sipped his brandy delicately.

"Well, I must say as it'll be bad times for English pluck when the poor old prize ring goes to squash," growled the Big 'Un, "'cept in a drunken row, Jolly Dogs has got no game in 'em."

George Grant deigned not to notice this hint from the low-bred speaker; but he fired up when Aubrey coolly rejoined, with a nod,

"'Gree with ye, Mr. Big 'Un. Bad day for this country when such displays of manly pluck are become things of the past. Still, you know——" and he finished off with a maddening whine, "*we can stick to the gloves.*"

A roar of laughter at George's expense followed this shaft.

"Do you intend that as an insult, sir?" panted George.

"An insult? Not for ten thousand worlds!" cried Aubrey, aghast. "If I have said anything that can give you offence, I eagerly retract my words, and make my frankest apology. After all, there seems a great deal of fuss about nothing. Surely a rough and ready round, all in good part, between friends, even if it results in a bit of a bruise or the shade of a scratch, is not a subject for a homily on the horrors of war—ha! ha! ha! Only the other day, Jolly Dogs, I narrowly escaped the pleasure of convincing my friends that I had some brains by having my poor quantum knocked out with a cricket-ball."

"You're right, quite right, Mr. Aubrey," cried George, gaily laughing. "Pshaw! of course it's nothing; a jolly lark, no more. Come, Big 'Un, what say to a turn up?"

"Done, my boy, done," cried the prize-fighter.

"Vell, I bet five to von on the Bethnal Pet," shouted Jemmy Gimp. "Hooray, Jolly Dogs, here's a sensation!"

"Come, then, gentlemen, choose your seconds and elect the referee," said Aubrey.

"We'll have you for our referee, Mr. Aubrey, if Mr. Grant's willin'."

"Certainly," returned George.

"I'm afraid you could scarcely have chosen a worse umpire," said Aubrey, smiling suavely; "but I've read the rules of the ring, and will do the best to see the fight conducted properly. Fair play, of course, is guaranteed?"

"Don't look wild, Puffy; I know I was wrong, and deserve a thrashing for my weakness, but I can't back out of it now," whispered George to his friend; "you must be my second."

"Well, I'll reserve my opinion till the fight's over; but, as you've let yourself into this stupid mess, you must fight your way out bravely."

"Jest allow me to hint, though, it can't werry vell come off here," said Jemmy Gimp, "not in this public room; better go into the lobby by the club-room."

It was arranged that but five or six of the company should be permitted to witness the battle; the rest were pledged not to give the alarm to the landlord or the servants of the house lest the scrimmage should be interrupted.

All arrangements being complete the two "men," with their seconds and backers, adjourned to the next apartment.

A sentinel was posted at the door to give warning of the approach of any unwelcome intruder.

The furniture was pushed to the walls, and a space cleared for the encounter.

The referee seated himself on a table, and the men and their seconds took their corners and stripped to their shirts.

The bystanders gave a cheer of surprise to find the two men so equally matched; for though the Big 'Un was undoubtedly the heavier and more powerful man of the two, yet Grant was better built, more firmly set on his legs, more agile, and his face wore a look of good-humoured determination.

The men shook hands, and the fight commenced.

The men moved cautiously round each other, and sparred for an opening.

The betting at first had been all in favour of the Big 'Un, but as the fight proceeded, the odds were laid on Grant.

It was some time before a blow was struck.

At last George, to force the fighting, rushed in; but his blow was cleverly stopped, and the Big' Un exchanged heavily on the breast; after more sparring and hitting, the men closed, and the Big 'Un went down.

So ended the first round.

Time being called, the men once more toed the scratch.

The Big 'Un was evidently "riled" at the chaff which assailed him on all sides, and swore he would smash the amateur in the next bout.

After some splendid sparring, feinting, and countering, the Big 'Un rushed in, and aimed a crushing blow at George's face; but George was away, and the blow landed at long reach on his cheek, not so lightly but that it left its mark.

In the next round, after much hard fighting and a display of science, which none but the initiated could properly describe, the Big 'Un landed one on Grant's nose, which had the effect of "tapping the claret."

The first event was claimed for the Big 'Un.

When the men once more faced each other it was evident that the Big 'Un, who felt his honour was at stake, had fully resolved not to spare his adversary, and the brutal cries of "Let him have it this round," "Force the fighting," from his backers, goaded him into ferocity, for though he smiled broadly, his was the grin of an automaton than the cheery smile of a man in good humour.

George saw his danger, and sparred very warily, and keenly watched for an opening. The Big 'Un at last, after drawing his man out, let fly a tremendous crusher, which landed on Grant's breast, and brought him to the ground.

The Big 'Un's backers cheered tremendously. George was voted nowhere, and any odds were offered on the professional.

In the next round, which was perhaps the prettiest in the fight, after some rapid, good fighting and some hot exchanges, the men closed for the fall, and the Big 'Un was under.

Time being called, the men once more put themselves in position.

They were evidently the worse for wear. George showed signs of punishment on his chest and in the red flush on his right cheek. After some slogging work, Grant landed a stinger full on his adversary's mouth, which seemed to stagger him; the Big 'Un, however, pulled himself together; and the Big 'Un, who was now riled, rushed in so recklessly, that Grant, springing backward, met his attack with such a downright blow, the professional pug was knocked down flat and clean out of time.

Yelps, cheers, and ecstatic yells greeted Grant's daring deed, and Jemmy Gimp rushed to his fallen man, whom he sponged and dosed with brandy, with fruitless labour, and tried to incite him to renew the contest, with unavailing prayers.

"Time!" shouted Renshaw.

The Big 'Un, evidently, had had enough of it, and responded to the call only by closing his eyes and dolefully shaking his head.

George was proclaimed the victor, amid general acclamation.

"Well, Geordie," chuckled Mr. Puffy, "it was my intention to have lectured you on your stupidity in being drawn into this foolish match with a professional pugilist; but, by St. George!—your patron saint, I should think——I'm forced to forgive ye. I'm proud of ye!"

George smiled.

"So am not I of myself," he said, "for I did not fight for the love of fighting, but only because I could not stand the Virginian rowdy's banter. Well, altogether, I ought to be ashamed of myself!"

"I should think the Big 'Un's of the same opinion," laughed Puffy; "he's a big 'un now about the 'dial case,' and no mistake!"

CHAPTER XXVI.

THE BURGLARY AT MAMMONSON'S BANK.—THE JOLLY DOG AND HIS ASSISTANTS.

NIGHT enshrouds the mighty city, now deserted by the busy throngs that all the fagging work day through have been pacing its pavements with busy feet ; at intervals a "growler" or hansom rattles past, a crew of Jolly Dogs stagger howling home, a shivering outcast limps dejectedly towards the park or the nearest casual ward, the manly policeman plods his weary beat, or a painted unfortunate flaunts along with her wretched professional smirk and her dreary assumption of gaiety.

Mammonson's bank was situated in a narrow court, surrounded on all sides by heavy blocks of dark buildings ; an archway gave admission to this court, and this archway is guarded by a pair of heavy iron gates, but they are never closed.

Two men are standing in the dark angle of a wall within the court.

"The crushers have passed on their beat, Neddy ; won't return for ten minutes. Now's the time !"

"I'm ready."

"Did ye take my advice about Grant ?"

"Yes ; but won't it be a dangerous trick ?"

"No ; you say you've cooked his books in such a way as to throw the blame of the defalcation on him ?"

"Yes, that's done."

"What's easier than to slip part of his swag into his room ? That'll fix him !"

"But why have you directed your spite against poor George ?"

"Because I hate him ! Hist ! time's up. They are gone far enough ; they'll turn presently. Quick, for your life, Ned !"

Dandy Jack went to a bar window in the opposite building, and gently tapped.

The heavy sash was lowered, and an arm was thrust out, which, grasping one of the bars, shook it out of its socket.

"The infernal window opens only atop," growled Dandy Jack. "Place your foot on my shoulder. Now, in with ye."

Wenlock crept in, Dandy Jack replaced the bar, and the window was carefully re-closed by the Lummy Cove, who had been secreted for hours in the house.

"You know the signal ; I'll stand in the archway, as if to keep out of the wet, for it drizzles rain, and when the peeler goes by, I'll whistle a tune."

"Aye, be off, yer fool !" growled the Lummy Cove.

The burglars were standing in a small waiting-room adjoining the clerks' office.

The Lummy Cove turned on his dark lantern.

"Had a quiet time ?" whispered Wenlock.

"On'y for the rats."

"Hist !"

"It's all right."

"The cussed rats is my avarsion. What the devil sich creetur's wants in a bankin' house licks me. They gets their grub for nuthun, and has no needs to trouble theirselves about the circ'lating med'um. Or, p'r'aps, they're gammoned by a fine name, like the poor devils of shareholders. This is 'Cornhill' yer know."

"Be quiet, I think I hear some one moving."

"So do I."

"Where ?"

"Hush !"

The burglar gripped his life-preserver.

They listened a long time, but the sound was not repeated.

"How many on 'em are there in the house ?" asked the Lummy Cove.

"Only the old porter and his wife."

"Gone to bed ; but, p'r'aps not to sleep," muttered the burglar, savagely ; "if there's any alarm, I'll settle 'em precious quick. Hark !"

A step was heard descending the stairs.

"Stand by, my pal," muttered the Lummy Cove.

Wenlock and his confederate crept into the darkest corner, and crouched behind a high-backed chair.

A key was turned in the lock, and an old man, wrapped in a dressing-gown and holding aloft a chamber-lantern in one hand, the light of which flashed on the steel barrel of a revolver which he held in the other, peered in.

"Is there any one here ?" he cried, between his chattering teeth.

"A cussed old fool, as if he expec's a answer ; if I'd brought my barker I'd give him one," muttered the Lummy Cove.

"Who's there, I say !"

The old fellow tottered into the room, and walked about, peeping into every corner.

The Lummy Cove had got his hands on Wenlock's neck, pressing him down, while he himself dodged the dancing light and cleverly eluded its glare.

"Oh dear, oh dear ! is there any one in the place ?" cried a woman's voice from the door ; "let's ring the alarum."

"You'd better not, old gal," muttered the burglar.

"No ; don't frighten yerself, missus ; seems all right, don't see as any one could get in ; besides, arter that affair a few nights gone, the burglary in Cannon Street, Mr. Wenlock's been more than common careful."

"But I'm confident I heard voices."

"Most likes from the streets, Betsey," returned the old man. "Come, let's back to bed ; t'aint the first time we've had a false alarm. Come, you see there's nobody."

And the old man paced round the room with evident conviction that he had been mistaken.

The porter and his wife retired.

They re-mounted to their room, and slammed to the door.

"It could be done easy," grumbled the Lummy Cove, with a foul oath, as he drew a dreadful-looking clasp-knife from his pocket and ran his thumb along the keen edge of the gleaming blade ; "you see if the old devils don't spile our little game unless we settles 'em."

"No, you wretch," gasped Wenlock, "wait ; they will soon fall asleep again ; besides, they won't hear us when we are at work, the room where the cash is kept is too far from their chamber ; let's get to work."

"Ready and willing, my pal."

"Come on, then ; don't turn on the light, catch hold of my coat, and keep close behind me," whispered Wenlock.

"Why, cuss me, if you ain't got yer boots on !" growled the burglar.

"Never mind, they're light ones, and if—"

"And don't creak like rusty bolts in a 'igh vind ! Why !" and here followed a string of fierce oaths, "there, take 'em orf, you blessed fool !"

Wenlock was forced to comply.

"Leave 'em there, along agen mine ; we shall find 'em when we comes back. Now, once more, I holds yer tight—go on."

Wenlock groped his way through the deep darkness down a narrow passage till further progress was stopped by a door.

"Has yer iled the lock ?"

"Yes."

"And ye've got the false key ?"

"Yes."

"Right you are, then ; open the door."

After fumbling with trembling fingers for some time, during which the burglar growled his impatience, Wenlock got the key into the lock.

"Clash !"

"S—sh !"

They listened a long time.

"It's all right, my kiddy, perceed," chuckled the burglar.

Wenlock thrust open the door, and again they moved along a dark and narrow passage, the Lummy Cove clutching fast hold of his confederate.

Another door barred the way.

This was opened carefully.

"Now turn on the light," said Wenlock, drawing a long breath.

The burglar complied.

(To be continued.)

the continued heat and the noxious fumes of the furnaces which were so often at work.

For more than ten minutes there was a dead silence in the room, and then he who occupied the chair said listlessly,

"Is there any change, Jasper?"

"Not much yet; but we must have patience, St. Leon."

"Ah, patience! The old story again—we must have patience! Patience to the crack of doom, I think."

"Nay," said the other, "you are unfit for these labours, if you cannot bear delay and disappointment. If the sublime secrets of nature, which we are intent upon discovering, were to be easily achieved, think you they would have remained so long unknown? No, no! The greatest discoveries are only to be obtained by the greatest energy, the greatest patience, and the greatest perseverance. Before we can hope or expect to be rewarded for our pains, we must see that those pains are not at all stinted, and that we repine not."

"But how long, Jasper, have we been already?"

"Are we old?"

"Old? No, we are not old!"

"Then we cannot have been very long. How many persons have consumed a long lifetime in vain upon these researches."

"Ah!" said he who was seated, "I can easily believe that, after a long lapse of years, the continuance of such studies as these become a part of the very existence of him who carries them on. But we are young yet."

"We are; and consequently have more time."

"But we have done nothing."

The one who was attending the crucible turned abruptly from his task, and looked the other in the face, as he said,

"Now, shame upon you, St. Leon. Is this like you? Is this carrying out the agreement into which we entered with the spirit it commenced? Truly I much regret, St. Leon, that you ever engaged with me in this matter, since you lack that kind of mental constancy which it requires. Go when you like, and how you like, and leave me here alone to pursue the favourable clue which I have now, as you well know, to one of the greatest of discoveries."

"You fancy you have such a clue."

"I am sure I have."

"You were equally sure many months since."

"No! no!"

"But, indeed, Jasper, you were!"

"Well, St. Leon, and if I were? You are dissatisfied—what then? I cannot help your being so; and I can but again tell you that I am willing you should go, and leave me to my resources; and the fortune, good or evil, which may attend my own researches."

"Jasper, if I intended to leave you, I should say so at once."

"St. Leon, if you intend to remain, let me beg of you to do so with a good grace."

St. Leon was silent for some few moments, and then he said,

"Jasper, you are right there; but still, intimate as we are, I did not think it at all necessary to look at my words before I uttered them. Nevertheless, if you dislike to hear any expressions of impatience or regret, I will school my tongue to utter none to you."

"I cannot but dislike to hear them," said Jasper. "They throw a damp upon my feelings and my enterprise. I pray you do not utter such remarks, St. Leon. You will yet, I feel convinced, be highly rewarded for all your trouble."

"Well, well! I hope so—I hope so!"

"You may well hope so; and Hope will play you no trick, believe me, on this occasion; I feel a kind of certainty that we are near some great discovery."

"Indeed!"

"Yes. A strange feeling to that effect has come over me. I am assured it will be so. Never since we have been at work have I felt so complete an assurance of such a fact."

"Well, there is hope in that!"

"Abundant! abundant!"

"How goes on the crucible?"

"Well! well! extremely well! Celsus tells us that the continuance of those yellow sparks, which you perceive shoot up so high, are indications that the experiment is succeeding well, and that we have hit the right proportions."

"I hope to Heaven we have!"

"See, there is an amber-coloured flame playing round the crucible!"

St. Leon rose and approached the furnace. He began himself to get wonderfully interested in what was going on, and to share in some of the sanguine hopes of his friend Jasper, who appeared so certain of a favourable result to the experiment they were proceeding with.

"You perceive the amber-coloured flame, St. Leon?"

"Yes! yes!"

"And see how it deepens. What would you say now were we to find some precious stone at the bottom of the crucible? Some rare jewel which would amply—ay, more than amply, repay us for all our trouble; what would you say then, good St. Leon? Might we not then go forth into the great world and achieve wonders?"

"We might, indeed!"

"Oh, this is indeed a moment of joyful expectation. Hold the lamp, St. Leon, while I attend to the crucible. There, now, you have a full light upon it, and the amber-coloured flame is waning, as you were aware it would do, after presenting itself to us in all its beauty."

"I recollect."

"Yes. If the flame were of that amber-colour, we might conclude that we should succeed in making a topaz; if the flame were green, an emerald would be the result."

"I remember it says so in the learned treatise which we consulted at Munich."

"True! true! And—what's that?"

Both the young men started, as well indeed they might; for something occurred at that moment which had never before occurred to them since they had inhabited that lonely mansion. There was a rapping at the door of the turret-chamber by some one.

"At such a moment," said St. Leon.

"When any interruption may spoil all," exclaimed Jasper.

"St. Leon, a human life must not now stand in the way of our experiments. You have arms."

At this moment the crucible, which they had been watching so earnestly, burst, with a loud report, into a thousand pieces, and all the labour which had been bestowed upon it, seemed in an instant to be lost.

They looked at each other for a few moments aghast. St. Leon tottered to his seat, on which he sank again with a feeling of deep disappointment; while Jasper followed him with his eyes, as if expecting to hear from him now some ebullition of impatience which would have been more justified than before.

The sudden bursting of the crucible seemed to have made them quite forget the knocking at the door of the turret-chamber; but now, when the noise of the report that had accompanied the bursting of the vessel had subsided, the application for admittance became much louder and more energetic.

A malediction came from the lips of Jasper, and in two strides he reached the small door which opened upon a staircase. He immediately flung it open, and cried aloud, in far from an encouraging tone,

"Who's there?"

The light from the room flashed out upon the narrow landing that was at the top of the staircase, and showed to Jasper's gaze the figure of a little old man, who, with body bent, and a lean shrivelled face, stood there, as if extremely doubtful about the sort of reception he was about to receive.

St. Leon, too, looked up from his despondent attitude with some degree of surprise at the stranger, who now, when he saw that no immediate violence was offered to him, advanced a step, and said,

"Gentle sirs, of course you consider this visit a great intrusion; but when I tell you that there is a storm without, which might well make the boldest tremble, and that no other shelter presented itself to me than this house, I am sure you will pardon the seeming rudeness."

The words of the little old man were as humble and proper as they could be; but for all that there was a something about his tone, and the general manner in which he spoke, that made both the young students strongly suspect that his cringing humility and courtesy were but assumed, and that he could, if he liked, speak in very different language indeed. Moreover, he kept advancing step by step, until he got into the very middle of the apartment, and then, turning towards the stove, he held his shrivelled hands close to it, saying,

"Ah, this is comfort. This is comfort."

"There is no storm without," said Jasper.

"No storm without, my young friend. Hark at the thunder."

The moment these words passed his lips, there was such a rattling peal of thunder, that the old turret seemed to shake again, and he added,

"No storm, indeed. Do you call that no storm? To my perception, young sirs, it is rather a serious storm."

"But this is the first I have heard of it," said St. Leon.

"And the same with me," said Jasper.

"Indeed! indeed!" remarked the visitor. "Then I'll be bound, young sirs, that your attention was minutely fixed by something. Ah! I perceive. How blind I was—ha—ha—I perceive now. You are adepts. Well, well, by the time your hair is silvered, you ought to have made some notable discoveries. Perchance, the divine elixir may yield to you its life-giving treasures; perchance the great secret of the transmutation of metals may be evolved from your researches, or the universal solvent may reward your labours.

Continued from page 56.

THE JOLLY DOGS OF LONDON.

THE EVENING'S AMUSEMENT—AS HAPPY AS A KING.

CHAPTER XXVI.—(continued.)

Illumined by the glare of the lantern, a strong-room appeared, with shelves piled high with boxes containing bonds, cash, and valuable papers; on one side of the room was a double window doubly barred, and opposite to that a large iron safe.

"Ah; now ve shall get on," said the Lummy Cove, drawing a deep breath.

He set down his basket of tools.

He took a survey of the place.

"That cussed winder looks into the court!" he said, savagely. "Sst! Jack's a whistling. Douce the glim!"

The steady tramp of a policeman was heard without.

The footsteps died away.

The men listened breathlessly.

"Now we can git on," said the burglar, with a leer. "Look alive, every minit's a minit. Pass over them files, and that ere centre-bit. No, not that von, fooley. Smash my heyes! you air a fine pardner, and no mistake. If I'd a had Black Bob wi' me, we'd a half done the trick by this time, and yet you calls yerself a man of edication. Sich is never no use for

No. 9.

nothin'. Now, then, there. Do jes' let's set up a kind o' light'ouse to d'rect the hintelligent crushers to our vorkshop, do. Oh! my body and heyes! can't yer stand out o' the way o' the winder, and throw on the light vhere it *is* vanted?"

Wenlock was fain to endure the abuse of his brutal confederate with forced patience.

He took his position as directed, and shading the light from the window poured the flashing stream upon the door of the safe.

The Lummy Cove set himself to work to prize open the safe.

For hours the two scoundrels toiled at the felonious work, each taking his spell, alternately watching and working.

From time to time their labours were suspended when the whistle without warned them of the approach of the police.

At last they paused from sheer exhaustion.

Great drops of sweat swelled like beads upon their quivering foreheads, and they trembled and panted as if they had been running a long, trying race.

"Here, old covey, freshen up a bit," said the Lummy Cove, holding out a brandy flask.

Wenlock seized it with eagerness, and drank a deep draught.

"Come, old chicken-heart, let's finish off the job."

Wenlock reeled to the safe, and re-commenced his labours.

"Yah! you mauls the jemmy like a young school gal a dandlin' her doll. Give's hold!"

Roughly pushing his partner aside, the Lummy Cove seized the bar.

Wrench!—scrunch!—wrench!

The door flies back with a sonorous ring.

"Humph! purty vell for von night's vork," said the burglar, scratching his head and grinning; "but stop!—the crushers again! Lay by! Now they're off. Let's see vot ve've got to reward our pains."

The shelves and drawers of the safe were found to contain valuable deeds, bonds, and bags of gold.

"Oh, Jemini! here's another vindfall for the noose-wenders! ''Nother bank smash in the City.' Blow me, here's enough for a moderate cove to retire on."

The burglars filled the tool-basket, a carpet-bag, their pockets, the linings of their clothes and caps, with plunder.

"Don't take those cheques; they're of no use," said Wenlock.

"Do for pipe-lights, bless ye. Come, make haste, 'I begins to snuff the mornin' hair,' as the rantin' hactor says. Ve must make tracks, my covey."

"I'm ready," said Wenlock, feebly.

The Lummy Cove led the way, close followed by his confederate.

They slipped on their boots, and then gently raised the window by which they had entered.

Dandy Jack was ready to receive them.

He assisted them to the ground, and replaced the bar.

"All right?" asked Jack.

"As a trivet," returned the burglar.

"A good haul?" asked Jack.

"Pretty tidy," chuckled the Lummy Cove. "But vhere's the cab?"

"Hard by, my tulips. I'll drive ye to the ken in a twinkling."

CHAPTER XXVII.

A JOLLY DOGS'S TREACHERY.

As the pale morning light began to break over the mighty city the cab with its rich freight drove down a narrow bye-lane in a low neighbourhood, and pulled up at the door of a high dingy house.

Wenlock and the Lummy Cove got out.

Dandy Jack leaped from the box.

A dirty, impudent-looking lad came forward, and offered to take the cab to the stables.

After a little rough chaff, Dandy Jack, who was much elated at the successful issue of the expedition, threw the boy a shilling, and told him to take away the "strawberry pottle," as he facetiously designated the ricketty carriage.

The boy drove off.

The burglars entered the house, the Lummy Cove opening the door with a latch-key.

The house seemed untenanted, and most of the rooms were void of furniture or inmates.

The three men entered a back-room at the second landing-place.

It was a dirty, ramshackle den, scantily furnished and begrimed with smoke.

The Lummy Cove went to the cupboard and brought out some bread, meat, onions, and a bottle of brandy, which he placed on the table.

He had previously lighted a lamp, which mingled its sickly glare with the cold, fresh, brightening rays of dawn.

Dandy Jack and the professional burglar partook of the coarse repast, but Wenlock refused to join them, and seated himself apart, his arms folded tightly athwart his breast, and his chin bent on them.

"Come; let's count our gains," said Dandy Jack. "Let's share h swag."

"Lors! I hearned mine 'ard. The t'other cove's no more use on sich a lay than a blind kitten at bird ketchin'," laughed the burglar; "but, howsomdever, Mister Venlock, take yer place at the council-board."

Wenlock rose, and passing his trembling fingers through his hair with a nervous gesture, seated himself with the rest.

Soon the lamp light blazed on heaps of bright, twinkling gold pieces, and piles of notes and cheques.

"Here's a feast for Midas!" cried Dandy Jack, rubbing his hands. "Come, Neddy, my hopeful son, let us go whacks."

The booty was portioned out in three lots, the Lummy Cove's share being equal to Wenlock's and Dandy Jack's combined.

This result was not arrived at without a good deal of bickering and swearing.

"And now about the paper," said Jack.

"Cuss the paper. You may take that," growled the Lummy Cove. "It were nothin' but them flimsies as led to my being lagged afore."

"Well, they want management."

"This is the best way to manage 'em, growled the burglar.

He snatched a handful of papers and held them over the lamp.

Dandy Jack seized his hand, and dragged it away.

"Stop! don't meddle with what don't belong to ye, Bill," he said. "We shall take 'em."

"But they're worth only the paper they're printed on," said Wenlock.

"If you were in the office, you could turn them into account, if you had 'em in hand?"

"Yes; if the robbery were not known to the firm."

"Well, George Grant shall have the benefit of 'em."

"How can that be?"

"I'll tell ye as we go along. Are ye too tired to go at once?"

"Whither?"

"Why, with me to Grant's lodging."

"You are mad."

"No; I'll explain."

"I dare not run further risk."

"There is no risk to be run."

"I'll have nothing to do with it."

"There's no need, Neddy; I'll manage all."

"What do you want to do?"

"I hate that George Grant."

"Why?"

"Because he has snubbed me, and more than once has thwarted me in my business; but come——"

"I am so weary, so excited, and have so much to do. In an hour the detectives may be on my track."

"At what time does your office open?"

"At half-past ten."

"Humph! it would look suspicious if you were behind time."

"Are you awake, Jack, or has this affair turned your head?"

"No, no, my boy, I'm wide, wide awake. Where was George last night?"

"Why do you ask?"

"Why don't you answer?"

"Because—I don't know where he was."

"Then I can tell ye," joined in the Lummy Cove. "He were at the ''Arp and Crown.'"

"And did he go straight home?"

"No; it seems he had a fight——"

"A fight?"

"Yes; a reg'lar merry mill with the Bethnal Big 'Un."

"Nonsense!"

"In course one 'd think so. I should a laid heavy on the Big 'Un; but blow me, if the swell cove varn't the better man; the Big 'Un were licked clean out o' time."

"And how do you know that? Were you present at the fight?"

"Me? No, I've withdrawed my paternage from the ''Arp;' 'cos, why, the landlord's a party as I don't like."

"What has he done to offend ye?"

"Pulled me, about some smashed money; but he couldn't rightwise 'stanstiate the evidence, so I were acquitted; but

I arn't acquitted him. I got my mark on him, believe me, and I means to see if I carn't jest relieve him of a little of the superfl'ous."

"Then how did ye hear of the fight?"

"Heard it at old Nat Sloggings, the 'Game Cock,' near Long Acre," returned the Lummy Cove.

"And was there a quarrel, then?"

"Ne'er a bit; it were all fair and square, jest a rough and ready set-to for fun and ten pounds; a rattling mill I were told."

"And George Grant make such a match? I'll never b'lieve it!" cried Wenlock.

"Why, yer see, it was as this way. A certain gent as was present, a awful flash cove, got a sneerin' about the last 'meet and shake hands' for the championship, and a calling all Britishers a set o' curs, and a darin' George to accept a challenge as the Big 'Un throwed out to fight any livin' man at catchweight on the spot. So I s'pose George got his dander riz, and that's what led to it. Howsoever, the strange cove's a stunner, been a 'Merican hofficer I'm told; a Fenian spy, no doubts; wears his arm in a sling!"

"Renshaw!"

"Eh?—who?—what? Why, dam'me, now you remind me on't, he is the werry pictur' of old Gentleman Dick!"

"I wish it were he," said Wenlock, with assumed calmness. "The poor devil's at Portland Island now; he wrote me a letter the other week; he's in a very sad way, quite broken down."

"Is he raally, now? Shouldn't a thought it of him; thought he were game for anythink."

"Why, you see, he was well brought up; can't stand the hard labour."

"There you have it agin; all this comes of edication. There's nothin' I hates so much as a schoolmaster, 'ceptin' a parson; I'd murder all on 'em as I met with, on'y it's a shame to be hung for such carrion."

"Well, but you haven't told us what Grant did with himself after the fight."

"Why, ye see, he'd given the poor Big 'Un such a stomaching over on the pepper-castor that he were knocked into the middle o' next week, as the sayin' is, and so he fainted, and rewived and fainted and rewived agin till some of the Jolly Dogs got funky; didn't want to call in the traps. In course that wouldn't do, so they quietly popped the Big 'Un into a cab, and carried him orf to the 'Game Cock.' This were early in the evening; I were forced to make off, but I heard him tell that fat cove, as is his constant chum, that he shouldn't return home that night."

"Where did he go to, then?"

"Lor' knows."

"Well," said Dandy Jack, musingly, "at all events, we'll try it."

"Try what, Jack?"

"To ruin him."

"Never! I will have no hand in it."

"You shall not, I tell ye; but I hate him. It's enough; besides, it will divert attention from us; put the traps on the wrong scent, and, even if he gets acquitted at length, he will be remanded from time to time, will suffer loss of time, lose pleasure, peace, money, and what I grudge him most of—reputation!"

CHAPTER XXVIII.

JACK BAITS THE TRAP.

IT was at about half-past nine o'clock that Wenlock and Dandy Jack stood before a neat and respectable-looking house in a pleasant suburb; it was George Grant's lodgings.

"Which is his window, Ned?"

"That one," returned Wenlock, pointing, "where the pane of glass is broken; George's terrier Snap did it yesterday springing at a bird that had perched on the sill."

"Ha!"

"I suppose his landlady knows you?"

"Oh, yes."

"Here, come out of the street, round this corner; you must not be seen."

"Well, what now?"

"You could have access to his room, I suppose, if you made some excuse?"

"At any time."

"Humph!"

"What's your game?"

"Dam'me, don't pester me; I'm thinking. Have ye one of his cards about ye?"

"Yes, I think so; here's one."

"Good; give it me."

"What will you do with it?"

"Aye, that's the question. Humph!"

Dandy Jack fell into a state of profound cogitation.

At this moment a Jew passed along with a frame of window-glass under his arm, and kept reiterating his nasal drone, "Vindesh sho mend, any vindesh sho mend?"

"Grant's evil genius assists me, Ned," he chuckled. "I have it," and he ran after the Jew and stopped him.

"Vindesh broke, shir?" snuffled the Jew.

"No; I want a word wi' ye. You know me, Bendie, don't ye?"

"Oh, shtrike me, sho I do. How ish ye, my poysh? Mishter Dandy Jack, very glad to shee ye."

"Will ye earn a couple o' quid, Bendie?"

"Ah, shtop; shince I come out of the—you knowsh vot I meansh—I never py any thingsh from shentlemen of your clash—no, s'welph me—neversh! I losht all my pretty shtock —three hundred poundsh—to the lasht shtiver, and vosh lagged for five yearsh. Holy Abramsh! I vill have noshing to do vit you, 'shept you vill shtand me a glash I vill drink your healthsh."

"All right, you shall drink my health, Bendie."

And the three men adjourned to a public-house.

Dandy Jack looked into the tap-room.

It was unoccupied.

He called for drink.

Then, seating himself by the side of the Jew, he conversed with him in a hurried under tone.

The Jew seemed to hesitate at some proposal made to him.

At length he seemed to consent.

The men changed coats, and Dandy Jack, taking the frame under his arm, bade Wenlock await his return, and left the house.

Dandy Jack, having equipped himself in the plumber's coat, and taking the frame of glass panes under his arm, proceeded to Grant's house, and knocked at the door.

The servant opened unto him, and stared rather wonderingly, for, though the betting man had assumed a partial disguise, still there was something in his manner which showed that he was not a mere straightforward mechanic

"I've come to mend the broken window in Mr. Grant's room, my dear," he said, with a smile.

"You ain't a plumber, are ye?" asked the girl, smiling.

"Why should you doubt it?"

"Oh, got no further reason than because you don't look like one."

"I wasn't aware that plumbers had any particular distinguishing appearance."

"Don't gen'lly wear white waistcoats."

"Well, you see, I am master man; my fellows are out on the spree, and as I know Mr. Grant I thought I'd slip on this coat, and get the job off hand as my men are not always to be depended upon."

"Then you knows Mr. Grant?"

"Of course, my dear; he sent me."

"He did, did he?"

"Yes. Of course you b'lieve?"

"Never listens to what the men says; never believes 'em."

"Not even when they tell you how pretty you are."

"I s'pose you'll charge extra on account of your white waistcoat?"

"One shilling, my dear."

"Come, that's reasonable."

"A respectable tradesman has no interest in over-charging his customers."

"Did Mr. Grant raally send you?"

"Yes, my dear. Oh, I forgot, he gave me his card."

"Got it with ye?"

"Yes, to be sure; here it is."

"Well, that's all right. This way please, sir."

The girl led him upstairs to George's apartment.

He set himself busily to work at the window.

A knock at the street door summoned the girl from the room.

For a moment Dandy Jack was alone.

He gave a rapid glance round the apartment.

A coat hung upon a chair beside him.

He slipped a bundle of notes and papers into the pocket.

He then crossed the room, and attempted to open a cupboard.

It was locked.

"If I could contrive to place these checks in this or some other place that he has secured it would strengthen the case against him," the rascal muttered, as he drew out a bunch of keys, and after some delay selected one which fitted the lock.

"Ha! open sesame!"

The door of the cupboard sprang back.

He found the shelves piled with books and papers, and among the latter he discovered an empty cigar-case.

In this he inserted the cheques.

He clapped to the cupboard door, and then returned to the window and set to work, rather clumsily, at mending the broken pane.

The girl returned.

Jack showed her his handiwork, received a shilling in payment, then left the house.

"It might have been better managed," muttered Jack, as he walked along; "but then this little plot was an afterthought. It is early yet, perhaps I can persuade Wenlock to return to the office and outbrave the suspicion. Pshaw! he is such a cur! Well, I am safe; I'll wait only till I can see this goshawk fairly caught in the toils. Yet this tit-bit of vengeance may cost me dear; but no matter, I cannot forego it. I hate the fellow, and I'll feed fat the grudge I bear him. This is a good beginning, and I'll follow up the work at once. I know a dodge to set the traps on his trail before he's an hour older."

CHAPTER XXIX.

THE PIC-NIC IN GREENWICH PARK.

THE first slant beams of the rising sun creeping in through the half-closed window curtains of Jemmy Gimp's bed-room, roused that gentleman from his dreams.

He jumped out of bed and consulted his watch.

"Vell, I'm blest if it ain't struck six, and I promised to meet the Jolly Dogs and their precious ducks at old Sprout's the greengrocer's at eight o'clock precisely?"

Jemmy hastened to dress himself.

"Vat vould Selina say if I vere to fail to keep my assignation? I shudder to think of the consequence. Vomen is my veakness, and there's nothing on earth I dreads like the female frown; Selina gives a look sometimes that runs through and through my fluttering heart like a pin through a butterfly. But, bless her!"

Mr. Gimp presently kissed a photograph, which he drew from beneath his pillow.

"Vot am I thinking about? I've fallen into a reverie, but there's no time to relieve my feelings by a soliloquy; I must attend to the cares of the tilette."

Mr. Gimp went to the door.

He found his boots brightly polished, and his shaving water at hand.

But Mr. Gimp was fastidious.

He leaned over the ballusters.

"Tom!"

A saucy-looking lad came bundling up-stairs.

"Well, Sir?"

"'Ave you any sense of propriety?"

"Essence of what, sir? The macasser ile and the little bottle of perfume is on the table, sir."

"Look at those boots!"

"Yes, sir; I can see my face in 'em."

"Do you see that spot? and then the 'eels. Take 'em away, sir, and remove that 'damned spot,' will ye?"

The boy grinned and carried off the boots, and to accelerate his passage to the nether regions slid down the ballusters.

Mr. Gimp ransacked his wardrobe, and having, after a great deal of consideration, made a "choice selection" therefrom, dressed himself with all the care of a belle of the season arraying herself for conquest.

Tom returned with the boots.

Mr. Gimp examined them critically, and after a little grumbling, put them on. They pinched his feet; but, there, something must always be sacrificed to appearances, and they looked so elegant.

Having given the finishing touch to his well-pomaded hair, and having daintily adjusted his cravat, Mr. Gimp took up his gold-mounted cane, of which he was prouder than a monarch of his sceptre or a mayor of his mace, descended to the parlour, snatched a hurried breakfast, and left the house.

Mr. Sprouts, the greengrocer, at whose house the party of Jolly Dogs were to assemble, prior to starting for Greenwich, where they were to spend a day of pleasure, was a very remarkable personage.

Though his shop was situated in the purlieus of Westminster, he carried on a literally "roaring" trade, and was in prosperous circumstances.

Mr. Gimp lost no time, but hastened to the rendezvous.

He found the shop closed, but the windows above were alive with expectant faces.

Mr. Sprouts in person admitted the laggard guest.

The jolly greengrocer was dressed in a dashing style, wearing a light grey coat, white waistcoat spanned by a massive gold chain, and pale primrose continuations.

"Well, here we har agen, Jolly Dogs!" shouted Mr. Sprout from lungs of leather, administering a sounding slap on Mr. Gimp's back, which sent him reeling into a bin of potatoes, "how har you? Shake hands!"

"Not if I knows it!" muttered Mr. Gimp with a ghastly grin and a visible shudder.

However, that he might not fail in showing the due amount of grateful cordiality, he took off his hat, and waved it with a hearty "hooray!"

"We thought you weren't coming, old son," roared the greengrocer. He had a loud, strong voice, and his laugh was like the successive explosion of an unlimited number of detonating balls. "Howsoever, the hour named is a hearly von for a Jolly Dog, which is a breed of canines decidedly resemblin' the jackals both for yelpin' and late hours; but I repeats 'ere we har agin, and we means to have a jolly spree; so—

"'Strike up the bagpipes, as all the folks may see
That we six magnificent bricks is bound to 'ave a spree!'

"Ha! ha! Tip us yer flapper; I must give yer a squeeze."

We have to record an instance of presence of mind which does credit to Mr. Gimp.

He snatched up an orange.

He held out his hand.

Mr. Sprouts gripped it in his iron clasp.

Squirt! the orange suffered, and Mr. Gimp's fingers escaped the torture of the thumb-screw.

Then Mr. Sprouts led the way upstairs.

A gay party were assembled.

It consisted of Mrs. Sprouts, her son Narcissus, and her three daughters, Violet, Rose and Camelia (in his younger days Mr. Sprouts had been a gardener, and, being very fond of flowers, had bestowed floral names on all his children), Mr. Harry Rattleton, the illustrious president of the Jolly Dogs, Mr. Graves, a most melancholy youth, who had the appearance of an undertaker's attendant, but was, in point of fact, no less a personage than the distinguished tenor, who enjoyed such an immense share of popularity amongst the intelligent and discriminating audience that frequent the "Fishmongers' Arms Free and Easy Concerts."

Mr. Graves was sitting beside a young lady of great personal attractions, pouring into her attentive ear a torrent of soft flattery.

The lymphatic-looking, sallow-faced youth glared into those deep blue eyes with a painful expression of subdued phrenzy.

The young beauty 'seemed so pleasantly and deeply interested by the discourse of her gifted admirer that she did not notice the entry of Mr. Gimp till a general rising of the company and a general shout of salutation caused her to lift her glance to encounter the stern and reproachful glare of her offended sweetheart.

"James!" she exclaimed, with a bright blush as she rose and flauntered across the room in her mist of muslin.

She offered her hand.

"Miss Selina Sparks!"

The words burst indignantly from the blue lips of her betrothed as he bent his head with profound and formal courtesy—cold, cutting, ironical.

Meanwhile, Mr. Graves drew himself up to his full height, solemnly placed his right hand in the bosom of his dress-waistcoat, thrust back a limp elf lock from his heavy brow, and assumed a look of passive scorn and defiance.

"La! we thought you weren't coming, James," said Selina, tossing her pretty head, and glancing slyly from the glaring eyes of her betrothed to the gloomy brow of his sombre-looking rival, and nipping her cherry lip with her snowy little teeth. "What makes you so late, sir? It's very ungallant of you, I'm sure, to keep us waiting; and, oh my! how ill-tempered you look. Pray, what is the matter?"

Mr. Gimp wrung her by the rosy fingers, gasped, and changed colour like a dying dolphin.

Mrs. Sprouts came to the rescue.

"Hoity, toity!" laughed the fat and jolly-looking matron, waddling up and forcing the reluctant Selina into Mr. Gimp's embrace. "Don't let's have no lovers' quarrels and sich-like nonsense, for gracious goodness sake! Jealousy's a green-eyed monster, as the sayin' is. Come, there, kiss and be friends, nobody won't tell. Lors, Tom "—this to her husband —"don't you mind how many a time you sp'ilt my pleasure for a whole week, through a gettin' riled about that little red-whiskered tallyman as used to ogle me through a gilt beye-glass? I considers it a mussy that our coortin' days is over. But let's make a start, and you, Mr. Rattleton, lend a 'and with the 'ampers.'"

The jovial party got into Mr. Sprouts's excursion wagonette and drove to Westminster Bridge.

Here they embarked on a steam-boat and reached the foot of London Bridge, the first of those mighty arched and pillared bulwarks which oppose the onward progress of ocean ships into the heart of the country.

The river at this point is nothing but a large settlement of steamers and boats of every description.

Our voyagers hitherto had seen many groups of small steamers and fishing boats with sails of dusky red; but the masts of the boats were lowered, and the steamers were lowered, and the steamers of a Lilliputian kind, undergrown, low-funnelled, small-engined, and paddle-wheeled.

They were passenger boats, plying between the bridges.

The class of vessels they saw here were of a more important appearance.

These were no water penny omnibusses, coasting it between the City and Putney Bridge.

Here were broad, black hulls, double funnels and capacious ones, high masts and boats hauled up at the sides; all told that these were hardy customers that could stand a stiff breeze in the Channel or elsewhere.

Some of them swing lazily on their moorings.

They had just come in from a voyage, and were taking their ease at home.

Others blow vast clouds of steam and black smoke.

Flags are being hoisted on them; hundreds of people cross and re-cross on the planks which communicate with the wharf or with other vessels.

They were just starting—whither?

Our party knew nothing about it.

A sailor could tell you all about them: he reads the character of a ship by the cut of her jib; but the Jolly Dogs were perfectly lost in this Babel of foreign vessels and seamen.

Here they are!

On a small steamer, next to a black Scotch coaster, crowded to suffocation, and just casting off.

The boy at the hatch is waiting the captain's signal.

The captain is walking the paddle-box and moves his hand.

The machinery is in motion.

The boy calls out and the engineer makes a corresponding movement and the steam rules the large cylinders.

The vessel has left the shore.

"Don't be in a hurry, miss! you can't leap that distance. You've missed the boat, as a thousand do daily amidst these vast comings and goings of London."

There will be another Greenwich steamer in five minutes, so the misfortune, after all, is not very great.

What an astounding spectacle the Thames presents at this very point below London Bridge!

In autumn, when the great merchantmen, heavily laden, coming in from all parts of the world, cast their bales and casks upon the shore, from whence a thousand channels of trade convey them to and distribute them over the whole earth—in autumn this part of the river presents a spectacle of a mighty, astounding activity, with which no river can vie.

The vessels are crowded together by fifties and hundreds on either side.

Colossal steamers, running between the coast towns of France, Germany and Scotland, have here dropped their anchors, waiting until the days of their return for passengers and merchandize.

Their little boats dance on the waves, their funnels are cold and smokeless, their furnaces extinct.

Sailors walk to and fro on the decks, looking wistfully at the varying panorama of London life and jolly doggism.

In a semi-circle round those steamers are the black ships of the north.

They are black all over; the decks, the bows, the sides, the rigging, and the crew have all the same dusky hue.

These vessels carry the dark diamond of England; they are colliers from Newcastle.

Our boat has just passed the Custom-House.

It is a splendid building, and it may be mentioned, in passing, has been burnt down six times, and six times re-built on the same site.

The vessels which come to London must all appear at the forum of this Custom-House, unless they prefer leaving their cargo in the docks or the bonded warehouses.

What crowds of sailing ships and steamers from all the harbours of the world!

What goings and comings; what loadings and unloadings; what a bewildering movement this Custom-House presents!

It is actually painful to the eye.

The further our pleasure party travel down the river, the more closely packed are the vessels on either side.

For above two miles the broad Thames is wofully narrow; and the steamers which run up and down must just pick their way through as best they can.

Accidents will happen, and the man at the wheel must keep a sharp look out.

Those who have never sailed the Thames have no idea of the number of black-funnelled steamers which continually whisk past each other.

There is one just now steering right down upon our own boat; within another second our sides must be stoved in.

Well done!

She has turned aside and rushes past.

But scarcely is danger over, when another monster of the deep comes paddling on.

A large schooner is wedging its way between us and the said monster of the deep; and on our right there is an awkward Dutchman, swinging round on her anchor; and on our left there is a lubber of a collier, with her gunwales just sticking out of the water; and there, goodness gracious! there it is, a very nutshell of a boat, and two women in it, passing close under our bows,

Why we did not upset them, and why the others did not run into us, is a wonder.

That nutshell of a boat had a narrow escape among the steamers, and these women are aware of it; and there is no end of accidents, and yet these people *will* row across the river.

It is a perfect blessing that the English know better than anybody else how to steer a boat under difficulties.

Look at that man at the wheel!

Immovable, with his head bent forward, his eyes directed to the ship's course, his hands ready to turn the wheel; that fellow knows what steering the Thames is!

To all appearance it is not so difficult as rope-dancing, but, no doubt, it's worse than rope-dancing; it requires the most consummate address.

And then there's the responsibility!

The sailors of all nations stand in great awe of the London Thames.

They navigate their vessels to the East Indies; they weather the storms of the Cape, and think nothing of its blowing "big guns;" but none of them would undertake to steer a vessel from Blackwall to London Bridge.

"It's too crowded for us," they say, "and the little nut-shells of steamers are enough to make an honest sailor giddy; and the river is so narrow. If you fancy you are clear of all difficulties and can go on, there's sure to be some impertinent boat in your way. Turn to the right! Why, there's not room for a starved herring to float!"

And the old steersman descends from his high place, and resigns his functions to the Thames Pilot.

If he is a conceited blockhead, let him try, that's all.

But if the vessel comes to harm the insurance is lost, for the underwriters at Lloyds' will not be responsible for any damage done in the pool, unless the wheel is in the hands of a regular pilot.

And they are right; for, with all the difficulties and dangers, there are few accidents.

Let us, then, trusting to the skill of that particular steersman who guide the destinies of our party, and those of our boat, look at the scenery around.

A forest of masts looms through the perennial fog, the banks of the river are lined with warehouses, some old and dilapidated, while others are new, solid and strong.

A stray flag fluttering in the breeze, a sailor hanging on the spars and chewing tobacco, a monkey of a boy sky-larking on the top-mast cross-trees of an Indiaman; these are some of the sights of the lower Thames.

Let us now look at the party on board our own vessel; for, after all, we ought to know the people who are in the same boat with us, and who, in case of an accident, would share one watery grave.

The boat is full.

A first-class ticket to Gravesend cost ninepence, and the society is of a mixed description.

It is not easy to look *into* people; and as for their exterior, their walk, manners, dress, and conduct, there is even among the poorer classes a strong flavour of the "gentleman."

The women of England, too, do not betray their social position by their dress.

Coloured silks, black velvets, silk or straw bonnets, with botanical ornaments, are worn by a lady's maid as well as by the lady.

Possibly, the maid's dress may be less costly; the lady, too, may sweep her flounces with a more distinguished air, there may be some difference or other, but who can see all and know all by just looking at people?

Here we are at the Tower.

There is nothing awful in its appearance from the river side, especially since it was repaired and white-washed after the great fire.

The outer wall is black, and two red sentinels creep to and fro along it.

As we advance the masts and the outline of the rigging come out well defined against the lurid sky; and just here and there an Indiaman deeply laden, turning out of the river, and proceeding inland, floating in locks.

What we saw were the basins of the various docks, which, hidden behind store-houses of fabulous size and numbers, extend deep into the heart of the country.

The river, broad as it is, cannot afford space for the hundreds and hundreds of vessels which lie snugly in these docks.

Our boat, too, turns to the left bank, and stops near an apoplectic grey tower.

A similar tower rises on the opposite bank.

These towers are the gates of the famous Thames Tunnel.

We leave the boat to look at this triumph of British science and perseverance.

The tower covers the shaft into which you must descend if you would enter the broad pathway under the water; and the sinking this shaft to the depth of eighty feet was the first step to an undertaking which, since its completion, has commanded the admiration of the engineers of all nations.

The broad, comfortable stairs, and the pathway beneath the river, devoid of ornament, and lighted with gas, do not, indeed, present any striking features to the unscientific visitor.

Our railway tunnels are a good deal longer, and what mortal, unless he be a practical engineer, has a conception of the difficulties of this particular undertaking?

Still those difficulties were enormous.

The breadth of the river is above two thousand feet at high water; the weight pressing on the arches is about double the low water weight.

Among the strata which the workmen had to pierce was a layer of floating sand, and, in spite of all precautions, the water broke in not less than five times, and several lives were sacrificed.

On one occasion Mr. Brunel the architect had a narrow escape.

Through a breach of several thousand cubic feet the water entered the tunnel, which had then advanced to the middle; the masonry and machinery were destroyed; it took many weeks before the water was pumped out and the disastrous hole stopped with sand-bags.

The workmen refused to go down again; the contractors had to double their wages.

The works had to be carried on by day and by night without cessation, and the strictest watch had to be kept on the river itself, its tides, and its movements.

At length, after an enormous outlay of capital and ingenuity, when even the most sceptical part of the public understood that the construction of a tunnel under the Thames was not an impossibility, it was found that the funds advanced by the shareholders were exhausted.

The parliament, however, granted a loan; the whole of England took an interest in the execution of this great undertaking.

Fresh machinery was invented, fresh workmen were engaged, and the second shaft was sunk on the Wapping side of the river.

The English carry out whatever they undertake to do.

Life in the Thames Tunnel is a very strange sort of life.

As we descend stray bits and snatches of music greet our ears.

Arrived at the bottom of the shaft there is a double pathway opening before us, and looking altogether dry, comfortable and civilized, for there are plenty of gas-lights, and in the passages which communicate between the two roadways are a numerous race of small shop-keepers, offering views of the tunnel and other penny wares for sale.

These poor people never see the sun except on Sundays.

The strangers in London are their best, and indeed it may almost be said, their only customers.

As we proceed the music becomes clear and distinct.

It is an Italian organ, played by a perfect doll of a Lilliputian steam engine.

That engine grinds the organ from morning till night; it gives us various pieces without any compunction or political scruples.

The Marseillaise, German waltzes, the Hungarian Rakowsky March, Rule Britannia, Yankee Doodle, &c., does this marvellous engine grind out of the organ.

In the present instance the organ and the engine are mere decoy-birds.

You stop, and are invited to look at the "panorama" at the expence of "only one penny."

Of such like spectacles the tunnel has plenty, but we cannot stop for them.

We hasten to the shaft, ascend the steps, and feel quite refreshed by the free air of heaven.

We are once more on the steamer.

There is scarcely standing room on the deck.

Besides the steamers there are Greenwich omnibuses, and there is an extra railroad running its trains every quarter-of-an-hour from London to Greenwich, and yet, look at the crowd which surrounds us on all sides.

London, too, has its tides, and its high and low water-mark ; its thousands and hundreds of thousands rush into the country and back again at regular periods from one twelve-month's end to another.

The majority of London merchants live in the country, and yet they are able to pass their days in the city.

Various means and modes of conveyance, and these quick, ready and cheap, enable them to accomplish that feat.

As we go down the river the banks recede, and the vessels lie in smaller groups.

In their place we see the very insignificant-looking yards of the London ship-builders, which extend almost to Woolwich, the seat of the government dockyard.

Woolwich is the second depôt of the country ; Portsmouth is the first.

The English ship-builders are cosmopolitans like the organ-grinders.

Little do they care for their customers' position, religion or nation ; they build ships for every man who offers his money, and for every country, too, for Denmark, Spain, Austria, Russia, and even for France.

But while we are describing the aspect of the river-banks we must not forget to record a little misadventure which occurred to Mr. Sprouts.

During the whole of the voyage that worthy gentleman, his spouse, and family, regaled themselves with biscuits and sundry potations from the brandy bottle.

Now, it happened that Mr. Sprout's youthful son dropped a "captain."

Mr. Sprouts, stopping to pick it up, he overturned the small boy, and with the cigar which he held in his hand burnt the hand of a lady near him, to the intense disgust of that respectable female, who vented her feelings in a piercing scream.

Mr. Sprouts, frightened and confused, made a leap backwards, and alighted with wonderful precision on Mr. Gimp's foot, and, to add to the luckless greengrocer's discomforture, a gust of wind blew his hat off his head, and lodged it safely on a large newspaper which a fat old gentleman was reading.

The biscuit, meanwhile, had been eaten by an Italian greyhound ; the small boy screamed, the fat old gentleman expressed his indignation. Some people are *so* awkward ; and even Mr. Gimp's temper is ruffled.

The inevitable personage who haunts all steamers, the man with the little book who takes the passage money from those who are without tickets, has at length found us out.

Here is Greenwich.

Here the façade and dome of the sailor's hospital, with a semicircle of wooded hills in the back ground.

We have left the fog behind us in London, and the morning sun once more breaks out from the clouds.

Our boat rushes past the "Dreadnought."

We touch the shore.

The engines are stopped.

We are at our journey's end.

We stand on the beautiful terrace in front of the hospital, the house in which Queen Elizabeth loved to dwell, and here at this very spot her courtiers used to take their walks.

Their gold-embroidered cloaks are gone, and in their stead you see long, blue, brass-buttoned on the mutilated or decrepid bodies of old sailors.

A blue coat, a white neck-cloth, white stockings, and a large, three-cornered hat with gold lace, that is the uniform of the invalids, who pass the evening of their life in this delightful place.

Greenwich Hospital presents the most beautiful architectural group of modern England.

Take the most gifted architect of the world, bandage his eyes, put him on the terrace on which we stand, and then show him this beautiful building, and he will at once tell you that this is and must be a royal palace.

How could he ever suspect that all this splendour of columns and cupolas to be destined to shelter a couple of thousand of poor decrepid sailors ?

But that it does shelter them is honourable to the founders, and to the English nation.

Those two hospitals of Greenwich and Chelsea, devoted to the disabled heroes of the navy and army, give incontestable proof of the grateful kindliness of feeling with which the English nation honours its old soldiers.

England treats her cripples as a mother would her sick and ailing children.

The architectural splendours of Greenwich Hospital are by no means destined to hide poverty and misery within.

The gates are open.

You may walk through the refectories, the kitchens, the sitting and sleeping rooms, wait while the "old gentlemen" sit down to their dinner, eat a slice of their meat, smoke a pipe of their tobacco, take a pinch from one of their snuff-boxes, admire the irreproachable whiteness of their cravats, take a seat at their side on the green benches which stand on the smooth lawn, from whence they view the Thames, its sails, masts, flags, the cherished scene of their early career.

Talk to them.

They like to fight their battles over again in conversation, and will tell you whether they have to complain of the ingratitude of their country.

All round the hospital, and, indeed, in its immediate vicinity, there are strange scenes of life, such as are not unfrequently met with in England.

A few yards lower down the stream stands, in aristocratic exclusiveness, the Trafalgar Hotel, which we beg to recommend to every one who wishes to pay for a dinner twice the amount that would suffice to keep an Irish family for a whole week.

The wines of the Trafalgar, like the Lethe of old, wash away the cares of the past ; for it is here that, according to an ancient custom, Her Gracious Majesty's ministers meet after the parliamentary session.

They drink sherry and champagne and eat white-bait, and thank their stars that there are no more awkward questions to answer.

As a contrast to this luxuriant hotel, we see, on the other side of the hospital, partly along the shore, and partly near the park, and in the interior of sundry lanes and alleys, a vast number of pot-houses, tea-gardens and places of a worse description, where every vice finds a ready welcome.

Boys and girls standing at the doors, invite the passing stranger.

"Boiling water, sir ; shrimps for tea, sir ; good accommodation, sir."

We know what that means, and go our way.

But that young fellow in the sailor's jacket with the girl hanging on his arm ; they are caught !

They enter the house.

Forward to the green, leafy, hilly park !

On the large grass-plots whole families are stretched out in picturesque groups, from the grandfather down to the grand-sons and grand-daughters, and along with them there are friends, country-cousins, maid-servants, and lap-dogs with a proud supercilious air, for they know, sagacious little animals, that their owners are continually paying dog-tax for them.

This is Monday, the Englishman's Sunday.

There they are chatting, laughing, and even getting up and dancing, eating their cold dinners with a good appetite, and a thorough enjoyment of sunshine, air and river-breeze, they are all cheerful, decent, and happy, as simple-minded men and women are wont to be on a holiday and on the forest green.

(To be continued.)

Have you ever seen a rare work of Marcus Aurelius, of which there are but two written copies extant, entitled, 'Ye Waye to Long Life and Abundante Wealthe?'"

The young men looked at each other in mutual amazement while the stranger spoke, for he seemed wonderfully familiar with those subjects upon which their own attentions had been fixed.

"What are you?" said Jasper.

"Aye," added St. Leon. "What are you? We can inform you, that be you whom you may, yours is the first foot, excepting our own, that has trodden in this apartment, since it has been in our occupation."

"I am highly honoured," said the little old man; "and as for what I am, I can call myself a student of nature. I have been compelled to fly from one of the petty Italian states where I had resided some years, because the vulgar people around me would have it that I was studying the black art."

"Then you are acquainted with alchemy?"

"A little."

The young men exchanged glances of satisfaction, and then Jasper continued,

"We are but tyros in a science in which, perhaps, sir, you have made great advances."

"Humph!" said the old man. "The science of alchemy is one which opens wider to the view at each forward step. I have made a few discoveries."

"Did you ever try," said St. Leon, hurriedly, "to consolidate the earths that enter into the composition of precious stones?"

The old man turned a keen eye on his youthful questioners, and with a short laugh he said,

"Aye, have I."

"And—and ——"

"And succeeded."

The young alchemists both gave a start of surprise at this communication, and after a moment's silence, Jasper said, with an eagerness that made him speak like one who from a race had lost his breath,

"Most honoured sir—we—we have been—been trying——"

"Ah!"

"Yes—yes. We tried according to the recipes of the great Calletti—and we thought that—that we ought to use some more subtle agent than the vapour of the aspen boughs, and we have dissolved some of the pure essence from the root called murdocke."

"Oh, oh!" said the stranger. "Of what colour was the flame you got?"

"Amber! amber!"

"Good. Did the sparks rise high?"

"Yes, very high. But, alas! when success appeared likely to crown our efforts, when it would have seemed that in another moment we should have been able to say we had conquered the greatest difficulty, the crucible broke to pieces with a loud report, and all our labour vanished."

"Of course," said the old man.

"Indeed, sir! Was it sure to do so?"

"Yes, if the process were successful. Have you raked out the furnace, to look for the topaz you have doubtless made? Why, the bursting of the crucible was the certain indication that you had succeeded. I wonder you knew not as much as that."

Before he had done speaking, both Jasper and St. Leon had flown to the furnace, and commenced raking out the live embers with a determination which would soon have tested the accuracy of the stranger's words. But he himself advanced to assist them, and taking up a pan full of the embers, he carefully raked among them with the charcoal-tongs.

"There is nothing here," said Jasper, in a tone of disappointment.

"Indeed!" said the old man. "What do you call this? What would this be, cut into shape, and more highly polished than it is?"

A cry of joy burst from the lips of Jasper as he received from the hands of the old man a large jewel, which, in some parts where it was most bright, was of surpassing lustre.

"'Tis done! St. Leon!" he cried, "'tis done! We are rich—rich beyond all expectation. Oh, what a glorious moment is this! Do you now grudge the labour you have bestowed upon this sublime pursuit? Do you now moan over the time you supposed you had lost? We are now magicians, and can vie with the emperor. Behold this jewel, St. Leon. Let me see you smile now, as I do, with exultation."

———

CHAPTER IV.

THE COMMUNICATION REGARDING THE MEANS OF LONG LIFE—THE PROPOSAL—THE DEATH AND THE SECRET.

THE little old man sat down and rubbed his hands together, as if

he still felt chilled and cold; while Jasper and St. Leon now whispered exultingly together, and proceeded to the window to ask each other in eager whispers what they should now do as regarded the stranger.

"A man," said Jasper, "who knows so much knows more. He may be some eccentric philosopher who, although in the possession of the greatest secrets of the art we are endeavouring to arrive at, may care nothing for those results which we pant for. Oh, St. Leon, this may be the luckiest chance that destiny ever threw in our way; who knows what we may prevail upon him to tell us if we but go the right way to gain his good feeling and confidence?"

"It may be so," said St. Leon.

"I am certain it is so. See how he at once told us concerning the jewel, which now we have, and which, although of great value, you perceived how little he thought of it, and how readily he handed it to us, without expressing the smallest desire to share with us in the profits."

"It seems that you must be right, Jasper. I am weak and tremulous myself. Do you talk to him, and, by remaining myself silent, I shall be the better able to pay the greater attention to what he says."

"A good thought, a good thought, St. Leon; I will endeavour to make much of him, while you will be careful not to lose a word of any communication he may make to us."

The mysterious old stranger was, during this colloquy, still warming his shrivelled hands by the fire.

He paid no attention to what was passing between the two young men; but now that they looked towards him again he moved complacently aside, and seemed waiting for them to address him.

"Sir," said Jasper, with an air of the greatest deference and respect; "sir, what thanks, or what recompense can we offer you for pointing out to us the jewel which we otherwise should most certainly have overlooked?"

"I want neither thanks nor recompense," he said.

"But our gratitude beats so loudly in our hearts that we would fain adopt some means of showing it."

"'Tis I who am and ought to be grateful for a shelter from the storm in this snug apartment. Hark how the rain beats against the casement."

Neither Jasper nor St. Leon had heard any rain beating against the casement before; but now there came such a sudden and tremendous gust of it, that the old turret-chamber shook again, and the window appeared to be threatened with instant demolition.

"It does, indeed!" said Jasper.

"And I am saved from the fury of such a storm, which, at my time of life," said the old man, "would have been by me severely felt, for which I cannot be too grateful to you. Is there anything you wish particularly to learn as regards the science you are pursuing here? If there be, and you are not working well with your crucibles and your alembics, for the love of the art, perhaps, I can save you some labour."

This was indeed coming at once to the very point which Jasper had intended to get round to as covertly and cleverly as he could, and the joy that sparkled in his eyes showed that he was sufficiently alive to the importance of what the strange visitor said.

"Good sir," he said, "you perceive that we are both very young men. I am but twenty-four, and my friend here is but twenty. We do not pursue this science of alchemy for the love of it, but for the results which may follow it. We hope, by sacrificing a few years of our youth, to be able to gild the remainder of our days by wealth, and all its attendant charms. We love the world, although you see us shut up here within the narrow confines of this apartment. We glory in the green fields, the songs of birds, and in the beauty of woman."

"Oh!" said the old man.

"And we hope with a longing expectation that language is weak to convey that the time will come when we shall be able to emerge from this our chrysalis state, if I may be allowed the expression, and bask in all the delights of the great world from which, for the present only, we have in some bitterness of spirit withdrawn ourselves."

"Ah! I understand," said the stranger.

"If then you, who, we are inclined to think, are an adept where we are but the veriest tyros, can, and will assist us, boundless shall be our grateful feelings."

"Well, well," said the old man. "I must confess that I do not set the same store that you do by the secrets of alchemy, because, perhaps, I have become tired of some of them. Listen to me!"

"With respect, sir, and attention."

"By pursuing a process which I shall point out to you, you shall be able to make diamonds."

"Diamonds?"

"Yes. Be calm. If you make too many you will defeat yourself, because upon their rarity depends their value; but you shall

(Continued from page 64.)

THE JOLLY DOGS OF LONDON.

THE MORNING'S REFLECTION—A MISERABLE DOG.

CHAPTER XXIX.—(continued).

And the deer, half tame, come out of the thicket and ask for their share of the feast, and we go our way up the hill lest we should disturb the children and the deer.

From the top of the hill we look down upon one of the most charming landscapes that can be imagined in the vicinity of a large capital.

That ocean of houses in the distance, shifting and partly hidden in the mist.

The docks, with their forests of masts; the Thames itself, winding its way to the sea; green, hilly country on our side, with the white steam of a distant train curling up from the deep cuttings; and at our feet, Greenwich with its columns, cupolas, and neat villas, peeping out from among shrubberies and orchards.

We share the hill on which we stand with the famous Greenwich Observatory.

Probably the building has a better appearance than it had at the time when Flamstead, with generous self-denial, established the first sextant on the spot.

But even in our days the exterior of the building is by no means imposing.

Here, then, we stand on the first meridian of England.

The road from the observatory to the back gate of the park leads through an avenue of old chestnut trees.

They are in a flourishing condition; and the chestnuts are quite as good as those of Italy and southern France.

Among these trees stands the official residence of the Ranger of Greenwich Park; a nobleman, or gentleman, whose duty it is, in consideration of six or eight hundred pounds per annum, to pass a few summer months in this delightful retreat, and to supply her Majesty's table with a haunch of venison once every twelve-month.

The post is a sinecure, one of those places which every one inveighs against, and which every one would be glad to possess.

We have crossed the park, and are on Blackheath, a sunny place, which derives its gloomy name from the gipsies who used to be encamped upon it in the days of "Auld Lang Syne."

Neat villas, covered with evergreens, surround this Blackheath, and a hundred roads and paths invite us to stroll on through garden-land and park-like domains.

We resist the temptation and return to our party of Jolly Dogs, from whom we have wandered away.

CHAPTER XXX.

THE APPREHENSION OF GEORGE GRANT ON A CHARGE OF
FORGERY, EMBEZZLEMENT AND BURGLARY.

UNDER a spreading chestnut tree a dainty cloth is laid, and
seated in a merry circle on the sunshiny sward the Jolly
Dogs are carousing.

At Greenwich the party was reinforced by George Grant,
Mr. Puffy, and several others of our acquaintance.

Poor George, while he laughed and chatted so gaily with
his fellow-excursionists, little thought of the storm that was
brewing at home.

Mr. Puffy and George were extremely diverted by the
humorous bluffness and simplicity of Mr. Sprouts and his
family, and though at first they created a little awe in the
breasts of the unsophisticated greengrocer and his troop by
their gentleman-like appearance and superior manners, they
soon ingratiated themselves by their frank and genial good-
temper, and were voted by Mrs. Sprouts as "'Werry nice
young men, reg'lar right sort;'" and by her liege lord they
were proclaimed "Magnificent bricks."

After they had finished their dinner George volunteered to
play some dance-music on a violin which he had brought
with him.

The proposal was hailed with great satisfaction.

So, behold Master George mounted on the stump of a tree
fiddling away right merrily, while his companions foot it on
the light and fantastic toe.

Mr. Puffy's performances cause much mirth; he waltzes
with Mrs. Sprouts, and the pair, scattering the smaller fry
before them, wave round and round with all the grace of
gambolling porpoises.

Then, during a rest, comic songs are sung, and Mr. Gimp
tricks himself out in bonnet and shawl, and affecting the
mincing gait of a very sentimental young lady, sings a serio-
comic ballad with expression.

Then there are races on donkeys and ponies.

Miss Selina Sparks is run away with by a ragged little nag,
Mr. Graves gets ignominiously thrown from his long-eared
courser, while the whole taboon of horses, mules, and
Jerusalems, take to flight with panic, snortings, neighings, or
brayings, at the very sight of Mr. Puffy, who threatens to
mount one of them—an infliction not to be borne even by the
proverbially patient animal.

But we have lingered too long on the road, and must not
enter into further details; suffice it to say that the day passed
right joyously, and when the night drew on apace the crew of
Jolly Dogs returned to town in high jubilee.

Humphrey Puffy and George Grant parted from the rest at
the railway station, and sauntered leisurely homewards.

"And what news of Angeline Lamonde? Have you seen
her, George?" asked Humphrey Puffy as they proceeded.

George's handsome face assumed a grave expression.

"Yes; she is looking very ill."

"Indeed? Yet at the stage she plays with unabated spirit
and energy."

"She does! She seems to have thrown all her heart into
her profession; but at home she is evidently labouring hard
against some hidden and exciting emotion. In company she
strains hard to appear gay as a lark: but in solitude, as
Lyddy tells me, she droops like a caged bird."

"And did she ever give Lydia any explanation as to whither
she went and in whose company, on the Derby Day, when she
broke her appointment with young Leoni?"

"No; when questioned she became so unmistakably alarmed
and distressed that Lydia would not persist in her enquiries."

"And has the mysterious visitor appeared at her house
since that occasion?"

"No, I believe not; but one night Angeline left home
late; in fact, after her return from the theatre, and just
before she started, Lydia caught her in the act of counting
out a large sum of money."

"All this is very mysterious. What can be the secret of
her strange conduct?"

"Heaven alone can tell; perhaps she is the victim of some
villain's extortion and intimidation."

"Or else, George, she may have committed some secret
crime."

"I will never believe it."

"Nor I. I will stake my life in her guiltlessness."

"And I, too, Geordie; but yet—Well, if that fellow Arthur
Aubrey is not a treacherous, cold-hearted, selfish scamp,
there's no such word as rascality."

"I do not think of him over favourably myself," replied
George; "but still I think he is deeply attached to
Angeline."

"Then, why don't he visit her?"

"She refuses to see him."

"Pshaw! a mere woman's waywardness. She would
rejoice to meet him, and frets because she thinks he slights
her."

"Has Lydia told him this?"

"Why, yes, she gave him a hint to that effect, as delicately
as possible, of course; but I see what the fellow is—a roué, a
spendthrift, a gambler, and a man of the world, of the earth,
earthy. He can no more appreciate the value of such a noble
heart as Angeline's than a swine the pearl he rolls in the mire.
I am sick of the rowdy."

"Well, talk no more of him."

"But I'll tell you what, Humphrey, I am sorry, for my own
sake, that Angeline should have fallen into this strange and
mysterious state of feverish excitement."

"For your own sake, Geordie? Does her distressful mood
affect your personal interest then?"

"Yes; and I don't mind telling you in what way it does,
Humphrey. I dare say it is no secret to you that I and Lyddy
—well—you understand—mutual esteem, and—and all that
sort of thing. Now, I have proposed to Lyddy."

"By Hymen's taper! And were accepted, Geordie?"

"Well—not rejected! but Lyddy refuses to marry me
till——"

"Till when?"

"Till she has unravelled the thread of Angeline's mystery—
till she has found out the cause of her disease of mind, and
has applied some remedy. The dear faithful girl refuses to
leave her beloved companion while she is in such a distressed
state of mind. I can't blame her resolve, though it's rather
hard upon me."

"Well, Geordie, we must not be over scrupulous in the
means we take to find out who this mysterious personage may
be who holds such a strange influence over the poor girl. If
we find that her secret is a dark one, at least it will be safe
with us; but unless something is done to save her, perish she
must, for her health is failing fast, and sometimes she is so
hysteric, abstracted, and strange in her manner that I almost
fear she is losing her senses."

"Yes, you are right, Humphrey, we must act with decision;
but we must first consult with Lyddy."

"Well, here we part, old boy; good night."

"No, Humphrey, don't leave me yet; it is not late; come
with me to my lodgings, and let's smoke a cigar together; I
am out of sorts to-night, and can't spare your society."

"Why, what's the matter? The green sickness?—a touch
of the heart complaint, eh?"

"Don't talk bosh."

"I wish I could fall in love. Cupid would be of more service to a man of my mould, even than Banting. Heigho! I
laugh and grow fat, but

'"Love wakes and weeps
While Beauty sleeps.'

"Perhaps a little watching and weeping would bring me down
a bit. But here's your street, Geordie; and, as you've beguiled
me thus far, I think I will turn into your crib just for half an
hour, and we will see if we can't come to some arrangements
as to what is to be done for poor Angeline. Why do you
pause so suddenly, like Macbeth at the air-drawn dagger?"

"I don't know what is the matter with me, but I have a
strange feeling of restlessness and foreboding. But here we
are at home."

As he said this, George was about to open the door with a
latch-key, when a man, close wrapped in a great coat, stepped
quickly up.

At the same moment the door was opened from within, and a stern-featured man appeared.

Both these persons seized George by the arms at the same moment.

"Why, what is this? What do you mean?" asked George, turning ashy pale. "Let go my arm, you rascals."

"I arrest you, Mr. Grant," said one of the men, in a stern, calm voice.

"Arrest me? What have I done? What is your charge against me?"

"You are charged, sir, with forgery, embezzlement, and burglary."

"Burglary? Come, that's good. What stupid joke is this?"

"You'll find it no joke, Mr. Grant, I do assure you," returned the man, grimly.

"And who the devil, sir, are you?"

"Inspector Pounce, of the detective force, at your service," returned the officer.

"Well, sir, and may I ask you by whom I am charged with such grave offences?"

"By your employers, Messrs. Mammonsons', bankers, Lombard Street."

"Mammonson!—pshaw! I don't believe that you are what you pretend to be; but if you think you can play me this trick with impunity you are much mistaken."

"You brave it well, sir; perhaps you would like to see my warrant?"

"Certainly, sir; produce it at once!"

"Very willingly, sir."

The detective placed a paper in his hand.

"There can be no mistake about this being a genuine warrant," said Mr. Puffy, examining the document; "this is a plaguy awkward business, my poor George; but take it easy, man. Of course you can disprove these absurd charges?"

"Of course," returned Grant, hoarsely; "but I can in nowise conceive upon what foundation these accusations can be based at all. I have heard of no robbery at Mammonsons', certainly of no burglary. When did the burglary take place?"

"You will know all in good time, sir," returned the officer. "Be careful what you say, as your word may be used against you."

"I care not what may be used against me; perjury, treachery, nothing can injure me, my character is too firmly established, and my innocence can be too easily made apparent."

"I truly hope so, sir," returned the officer.

"Well, what is to be done now? How do you intend to proceed? Of course it is useless to resist your authority? I am ready to go with you; but let us call a cab to escape the scandal of a march through the gaping crowd."

"First, sir, we must adjourn to your apartments."

"Aye, do, and if you can find anything there to criminate me I will plead guilty at once."

"Be it so; please follow me."

"Come you, too, Humphrey."

"My dear boy, I will never leave you till I am forced from your side. Cheer up, right is might, and justice will prevail."

The policemen conducted George to his room, one preceding and the other following him.

"Now," said Grant, boldly, "ransack the place, turn every box and cupboard inside out; let the place be gutted if you please, and if you find one tittle of evidence against me I am ready to take the consequence. Commence the search."

Grant seated himself calmly and folded his arms.

One of the officers took down a coat from a rail behind the door.

"You wear this coat at the office, do you not, Mr. Grant?"

"Yes, certainly; I brought it home with me at the beginning of the week, as I was leaving the office for my annual holiday; it is getting too shabby for use."

"Do you adhere to that statement, Mr. Grant? Remember, I cautioned you."

"Yes I do. Why should I not? I have no cause to be afraid of the truth?"

"It is my duty to examine the pockets."

"Hang it! do your duty, then; and if a play-bill, a watchkey, and an old tune-book will form links in the chain of evidence against me you are welcome to make the most of them."

"A tune-book, eh?" grinned the detective, producing a packet of papers. "Here are some notes, certainly, to the tune of five thousand pounds!"

"Great God!" cried poor George, leaping to his feet as if he had been shot.

"Can this be true, George?" asked Humphrey, in great dismay.

"Do you plead guilty now?" asked the detective, leering.

"It is a foul conspiracy; the notes have been placed where you find them by some other hand than mine. I know nothing about them!"

"Well, we must now search the cupboard."

"Yes, yes," cried George, eagerly; "here is the key. I always keep that cupboard locked; that at least cannot have been tampered with; this key has never before been out of my possession since I've lived here."

"Hush, George! you must be careful even though you are innocent," said Humphrey. "Remember, your words may be used against you."

"Against me? God help me!" murmured George, covering his face with his hands.

Then he bravely uplifted his glance, and exclaimed, firmly,

"But God, who defends the right, will help me! Open the cupboard at once, sir, and bring out my papers."

The detective complied with this request.

Poor George's horror and confusion may be well imagined when a cheque-book, a bundle of notes and bonds, and other valuable papers were produced.

George seized Humphrey's hand.

"Pardon me, my dear friend," he cried, wildly, "if for a moment I am unmanned by this sudden and astounding stroke from the hidden hand of some dastardly enemy. Oh, spare me the worst bitterness; say that you at least believe me innocent, and then, come what may, I am resigned to my fate!"

"Resigned, George! Pshaw, man, you need not ask me if I think you are innocent; that you could have been guilty of these acts is sheerly impossible; you are as innocent of them as I myself; but don't talk of resignation, Geordie, let the word be 'reparation.' The arch-villains who have concocted this precious plot, clumsy as it is, shall dearly rue their scoundrelism. Cheer up, all will soon be cleared up, I am sure of it; meantime I will be bail for you, and I will strive my uttermost to unmask the monstrous traitor who has played you this foul trick. I almost think I know him."

"I will not feebly protest my innocence, I will prove it!" cried George, fiercely.

The detective looked at the anguished, but noble and frank face of his prisoner, and his own stern countenance softened.

"May I ask you, Mr. Grant," he said, "did you sleep at home on last Wednesday night?"

"No."

"Where did you pass the night, then?"

"At a public-house near Long Acre, the 'Fighting Cocks.'"

"Phew! the haunt of thieves and characters of the worst class."

"I can explain about that," said Humphrey, quickly.

"No need, sir; I asked Mr. Grant the question in hopes of being able to re-assure him, but what he has spoken I will not mention, I give you my word of that. But come, sir, we must be going, a cab waits; we must get off to the station. I'm very sorry for you, sir, but I must do my duty."

"Of course, of course; I'm ready," gasped the unfortunate victim of Dandy Jack's treacherous plot.

He rose firmly and followed the officers from the room.

CHAPTER XXXI.
JOE CURTIS ON THE SCOUT.

DARREL and Black Isaac alighted from the brougham at the door of a little cottage in one of the most quiet and retired of the rural suburbs.

It was a neat and pleasant dwelling, adorned with a pretty little garden in front, and an orchard at the back.

There was an air of quietude and repose about the place very grateful after the dust and glare of the high road by which the travellers had come.

Before the driver could reach the little garden gate the door was opened by a tidy-looking girl, who apparently expected the arrival.

Darrel, who bore little Elfie in his arms, gave one hurried glance around as if to assure himself that their movements had not been watched, and then, with the gipsy, entered the cottage.

The door was immediately closed.

The man who drove the brougham re-mounted the box, shook the rein, and drove off.

Scarcely had the vehicle disappeared round the corner of the quiet street than a man, closely wrapped in a long grey coat, stepped from behind the portico of a neighbouring villa and cautiously approached the house into which the child had been taken.

The Venetian blinds were still drawn.

The man passed on.

He retraced his steps.

He loitered irresolutely near the place, keeping his eyes upon the gate.

The maid was presently seen to leave the house by a little side entry, and to approach him.

He looked at her fixedly, and smiled in recognition as she drew near.

"Why, Mr. Curtis!" cried the girl, extending her hand, "I thought I should never see you again; what brings you into this part of the world? Come to pay us a visit I hope?"

"No," returned Joe, in his short manner.

"That's a shame too. Mrs. Willis often speaks of you; she thought, perhaps, you did not know her address."

"Didn't."

"Well, you'll come in now, won't ye?"

"Yes."

"And how have you fared all this time?"

"So, so."

"In work?"

"Yes."

"As a coachman?"

"No."

"What then?"

"On my own book."

"Drive a cab?"

"Sometimes."

"Do you own one?"

"No."

"What do you do then?"

"Odd work."

"Sorry you haven't something better in hand."

"Where's the use o' strugglin'?"

"Well, I know you've been shamefully used."

"Yes."

"But not so badly as poor Mr. Darrel."

"No."

"Do you know, Curtis, Darrel is here with another person?"

"Missus not alone then?"

"No."

"What's Darrel want here?"

"Can't say."

"Won't say, is that it?"

"Well, it's very strange I should meet you just at this time, it is indeed!"

"Why?"

"Oh, because——but never mind, it is not our business."

"Summut up?"

"Something very strange."

"Ho!"

"I can't make it out at all."

"What?"

"Such a pretty little darling of a girl, and the very picture of——"

"D'zactly. I say, Lucy?"

"Well, Curtis?"

"Do me a favour?"

"If it's possible; what is it?"

"You won't do it?"

"Yes, I will, if I can."

"No, you won't."

"Why, what is it?"

"Know what became of Edith Harding?"

"No, indeed, poor girl. Do you?"

"Yes."

"Where is she now?"

"Ha!"

"The earl is married; they say his wife is a very lovely lady, and very good to the poor on the estates at Northminster Hall, but I never heard what became of poor Miss Edith. She acted very badly and foolishly of course, but the master played the villain to cast her off without making any provision for herself and the child, poor creature. What became of her?"

"Took the leap."

"The leap?"

"Yes, from Chelsea-bridge. Drowned herself."

"Great Heavens! but can that be true?"

"Why not?"

"Poor girl! we all loved her dearly."

"Yes."

"Then, perhaps—why, yes—did the child perish, too, Curtis?"

"No."

"Then, this little one must be her daughter."

"What little one?"

"It must out. Curtis, I will tell you; though, perhaps, I am doing wrong."

"No, you're not."

"I know you may be safely trusted, Curtis."

"In course."

"Well, then, Darrel has brought a pretty little thing, a child of five or six years of age, to Mrs. Willis."

"When?"

"Why, now."

"Ha!"

"And I shouldn't wonder if this child proves to be poor Edith Harding's daughter, and Darrel has confided her to the old housekeeper's care."

"Lucy?"

"Well, Mr. Curtis."

"Sorry for poor Edith Harding, eh?"

"Poor girl! poor girl!"

"For her sake."

"What's for her sake?"

"For the child's sake—the motherless child."

"Yes, yes."

"Do me this little favour?"

"What is it?"

"Darrel is holding a private conference with Mrs. Willis, ain't it so?"

"Yes, and gave express orders that she should not be disturbed."

"Don't want to disturb her. I say, Lucy, couldn't let me into the house, and post me where I could overhear their conversation, could ye now?"

"Really, Mr. Curtis——"

"Ah, thought ye wouldn't."

"Is it likely, now?"

"So ry, for the child's sake."

"What do you suspect? Is there any plot against the poor little orphan?"

"Don't know; want to find out."

"Well, surely Mrs. Willis will tell you all that you want to know?"

"Not after she has talked with those fellows."

"This is all very strange."

"Ain't it? Hark'ye, Lucy. I don't want to appear in this business; I want to learn all without being seen in the matter. Do ye understand, eh?"

"But what can be your motive for such strange conduct?"

"The interest of Lady Lindenwold."

"What, the poor countess? She has discovered her husband's perfidy, and she employs you as a spy upon his actions? Oh, shame, Curtis; I did not think you would undertake such a treacherous office."

"Stop a bit. Who spoke of the countess?"

"Why you did, of my Lady of Lindenwold."

"There is no Lady of Lindenwold except the heiress."

"The heiress? Then this child——"

"Hark ye, Lucy. You were ever a kind-hearted lass, and in this affair I must have some one to aid me. If I convince you that it is for the benefit of the child of the poor young lady we all loved so well——"

"I will do anything; but you must give some proof—some sterling proof. I won't act without some warrant for what I do."

"You shall see the proof, Lucy," returned Joe, with a smile.

He drew a letter-case from his pocket, and, opening it, took out a paper, which he placed in the girl's hand.

"A certificate! A marriage certificate, by all that is sacred and true!" cried the girl, with a cry of boundless astonishment. "Then the earl really married this hapless girl? She really was his wife and countess? she is not dead? Surely it was a false report you heard, Curtis?"

"No, Lucy," returned the honest fellow, shaking his head sadly, "it is but too true; but quick, if you would help me as you promise. Get me into the house. Let me hear what Darrel is saying to your mistress. We have already lost too much time."

"Come quickly, then," whispered the girl.

She admitted the man into the cottage and concealed him in a room adjoining that in which Mrs. Willis was holding the interview with her visitors.

Joe listened intently, and the working of his features betokened the deep impression made upon his mind by what he heard.

The men left at length, and Lucy let Curtis out by the backway.

"Is all well?" she asked.

"One thing is well. Darrel may be depended on; but I must save him from my comrades."

"Your comrades?"

"Yes, Lucy, it may as well out. I am now an officer in the detective force, and for months I have been employed in a dark and mysterious case; but I have great hopes that I shall be able to follow up the clue I have found; I shudder to think whither it may lead me."

"The poor injured countess—she was murdered!"

"Murdered, indeed! and yet the villain who destroyed her will escape the extreme penalty of the law."

"Oh! is there not one thunderbolt can be spared to strike such a villain—but stay, Curtis, you have not answered half the questions I wish to ask."

"Nor should I. Keep your council, Lucy; I know you are a discreet girl, or I should not have told you so much. Good bye, I must hasten back to the city, I have more than one case in hand. My next affair is with one of the crew of Jolly Dogs. Good bye, and keep our secret."

The detective strode away, leaving the girl gazing after him bewilderedly.

While Joe Curtis is hastening townwards it may not be amiss to lay before our readers a paper which contains a most instructive and amusing account of the character and functions of the London Police, both of the Detective and the Preventive force, and we do so in accordance to our promise that this romance should contain an admixture of interesting fact with sensational fiction, and on the full conviction that the following pleasant account will deeply interest our readers.

CHAPTER XXXII.
THE LONDON POLICEMAN.

THE London policeman knows every nook and corner, every house, man, woman and child on his beat.

He knows their occupations, habits, and circumstances.

This knowledge he derives from constantly being employed in the same quarter and the same street, and to—and surely a mind on duty bent may take great liberties with the conventional moralities—that platonic and friendly intercourse which he carries on with the female servants of the establishments which it is in his vocation to protect.

An English maid-servant is a pleasant girl to chat with when half shrouded in the mystic fog of the evening; and with the smart little cap coquettishly placed on her head, she issues from the sally-port of the kitchen, and advances stealthily to the row of palisades which protects the house.

And the handsome policeman, too, with his blue coat, and clean white gloves, is held in high regard and esteem by the cooks and housemaids of England.

His position on his beat is analogous to that of a porter of a very large house; it is a point of honour with him that nothing escapes his observation.

The "police honour" constitutes the essential difference between the English and the Continental police.

Even the most liberal of politicians—not a visionary—must admit, that it is impossible for a large town, and still more impossible for a large state, to exist without a well-organised protective force.

It matters little whether the force which insures the citizens against theft and robbery, as other associations insure them against fire and hail-storms, is kept up and directed by the state, or whether it is maintained by private associations, as has been proposed.

The police, whenever or wherever it answers its original purpose, is a most beneficent institution.

Its unpopularity in all the states of the continent is chargeable not to the principles of the institution, but to their perversion.

It is the perversion of the protective force into an instrument of oppression and aggression which the German hates; but he has no aversion to the police as such.

The policeman, no matter whether in uniform or in plain clothes, is a soldier of peace—a sentinel on a neutral post, and as such he is as much entitled to respect as the soldier who takes the field against a foreign invader.

This is the case in England.

The policeman is always ready to give his assistance and friendly advice; the citizen is never brought into an embarrassing and disagreeable contact with the police; and the natural consequence of this state of things is, that the most friendly feelings exist between the policeman and the honest part of the population.

Whenever the police have to interfere and want assistance, the inhabitants are ready to support them, for they know that the police never act without good reasons.

The detective police, who act in secret, do not stand on such intimate footing with the public as the preventive part of the force; but whenever they are in want of immediate assistance for the arrest of an offender, the detective has but to proclaim his functions, and no man, not even the greatest man in the land, would refuse to lend him assistance.

In Germany and in France no one will associate with an agent of the secret police, a *mouchard*, or by whatever other name those persons may be called.

Every one has an instinctive aversion to coming in contact with this species of animal, for they are traitorous, venomous, and blood-thirsty.

And that such is the case, is another proof of the vast superiority of the British institutions over those of the continent.

That London has not in the fulness of time come to be a vast den of thieves and murderers, is mainly owing to the action of the detective force.

Here, where the worst men of the European and American continents congregate, the functions of a detective are not only laborious but dangerous.

The semi-romantic ferocity of an Italian bandit is sheer good nature, if compared to the savage hardness and villany of a London burglar.

The bandit plies his lawless trade in the merry green wood and mossy dell; he confesses to his priest, and receives absolution for any peccadilloes in the way of stabbing he may happen to commit ; in moonlight nights his head rests on the knees of the girl that loves him, in spite of his cruel trade.

He is not altogether lost to the gentler feelings of humanity, and, in a great measure, he wants the confounding, hardening consciousness of having, by his actions, disgraced himself and his species.

But the London robber, like a venomous reptile, has his home in the dark holes under ground, in hidden back rooms of dirty houses, and on the gloomy banks of the Thames.

He breaks into the houses as a wolf into a sheep-fold, and kills those who resist him, and, in many instances, even those who offer no resistance.

There is no sun or forest green for him; no priest gives him absolution ; the female that herds with him is, in most cases, even more ferocious and abandoned than himself ; and if he be father to a child, he casts it at an early age into the muddy whirlpool of the town, there to beg, to steal, and to perish.

The streets that skirt the banks of the Thames are most horrible.

There the policeman does not saunter along with that easy and comfortable air which distinguishes him in the western parts of the town.

Indeed, in many instances, they walk by twos and threes with dirks under their coats, and rattles to call in the aid of their comrades.

Many policemen and detectives, who, hunting on the track of some crime, have ventured into these dens of infamy, have disappeared and no trace has been left of them.

They fell as victims to the vengeance of some desperate criminal whom, perhaps, on a former occasion, they had brought to justice.

And it would almost appear to be part of the politics of London robbers, that some policeman must be killed from time to time as a warning to his comrades.

The guild of assassins, too, have their theory of terrorism.

Another remarkable fact is, that the London policemen, though their duty brings them constantly in contact with the very scum of the earth, contract none of their habits of rudeness, which appear to be an essential stock-in-trade of the continental police.

One should say that the "force" in England is recruited from a meritorious class of society—one in which patience, gentleness, and politeness are hereditary.

Look there !

A fine, strapping fellow crossing the street with a child in his arms !

The girl is trembling like an aspen leaf, for she was just on the point of getting under a wheel.

That fine fellow has taken her up, and now, you see, he crosses again and fetches the little girl's mother, who stands bewildered with the danger, and whom he conducts in safety to the opposite pavement.

Who and what is that man ?

His dress is decent and citizen-like, yet peculiar ; it differs from the dress of ordinary men.

Coat and trousers of blue cloth ; a number and a letter embroidered on his collar, a striped band and buckle on his arm, a black helmet-shaped hat, and white gloves—rather a rarity in the dirty atmosphere of London.

That man is a policeman, a well got-up and improved edition of our own German *Polizeidiener*, those scarecrows with sticks, sabres, and other military accoutrements, standing at the street corners of the German capitals, and spoiling the temper of honest men as well as of thieves.

It is, however, a mistake to believe, as some persons on the continent do, that the London police are altogether unarmed and at the mercy of every drunkard.

Not only have they, in many instances and quarters, a dirk hidden under their great coats, but they have also, at all times, a short, club-like staff in their pockets.

This staff is produced on solemn occasions ; for instance, on the occasion of public processions, when every policeman carries his staff in his hand.

The staves have of late years been manufactured of gutta percha, and made from this material they are lighter and more durable than wooden staves.

In the name of all that is smashing, what a rich, full sound does not such a gutta percha club produce when in quick succession it comes down on a human shoulder !

That sound is frequently heard by those who, on Saturday or Monday night, perambulate the poorer or more dissolute quarters of the town, when all respect for the constable's staff has been drowned in a deluge of gin.

Matters on such occasions proceed frequently to the extremity of a duel.

The policeman, like any civilian, fights for his skin ; he gets a drubbing, and returns it with interest.

But since his weapon does not give him so manifest an advantage as a sword would, the public consider the fracas a fair fight.

And after all the combatants must appear before a magistrate.

In the police court they are on equal terms, and witnesses are heard on either side.

There is no favour in prejudice of the policeman.

But stop !

Look at the crowd in the street.

Two policemen are busy with a ragged creature of a woman, whom they carry to a doorway.

An accident, perhaps ?

Nothing of the kind.

The woman is drunk, and fell down in the road.

The policemen are taking her to the station, where she may sleep till she is sober.

But it was a strange spectacle to see those two men in smart blue coats, and white gloves, rescuing the ragged woman from the mire of the street.

Let us go on.

At Temple Bar there is a Gordian knot of vehicles of every description.

Three drays are jammed into one another.

One of the horses has slipped and fallen.

The traffic is stopped for a few minutes, and this is a matter of importance at Temple Bar.

Just look down Fleet Street ; the stoppage extends to Ludgate Hill.

But half-a-dozen policemen appear as if by enchantment.

One of them ranges the vehicles that proceed to the City in a line on the left side of the road.

A second lends a hand in unravelling the knot of horses.

A third takes his position in the next street, and stops the carriages and cabs which, if permitted to proceed, would but contribute their quota to the confusion.

Two policemen are busy with the horse which lies kicking in the road.

They unhook the chains and straps, get the horse on its legs, and assist the driver in putting him to rights again.

They have got dirty all over, and they must, moreover, submit to hear from Mr. Evans, who stands on the pavement, dignified, with a broad-brimmed quaker's hat, that they are awkward fellows, and know nothing about the treatment of horses.

In another moment the whole street traffic is in full force.

The crowd vanishes as quick and as silently as it came.

The two policemen betake themselves to the next shop, where the apprentice is called upon to brush their clothes.

The continental policeman is the torment of the stranger. The London policeman is the stranger's friend.

If you are in search of an acquaintance, and only know the street where he lives, apply to the policeman on duty in that street, and he will show you the house, or, at least, assist you in your search.

If you lose your way, turn to the first policeman you meet ; he will take charge of you, and direct you.

If you ride in an omnibus without being familiar with the comings and goings of those four-wheeled planets, speak to a policeman, and he will keep you by his side till the "bus" you want comes within hailing distance.

If you should happen to have an amicable dispute with a cabman—and what stranger can escape that infliction ?—you may confidently appeal to the arbitration of a policeman.

If, in the course of your peregrinations, you come to a steamboat wharf, or a railway station, or a theatre, or some public institution, and if you are at a loss how to proceed, pray pour your sorrows into the sympathetic ear of a policeman.

He will direct yourself and baggage ; in a theatre he will assist you in the purchase of a ticket, or, at least, tell you where to apply, and how to proceed.

The London policeman is almost always kind and serviceable.

At night, indeed, he is rather more rough-spoken than in the day-time ; and when you meet and address him in some solitary street, he is reserved, and treats you something akin to suspicion.

Whether or not this remark applies to the force generally, we will not undertake to decide.

But it is quite natural that they should not be altogether at their ease in solitary or disreputable quarters.

A glass of brandy now and then may also contribute to produce the above effect.

But the English climate is damp ; the fog makes its home in the folds of the constable's great coat, and the rain runs from the oil-skin cape that stands the policeman in the stead of an umbrella ; the wind is cold and bleak ; and we leave the policeman on his beat with the " stranger's thanks and the stranger's gratitude."

———

CHAPTER XXXIII.

ANGELINE AND THE RUFFIAN.

RAIN, rain, rain ! Floods of rain are deluging the turf and pathways in St. James's Park, and through the hurtling showers poor cowering wretches slink on to seek what shelter they may beneath the dripping trees, or under the covers of the shrubberies.

It is night.

The great broad face of the lantern clock of Westminster Palace glows dimly through the dank grey mists.

Entering the Mall by the court-yard gates of St. James's Palace, a fair young lady, enveloped in a fluttering mantle, looks anxiously from side to side.

The lamplight falls upon her pallid face, and glints on her golden hair.

Her features are perfect as those of the finest master-piece of statuary ; but oh ! so pale—so marble pale and rigid.

Her arched lips trembled.

The half-frozen tear dims her noble blue eyes.

She shrinks timidly across the broad avenue.

Like a sylph of the mists she glides along under the iron pales of the park enclosure.

At last she pauses ; a visible shudder runs through her delicate frame.

She suppresses a shriek and supports herself by clutching at the iron palings.

Looming through the drear fog the burly form of a man is seen advancing.

The fair young lady recoils from him.

She turns as if to flee.

Then, as if fascinated like a bird by the deadly glamour of a snake's eye, she stands stone still.

The man advances.

He is an evil-looking ruffian, coarsely dressed in a dirty suit of fustian, with a flap-eared fur cap drawn down close over his brutal brow.

He holds out his hand.

" Well met, miss," he growls ; " sorry as it's sich weather for ye to come out in ; if I'd a knowed as the rain were a comin' down so sharp I'd a run over to yer own 'ouse and paid yer a wisit. Never mind, my dear, we can settle our little business in a jiffey, and then I wotes as we goes in somewheres, and, as I'm awful gen'rous—it's my failin'—I'll stand yer a glass o' brandy, hot. Lors, miss, dessay you sometimes thinks me rayther hard, don't ye now ? Well, well ; I am so poor, I am ; and on'y consider if I weren't good-natured, now, what *would* become on ye some black Monday mornin', eh ? Hail, rain or shine, you must go then. Who to meet, eh, my dear ? The Lummy Cove ? No ; some devils is blacker than t'others, and, if you don't like me, I'm 'feared you'd find Mr. Calcraft,

with his 'ily smile, and his horrid, hoary beard and his bald head, a tidy sight wuss ; instead of smoothin' down that bootiful golden hair with his fingers as I does, he'd jes' lift 'em, in a perlite kinder manner, and, with his scissors, sinp, snip, yer know, to make way for the neck orniment, yer know ! Ho, ho ! but they does these things so charitable, bless ye ! Yer may feed, yer last time, like a prince or princess ; they gives yer short, and 'ands yer up the steps of the purty little platform as tender and respectful as if yer were a bride bein' 'anded into a chariot ; and they attends on yer to the last, they even sets the bells of the big church a tollin', and they perwides a diwine to ac' as chapl'in, and, when it comes to the last, it's jes' like a cor'nation, for they puts a kinder white crown on yer nut, and they pulls it down, and down——"

The girl uttered a wild shriek.

The brutal ruffian, whose vile ribaldry fell into her ears like a stream of molten lead, stumbled aside for an instant, for he was in a beastly state of intoxication, and propped himself against the iron rails.

" Here, Miss Angeline, shake hands ; I hadmires yer, I raally does."

The girl shrunk away from him with an insane look.

" Catch hold, gal ! Catch hold, cuss yer, and think yerself honoured as even sich a cove as I will shake hands with a murd——"

Angeline once more uttered a maniacal shriek.

She thrust her hands to her ears, and glared at him with an insane, vacant stare of deadly horror.

" I have not deserved it. No, no ; this will not be permitted, even though I am to be punished for that which I did unwittingly ; an accident is not a crime. I am not a murderess ! I will not touch your hand, strong, cruel, bloody man ! It is you who are the murderer ; fiendish in cruelty, you are driving me mad. Have a care, you prize the money I win so hard for you ; do not drive me to despair or I shall kill myself, and the secret you trade upon will die with me. Yes, you will make me a murderess ; I shall destroy myself."

The girl reels giddily, clutched the iron rails, and dropped her golden brow on her marble-white and quivering hands.

" Strike me dead ! if I'll stand any o' this kinder humbug ! Haccident ? that female poisoned by haccident ? Well, certn'y, it's a case for the coroner, and for a jury o' yer peers to decide. Arter all, I don't think the judge could ever 'ang sich lovliness, 'ceptin' round his own neck, and that's vhere I means to 'ang her—right over my faithful bussum, for I loves yer, Angeliner, blow me if I don't. I means well by yer, too. How much have yer brought ? Twenty quid, ain't it ?"

" Yes, yes ; here it is ; but do pray have mercy on me, I am almost beggared, I am in debt."

" You in debt ?—you in want o' money ?—yah !"

" Oh ! believe me it is all true. You are so extortionate. Sometimes I have scarcely enough money to meet the expenses incidental to my profession : sometimes I am penniless."

" Gammon ! with sich a face is that ?—and sich limbs ?"

" Here—take it. Let me go," cried the girl, fiercely.

" Not till you've guv' me a sweet little kissiwissy, and told me vhen you'll meet me by moonlight alone vonce more, my precious."

The ruffian passed his strong arm round her slender waist, and drew her towards him.

Her great blue eyes flared, her golden tresses broke from their bonds, and fluttered in the driving rain storm.

She fixed her thin fair fingers in his throat, and thrust his head back against the rails.

The prestige of beauty, the passion-power, the force of madness cowed the brutal ruffian, and he shrunk down growling like a hyena in the hunter's grip.

" I am armed !" gasped Angeline, " for my own protection, after your insult at our last meeting. I prepared myself for this. One breath, one movement, and I will drive this dagger blade into your foul throat. Here is your blood-money. At your peril let me go."

Angeline had drawn a poignard from her bosom : she pressed the point to the ruffian's throat.

(To be continued.)

be able to make more than enough to supply you with earth's choicest luxuries."

"Oh, what glorious tidings!" exclaimed St. Leon. "Jasper! Jasper! we shall indeed be princes."

"Yes," said Jasper, throwing his arms above his head. "Yes. What shall stay us in our career of fame, of pleasure, and of exquisite enjoyment? Oh! what a glorious future is open to us. How we shall pass our time now in an endless career of never-failing enjoyment. The days will appear to us but as pleasant hours; the hours will dwindle into mere minutes, and we shall be kept in so continued a whirl of enchantment that we shall have no time to dream of care."

"We shall be courted by all," said St. Leon. "Thousands will bow down before us in acknowledgment of the majesty of wealth."

"And beauty will smile upon us."

"Ay! and——"

"Hold!" said the old man. "Hold! a slight cold—a fall—the merest accident in the world, may place you in your graves. Some envious or malicious beggar may place poison in your cup, and lo, you die!"

"True! true!" said Jasper, as his tone lowered from one of the greatest exultation to a mournful cadence. "I—I did not exactly think of that."

"Nor I," murmured St. Leon.

"I know you did not," said the old man; "but there is a mode of escaping even from such a consummation as that. It may be a mode which neither of you choose to adopt. It is saddled with some conditions. But, then, they are not hard ones. You must both consent to pass out of this mortal life before you can be endowed with that new existence which is eternal."

The young men looked at each other aghast.

"Yes. That is a condition of things," added the stranger, "which brings with it a pang from which, for all I know, you may shrink. What say you now?"

"We—we—would fain hear more," said Jasper, while St. Leon shook his head as if he had heard already quite enough.

"You shall hear more, then. No human power whatever, or supernatural power, short of that possessed by him who gave you your existence, can protract that existence beyond the limits he has set to it."

"Then there is no hope," sighed Jasper.

"Hear me out. There are means of resuscitating the mortal frame, and of bestowing upon it a new vitality after the breath of life which at first has inhabited it has passed away."

"Indeed!"

"Yes. And therefore is it, that, to live for ever, you must pass through the gates of death first. Possibly you may doubt, both of you, if such be the case; but to resolve such a doubt, you have but to take some corpse before it be cold, and before the breath of life has left it many hours, and, by the experiment, you will revive it, although the same causes which led to its death, if they are causes which have destroyed some of the actual animal structure, will again operate in producing death. You two, however, who are both well, will not, after passing through death, be liable to the disorders of humanity."

"And would youth be perpetual?"

"Why, yes; upon renewing every ten years the draught."

"And you spoke of a condition."

"Yes, I did. The condition is this—that every ten years you exchange forms. That is to say, that, let your individual positions in life be what they may, you will meet and exchange personal appearances, each of you bearing the exact likeness of the other."

The young men looked for a moment at each other, as if the condition was not the pleasantest one in the world, which the old man observing, he said to them,

"There is no compulsion in the matter. Take the gift or leave it, as you please, I care not. Perhaps, however, you have not considered yet the many advantages which it would give you. Living for some time, as you have been, apart from the world, you do not know that the most exquisite enjoyments can be commanded by those whose means are sufficiently extended to enable them to purchase them. You have probably forgotten, in this your retirement, some of the delights of that great world which is around you. Just for a few moments fancy yourself in possession of unbounded wealth, and of such a lease of existence as shall with care be endless. What magnificent advantages you will have over every one else. What exceeding powers of enjoyment."

"But that's a very awkward condition," said St. Leon; "and one which is enough to poison the gilt."

"Think you so?"

"Indeed I do. What say you, Jasper?"

"I know not what to say. I know not what to think. Sir," said he to the old man, "how is it that such a condition becomes attached to one of the greatest secrets of alchemy?"

"I cannot tell you. Come, the storm abates. Let me have your answer at once. If you consent, by bestowing upon you a small phial of this liquid I get rid of the debt of gratitude which I owe to you, and am content."

"But, good sir," said St. Leon, "what if in this chamber you had found but one student of alchemy, would your gift then have been tendered without its accompanying condition of the change of forms?"

"True!" said the old man, "your remark is just enough; and the only thing that can relieve either of you, would be voluntarily giving up one of the other of the conditions."

"Can we either of us be killed by mortal means?" said St. Leon.

"Yes. Certainly."

St. Leon appeared to be musing for some seconds, and then he said,

"Jasper, what say you to all this? Speak freely. I will be much guided by your judgment. Shall we embrace this strange gift, or shall we reject it?"

"What sound is that?" said Jasper.

"It is the church bell of the village," replied St. Leon. "Some one has died, and those solemn notes are proclaiming the fact."

The old man rose hastily.

"I cannot stay here all night," he said. "Look here. In this small phial, which has a red aspect, is the means of long life. One drop of it is enough at once to renew the corporeal frame for ten years. In this one, which has a greenish hue, is a subtle liquid, the mere odour of which enables a person to become invisible to mortal eyes. A smart stamp with the left foot will restore the person to a visible appearance again. Here are the gifts. Make what use of them you like. You know the conditions, and you know how to make precious stones, by which you may enrich yourselves to any extent you like. Farewell, we may meet again, but when and where I cannot tell. But be mindful, both of you, you are as liable to death from mortal means as you were before, and in that case the liquid of life would only restore you to give you the pain of enduring a few more troubles, and then dying again."

The old man waited for no reply, but at once quitted the chamber. The sound of that church bell seemed very much to have disturbed him indeed.

The two little bottles he had placed on the top of the furnace before the faces of the young men, and as the fire flickered and danced, now and then receding with an evanescent pale blue flame, the difference of colour in the two liquids, contained in the small bottles, was easily apparent.

The two students remained for some moments exactly in the attitudes they had been left by the old man, and then, when they recovered sufficiently to speak, it was but to utter each the name of his companion.

"Jasper!"

"St. Leon!"

"What—what think you of all this?"

"I am bewildered!"

"And I. Where is the topaz?"

"'Tis here; and I am certain it is of great value."

"There—there then is boundless wealth."

"Yes. And in this small phial is long life and eternal youth."

"And in the other, not the least entertaining and curious gift of invisibility. What a world of delightful adventure does not that power open to us."

"Most true! Most true! But——"

"But what?"

"What, if sudden death, instead of immortality, should come upon us, by taking any portion of this draught. We may be deceived."

"I understand you, Jasper; although that tolling bell so confuses me, that I lose some of your words."

"The casement is open, and the sound is conveyed by the wind most distinctly into this chamber. I will close it, and then we can discourse more freely."

Jasper did so, and the moment he had closed the window he turned suddenly to his companion, as he exclaimed,

"A lucky thought! A lucky thought, St. Leon!"

"What is it?"

"Life has just quitted the body of the being for whom that bell is tolling. Let us hasten to the house of mourning, and test the virtue of the wonderful elixir."

"A good thought, Jasper; and so before we involve ourselves in any danger, we shall be able to come to a judgment with regard to one of the assertions of the strange visitor we have had. If we find him correct in one instance, it will, at all events, be presumptive evidence that he is so in others."

"Come along then, at once."

"Does the storm continue?"

"There is no appearance of it. It is a very strange thing, but the sky is covered with stars, and there is not the least appearance of a storm having taken place, and yet we heard the thunder, and the dashing of the rain against the casement."

Continued from page 72.

THE JOLLY DOGS OF LONDON.

THE JOLLY DOG ENDEAVOURS TO RAISE THE WIND.

CHAPTER XXXIII.—(continued.)

He quailed and kept silence, staring stupidly at her flashing eyes, quite quelled and entirely at her mercy.

But the momentary power that passion lent her vanished away, and Angeline's hand quivered.

In an instant the ruffian recovered his presence of mind, and knew the powerlessness of his victim.

He seized her roughly, snatched the knife from her hand, and hurled her savagely against the rails.

The next moment he was hurled head over heels, and a stately, elegantly-dressed gentleman bestrode his prostrate body.

"Arthur!" shrieked Angeline. "Oh! save me, Arthur!"

The Lummy Cove rolled over on the ground, uttering the most fearful blasphemies.

Angeline clung to her protector's arm.

Aubrey glared with intense, but subdued fury upon the prostrate ruffian.

The Lummy Cove raised himself on his hands and knees.

He looked up into Aubrey's flaming eyes, and snarled like a savage but half-cowed hound.

No. 11.

"Off, you beast!" cried the pretended Aubrey, in a tone of startling fierceness.

The Lummy Cove staggered to his feet.

He recovered his bludgeon, which had fallen to the ground.

He was about to attack Aubrey.

The adventurer, however, was too quick for him, and growling an oath which caused Angeline to recoil with amazement, he seized the burglar by the throat, and dashed his head voilently against the iron railing.

It was well for the Lummy Cove that his skull was of more than ordinary thickness, or his brains would have been dashed out.

Angeline became alarmed for the brute's life, and caught Aubrey's arm and whispered imploringly—

"Release him, Arthur: let go your hold; you will kill him."

Aubrey relinquished his grasp, and though he stood still glaring furiously upon the ruffian, re-adjusted his dainty white wristband which had been ruffled in the encounter.

"P'r'aps, my flash cove," panted the burglar; "p'r'aps you thinks as I'm a goin' to put up with this yere kinder usage; p'r'aps you thinks I'm the sort o' feller to be pitched into by a bloated haristocrat, and take it like a lamb; it's a reg'lar honner, ain't it? Hulloa! jes' let me have a look at yer hansome phizog. Oh! it's *you*, is it?"

He peered curiously into Aubrey's face.

It would have been better for him to have been less curious in scrutinizing the fierce countenance of his opponent, for Aubrey let fly a tremendous blow with his right hand, which sent the burglar reeling backwards.

He reeled giddily for a moment, and then dropped on his knees.

He seemed half stunned.

It was some moments before he could sufficiently collect his shattered faculties so as to stagger to his feet.

With a horrid oath he dashed the blood from his cut cheek.

"You've done for yerself," he hissed savagely; "for all your flash toggery, I know ye, Dick Renshaw; perdooce yer ticket of-leave, you ——— convict; see if I don't gaff on yer, that's all. I'll mark ye and this fine Lady Finikin, as is nothing better nor a ——— murderess. She dances on the stage do she? Bless my eyes if she sharn't dance without music on a hopen-hair platform."

Aubrey looked upon the broad brutal face of the ruffian with a glare of contemptuous defiance, and clubbing his walking stick advanced stiffly towards him.

But the Lummy Cove was vanquished.

He hopped backwards with more agility than could have been expected from one in his half-drunken condition.

"You frowsy blackguard, do you pretend to know me? I am Arthur Aubrey. I know nothing of the man you mention," said the daring adventurer, with thrilling calmness; "but you shall have ample opportunity of proving my identity, for I mean to give you in charge for insulting this lady."

With the growl of a bull-dog the burglar leaped upon him, upraising his dreadful bludgeon.

Aubrey, as agile as a deer, sprang lightly aside.

The burly ruffian blundered on.

Aubrey caught his wrist, and with a powerful, dexterous wrench, snatched the bludgeon from his grasp.

Then striking his knees against the ruffian's sturdy calves, he hurled him over, and brought him once more to the ground.

"Hi, there? Policeman!" he shouted.

Angeline rushed to his side, and wildly clutched his arm.

"No, Arthur, no, for God's sake!" she muttered, in excited tones. "I am in the wretch's power—you will destroy me."

She pulled him away.

"And I am Mike Fanshawe or Ranshawe, am I?" growled the bolder scoundrel to the subdued robber. "An accomplice, I suppose! What do your fellow-blackguards do when you betray them? Is there no punishment for traitors in your beastly gang? Pah! you filthy rough; do you think that because you can bully your own dirty 'pals,' that you can insult and assault a gentleman? With all deference, Miss Lamonde, I *must* give this villain into custody. It is a duty I owe to society. My friend, Mammonson's, office has been broken into, and when I went thither to draw some cash yesterday, I saw this same scoundrel loafing about near the house. I am firmly convinced he had a hand in the robbery; it is plain, too, he has used threats to extort money from you. I swear he shall be locked up. Ho! help, there—police!"

Considering how firmly and resolutely Mr. Aubrey seized the ruffian, it was rather remarkable that he let him escape so easily.

Perhaps this was owing to his yielding to the fervent entreaties of Angeline, who clung to him imploring his forbearance.

At all events the Lummy Cove freed himself after a sharp tussle, and taking to his heels, made off as if a pack of bloodhounds were behind him.

A policeman came up.

"Did you not call for help, sir? Have ye been robbed?" asked the constable.

"No; but this lady has been insulted," returned Mr. Aubrey.

"Ho, indeed, sir! Where is the rascal?"

"He broke away."

"Which way is he gone, sir?" asked the policeman, drawing his staff, and preparing to start in pursuit of the fugitive.

"That way, that way!" half-screamed poor Angeline, pointing in an opposite direction from that the robber had taken. "Through yonder gate."

The policeman darted off in the direction indicated.

Now it happened, somewhat strangely, that Wenlock had appointed to meet the Lummy Cove at the gates of St. James's Palace.

There he paced, his eyes bent on the ground, his umbrella drooping in his hand, though the rain was pouring fast, wrapped in gloomy reverie.

He heard the quick tramp of the policeman's step on the slippery rain-washed pavement.

He turned.

For a moment he stood startled and irresolute.

In the next instant he dashed off.

The policeman sped after and overtook him.

There was a sharp struggle.

The policeman pinned him against the wall.

"Come, it's no use, my fine fellow," said the constable, "you're my prisoner, you'd better take it quiet."

"Is it for—for the—" gasped Wenlock; the word "murder" stuck in his throat.

"For insultin' a lady. Come along, she'll be here in a moment to identify ye."

"This is a mistake, my good fellow," returned Wenlock, recovering his presence of mind, though he still quivered and grew deathly pale.

"If you wasn't guilty, what did you cut and run for? Come, you don't gammon me," said the policeman.

"It's a mistake, I assure you," returned Wenlock, with forced calmness; "take me to this lady, she will exonerate me."

"Come along, then."

They entered the Mall.

But Angeline and her chivalrous defender were nowhere to be found, and the policeman was forced to liberate his prisoner.

CHAPTER XXXIV.

ANGELINE REVEALS A DREADFUL SECRET TO RENSHAW.

MEANWHILE "Arthur Aubrey" and Angeline had hurried off towards the Horse Guards, and passing through the archway, had entered Parliament Street.

Angeline had not spoken.

She clung to her gallant with nervous tenacity.

"Arthur," she whispered faintly, "do not frown so darkly. Oh, if you knew what I have suffered; from what a horror I am vainly struggling to escape! Come home with me, I will tell you my dreadful secret; you will believe me, I know, my dearest Arthur; I am innocent of this awful crime—innocent in intent at least. Oh, I shall go mad!"

"Crime! Angeline, crime!" gasped Aubrey.

"Yes, yes; I dare not name it!" returned the shuddering girl; "but let us get home at once, and I will tell you all. This is no time to stand upon nice points of conventional propriety. At home I shall be safe! Safe? Where am I safe? Oh, that villain will betray me; what he said was true. I draw my breath on sufferance. I am doomed, doomed to a fate that will not bear contemplation."

"Impossible, dearest Angeline! This miscreant has evidently found some means of holding you in a state of terror by affecting a knowledge of——"

"Alas, dearest Arthur, he *does* know my fearful secret! he knows all! I am at his mercy—and the mercies of such a fiend must be cruel. Oh, I am but a frail, timid, young girl. I am no Spartan maid, or my course would be simple and easy. I shudder at the thought of self-murder! but then the grim, chill, awful alternative!"

"Well, dearest, you must tell me all; if you are really in danger, we must find some means of escape: but, if, as I am sure is the case, you are the victim of a foul conspiracy formed by that brutal scoundrel and his associates, for the purpose of extortion, you may rest assured that I will have justice done, and you shall be at once relieved from the horrible incubus which is weighing you down to the grave."

Aubrey called a cab, and handing in the trembling Angeline, bade the cabman drive to her suburban residence.

The girl rested her head against the panel of the vehicle, and closing her fringed lids, sank into a state of semi-insensibility.

More than once Aubrey spoke to her, but she raised her hand feebly, and by faint moaning seemed to deprecate conversation.

Aubrey gazed gloomily upon her pale, but lovely face, and a dark thoughtful look settled on his bent brows.

After a long drive they arrived at the quarter in which the dwelling of the beautiful actress was situated.

Angeline aroused herself.

"Arthur, we will get out here," she said ; "I do not wish the servant to be disturbed. We will enter the house quietly. Lydia is from home. My secret is fit to be whispered only in the dull ear of night ; we must have no eavesdroppers."

Aubrey handed her from the cab.

The driver looked at the handsome young couple with a softened glance.

He mounted the box, and before driving off cast a curious glance at the retreating figures.

"Case of 'lopement, I dessay," he muttered ; "reg'lar swell people they seems. Poor gal, she's a fine creetur and no mistake. Well, it's a rum world, and every 'art knows it's own bitterness, as the parsons says. I should like to know the cause of her grief ; p'r'aps her parients is set agen her lovier. Hiegho! can't afford to be sentimental ; but, blow me, if I don't allers feel for beauty in distress."

The gallant cabby shook the reins and drove off.

Angeline opened the little green door in the garden wall belonging to her little villa, and followed by Renshaw, crossed a neat, smooth-shaven lawn, and entered the house by a glazed door on a verandah.

She ushered Aubrey into a little sitting-room, and having lighted the lamp, left him alone for an instant, while she retired to change her dress, which was soaked with rain.

Aubrey had shaken his cloak in the hall, and he now seated himself in a chair by the table, and buried his face in his hands.

"Oh, this is horrible !" he muttered, half aloud, in his anguish of soul. "And this beautiful and noble-hearted girl is about to confide to me her dreary history. To me !—her lover's murderer !"

The rustle of a dress was heard in the passage.

Angeline entered the room.

She seated herself disconsolately upon a couch, and hid her face in the damask cushion.

Aubrey threw himself by her side, and took her trembling hand in his own.

She shrank from him, and waved him away.

"Do not speak to me," she said, hoarsely ; "do not mock my despair by any fruitless efforts to console me, but listen patiently to my sad, sad story."

Aubrey made no reply, but sat gazing with a sickly smile upon the girl.

Then he started up.

For a few moments he paced the room in a state of intense agitation.

Then he re-seated himself by the side of the half-frantic Angeline, and once more took her hand.

Almost as much moved as herself by the violence of his emotions, he preserved for a long while a deep and conscious silence.

At length he spoke.

"Angeline, after our long parting, is it necessary that we should speak of sorrows that have befallen us in the dark interval of our separation ? Let us rather talk of the joy of our happy re-union, of the bliss the future has in store for us."

These words were spoken in a tone of calmness that was forced and affected. Angeline seemed conscious of the fact,

for she regarded the speaker with a look of surprise almost amounting to alarm.

"You are strangely altered, Arthur," she said, coldly ; "or it may be, you do not believe in the reality of my danger. Well, when I have told my story you shall judge for yourself whether or not I have cause to dread that fearful man."

Aubrey made no reply, but listened with deep interest.

"You remember, Arthur, that when we first met I was living at home with my grandmother—if I can call that wretched abode, which was a place of terrors and miseries, my home. I was at that time studying for the stage, under her severe tutelage. In her youth she had been an actress ; she was one of those remarkable women that are sometimes met with, who seem to set age and distress at defiance ; though she had lived threescore hard years in the very vortex of the stormy world, her form was unbent, her dark hair was but slightly silvered, her fierce, fine black eyes shone with intelligence and fiery passion. She was a woman of great force of character, imperious, I may say savage temper, and of vicious habits ; miserly to a degree, she had managed to save money ; what sum no one ever knew, but it could not have been much that she was able to set apart, her hard earnings were so small. We, that is myself and my cousin Mabel, who both of us became orphans at an early age, were left to her charge. She treated us very harshly ; but I must do her this much justice, she spared no pains to fit us for the different positions she had marked out for us. I was trained for the stage, Mabel educated to become a governess."

"But your grandmother's three daughters, will it not be better to glance at their history, Angeline ?" said Aubrey with some excitement.

"Yes. I will begin with the youngest, Christine, my own mother ; she married Lamonde, the French actor, who was killed at the barricades in the insurrection of '48 ; my poor mother did not long survive him. The second daughter, Edith, married a poor artist, and she and her husband died in great poverty, leaving Mabel to grandmother's care. The eldest daughter's history was long unknown to Mabel and myself, for the name was never mentioned in our presence ; but I have lately discovered that she was older than her sisters, and had long ago married a Virginian planter, who's name was Reginald Aubrey ; and, what is stranger than all, dear Arthur, I have discovered that you are her son, and, consequently, my own first cousin !"

"You amaze me !"

"But it is so, nevertheless ; I am convinced of it, and will show you letters and documents that will put the fact beyond the possibility of doubt."

"Then, dearest Angeline, I am really your near kinsman ?"

"Yes ; and do you not remember, Arthur, when you were first introduced to my grandmother, that she betrayed strange and unaccountable emotion, and, for a wonder, as it seemed to me, did not oppose your love suit, though she had compelled me to refuse the most brilliant offers. I say compelled me to refuse them, Arthur ; but the 'compulsion' she used in the case was of little consequence, as I never loved any one but you ; yet, I am fain to confess, base and selfish as it may sound, I was so cruelly used, so wretched at home, that I would have gladly sought refuge in marriage."

"But her name ?—your grandmother's name ?"

"Why, as of course, you know, was Margaret Herbert."

Aubrey received this announcement with a bewildered stare.

"Yes, yes ; go on," he cried, excitedly.

"Before I proceed with that part of the sad story which affects myself, I must tell you of a strange report that came to my knowledge, the truth of which, however, I will not vouch for. You were born in England, as you know, and it seems, Arthur, that you had a twin-brother, who was stolen away by my grandmother, but for what motive does not appear."

"God of justice !" murmured the guilty wretch, burying his face in his palsied hands.

"This brother is not dead ; they say he lived with grandmother as an adopted foundling ; but being a wild and wilful lad, ran away from home. This happened before I or Mabel were born. Rumour says that he took to evil courses, and even that he outraged the laws, and was transported; but you must not put too much stress upon this strange story; for my own part I don't credit one word of it."

"Margaret Herbert! It must be so; the stranger was my brother!" gasped Aubrey.

There was a long pause.

Angeline was about to continue her story.

Aubrey caught her wrist, and asked, in an eager, hoarse voice,

"Tell me—this brother; by what name was he known?"

"By the name of Renshaw."

"Is it possible?"

"Have you met him, then?"

"Never, never!"

"Heavens! how very strange! Why, Arthur, the miscreant from whose insults you defended me this very night, called you by that name, declared you to be an escaped convict, and threatened to betray you. He has doubtless seen your outcast brother, who must closely resemble you in features; and now I think of it, that night at Cremorne, a rude, ill-dressed fellow——"

"We will recur to this subject anon; now for your fatal secret, Angeline," interrupted Aubrey, with a ghastly smile.

"Yes, I am coming to that," returned the poor girl, with a deep sigh. "Imagine, then, all her daughters dead, Margaret Herbert the guardian of her two grandchildren—myself and hapless Mabel. It is of Mabel I am about to speak. She, as I told you, became a governess, and was engaged in the family of the old Earl of Lindenwold. The eldest son, the heir, fell in love with his sisters' lovely tutoress, and married her secretly. She resigned her situation, and lived in seclusion, visited from time to time by her high-born husband. The old earl was a proud and hard-hearted man, who, if he had known of his son's *mésalliance*, would have disinherited him, as far as his personal wealth, which was great, might be concerned, so Lord Lindenwold kept his marriage a dead secret; and when his wife was about to become a mother he had her removed to our house. Neither I nor my grandmother, you must note, were aware, at that time, that Mabel was really married to the young lord."

"Did he visit her often? Was he kind and devoted to the poor girl?"

"Alas! far otherwise. He treated her with cruel neglect; no doubt he had repented his hasty marriage with the poor girl. He had bound her by an oath not to reveal the truth to any one, and she kept her vow to the last."

"Well."

"One day, while poor Mabel was very ill, there came to our house a strange-looking gentleman. He appeared to be a lawyer, stated that his name was Vincent, that he had come from Lord Lindenwold, and that he wished to be alone with Mabel for awhile. We left him with her, and when he retired I entered her room to find her face suffused with radiant smiles; she seemed half wild with joy, and said that all would be well, and that she had received the kindest message from Lord Lindenwold. She showed me a packet, which she said she would be at liberty to unseal when her child was born; and that its contents would bring the sunshine of gladness even to our wretched, poverty-stricken home. Mabel had many little mementoes of her cherished husband—one, that she specially prized, was a faded wreath of white roses, which she had worn at a rustic fête some time previous to her marriage with young Lord Lindenwold. It was quite withered and falling to decay, and, in order to preserve it, I persuaded her to let me sew up the sere petals in a little bag of silken network. She kept the little satchel on her pillow, and would often bedew it with tears, press it to her lips, or inhale its lasting fragrance. On the day of the lawyer's visit, it lay, as usual, upon the bedside, and after his departure, when the poor girl had wearied herself out with talking, I noticed, while I was busying about her room, that when she kissed it more than once her eyes seemed to glitter with unnatural brilliance, her cheeks flushed with a hectic glow, and she reclined heavily backwards, and soon sank into a deep, trance-like sleep. Judging her to be exhausted by the excitement through which she had passed, I drew close the window-curtains, picked up the packet which had fallen from her hand and locked it in my box, for I did not wish my grandmother to find it; then, softly shutting the door behind me, I crept from the room."

Angeline paused in her recital, burst into tears, and wrung her hands in silent despair.

Many moments elapsed before she could proceed.

At length she recommenced, in a quivering tone,

"I little thought, when I left my poor cousin to all appearance calmly sleeping, that I should never behold her waking—never hear her dear voice again. I went below; my grandmother was in a bitter mood. She asked if the lawyer had brought any money for Mabel's use. I gave her a few sovereigns which he had left. She snatched them eagerly, reviling Lord Lindenwold for his meanness in sending such a paltry sum, and cursing poor Mabel for the shame and trouble which she had brought upon our house. Then she carried off her prize, for she appropriated every farthing that was sent for Mabel to her own room, which she never suffered us to enter."

"The cursed old hag!" muttered Aubrey.

"I was about to return to my cousin's bedside, when I was startled by a loud knock at the door. The lawyer once more stood before me. I thought he looked pale and agitated. He was not alone. A tall, dark man, who, he said, was a doctor, was with him. I was not much surprised at seeing him, for Mabel had told me of Lord Lindenwold's promise to send his own physician to attend her. As I was closing the street door, I observed a rough-looking fellow sauntering on the opposite side of the way. He was the same ruffian whom you encountered last night."

"Phew! the Lummy Cove!" muttered Aubrey.

"Mr. Vincent! for so the lawyer styled himself, enquired if he and the physician could be permitted to see Mabel. I told them that the poor girl was in a deep sleep, and that it would be wrong to wake her; however, as they were urgent in their request to be brought to her, I retired to see if she were still sleeping. When I peeped into her room, I found her still sunk in the same trance-like slumber. I returned, and told the two gentlemen the result of my visit to her chamber; the physician rose, and expressing a desire to see her as she slept, I conducted him to her room."

Again Angeline paused, as if overcome by a terrible reminiscence.

"Mabel was sunk in no gentle sleep; her's was a death-like swoon, from which, with all our efforts, we could not arouse her. I rushed wildly down stairs. I found the lawyer deep in conversation with my grandmother, whom I observed at the moment I entered to thrust hurriedly into her bosom something which appeared to be a pocket-book. She and Mr. Vincent accompanied me to Mabel's room. The poor girl was apparently lifeless; but the doctor insisted that she should be at once removed to his house; that the trance was the effect of exhaustion of the powers of nature, and that the patient would require a course of treatment such as she could not obtain in this house. He said he would take her to his own home, and tend her there. He handed his card to my grandmother, who, to my horror and surprise, at once agreed to this arrangement; and when I protested, menaced me into silence by her fierce looks, for I held her in mortal dread. I pleaded that, at least, I might be allowed to accompany my poor cousin. To this the physician readily consented; but Mr. Vincent and my grandmother said that it would be better for me to remain behind, to pack up and bring away a few necessaries for the patient, with her clothes and letters. Before my grandmother's blasting glance I was powerless, bewildered. I suffered them to carry off my darling, and then, being left alone, I implored Heaven's direction in this terrible emergency. Ah! why were my prayers unanswered? She was gone—gone like a lamb to the wolf's lair. I saw her again no more!*"

Angeline resumed,

* This incident is founded upon a fact which occurred some years ago in France.

" I packed up the few clothes, trinkets, letters, and the like, belonging to my sister, hurrying as fast as possible ; for I was dying with suspense and the agony of evil presentiment. As I removed the little satchel of rose-leaves from my own box to hers, I noticed that it was impregnated with a strange, sickly odour, which induced a feeling of faintness and irrepressible languor. I felt quite giddy, and almost fell to the ground. My grandmother at the moment burst open the door ; she wore her bonnet and cloak, and told me that she was going out on business, and forbade me with threats to tell any one what had happened to Mabel. I asked her for the card on which the physician's address was written, that I might hasten at once to my sister. She said that to-morrow would be time enough ; and though I tried to detain her, she left the house and did not return till the evening of the next day, when she told me that she had visited the house of the physician, and that she had learned that Mabel was dead. My horror may be conceived, and it was increased when my grandmother told me that orders had been given that Mabel should be buried quietly, and that none of her family should attend the funeral."

" What a monster this old woman must have been !" cried Aubrey. " Can you imagine what could have been her motive for lending herself to such an infernal plot ? Mabel, no doubt, was murdered !"

" Yes ; murdered—poisoned by those rose-leaves,"murmured Angeline, through her white lips. " My grandmother, in her youth, had been a woman of vile and violent passions ; her husband deserted her for sufficient reasons, they say. He was wrecked on his passage to America. In her old age she became as malignant as an old Indian squaw or an African Obi woman. She thought of nothing but money, and God forbid my uncharity ; but unless I tell you all the truth, Arthur, my story is nothing. I believe that she would have sold both me and Mabel, body and soul, for gold, dear gold ! Well, I must come to the catastrophe : within a week of poor Mabel's death, my grandmother broke up our home, and removed to a distant part of the town, and despite my utmost efforts, I could never find out whither poor Mabel had been carried, and under what circumstances she had died."

" But the packet, Angeline ; the papers that had been sent to Mabel. Did you not open them ?"

" I did, Arthur."

" And their contents ?"

" They contained a roll of bank notes, but not a line, not a word in writing."

" Did the old harpy get possession of them ?"

" No ; she was not aware that Mabel had received them. On the night preceding the day of our flitting from the old house, my grandmother left me alone ; two men called, one of them was William Saunders, the man you saw last night ; his companion said he was a detective, and produced a warrant authorising him to search the house ; he said that a suspicion had arisen that my sister had been poisoned, and that he was commissioned to make enquiries prior to her body being exhumed for medical examination. I asked him where my sister had died, the circumstances of her death, where she had been buried ; he would tell me nothing. He searched my boxes, the little satchel of rose leaves were fond ; he declared they had been poisoned, and charged me with having administered poison to my sister ; he found the money also, and said that my motive for perpetrating the fatal deed was clear. But, worse than all, in my work-box was found a packet, which I had not placed there, which I had never seen before, and which he declared to be a deadly poison. I was bewildered, maddened ; I had rashly placed the rose leaves to my lips, and was in a state of indescribable apathy. I scarce knew what I said or did. The detective declared that it was his duty to take me into custody, and that I must at once prepare myself to accompany him to a magistrate. Saunders took me aside, said that he pitied my youth and would do what he could to save me ; he added that poor Mabel's money was a good round sum, and that the officer would, no doubt, accept it as hush-money, if I would make the proffer of it to him. Half-dead with terror, half-stupefied by the poison I had inhaled, I did so ; he then told me that before he could get change for so many notes, he must have

my signature to a certain paper. I wrote it blindly—I signed I knew not what !"

" Angeline, is it possible that you could be duped by such a shallow plot !"

" Had I been in possession of my senses I should not have done so ; but, as I tell you Arthur, I was maddened by the poison I had inhaled !"

" And the detective took all the money ?"

" He took it all ; the men both left with many cautions, accompanied by threats, that I should never divulge what had passed between us on that fatal night ; he exacted an oath from me that I would preserve the dreadful secret, an oath which I have never broken till now. I fled from home. In my agony and desperation I could no longer bear my grandmother's tyranny ; we quarrelled and parted ; what has become of her I know not."

" And the Lummy—hem ! Saunders, I conjecture, paid you another visit to intimidate you, to extort more money from you ?"

" He did. It was soon after my engagement at the theatre, where I made my *debût* with such success. I was at that time courted, flattered, and I think respected by a crowd of friends. As an actress I was earning fame, and fame's guerdon—gold. When he came he brought with him the paper I had signed in my delirium."

" And that, Angeline——"

" Was—*my confession of my cousin's murder !*"

" Good God !"

" Since then I have been his slave—his abject, miserable slave ! I have lived in constant dread of him. He has visited me from time to time, and he has come when I have least expected him. For his sake, that is, to purchase his forbearance, I have struggled and toiled ; for him I have been a heartless coquette, cold, cruel, and rapacious, all to find gold to insure his silence and mercy. Sometimes I have thought to defy him, to trust my case to a jury. But many have perished innocently. It is the curse of the criminal procedure of our boastful country that, like all mere human institutions, it is fallible. If right were might, if innocence were always a sure safeguard, then I would bid this miscreant defiance ; but should I stand the test, and then—ah, God !"

The wretched girl dropped her head upon the cushion of the couch, and a violent shudder convulsed her delicate frame.

She started up wildly, and caught Aubrey's hand.

" Tell me, dearest Arthur, tell me truly ; set all scruple aside. We live but a day, but if that day is one of insupportable misery, what harm — what crime to shorten its agonies ? Tell me, could you forgive me if I sought refuge in self-dealt death ? How else can I escape this monster ? Damning proof overwhelms me, and his forbearance lasts only so long as I can pay for it ; a short time, for my health and energies are failing fast. Oh, shall I die ?"

" Hear me, Angeline," said Aubrey, hoarsely ; " I will not underrate the difficulty of your position, yet it is rather delicate than dangerous. I am not one to promise more than I am able to perform ; I can, I will save you from the effects of your indiscretion in allowing yourself to be intimidated by these base and clumsy schemes. I can, I repeat it, and I will, but it must be on one condition."

" Yes, dearest Arthur ; speak. Surely I have learned prudence bitterly," said Angeline, drooping her head on his shoulder.

Aubrey grew sick with horror, and gently disengaging himself from her embrace, and drawing himself away.

Angeline glanced at him, and wailed her utter anguish.

" Arthur, do you not believe that I am guiltless ? Have I told my dreadful story in vain ?"

" No, no, dearest Angeline," he replied, faintly ; " it is I who am guilty, it is I who have a secret far more terrible than yours which you have confided to me. I will save you from the persecution of these miscreants ; but you must never, never speak to me of the past—of—of love. I am not what you take me to be ; I am what I dare not acknowledge myself even to my own heart. When the worst is known to you, you must think of me with what charity you may, and— but I will break off—I dare not speak more lest I should betray myself, even to you. I am gone, Angeline; think of me as of one dead; forget me! forget me! Neither approach me, nor speak to me; I dare not even bless you from my lips, the words would be profanation. Away!"

The guilty wretch shrank from contact with the pure and beautiful girl, who had thrown herself imploringly at his feet.

He cast a wild and haggard look upon her upraised wondering face, and rushed from her presence.

Angeline stood petrified.

She raised her hand to her throbbing brow.

"It must be a dream!" she murmured. "I walk in my sleep! Was Arthur here? Did I reveal my dreadful secret to him? and did he doubt me, reject me, flee me, as if the taint of blood were on me? Oh! this worse than the worst! He upbraided himself. Why? What has he done? There was something strange in his voice. I am bewildered—mad, perhaps! Ah, me, what wonder?"

Angeline sank upon the couch and fainted away.

— —

CHAPTER XXXV.

LIFE IN LONDON STREETS—DANDY JACK AND WENLOCK'S WALK THROUGH DRURY LANE.

DANDY JACK and Wenlock are wending their way through the slums of Drury Lane in their way to the burglar's den.

Let us extract a few graphic sketches of the neighbourhood through which they are passing.

In Drury Lane the deadly sins which revel in more aristocratic neighbourhoods do not use paint, and scorn to use the blandishments of seduction.

Their names are Poverty, Drink, and Dirt.

In the Strand, just opposite to the majestic Somerset House, and half hidden by the railings of the churchyard, which encroaches upon the natural dimensions of the street, there is a narrow passage which turns up into Drury Lane.

That lane, though of unequal breadth, is always narrow, and numberless are the blind alleys, courts, and passages on either side.

The first and second floors of the high and narrow houses shelter evidently a class of small tradesmen and mechanics, who, in other countries, would pass as "respectable," while here they work for the merest necessaries of life, and, like their customers, live from hand to mouth.

A few of them are usurers, preying upon poverty, coining gold from its vices and morbid longings.

As for the garrets of those houses, we would not for the world answer for the comfort of their inhabitants.

All the lower floors are let out as shops, in which are displayed dingy dresses and other articles of female ornament, coarse eatables, cheap and nasty literature, shockingly illustrated; thick-soled shoes, old clothes, awful cigars—all at very low prices.

But the gin-palaces are the lions of Drury Lane; they stand in conspicuous positions, at the corners and crossings of the various intersecting streets.

They may be seen from afar, and are the light-houses which guide the thirsty "sweater" on the road to ruin.

For they are resplendent with plate glass and gilt cornices.

On the walls of each establishment you are are informed in green letters that here they sell "The only Real Brandy in London," and a set of scarlet letters announces to the world that in this house they sell "The Famous Cordial Medicated Gin, which is so highly recommended by the Faculty."

Cream gin, honey gin, old Tom, sparkling ale, genuine porter, and other words calculated utterly to confound a teetotaller, are painted up in conspicuous characters, even so that they cover the door-posts.

It is a remarkable fact that often the houses which are most splendid from without appear most dismal and comfortless from within.

The landlord is locked up behind his "bar," a snug place enough, with painted casks and a fire and an arm-chair; but the guests stand in front of the bar in a narrow, dirty place,

exposed to the draught of the door, which is continually opening and shutting.

Now and then an old barrel flung in a corner serves as a seat.

But, nevertheless, the "palace" is always crowded with guests, who, standing, staggering, crouching or lying down, groaning and cursing, drink and forget.

On sober working days, and in tolerable weather, there is nothing to strike the uninitiated in Drury Lane.

Many a capital of a small German country is worse paved and lighted.

Nor is misery so conspicious and staring in this quarter as in St. Giles's, Saffron Hill, and other "back slums" of London.

But at certain bestial periods, misery oozes out of all its pores, like Mississippi mud. Saturday and Monday nights, and Sunday after church time, those are the times when Drury Lane appears in full characteristic glory.

A Sunday afternoon in Drury Lane is enough to make the cheerfulest splenetic, for the Lord's day is to the poor labourer a day of penance or dissipation.

The cotton frock, or fustian jacket, are scared away from the churches and the parks, by their respectful awe of rich toilettes and splendid liveries.

The poor man in England is ashamed of his rags; he has no idea of arranging them into a graceful *draperie*, in the manner of the Spanish or Italian Lazarone, who devoutly believe that begging is an honest trade.

Even the lowest among the low in England are proud enough to avoid the society of a higher caste, though that superiority consists but in half a degree.

They consort with persons of their own stamp, among whom they walk with their heads erect.

Church and park have, moreover, no charms for the blunted senses of the over-worked and under-fed artizan.

He is too weak and fatigued to think of an excursion into the country.

Steamers, omnibus, or the rail, are too expensive.

His church, his park, his club, his theatre, his place of refuge from the smell of the sewers that infect his dwelling—his sole place of relaxation—is the gin-palace.

To provide against the Sunday, he takes a supply of fire-water on Saturday evening, when he has received his week's wages, for with the stroke of twelve the Sabbath shuts the door of all public-houses, and on Sunday morning the beer or brandy paradise must not open before one o'clock in the afternoon, to be closed again from three to five.

Hence that unsacred stillness which weighs down upon Drury Lane on Sunday mornings.

The majority of the inhabitants sleep away their intoxication or *ennui*.

Old time-worn maudlinness reigns supreme in the few faces which peer from the half-opened street-doors; maudlinness pervades the half-sleepy groups which surround the public-house at noon to be ready for the opening; chronic maudlinness pervades the atmosphere.

If a stray ray of light breaks through the clouds it falls upon the frowsy loungers, and the dim window-panes in a strange manner, as though it had no business there.

It is Saturday night, and the orgies of Drury Lane have commenced.

A dense fog, with a deep, red-colouring, from the reflection of numberless gas jets, and the pavement flooded with mud.

A fitful illumination, according to the strength of the gas, which flares forth in long jets from the butchers' shops, while less illumined parts are lost in the gloomy twilight.

If your nerves are delicate, you had better not pass too close to the gin-shops, for, as the door opens—and those doors are always opening—you are overwhelmed with the pestilent fumes of gin.

The pavements are crowded.

Slatternly servants, with baskets, hurry to the butchers' and grocers', and haunters of the coffee-houses of Drury Lane elbow their way through the very midst of the population, the sweepings of humanity.

A wicked world this; but the only one fit for those forms of woe and livid faces, in which hunger contends with thirst and vice with disease.

What subjects for Hogarth on the narrow space of a couple of flag-stones !

How ravenous the craving which flashes from the eyes of that gray-haired woman, as she drags a slight, yellow-haired girl, perhaps her own child, to the gin-shop !

The little girl follows in a dumb, wondering way ; but her small slight hand is shut with an anxious grasp, as though she feared to lose her weekly earnings—the wages, perhaps, of hard work, or still harder beggary.

She stumbles at the threshold, and almost falls over a couple of children that are crouching on the ground, shivering with cold, and waiting for their father within.

The father comes staggering and kicking the air, with manifest danger to his equilibrium, and cursing awfully.

The kick was meant for his wife, a thin woman, with hollow, yellow cheeks, whose long, serpent-like curls, are covered with an old silk bonnet, while her stockingless feet are contained in large slippers.

She counts five copper pence in her bony hand, looks at her drunken husband and the fatal door, and at the costermonger's cart in the middle of the street, and she counts her pence and re-counts them, and cannot come to the end of them, though they are but five.

The large oysters in the dirty cart excite her appetite.

Which is it to be ?

The public-house or a lot of oysters ?

" Penny a lot, oysters !" shouts the man, as he moves his cart forward.

A dozen greedy eyes watch his movements.

Similar groups are met at every step.

At the door of almost every gin-shop you see drunken women, many of them with children in their arms ; and wherever you go, amidst the confused noise and murmur of many voices, you hear distinctly the most awful oaths.

It is not at all necessary to repeat these oaths.

Let it suffice, that one of these, beginning with a B, startled our ears a hundred times at least during our walk through Drury Lane.

And now let us enter that temple of art—a penny theatre ! We pass through a low door and enter a kind of antechamber, where we pay a penny each.

A buffet with soda-water, lemonade, apples, and cakes is surrounded by a crowd of thinly-clad factory girls, and a youthful cavalier is shooting at a target with a cross-bow, and after each shot he throws a farthing on the buffet.

Passing through the ante-chamber and a narrow corridor, we enter the pit of the penny theatre, a place capable of holding fifty persons.

There are also galleries ; a dozen of wooden benches rise in amphitheatrical fashion up to the ceiling, and, strange to say, the gentlemen sit on one side and the ladies on the other.

This separation of the sexes is owing to a great refinement of feeling.

The gentlemen, chiefly labourers and apprentices, luxuriate during the representation in the aroma of their " Pickwicks," a weed of which we can assure our readers that it is not to be found in Havanna.

But they are gallant enough to keep the only window in the house wide open.

Just as we enter we see the director, a small curly-headed man, with a red punch face, ascending the stage by means of a ladder.

He makes two low bows, one for the ladies and one for the gentlemen, and delivers himself of a grand oration, to excuse some small deficiencies in his institution. At every third word he is interrupted by the cheers and remarks of his audience.

" Ladies and gentlemen," says he, " I am sorry I cannot produce a prima donna to-night. Jenny Lind has sent me a message by the submarine telegraph, asking for an extension of her leave. You would not surely shorten the honey-moon of the nightingale? Why, to do that, would be as bad as cruelty to animals. Madame Grisi tells me, quite in confidence, that she is falling off, and that though her voice is good enough for Yankee ears, she wants the courage to make her appearance at No. 17, Broad Street, London. Madlle. Wagner was at my service, cheap as any stale mackerel ; but could I insult you by producing her ? Would not every note have reminded you of the fact that she values nothing in England but the copper pence? Besides the terms of friendship which subsists between myself and Mr. Lumley, there are other considerations. I hope you'll understand me, ladies and gentlemen !"

" Question ! question !"

" Maybe you are astonished that these boards are uncarpeted, and that no painted curtain displays its glories to your eyes ?"

A voice from the gallery,

" At your uncle's, eh ?"

Another voice,

" Nonsense ! His wife has turned the stuff into a petticoat."

" How little you understand me, ladies and gentlemen ; it is but decent that our stage should lament the death of the Great Premier—"

Interruption.

" No fast place !"

" Don't you try to be funny, old feller !"

Blasphemy !

Groans !

" Ladies and gentlemen, pray listen to me. Let all be serene between us. I have nothing to conceal. Ladies and gentlemen, the overture is about to commence !"

The speaker vanishes through a trap-door, through which two fellows presently ascend.

One is dressed up to represent an Irishman, the other wears the characteristic habiliments of a Scotch Highlander.

They play some national airs, and while thus engaged, strip themselves of every particle of their outer clothing, and appear as American planters.

Some one from below hands up a couple of straw hats which they clap on their heads, and the metamorphosis is complete.

They then go to the back of the stage, and return with an unfortunate " African."

The part is acted by no less a personage than the director himself.

His face is blackened, he has a woolly wig on his head, and heavy chains on his wrists and ankles ; and to prevent all misunderstanding, there is pinned upon his waistcoat an enormous placard with the magic words " Uncle Tom."

The planters produce, meanwhile, a couple of stout whips, which instruments of torture they use in a very unceremonious manner in belabouring the back of the sable protégé of the Duchess of Sutherland and the women of England generally.

All of a sudden that illustrious negro exclaimed, " Liber-r-r-ty ! Liber-r-r-ty !"

He breaks his fetters, and turning round with great deliberation descends into the pit.

Exeunt the two planters, each with a somersault.

Transformation :—The forms issue from the back door ; a colossal female, with a trident and a diadem of gilt paper, bearing the legend " Britannia ;" after her, a pot-bellied old gentleman, with a red nose and a spoon in his right hand, while in his left he holds an enormous soup-plate, with a turtle painted on the back of it.

Britannia, heaving a deep sigh, sits down on a stool, adjusts a telescope, which is very long and dirty, and looks out upon the ocean.

The gentleman with the red nose, who of course represents the Lord Mayor of the good City of London, kneels down at her feet, and indulges in a fit of very significant howlings and gnashings of teeth.

The third person is a sailor-boy complete, with a sou'-wester, blue jacket, and wide trousers, who dances a hornpipe, while Britannia sighs and the Lord Mayor howls.

Now comes the great scene of the evening !

Somebody or something or other diving from up the very centre of the pit, makes a rush against the stage.

(To be continued.)

"We did indeed. I feel a strange sense of bewilderment, which probably the open air will remove. Come along, Jasper, and bring with you the phial; this night may be the most important one in our existence."

"It must be."

Jasper took the phial which contained the elixir of life with him, the other one he placed carefully on one of the shelves in the turret-chamber, and then the two young men slowly descended the narrow and intricate staircase; and crossing the lower rooms of the mansion, they soon emerged into the gardens, and then proceeded at a rapid pace towards the village.

CHAPTER V.

THE HOUSE OF DEATH—THE RESUSCITATION.

It was a great relief to St. Leon to feel the cool fresh open air, after inhaling, for so many hours as he had, the hot stagnant atmosphere of that small turret-chamber, impregnated as it was with the deleterious vapour of the burning charcoal, and the many strange chemical compounds which those ambitious young men were in the habit of using. Not even the intense excitement, which might well be supposed to arise from the singular circumstances that had recently occurred, could produce such a degree of mental enjoyment as came over the mind of St. Leon; he drew himself up, and expanded his chest as he breathed more freely, feeling, as he did so, sensations of youth and health, to which within that turret-chamber he was a stranger.

"Jasper," said St. Leon, "I almost tremble at the rush of mingled thoughts and sensations that now beset me! Should we obtain full proof, in the experiment we are about to try, of the truth of those words spoken to us by the stranger, what a glorious future opens before us!"

"True!" said Jasper, "true! and hark! St. Leon, how solemnly the bell still tolls for the departed soul! St. Leon, tell me truly, as we now proceed, what your own impression is concerning him who visited us in the turret-chamber."

"I almost dread to think," said St. Leon, in a low tone; "he said there was a storm without, but we see no indications of its presence."

"And yet, in our chamber, we heard the rushing of the wind, and the wild dashing of the rain!"

"We did, indeed! and at the moment I fancied the very turret shook again with the blast."

"And I, and I;—but no matter; I am not one to be deterred by foolish fears from grasping at the good which I may be enabled to see. I am not one, St. Leon, who would reject for idle superstition sake the benefits which may result from that science in which we, tyros as we are, have achieved one such glorious result. But, hush! we are now in the village; let us immediately seek the house of death."

There were evident signs of confusion among these villagers, and lights flashed from house to house, and even if the solemn bell had not announced the fact, any one might well have supposed that death had been busy, and had taken from that small community of persons surely one of its most valued members.

The students passed on until they saw an old dame leaning over the low hatch of her door, and apparently at leisure for anybody's questioning.

They approached the woman, to whom Jasper said,

"Mother, what is amiss? There appears to be consternation on every face we meet."

"Ah," said the woman, with a slight chuckle, "and well there may be. Death is an impartial guest. He has passed the cottage doors of the aged, the poor, and the helpless; he has gone by those whom nobody would mourn—for whom, perhaps, yon passing-bell would not toll; and he has taken away the pride of her beauty, the young, and the loved."

"Indeed! and at what house has this calamity occurred?"

"There," said the old woman, as she pointed to one of the cottages; "there, there lies the corpse, the still warm corpse of the hope and pride of those who are now weeping. 'Twould be worth your while to go and look upon her while the flush of beauty yet lingers on her cheek. I have been, for I was young once, and there are those now in the cold grave who have called me beautiful. Look at me now."

"In truth, good mother," said Jasper, "you are strangely altered, or those who called you beautiful looked upon you with too partial eyes. Come on, St. Leon; come on."

"Now curses on you both," said the old beldame, as the students passed on; "curses on you both; but I might have been sure of that; a smile and a well-turned compliment for the young; but a gibe for the old. Yes, yes; I might have been sure of that; but I can curse now, that is a consolation."

She shook her gaunt arm after the young men, and screamed a malediction on them which they did not hear, and which, if they had heard, they would not have heeded.

They passed on towards the house which they had indicated, and from which they distinctly heard the sounds of lamentation.

"The bitterness of grief is here," said St. Leon; "what if we could retain the life we expect to restore?"

"You forget," said Jasper, "we may call back, by means of the subtle fluid contained in this small phial, the wandering spirit of its earthly tenement; but the same cause that produced the death in the first instance will again operate."

"True, true; let us enter the house."

The scene within that small dwelling was an appalling one. In the first room in which they entered was the whole family, with the exception of that one member of it who now lay in the chill arms of death. The utmost agony of woe was upon every countenance; it seemed as if that stern blow of fate had destroyed for them the world and all its enjoyments.

There is something in such grief that commands respect. The students walked stealthily, and each took off his hat, as if in mute acknowledgment of the majesty of death.

Silently one of the family pointed to a narrow staircase; the students understood the mute invitation, and in their own minds congratulating themselves upon the ease with which their experiment could be tried, they noiselessly ascended to the room above.

The door was partially open, and a faint glimmering light came out upon the landing. They spoke not, but passed into the chamber of the dead. It was a small room, but the very spirit of neatness and cleanliness pervaded it. On a humble bed, the snow white hangings of which were scarcely paler than the cheek of her who lay in death beneath them, reposed the corpse.

It was that of a young girl who had scarcely numbered sixteen summers; she was beautiful—most beautiful even in death; decay's offensive fingers had not yet

"Marr'd the lines where beauty lingers."

She seemed but slumbering—and one could almost fancy that some gentle breath of life yet lingered between those slightly parted lips.

Jasper laid his hand upon her brow.

"St. Leon," he said, "it is icy cold."

St. Leon trembled.

"Quick, quick," he said, "let us do that which we have to do; we may be interrupted. Have you the phial?"

"Yes, hush!—I thought I heard some one move below. I will keep watch at the chamber-door, while you place in her mouth one drop of that divine elixir."

"Be still—be still; you speak too loud. Will you not stay by the bed-side, and look upon the result? Do you shrink now, St. Leon?"

"No, no, but I am sure they must be listening below. I do not hear the sounds of grief."

"Then is there no time to lose."

At the head and foot of the corpse burnt candles, whose long unsnuffed wicks cast a melancholy glare on the face of the dead. Some salt, too, and twigs of rosemary were on the breast; the hands were crossed as if in devout supplication; upon the closed eyes were placed two silver coins. Jasper knelt beside the couch—there was a slight tremor even about his frame as he produced the mysterious little phial, and removed from it its tight-fitting glass stopper. St. Leon's hands were clasped with the most painful tension, and he stood in such an attitude of intense expectancy, that an actor would have been delighted to catch it for imitation. Not a sound disturbed the serenity of the silence that reigned around; it seemed as if the whole world had paused in its millions of actions and emotions, while that magnificent experiment was about to be performed.

One drop from the bottle fell between the parted lips of the dead—a convulsion shook the limbs, and such a cry of anguish filled the air with horror, that Jasper even staggered from the couch with an answering shout of dismay, and St. Leon placed his hands over his ears, and he cried frantically,

"Heaven help us now! Heaven help us now!"

The young girl sprung half from the couch, dashing down the spectral looking candles that were at the bed's head.

"Fly," said Jasper, "fly, St. Leon! this is too terrific!"

St. Leon rushed to the stairhead, but he was seized in the nervous grasp of a young athletic man, who shook him as though he had been but a child, as he exclaimed—

"Villain! monster! disturber of the sanctity of death, what horrible profanation is this?"

"D———n!" said Jasper, and he rushed to the rescue of St. Leon.

In the next instant, locked in each other's grasp, the whole three rolled down the narrow staircase into the room below.

THE JOLLY DOGS OF LONDON.

THE JOLLY DOG HAS A DAMPER PUT ON HIS PLEASURES.

CHAPTER XXXV.—(*continued.*)

It is the Uncle Tom of the last scene; but surely even her Grace of Sutherland would not know him again.

His face is as black, and his hair is as woolly as ever, but a cocked hat, a pair of red trousers and top boots, and an enormous sword, brings it home even to the dullest understanding that this is a very dangerous person.

Besides, on his back is a placard with the inscription, " Soulouque—Napoleon—Emperor !"

The monster bawls out "Invasion !" ·

Then, to the great delight of the ladies and gentlemen, he bumps his head several times against the chalky cliffs of Britain, which, on the present emergency, are represented by the wooden planks of the stage.

The very sailor-boy dancing the hornpipe shows his contempt for so much dulness and ferocity.

He greets the invader with a scornful " Parli vow Frenchi ?"

At this juncture the conqueror becomes aware of the presence of the short ladder, and mounts it forthwith.

The boy vents his feelings of horror and disgust in an ex-

No. 12.

pressive pantomime ; the Lord Mayor howls louder than and the gnashing of teeth is awful to behold.

Just as the invader has gained the edge of the stage he is attacked by the sailor, who, applying his foot to a part of the Frenchman's body which shall be nameless, kicks that warrior back into the pit.

The public cheer.

Britannia and the Lord Mayor dance a polka.

The sailor sings " God save the Queen !"

Woe to the "entente cordiale" if the French ambassador could know of this ; alas ! for the liberties of old England.

The fog has vanished in Drury Lane, for about midnight the London sky is usually clear ; the moon looks out from behind the steeple of St. Mary's church in the Strand, and at each street corner stands a policeman, he being on the look-out.

Dandy Jack and Edgar Wenlock are stopped in their progress by a dense crowd, surrounding a couple of Irishwomen, who are settling a "little difficulty" of their own.

Ragged little boys stand in dangerous proximity urging

them on, and making very laudable exertions to procure for the street the gratification of a "real fight," for hitherto the two amazons have used their tongues rather than their fists, and indulge in an interchange of choice epithets, one of which, the foulest, is repeated with extreme volubility an incredible number of times.

"You've got no pluck, you old daughter of a dog; that's what you hasn't!" shouts a little imp of a fellow, jumping right between them and splashing all the bystanders.

With bursts of laughter and many curses the crowd disperses down the street, and follows a stretcher, carried by two policemen, who have just issued from a dark gateway.

On the stretcher, her head and legs hanging down, is a tall, consumptive-looking girl, with her loosened hair sweeping down like a black veil.

"They're taking her to the station-house," says a woman, with a pipe and a strong Irish accent, "taking her to the station-house for the blessed dthrop that is such a stranger in her throat. Poor Poll! belave me, gintlemin, it's only hunger has made her drunk—only hunger!"

Through all the various sounds of yells, groans, and curses is heard at the distance the inharmonious concert of two barrel organs, one of which is grinding a woeful caricature of the Marsellaise, while the other, addressing itself to the human family generally, informs them with an awful screech, that "There's a good time coming, boys," which cheering intelligence is in the end qualified by the growl, "Wait a little longer."

A few yards on a beggar-boy, with naked feet, and with an almost naked back, has taken up his post where the mud is deepest in the road, and sings with a thin, small voice, "Ye banks and braes of bonnie Doon."

Nobody cares for him, for the public are attracted by two artists who are performing in the next street.

They are brothers, by their looks, and work together.

The younger, a tiny boy, with an aged face, taxes the ingenuity of the public by conundrums, whose chief characteristic is that they are always political or smutty.

He shouts them out—they are too indecent for publication—in a tone which would do honour to a trained schoolmaster.

While the public are trying to find the answer the elder brother imitates the songs and voices of birds and beasts.

They all give it up.

The little boy shouts the answer, with a most indecent wink at some females.

And the songs of birds and voices of beasts are again imitated, and conundrums of a still grosser description propounded and explained, and the hat goes round and comes back with a few pence and half-pence in it.

And this classic soil!

All of a sudden the lights are put out in the gin-palaces, the barrel-organs are silent, the howling and cursing shrinks into a hoarse murmur.

The multitude disperse gradually, like muddy water which runs through the gutters, and is lost underground.

The street is all silent and lonely.

Only one tall figure comes with rapid and noiseless steps out of one of the alleys.

It looks round in every direction.

It steps up to our two pedestrians, and looks at them with staring, glassy eyes.

It is not the spirit of midnight, nor is it a ghost, but neither is it a form of flesh and blood, for it is all skin and bones.

And the clear light of the harvest moon displays a half-starved woman, with an infant on her arm, to whom her bony hand is a hard death-bed.

For some minutes she stares at the strangers.

Wenlock puts some silver into her hand.

Without any remark or thanks, she turns round and walks slowly away.

St. Mary's clock tolls one!

CHAPTER XXXVI.

THE LUMMY COVE AND HIS CONFEDERATES PREPARE FOR A BURGLARY.

THE Lummy Cove was leaning from the window of his squalid den.

He was on the watch for his confederates.

Unusual quiet prevailed in the foul, packed court where the burglar dwelt.

The broad, bright, golden moon, looked calmly down from the deep blue sky, flooding the filthy pavement and the festering walls with her pure radiance.

The burglar seemed to be in an evil mood.

He was smoking a short black pipe, which, ever and anon, he removed from his mouth to give vent to an explosion of savage oaths.

His face still bore the traces of his encounter with Aubrey, his cheek was blackened and swollen, and his forehead swathed and plastered.

By his side on the window-sill stood a little black bottle of brandy, which he put to his lips at very frequent intervals.

An old Jew glided into the court, and looking up to the window at which the Lummy Cove was taking his ease, made a peculiar sign with his hand.

The burglar leered, and nodded his bullet-head.

He then descended, and opened the street door.

"Vell, have yer brought him?" he asked, in a surly tone.

"Yesh, ma tear, brought 'em bothsh. O! shtrike me! if he isn't the cleverish poy that ever worked on a plant. Von of my besht cushtomersh."

"Is Bob with 'im?"

"Yesh, my poy. Black Bob. They're outside the court. 'Feared you might be out, you know. Didn't want to show themshelves for nothing."

"Bring 'em in."

The Jew grinned, and displayed his yellow fangs.

He went off to the little blind alley that led into the court, and presently returned followed by two sturdy fellows dressed in suits of fustian, and carrying heavy club sticks in their hands.

One of these worthies was a very savage-looking ruffian with black eyes and hair, and a complexion as dark as a mulatto's.

He had an ugly gash on his lip, which gave his face a peculiar and sinister expression.

His companion was a sturdy, sullen-faced, swarthy man, with a keen, grey, restless eye.

"Vell, my pal, how goes it?" asked the Lummy Cove, gruffly saluting Black Bob.

"D——d bad."

"Vhy, what's hup?"

"Nothin' doin'," grunted the other. "There's been a smash in the gang. Some of the leary coves in the Dials has been gaffed on and shopped; been forced to keep out of daylight myself."

"Vell, that's all in the day's vork, my pal. To day hup and to-morrow down, von month in and t'other out; but come under kiver."

The burglar led the way down into his dirty lair, and his three guests seated themselves.

The Lummy Cove produced the inevitable brandy bottle, and handed it round.

"Petter luck, my poysh," said the Jew, wiping the mouth of the bottle with the cuff of his greasy sleeve.

"So this is the new cove, eh?" asked the burglar, scrutinising Black Bob's companion.

"Yes; and a clever 'and, though I says it afore him. Ve calls him Sam Short, a'cos he's so short-spoken."

"Ha! that's a good quality that is. Vell, my pal, are you on for this 'ere plant at the jeweller's?"

"Yes."

"Think yer compertent ?"

"Yes."

"Ha !"

"Bless yer heyes, Bill, he's up to everythink."

"That's right. Ever served time ?"

"Yes."

"Vhere ?"

"Pentonville."

"Ho !"

"How long ?"

"Six stretch."

"Phew ! Got a ticket ?"

"Yes."

"Ah ! that's bad !"

"Yes."

"Crushers down ye ?"

"No."

"Vell, the screws allers were dead nuts on me ; but I've managed to bilk 'em so far. I say, now, this yere plant as Bob told ye on is a thundering good lay, there's about fifteen thousand pounds' worth of swag. What say to that, old cove ?"

"Plummy !"

"Ain't it ? Well, now, you look here ?"

"Well ?"

"I don't want no ——— blow-up on this plant."

"Course not."

"No, I don't."

"Nor I neither."

"It'd corst me a fifteen stretch !"

"I should be lagged for life."

"'Spose so ?"

"Yes."

"And there's another consideration as has a great inflooence with me."

"What's that ?"

"Vhy, yer see, I've done purty well lately, do ye mark ?"

"Glad to hear it."

"Yes ; purty well."

"In what line ?"

"Ax no questions, you'll be told no lies !"

"Right, my pal."

"Smash my heyes, if you ain't a rum 'un !"

"Think so?"

"Rayther. Is yer name Short ?"

"Yes."

"And you're Short by name and short by natur'."

"Well, as I were a sayin', I've done a purty good thing lately, and I intends to strike off."

"Give up the lay ?"

"Yes ; I means to retire."

"What to do ?"

"Vell, I think as I shall emigrate to Amiriky or Australey, and take a public."

"Allers a payin' game."

"Jes' so."

"And now, my fine fellers, let's come to business," said Black Bob. "How many on us are there in this plant ?"

"Four on us—us three and Dandy Jack."

"Too many," said Mr. Short.

"Ah, well, p'raps so," returned the Lummy Cove, scratching his head ; "on'y, yer see, it's a heavy job !"

"In course we all goes reg'lars ?" said Bob. "No two ways about that."

"And who's to act capt'in ?" Bob asked.

"Why, cuss it all, who fust proposed the job ? Who's been head director of our firm goin' on a twelvemonth ?"

"Why, cert'ny, you have, Lummy."

"Vell, then, vat do yer vant a change of ministry for ?"

"Oh, ve're satisfied."

"Werry well, then ; no jaw !"

"Oh ! it's all the same to me, on'y———"

"On'y what ?"

"Dandy Jack———"

"What of him ?"

"He knows the plant ; vonce lived on the premises."

"'Struth ! vot o' that ? He can hact as guide, but I don't go out of hoffice for no hopposition whatsumever."

"Well, we'll put it to the vote."

"Cuss the wotes ! I appeals to the nation if I arn't allers done my dooty ?"

"Shwelp me, thatsh right ; there ain't a petter hand than the Lummy to pe found, he dosh honner to his perfessionsh !" said the Jew.

"Well said, old son of Israel ; but, I say, Abrams, vot about these 'ere flimsies ?"

"Shtrike me the shoft ish never vorth a cush ; I shall have to shend all down into the countrish."

"Humph ! how much will yer put down, then ?"

"Three per shent ; too mush. Shtrike me, it is my failin' to deal too liberalsh ; but you're old cushtomersh———"

"Liberal ! Don't yer think that this yere old wulture orter be scragged, Mr. Short ?"

"Yes."

"Don't you never let me hear you mention sich a word as 'three per cent,' old hawk ; I von't take a mag less than twenty, and vouldn't take that on'y I can purty well afford it, and don't vant no kinder row atwixt us, 'cos, I tells yer, arter this plant is polished off I means to make tracks for a furrin country. But the clock's a strikin' von ; I expects Dandy Jack and a friend here d'rectly, so you'd better make yerself scarce, old Houndsditch."

"Pery goot, my tear poy," said the Jew, rising.

"I've interdooshed my novish according to the promish I made ye ; you'll find him a perfect shentleman, I've no doubtsh. Versh shall ve meet ?"

"At the 'Fighting Cocks ;' to-morrer, p.m. ten thirty," returned the Lummy Cove, with a grin.

"Pery goot, pery goot ; I vish you good-night, shentlemen.' And the old Hebrew shuffled out of the kitchen.

He had not been gone long when Dandy Jack and Edgar Wenlock arrived.

The former was dressed in a workman's suit, while the latter was wrapped in a large and shabby great coat.

They were received cordially by the Lummy Cove, who stirred up the fire which was roaring half up the chimney, although the night was close and sultry ; he produced another flask of brandy and drew up a rude settle to the table.

He then crossed the room, opened the door, looked out to see that there were no listeners, re-closed and locked it, and then took his seat at the head of the table.

"Now, my hon'ble fren's, ve'd better at vonce go into committee of vays and means," said the burglar, with a leer.

The men seated themselves at the table.

"Pipes round," said the Lummy Cove, refilling his little black cutty and blowing a dense cloud.

Mr. Short and Black Bob imitated his example, and Dandy Jack lighted a fragrant cigar.

As for Wenlock he drew off to the end of the table, and, leaning his pallid cheek on his hand, fixed an uneasy look upon Mr. Short who sat next him.

The Lummy Cove noticed this.

"Make yerself comfortable, my tulip," he said, with a sneer, "you're among fren's and pals, and I can tell yer that yer'll find that there ain't 'arf the black treach'ry in yer present spere as there were in the vorld you've descended from."

Wenlock tried to look indignant, but failed miserably ; a look of unutterable shame and self-abasement setting on his handsome features.

The burglar grinned with insolent malice.

"First and foremost, Jack," said the Lummy Cove, "how about that 'ere last little affair? Did yer succeed in gettin' this feller Grant in a line ?"

"To perfection!" returned the swindler, rubbing his hands and chuckling. "Our talented friend here——"

"Mr. Wenlock?"

"Yes—but no names!"

"Yah! it's afore the public in all the papers."

"Well, then, our gifted friend here, managed the books most cleverly; all the 'cooking,' is found to have been in Grant's department; and another intimate friend of mine, with a queer penchant for mending broken windows, contrived with admirable skill to slip certain cheques and documents into the very pockets of the poor scape-goat, into the cupboard of his room, into his desk—ha! ha! ha!"

"The d——d fellow, how I hate him! I never feel spite but I make any sacrifice to gratify it. To feed fat a grudge is a feast to my soul!"

Mr. Short puffed away at his short pipe, and appeared to be the only uninterested person of this pleasant story.

"Is the cove committed?" asked Black Bob.

"No," returned Dandy Jack, "but he will be, and convicted, too, as safe as Newgate. His fancy gal has been to visit him."

"Who is she?"

"The famous dancer, Lydia St. Clare."

"My heye! And who has charge of the case?"

"Which of the crushers, you mean?"

"In course."

"Inspector Pounce."

"Phew! He's the cove to make a case," said Black Bob.

"Vell, I don't know so much about that," dissented the Lummy. "You remember that gal as were tried for murder; he got her off."

"That's true," said Dandy Jack, with a start.

"Yes," rejoined the Lummy Cove, in an oracular tone, "that 'ere hinspector is a hexception."

"How so?"

"Why, Jack, yer see as he *will* have his man. But that don't satisfy him."

"What more does he want?"

"He will have the *right* man; nothing else will suit him."

"I wish we could trap the infernal bloodhound."

"So do I, Jack; he's a dangerous dog. I were bit by him once. Squelch me, if I wouldn't slit his throat if I'd got the chance!"

"I seconds yer good intentions," added the Lummy Cove. "I on'y wish as we had 'im here now; he's allers goin' about in disguises, and they say he b'longs to more than one leary gang—reg'lar downy peach he is, and no mistake; ain't he, Mr. Short?"

"Yes."

"Right you are, my son; he orter be put down, what say?"

"Who's to do it?"

"Ah, there it is. Do you know him?"

"Yes."

"Did yer know him when you was in the jug?"

"Yes."

"Lors; seen him since yer come out?"

"Often."

"Does he know yer?"

"A little."

"Has he been yer enemy?"

"Yes."

"He's a feller yer loves, I know."

"Yes."

"Ho—ho; you wouldn't like to have the shavin' of him?"

"Yes, I'd like to do that job myself."

"I dare say you would; vell, his time 'll come; I've got my eye on 'im."

"Which eye?"

This allusion to the Lummy Cove's visual defect—for it will be remembered he was one-eyed—caused a general laugh.

"Well, he's one of the wustest of his clarss," said Black Bob, "'cos he been lagged hisself."

"The devil he has!" cried Dandy Jack.

"Yes; don't yer know?"

"No, I don't."

"Why, 'is name ain't Pounce at all."

"What is it then?"

"Joe Curtis."

"Who was he?"

"Lord Lindenwold's coachman."

"And how did he get flummexed?"

"He were charged with robbery."

"And convicted?"

"Yes, to ten stretch."

"Oh, crickey; and did he get a ticket?"

"Do ye think they'd have a ticket of leave in the force?"

"How was it then?"

"His 'doctor,' Lawyer Lynx—you know the cove—got him off; proved a clear halibi."

"Ho! that was it."

"Yes, and Her Majesty graciously pardoned him for bein' innercent."

"How werry gracious."

"And constitootinal."

"Warn't it?"

"Thank ye for nothin', as the sayin' is."

"Well, I should like to catch him, that's all," grumbled the Lummy Cove. "And so yer think, Master Jack, that you've 'fixed,' the quill-driver to rights?"

"No fear."

"Got plenty o' witnesses?"

"Want one more."

"Ha!"

"Yes; the prisoner spent the night that the robbery took place at the 'Fighting Cocks.'"

"Can he prove that?"

"No."

"Why not?"

"That very night he had a round with the Bethnal Big 'Un, and licked him out of time; the poor 'pug' was carried off to the 'Fighting Cocks' in a state of insensibility. Grant left his friend and went to look after his defeated man."

"What a S'maritan!" chuckled the Lummy.

"What a fool rather; the Big 'Un was put to bed in a little room in the first floor; there was a dog fight on that night, and nobody cared to look after the chap, and Grant spent the night in the Big 'Un's room. I've given the landlord and the barman the tip to swear that Grant left the house before it was closed."

"What do you want more than that?"

"I want the Big 'Un's evidence."

"Want him to swear to the same story as the cove of the ken?"

"Exactly so."

"Have you seen him about it?"

"Not yet."

"Think he will swear as you wants him to?"

"Why shouldn't he?"

"Cert'n'y, why not?"

"I'm sure he will."

"Cock sure?"

"Yes, Bill, of course he will; wouldn't you?"

"For a consideration."

"That's understood. I'll offer him twenty quid, and double it rather than lose my point."

"It's a case for poor Grant, then; he's in for it."

"Yes, he has done the Big 'Un a mortal injury, and the 'pug' will have the chance of clearing scores with him, and doing a good thing for himself."

"Done him a mortal injury? How's that? Has he broke his ribs, then?"

"No, but he's smashed up his reputation."

"Oh!"

"Destroyed his reputation for ever."

"Is that all?"

"All? You may well say all! Don't you see it? The

Bethnal Pet has been thrashed by an amateur; he was backed to fight Bos Hammers, but after this shameful defeat by an outsider not one of his backers will lay a stiver on him."

"That's werry evident."

"Yes, he's a ruined man. Grant was the cause of his ruin. Do you think that he won't take his revenge, especially when that revenge, for a wonder, is profitable to himself?"

"As I said afore, Grant is a gone coon. But now let us return to the subjec'—the plant—as we're met to arrange."

"Hear, hear!"

"Where is it?" asked Mr. Short.

"In the Lothbury."

"Orkard."

"Yes, it's a delicate plant, and wants proper treatment," returned the Lummy Cove. "But, my heyes, it'll make our fortun's. There's nothin' but what'll go into the pot at once, 'ceptin' the watches, and they're so easy altered and re-numbered. Abrams has got a fust-class engineer."

"What firm is it?"

"Hall, Marks & Co."

"Everythink they stamps is gen'wine."

"Yes; there's no bouncing about them."

"Here's their health."

"Yes, fill up, gentlemen."

"We're all in the lay?" asked Black Bob.

"Yes, 'ceptin' my friend Wenlock, and he's trustworthy; our hinterests is one. I drinks to you, Mr. Wenlock," said the Lummy Cove, with a leer.

"If you wish it, I'll leave the place while you settle this business—I would rather. I can meet you, Jack, to-morrow night at the 'Jolly Dogs' club; I would rather not be present at this council."

"Bosh! sit down, man; it will be settled presently."

The robbers then proceeded to make their plans for the intended robbery.

It will be needless to detail their elaborate schemes, and we will, therefore, pass over the consultation, which lasted nearly an hour.

At its close the robbers left their seats, took up their hats and bludgeons, and departed, all but Dandy Jack and Wenlock, who lingered on the threshold to exchange a few parting words with their respectable host.

"The blunt is all safe, my ben cove," said Dandy Jack, "and if this plant turns out well, we shall be able to pay for a fust cabin passage to the New World, where we can enjoy the fortune we have won so manfully. I say, Bill, there's a question I would ask ye."

"Speak up, my sportive kiddy."

"Who is that Short?"

"One of the fly."

"Who introduced him?"

"Abrams."

"I don't trust that old fence."

"Oh, he knows his book. It's all right."

"I hope so. What the devil have you done to your face?"

The Lummy Cove burst into a paroxysm of rage and blasphemy.

"Look ye here, Dandy Jack," cried he, "if you're a feller as never forgits or forgives a injury, here's me o' the same kidney. Some infernal gilt-cove pitched into me last night in the park. I were drunk, and he had the adwantage; but I means to take my time, never fear; I'll wreak my vengeance. I'll have his blood!"

"Who was he?"

"A flash swell."

"A mobsman?"

"As likes as not; he were for all the world like Dick Renshaw, who broke the jug."

"I shouldn't wonder if it were the American—young Aubrey, who lately joined the Jolly Dogs. Was he richly dressed, with a soldier-like bearing?"

"He were."

"And why did he attack you?"

"That's my business."

"Were you sweet on his tatler or fawney?"

"No, that ain't my line. I scorns the moochin' lay. I'm a honest, respectable cracksman."

"Renshaw. I wonder, Bill, what became of that fellow?"

"So do I."

"Hulloa, Neddy, the old fit returning; you're quaking again like a school-girl at a meeting of spirit-rappers. Take a drain, man. I'm disgusted at such weakness! Blood and hounds! the clock is striking three. Let us be going."

Meanwhile, Mr. Short had parted from Black Bob at the corner of Wellington Street.

He was plodding thoughtfully westwards, muttering to himself.

A man passed him.

"Good night, inspector."

Mr. Short started from his reverie.

"Egad, I didn't see ye, Dogget."

"Any orders for me, sir?"

"Yes; you know where the Lummy Cove lives?"

"Yes, sir."

"Watch his house."

"Very good, sir."

"And there's an old fence—Abrams; know him?"

"In Slime Alley?"

"That's the man. Set one of the division to keep a sharp look-out in that quarter."

"Yes, sir."

"And send a man to the policeman on the beat on the right side of the Lothbury. The Lummy and Black Bob have laid a plant at Hall, Marks & Co., the jewellers."

"Is that to come off to-night, sir?"

"No; but tell the constable on duty there to keep a watch on the premises."

"Anything further?"

"No. Good night."

"Good night, inspector."

It was early morning, and the summer sun was shining brightly, when Mr. Short reached Chelsea, where his home was situated.

He opened the door with a latch-key and entered.

All was quiet.

The clock in the parlour was ticking.

A huge bloodhound came bounding down the passage.

The police officer patted the noble head of the lion-like brute, and then motioned him back to the mat on which he had been sleeping.

Obedient to the gesture, the magnificent animal crouched down on his bed, but watched the man with a sagacious look, as he softly mounted the stairs.

Mr. Short paused at the first landing and listened.

He then secretly opened the door.

On a bed in the centre of the room lay the pale, emaciated form of a sick man, as motionless as if life had left it.

"He sleeps better now," muttered the detective, as he carefully reclosed the door. "His reason is returning—he will soon be able to take charge of his own affairs. Meanwhile, they might be in worse hands, I fancy; yet I shall be glad when mine are clear of them—and that will be soon I hope. Gentleman Dick's game is nearly played out! Well, I have done a good day's work, and if I can capture the Lummy Cove and his gang my fortune is made. They are the most desperate set of ruffians in the town, and every one of them once belonged to the same gang as those unheard-of scoundrels that robbed and nearly murdered the poor gentleman in Aldersgate Street. But I'll to bed."

As our readers may not be acquainted with the details of this extraordinary case, in which some of the Lummy Cove's associates were concerned, and which occurred a few years ago, we lay before them the report which appeared in the papers at the time when the occurrence took place.

Mr. Cureton, of the British Museum, was robbed and nearly murdered in an extraordinary manner on the 20th September.

Mr. Cureton lodges on the second floor of a house in Aldersgate Street. In the afternoon three men, fashionably dressed, inquired for him in the lower part of the house, and were directed to go upstairs; they did so, and in about a quarter of an hour descended, and left the place.

A few minutes later a Mrs. Wilson took some milk for Mr. Cureton's tea, and on entering his room she found him extended on the floor insensible, his face quite black, and blood flowing from a wound in his forehead.

Seven hours elapsed before Mr. Cureton was restored to consciousness. He then intimated that he had been robbed.

It seems that the three men pretended that they wished to purchase a crown-piece of William and Mary. Mr. Cureton showed them one. While two of the gang were inspecting it, the third stood by the door, probably watching if any one ascended the stairs.

Mr. Cureton turned to ask him to be seated; at that instant an instrument was pressed round his throat, depriving him of all power, and he was struck a violent blow over the right eye which made him fall senseless; then it appears the villains ransacked the place, carrying off a watch, a diamond pin, a box of cigars, and old coins worth from £300 to £400 as antiques, but not so many shillings if melted down for silver.

It is supposed that the vice in which Mr. Cureton's neck was grasped was formed of two "life-preservers" tied together at one end.

Fortunately the villains missed the most valuable articles, having overlooked a number of gold coins while sweeping away the silver ones. Two rewards were offered for their conviction—£50 by government and £50 by Mr. Cureton.

On the 2nd October the police produced Henry Denham, a rough-looking young man, at the Mansion House, and charged him with having been concerned in the robbery and outrage. It seems that this person is a thief, and has been convicted, and the police had received information that he was one of the robbers.

Mrs. Wilson, who lives in the house where Mr. Cureton lodges, and who admitted the three men on the 20th of September, stated that she could not swear to the prisoner, but she believed that he was the last of the three who entered the house.

The noise of the violence and robbery had attracted the attention of Mrs. Edwards, who lives in the first floor, and as Mr. Cureton was usually very quiet, she went to speak to Mrs. Wilson about the noise, but could not find her. Mrs. Edwards saw the three ruffians descend the stairs; but, unfortunately, did not particularly notice them.

Denham protested his innocence, and said he was an outpatient at St. Thomas's Hospital at the time of the robbery. He was remanded and brought up for further examination on the 9th, when he was again remanded for the production of additional evidence, and the magistrate directed him to be placed in the infirmary, as he complained of illness.

While he was being removed, the magistrate was informed that a gentleman was in court who had recognised him as one of a gang who made an attack on him similar to that which had been made on Mr. Cureton.

The prisoner was again placed at the bar, and a gentleman presented himself in a state of great agitation.

He stated that his name was Thomas Miller, a colourman in Long Acre; that about a month ago an attempt was made to rob him as he was returning home about midnight; he was seized by three or four men, who caught him round the throat with an instrument like a walking-stick, made of gut or some pliable substance; he felt suffocated, and was thrown with violence on the kerb-stone, one of his teeth being broken and his chin severely hurt.

Alderman Gibbs: Look at the prisoner at the bar, and say whether you know anything about him?

Witness: I have no hesitation in saying that the prisoner is one of those who attacked me. I have a recollection of his face from the strong reflection from the gas lamp upon it. My recollection was so strong that the moment I looked at him at the bar I was almost ready to sink.

The Prisoner: Oh, Lord! Oh, Lord! how wicked!

Alderman Gibbs: Do you apprehend that he was the man who put the instrument round your neck?

Witness: I do.

Alderman Gibbs: Did you lose any property?

Witness: No; my pockets were tightly buttoned up. I struggled, and struck one of my assailants, I think I must have marked his face with my knuckles.

Alderman Gibbs: How many were at you, to the best of your belief?

Witness: I believe there were three at me, and that one was on the look out. When I was assaulted, it was a quarter past twelve o'clock to a moment.

The Prisoner: Oh, it's a cruel thing—a most cruel thing. No sooner does one charge fail than another wicked charge is brought on. Oh, I was not out of my bed at the time he speaks of. I was seriously ill at the time, and I can prove it.

Witness: I wish to see the prisoner with his hat on his head.

The prisoner put on his hat.

Witness (having looked steadfastly at the prisoner): I cannot alter my opinion as to his identity.

The Prisoner: It was only a few moments ago I had my solicitor here. Why was not this charge brought forward in his presence? Oh, you may as well hang a dog as give him a bad name. I know nothing at all about these wicked charges.

The prisoner was then removed from the bar.

On the 16th Denham was re-examined, and committed on the charge of assailing Mr. Miller.

———

CHAPTER XXXVII.

JAMES GIMP AND SELINA SPARKS AT HIGHBURY BARN.

MR. JAMES GIMP and Selina Sparks are standing on the dancing platform in the illuminated gardens at Highbury Barn.

It is a grand gala night, and there is a gay assemblage of fair women and brave men.

The youthful pair are dressed in the height of the prevailing fashions.

They appear to be in buoyant spirits, and intent upon thoroughly enjoying themselves.

There was a sound of revelry by night, and England's capital—at least that part of it known as the populous district of Islington—had gathered there her beauty and her chivalry, and bright lamps shone on fair women and brave men.

Music arose—"But halt!" cries the discerning reader, "that horse is not yours; get down from Pegasus, and continue your own limping foot pace."

The quadrille is over, and the crowd of gallants and their ladies fair are promenading the platform, or whispering beneath the waving trees that respond to their soft sighs of sighing softs.

Then—yes then—music arose with its voluptuous swell; said voluptuous swell the leader of the band, who takes his place with an air of imposing grace and dignity, and waves aloft his magic wand. Crash! And once more the dancers are whirling round.

(*To be continued.*)

CHAPTER VI.

THE ATTACK ON THE MOAT-HOUSE, AND THE ESCAPE OF THE STUDENTS.

FORTUNATELY for the students, their opponent was more stunned than they by the fall down the narrow staircase; indeed, this young man was half rendered insensible; and, but for the fact that the mother of the dead girl had rushed screaming for help into the village, they might have escaped.

"Help, help!" screamed the old woman! "help, neighbours, help! they are spiriting away the dead, they are desecrating the chamber of death, and our daughter is being plagued by the evil spirits that are conjured up! Help! help!"

The old woman's cries soon brought out the majority of the neighbours, the sole inhabitants of the village, and as each cottage door was flung open, a broad red glare from the interior spread itself across the road, and threw the figures that darkened the doorway into strong relief.

Every one was anxious at the import of those strange sounds coming so clear and strong upon the night air. They disturbed the peasant who sat by the fire on the hearth, and causing him to start as the sound of distress—that piercing scream—that shrill cry for help came suddenly on his ear.

It was such an hour, too, when the villagers were all within doors, and all going out had been done for the night. Their discourse, too, was all upon death—the death that had taken place in the little community—so well known to them all, that it seemed as though the attack had been made upon the lives of one of their own families.

"Help, help!" screamed the old woman, as she held her hands aloft; "help, neighbours, they would bear away the dead, or do some devilish deed to her who lies a corpse up those stairs!"

"D———n!" reiterated Jasper, "rise, St. Leon, or that old beldame will rouse half the hinds of the village upon us. Be quick! be quick!"

"I am ready," replied St. Leon; "now for the door, and then for the old moat-house. I fear that will be the only shelter for us."

"And lucky if it prove effectual. Push on—push on, and escape while the play is good."

They both rushed to the door, as a number of persons came up, exclaiming,

"Well, dame, what is the matter?—what's amiss, dame, what is amiss?"

"Those men have been in the chamber of the dead, desecrating the remains of her who once lived, and whom I love. Now, hasten to avenge yourselves upon them!"

"Aye, aye, dame, we'll have them well ducked in the pond; and if they don't deserve it, why, they'll soon show it, and sink in the water."

The two students endeavoured to escape from the house, but they were frustrated in their attempt by several persons, both male and female, all of whom believed that some dreadful outrage had been committed, but they could not tell precisely what it could be.

"Out upon you, spawn of the evil one!" exclaimed the old woman, "out upon you! Cannot you let our dead rest in peace? Cannot even the departed soul seek the realms of paradise, but you must put some necromantic horror upon us? Veng-ance! vengeance!"

With a loud shout, the people ran upon the two young men, who endeavoured, by a sudden dash, to pass through the midst of them.

Indeed, there was no other mode of getting off, for people came from all sides alike, and there was but an example required to set them all on the students at once.

The coup, however, was foiled; for the very attempt was productive of immediate violence; and then commenced a serious and murderous assault upon them.

One man had seized Jasper by the throat, while a virago was about to deprive him of his hair; but, drawing his sword, St. Leon cried out to the man,

"Release your hold!"

"When he's ducked in the horse-pond, and you—or maybe, hung to a tree."

"Yes, hang them! hang them!" cried several voices at once.

St. Leon, seeing that Jasper was not in danger of being dragged away, but in danger of being choked, cried,

"Then, if you will have it, take it at the sword's point!" and by a desperate effort he shook off those who were endeavouring to bring him down, and, making a plunge at the man who held him, the sword passed through him below the armpits, and stopped only when the hilt struck against the ribs of the man, who instantly relaxed his hold with a loud and sudden "Oh!"

Jasper, feeling his throat freed from the rude grasp that had pressed it so strongly, now got himself from the female by a very ungallant salute upon the bridge of her nose.

A thousand lights danced before her eyes, and she relaxed her hold.

As the wounded man fell to the ground there was a general pause; the event was so unexpected that they all stood mute and still.

"Quick! quick!" said Jasper, in a husky voice, to St. Leon, "hasten—fly! fly!"

They immediately made a rush to get out of the village, and had done so but for an unlucky incident.

St. Leon and Jasper were exerting themselves to the utmost in rapid flight when they encountered some old cart or waggon, that had been placed on one side of the road.

Coming with great force against this, they were both flung back into the road; and before they could recover themselves they could hear a mighty scream and shout.

"After them—the murderers! after them—seize them, and kill them! After them! destroy them, the murderers!"

And then the sounds of footsteps coming forward upon the hard road were heard, and ere they had again dashed forward the peasants were hard upon them.

St. Leon and Jasper ran with all the speed they were master of towards the moat-house, but the peasants gained upon them, and St. Leon found himself so closely pressed that he could not escape being seized, and the next moment he heard the peasant exclaim, close by his head,

"Villain! murderer! you shall not escape: but blood for blood!"

As he spoke, he aimed a tremendous blow at St. Leon's head.

It missed it aim; had it not done so, he had been stunned beyond recovery; but as it was, he felt a tremendous blow on the back part of his shoulders, that caused him to spring forward with a shout.

Jasper turned round, and saw the fellow about to repeat the blow, when he drew his sword and pinked him on the arm, just enough to cause a pause in his career.

These little interruptions gave time for the more later portion of the pursuers to come up, but the students again started forward. Now, however, they were assaulted by sticks and stones, which were thrown after them, and every now and then they felt a blow in this manner from hands that could not otherwise reach them.

Thus it was that St. Leon and Jasper had more than once been nearly beaten to the ground, and every now and then they were compelled to skirmish with the foremost of the mob—for such it was—of men and women, who came on resolutely with shouts and screams in pursuit of the students.

They could hear their sanguinary and bloody threats—their stern determination dreadfully expressed by their perseverance, and full did Jasper and St. Leon know what they had to expect should accident place them in the hands of the infuriated villagers, who were close to their heels.

"We must get clear, St. Leon," said Jasper, "or die! There will be no mercy shown us."

"None, none! I know full well we must die fighting, or a death of torture! Curses on the gift, say I! 'Tis death, not life, it brings to us!"

"You know not that till the issue; but hasten to yon stile, we may make a stand there against these men."

"These infuriated demons, rather."

"Yes."

They now reached the end of a lane, and, though closely pressed, yet they contrived to cross the stile, and place themselves at the other side.

"Now," exclaimed Jasper, "make this good for a time, at least. My brain reels, and ——"

He could say no more, for on came the villagers, rushing and cursing as they came.

"Down with the murderers!" exclaimed one.

"Kill! destroy the necromancers!" cried another. "There won't be a cottage in the village that won't be visited by misfortune before morning if you don't. Destroy the vile spawn of Satan!"

They now made a rush at the stile; this the young men defended with their swords, inflicting many serious wounds upon those who, in the fury of the moment, dared to attack them. But they soon found, by the groans and curses of the wounded, they had resolute armed men to deal with.

"Over the hedge!" cried one. "Come round this way, and we may surround them."

They then dashed through a hedge, a part of the villagers at the same time seizing heavy hedge stakes, which they tore out of the ground, to use as offensive weapons, and a furious attack was made upon the stile.

Notwithstanding this, St. Leon and Jasper used long swords that gave fearful wounds, yet the peasants with their heavy sticks beat down their guard, and they received many a heavy blow.

At length, those who broke through the hedge came round, and were about to break through the hedge that separated them from the lane in which the students now stood.

"Fly! fly! St. Leon!" cried Jasper; "fly! or we shall be surrounded! I have lost my sword. Hasten on to the moat-house, and we may yet do something there to preserve ourselves."

St. Leon turned from the stile, which his single efforts he found insufficient to make good against such a host of enemies. He had scarcely done so before new enemies presented themselves. The men were coming down through the hedge, and were about to cut off their retreat.

Rendered desperate by this the two students dashed onward, and, one man in particular, stood across the road with his stake uplifted to crush to the earth any one who should think of passing him.

By a sudden bound St. Leon brought himself within the sweep of his weapon, and before he could strike had effectually disabled him; but St. Leon had the misfortune to lose his own sword, which got somehow into the bones of the man and stuck there. St. Leon was compelled to abandon it, and hasten on.

"Jasper," said he, "on, on, on! I have lost my sword now! Flight is all that is left us!"

St. Leon at that moment was seized, and a heavy blow was dealt him, followed by several others. He was in the grasp of a man whom he could not resist. He panted for breath, but still kept on running.

"Jasper! Jasper!" exclaimed St. Leon.

"Come on!"

"I am seized!"

Jasper turned round, and by the light of the moon he could see that St. Leon had been stopped.

Slackening his own pace he struck the man a blow on the side of the head which caused him to reel, and St. Leon was free.

"Now, now," he exclaimed, "exert yourself, St. Leon. We may yet get to the old moat-house in time to save ourselves, for, decayed as it is, it will resist the mere efforts of animal strength, unaided by art."

St. Leon spoke not; he felt it was no time to answer, when he could hear the infuriated villagers, like demons, threatening vengeance—the deep curses of the men mingling with the shriller imprecations of the females.

The old moat-house now rose to their view, and never was there a welcomer sight to human beings than the time-worn walls and turrets of the ancient mansion to these two young men. They were at the last extremity, and a few moments more must have ended their earthly career, for no mercy would they have found from their enemies, whose fury and feelings of revenge were fully aroused, and nothing but the most unexampled vengeance could appease them, and to obtain this Heaven only knows what cruelties they would commit, or what tortures they would inflict.

They heard the yell of the mob—that mob who, singly, would have shrunk from approaching this very spot—but now, under their excited passions, fear was unfelt and unknown among them.

The students gained the precincts of the house, and this success inspired them with momentary vigour and swiftness.

"Hasten, St. Leon!" cried Jasper, as he quickened his own pace, "else they will enter before we have time to barricade and secure the door."

St. Leon did exert himself, and they both dashed into the house; but they were projected some yards forward by the force of their own speed before they could turn and close the door. This Jasper did, and scarcely had he done so when the foremost of the peasants rushed headlong against it.

The door was massive, and the fastenings were there, but rusty, and it was scarcely possible to draw them, but they contrived to do so.

"Now, if the staples hold good," exclaimed St. Leon, "we may expect to hold out against them till they are tired."

"No, no," replied Jasper, "the dogs will get in by some means. There are several likely places, and they will do so before long."

"Then let us secure what doors we can, and barricade them," said St. Leon.

"Yes, yes—quick, too! We can offer them impediments that will so tire them that they may give up the attempt."

"Do you think they will, Jasper?" said St. Leon, panting with exertion.

"I hope so," replied Jasper, also panting, and speaking only at intervals. "I think there is a chance of it if we go to the top, and throw down upon them some of those loose stones and bricks that are easily moved at that spot."

"By heaven," said St. Leon, "a good thought! We may yet give the dogs such a taste of what is in store for them that they may sicken of it."

"Let's secure the lower place first."

This they immediately set about, and with much labour and exertion placed some old lumber against the doors in such positions that, if it did not render them perfectly secure, at least, they would require much force and trouble to open them.

"Now, then, for the roof," said Jasper, as they secured all the places below that were capable of it; "now, then, for the roof!"

They both now got on to the roof through a trap-door, and here they found a whole magazine of the kind of artillery that was considered effective in the extreme—namely, loose stones and bricks—the former about the size of one's clenched fist.

"What could be better?" exclaimed St. Leon.

"Hush!" said Jasper.

"What now?"

"Speak not. We can remain here for some time unsuspected, and commit much mischief before they know whence it comes. Keep close, and stand behind this projecting point while I reach that one yonder. We shall be concealed, and there will be no danger."

"That's a recommendation, certainly," replied St. Leon, as he gathered up about ten or fifteen good-sized bricks or stones.

Jasper now reached his post, and having followed the example of St. Leon with regard to the bricks, he looked over the parapet upon the noise and tumult below. It appeared that they were destitute of any means of forcing the door, and they were hammering, kicking, and bouncing against the large oaken door—cursing and invoking imprecations upon themselves, the door, and the students indiscriminately in their rage.

"Now," said Jasper, "now, St. Leon, they are thickly wedged together, and we are sure to make some of them recoil."

So saying, he flung a large flint stone in the midst of them, which was followed by a deep groan, and a movement among those below. St. Leon followed with the like result.

"I think," he said, "that this will tire them, and if they can stand much of this they are certainly less human than I could have imagined."

They went on thus for several minutes, and, pelting the mob with these heavy stones, a visible disturbance took place among them, for they could not imagine where the assault came from.

"They are necromancers," said an old man, "and can make the very stones fly up and injure men. They will not be taken."

"We will try," said a young man, rushing forward; but he was immediately felled to the earth by a stone thrown from above.

The mob gave way a little at this, and, many more stones falling, they looked upward, and then at length they detected whence they came.

"There they are!" said one, pointing upward, "there they are!"

A general execration followed this announcement; hootings and yellings were heard on every side, and so dreadful were the sounds that even Jasper quailed when he heard them, and St. Leon believed there was no hope.

Animated by despair, however, the two students exerted themselves to use their means of defence to the utmost, and they kept up such a shower of stones that in many cases the mob recoiled.

"Burn them out!" cried the old woman. "Burn the place down! burn—burn! and destroy them and their habitation together!"

"A light! a light! a light!" echoed the peasants, as this notion spread like lightning among them; and the words were scarcely uttered before several torches were seen advancing in the hands of the infuriated peasantry, while others brought fire-wood to the spot.

St. Leon and Jasper could not conceal their surprise and terror at these words, for full well they knew their meaning.

"Fire!" said Jasper, "fire, St. Leon! They will smoke us out like rats! See—see! they come! Now use your missiles, and keep them off!"

As he said this, he himself threw a flint stone on a man who carried a torch, while St. Leon struck down one who carried some fire-wood.

The two students continued throwing for some time, but the peasants placed their faggots on their heads, and, protecting themselves, they at length set light to them, and the old moat-house soon caught fire. This was announced to those above by a loud shout from below.

"St. Leon, the house is on fire, and we can do no good here. We can escape by means of a rope. The danger is very great, it is true; but if we are not seen, which I most fear, we may yet cross the moat."

"In God's name, be quick then!" returned St. Leon; and the two young men, as quick as thought, immediately executed the project they had formed, and in a few moments more they stood on the brink of the moat.

"Look," said St. Leon, "how the old house blazes! see how rapid it burns! There is not a room which the fire has not reached! We should have been dead ere this had we been there!"

"See—see! they come, St. Leon! The moat! the moat!" and he dashed into its dark waters.

Jasper was immediately followed by St. Leon, and they had scarce reached the opposite side when they beheld the peasantry, like so many imps of darkness, rushing wildly round the old moat-house, with frantic gestures, in the red glare of the fire, which reflected upon themselves. The students, fearful of being seen, fled swiftly from the spot.

Continued from page 88.

ANGELINE.

CHAPTER XXXVII—*(continued.)*

"Selina," said Mr. Gimp, taking his inamorato's hand, and gazing upon her pretty face with a languishing air, "vords is too veak to express the emotions of my 'art; the vorld is vide, and the poet says it's a 'rosebud gardin' of gals;' but, then, how much von beauteous flower excels all others."

"La, now, don't be stupid," simpered Selina; "but talking of flowers reminds me of your promise to take me to the flower show at Sydenham."

"Vhen did I break my wows, Selina? But, as I was a sayin', vhere——"

"In the world is poor Mr. Graves? I promised him my hand——"

"Your hand?"

"For the next dance, silly. How jealous you are; I can't abear a jealous disposition."

"Selina, I am not jealous, not the least in life; but that fellow is a scorpion! I could crush him," growled Mr. Gimp, stamping his foot.

Selina uttered a shriek; her luckless swain had accidentally trod upon her light fantastic toes.

He was profuse in his expressions of regret, and frantically implored her pardon.

No. 13.

But it was long before she would be appeased.

"I'm quite shocked at ycur displays of temper, James," she said, pouting; "I'm sure poor Mr. Graves is much more amiable than you are; he wouldn't go on so. It is very mean of you to be so envious, so jealous!"

"Envious! jealous! I scorns the thought! But, then, Selina, the pref'rence you shows to the murderer of 'Pretty Jane' and 'Phœbe dearest,' and the rest of the pop'lar musical favourites, is quite unaccountable. Why, he's a feller, as Shakespeare calls, 'most musical' (not as I agrees with the immortal bard, there), 'most melancholy' (vhere I quite concurs in the opinion.) Look at your own Jemmy, my dear Selina; in what respect can this sallow-faced squaller of trumpery ballads wie with me?"

"Oh, but just consider his talents."

"His talents? What colour?"

"Colour?"

"Yes; talents of gold or silver! Vhy, his salary is von pound a veek, and he finds his own properties. Vhot a prospect for a vife and fam'ly!"

"But, then, if his income is small, his manners are so refined!"

"Werry refined, like his income. Selina, he's a hidgeous mockery, and as for his making a home for any deluded female, as he might lead like a lamb to the altar, it would dissolve, like the baseless fabric of a wision, before the broker's warrant, and leave not a stick behind!"

"Heigho!" sighed Selina.

Mr. Gimp glared at her with a look of serio-comic agony, and then rising offered his arm, with some trepidation, for afar down the leafy vista he espied the tall, gaunt form gliding with a slow and stately march like Hamlet's ghost.

"That's the new polka," he said, quickly. "Come, Selina, let's have a dance."

"I hate the polkas, they're so common, so stupid; we'll wait for a waltz."

Mr. Gimp threw himself upon a seat with a look of jealous despair.

"I'm so faint," said Selina, fanning herself with her handkerchief. "James, there's a dear, bring me a glass of lemonade."

Nearer and nearer stalked the gloomy figure of the tall and moustachioed Graves.

Fiercer and fiercer grew the scowl upon Mr. Gimp's face.

He looked hurriedly round for a waiter.

There was no attendant within call.

He started up.

He glanced vindictively at his rival, entreatingly at the lady fair.

"Iced!" said Selina, naively. "Now don't run off so fast, it looks so absurd. Go quietly, James dear; you need not hurry, Mr. Graves is a charming companion, and I shall be entertained——"

Mr. Gimp stayed to hear no more.

He rushed away to the refreshment bar, obtained a bottle of lemonade, and, dashing madly through the gay crowd gathering round the platform for the dance, returned to the bower where he had left his fickle charmer.

The bird was flown!

He threw down the bottle and ran back to the platform.

Then, whirling round amid the throng of dancers, he beheld his inconstant fair one fast clasped in the embrace of his detested rival.

This was too much for poor Jemmy.

He rushed on to the platform.

He made a dash at the celebrated tenor, intent upon tearing him from the side of the fickle beauty.

But he found that it was less easy to reach him than he had expected.

A fat couple bounced against him, and sent him reeling against a gaunt volunteer of irascible temper, whose fair partner shrieked her alarm.

The gallant warrior resented the obstruction by a kick, which sent poor Jemmy spinning against the orchestra.

He recovered his footing, only to find himself carried along by the bumping, swirling tide of Terpsichoreans, who were swaying round and round in a dense mass, for it was a grand gala night, and the place was awfully crowded.

He lost his hat.

His coat was torn.

He was maddened to such a pitch of fury by the rough usage he met with that he felt inclined to run amuck in the throng like a Malay savage.

However, he contrived to struggle to the outskirts—the word is appropriate—of the whirling crowd, and, gnashing his teeth, and rolling his angry eyes, he leaned against the palisades breathless and half frantic.

The chaff, laughter and derision which assailed his ears were not calculated to assuage his aroused indignation.

He glared wildly about him.

Mr. Graves and the false Selina came gracefully floating past.

He flung himself in their way.

His foot slipped.

He fell prone.

The couple stumbled over him.

He leaped up.

Seizing Mr. Graves by his limp white cravat, and nearly strangling him, he dragged him from the platform on to the lawn.

He shook him off.

"Sir-r!" gasped the man of genius, "to what must I attribute this outrageous conduct?"

"To the outraged feelings of von you have vilely insulted, of von who von't brook insult from the—the Pope!" roared Mr. Gimp, beginning to strip off his coat.

"James!" screamed Selina, throwing herself into his arms.

"False and abandoned voman! Avay!" cried the irate Mr. Gimp, thrusting her aside. "Speak! Vosn't ve engaged for the next dance? Haven't you tvitted me with jealousy? I am not jealous, Miss Selina Sparks; you may scorn and slight me if you vill, for, as the poet says, there's as good fish in the sea, though that don't matter; but don't you think I'm going to be cut out by this wile, designing, vanderin' minstrel. Stand out of my vay vhile I smash him!"

Mr. Gimp rushed upon his luckless rival, and dealt him a fearful blow on the nose.

The tenor, who was showing off, finding the "Even tenour of his way" thus rudely intercepted, turned like a tiger.

Mr. Gimp threw his arms well before him, and capered round his adversary with due intent to "polish him off," as he stated.

Mr. Graves, however, who considered himself sufficiently polished already, backed before his advancing foe, and jerked his arms and bobbed his head in a very helpless and contemptible style.

The valiant James rushed in, then a smart "thwack," and the luckless Graves was knocked flat on his back.

He rose to his knees, yelling for help.

This remorseless rival was about to renew the attack.

There was a great fracas.

Growling his wrath, Mr. Gimp crouched, in order to make a spring upon his cowed adversary.

Selina threw her arms about him and dragged him off.

"James!" she shrieked, "O, spare him! For my sake, dear James! You know I never slighted you. O, you would not murder the poor fellow! you see that he is no match for you. You are the best man, dear, and——"

"The best man!" reiterated the indignant James, in accents that bespoke his sublime contempt. "Go, deceitful voman, and 'vhen other lips and other 'arts their tales of love shall tell,' vhy then——" Mr. Gimp's voice failed; and, after struggling a moment, he sobbed forth, "'then you'll remember me!'"

He turned, and took a forward step.

The crowd gave way with a cheer and a laugh, as with bantam strut, the little fellow marched past his tall, but discomfited rival.

"You will not leave me, James!" cried Selina, trying to detain him.

But he cast her off.

"You have roused the lion in my chest—I mean my breast!" returned her enraged lover, with a withering glance, "I leave you to reflection and repentance. Adoo! Remember me!"

"Stop him!" cried Mr. Graves. "Where's a policeman? He has assaulted me. I give him into custody."

Several persons rushed upon the hero and seized him.

"Unhand me, gentlemen!" shouted Mr. Gimp, struggling hard to liberate himself. "You will not take part with yon designing betrayer of genuine friendship; he owes me five pounds seven and sixpence; I bestowed on him a pair of boots as good as new; he borrowed my umbrella, and never returned it; and I gave him all my old hats, to say nothing of the applause I've lavished upon him, when others tried to hiss him off the platform at the music-hall, and you behold how he returns my kindness? He tries to supplant me in the affections of my betrothed; but justice will overlook the miscreant, and he will be both personally and professionally damned for his perfidy!"

With this fine alliterative denunciation Mr. Gimp hurled off his intending captives, and ran off towards the gates of the garden.

The crowd set up a wild halloo, and followed in hot pursuit.

Selina swooned, but not in the arms of Mr. Graves; for, when he darted forward to support her, she recoiled, and threw herself plump into the embrace of a stout, apoplectic old gentleman standing near.

Meanwhile, Mr. Gimp had reached the gate.

Here he found the way stopped by a posse of policemen.

He doubled, and clambering the walls, escaped into the streets.

Hatless, coatless, and breathless, he called a cab, and giving the cabby a hurried explanation, desired him to drive to the house of Mr. Harry Rattleton.

That gentleman and Mr. Humphrey Puffy were sitting by the open window, smoking their cigars, and sipping their wine.

Mr. Gimp rushed into the house.

The two Jolly Dogs received him with a shout of astonishment.

"Why, Jemmy, what on earth is the matter? Whence have you escaped?—from Colney Hatch or White Cross Street?" laughed Harry Rattleton, as his friend threw himself down upon a sofa in a state of exhaustion.

"From 'Ibury Barn," gasped Mr. Gimp, "and from one of the most deceitful flirts that ever broke a feelin' 'eart."

"But, hang it, you look as if she had broken your head also."

"My 'ed? I smashed that distracted globe in climbing the wall to escape from the minions of the lor and the t'other sycophants that took part with that despicable feller, Horatio Graves, the concert singer. You know the willain; but I fancy I've spoiled his complexion. All the rouge in Regent Street won't plaster the bruises on his tallow cheek. He won't be able to appear at a concert for a month to come. He was defeated in his engagement with me, and he'll lose his engagement with his guv'nors. Surve him right, the designing libertine, to think he's a goin' to play Don Juan with such a phiz as that."

"Oh! I see, there's a lady in the case. Tell us all about it."

Poor Mr. Gimp, in dolorous accents, gave a moving account of his disastrous adventure.

"At least, Jemmy, I must congratulate you upon the spirit you displayed; your mistress will love you all the better, for it's in the nature of woman to adore a bold wooer—

"'Gin' a laddie woo a lassie,
He must not be shy;
If he find the maid unkind,
He mustn't pipe his eye.
Every lassie lo'es the laddie
That she fears to lose;
But he may go to Jericho,
His head once in the noose.'

"So cheer up, my lively pup. Let us adjourn to the 'Jolly Dogs,' there's harmony to-night, and, remember—

"'Care's a thing that profits none;
What were life if not for fun?
A man of sense, and genial soul,
Will drown his sorrows in the bowl.'

"So slap on the coat that hangs yonder, and let us be off at once, and—

"'We'll all get blind drunk,
And then come stumbling home.'"

"Noble resolve, and worthy of a Jolly Dog. Vive la bagatelle! Let us eat and drink, for to-morrow we die."

The "noble resolve" was faithfully kept by the young roués, and the "small hours" were far advanced when, assisted by the cabman, Jemmy Gimp stumbled up the steps of his house where he lodged.

The next morning he found that his watch was missing; but whether it had been lost or stolen there was no evidence to show.

The day after the carouse found him a miserable dog, feverish, aguish, stupefied and giddy, for Nature exacts a severe penalty from those who infringe her laws of temperance and moderation.

If our readers desire to witness the pitiful condition of poor Jemmy Gimp after his night's debauch, we refer them to our artist's clever sketch of "The morning's results of a night's amusement."

May all young dogs who are inclined to be too "jolly," profit by the graphic illustration of the bitter fruits of intemperance.

CHAPTER XXXVIII.

WENLOCK'S RESOLVE – LYDIA'S INTERCESSION—DANDY JACK REMAINS IMPLACABLE.

"HE is innocent, Mr. Wenlock; you know he is innocent!" said Lydia St. Clare, with passion, addressing the caitiff who had so basely betrayed her injured lover, George Grant. "He is the victim of some foul conspiracy got up to ruin him by some unmanly, detestable miscreant, seeking to shield his own guilt."

"He may be innocent. I trust it will prove so," returned Wenlock, coldly.

"Do you doubt for a moment his integrity?" she rejoined, with indignation. "You, who have known him so long, who are so intimately his friend? You know that his character has always been irreproachable."

"It is hard to believe that George Grant can be guilty of such a crime as that laid to his charge; unfortunately the evidence against him is very strong. But I have not heard the other side of the question; he may be able to get up a faultless defence."

"And you can talk so coldly, in a tone implying such distrust, of one who has been your constant companion, your friend, for so long—— Oh, Edgar! but your treatmen of your friend accords with your ruffianly usuage of her whom you pretended to love!"

"You are unjust, Miss St. Clare," returned Wenlock, with agitation. "You know that I was rejected by Miss Lamonde, and if I have abstained from persecuting her with attentions distasteful to her, I think in that I am deserving rather of credit than censure."

"But that night! Well, Edgar, I do not wish to recall the past. I look to you for a future justification of that good opinion we always had of you till it was shaken by your strange, unwarrantable conduct on one occasion."

"Can you make no allowance for the weakness of slighted passion? I do not remember that I was violent on the occasion to which you allude; I was maddened by the preference shown to another, by the rejection of a suit which Miss Lamond so freely favoured, but I was not violent."

"What! Did you not use threats? But there, that is all forgotten. As you say, there is much allowance to be made for one in your position. I believe that you were in some measure ill-used, Edgar. You are quite forgiven. I am sure your love for Angeline was fervent and honourable. But tell me, you will not appear as a witness against poor George?"

"What can I do?" said Wenlock, shrugging his shoulders. "I am subpoenaed for the trial. What then? I know nothing of the robbery. I can speak of George as I have found him; a man against whom the veriest scandal-monger could find no fault. All that I shall be bound to confirm is the state of the account-books, in which there are several false entries."

"You may well say false!" rejoined Lydia, indignantly. "There can be no doubt the books have been tampered with."

"And I'm sorry to say it remains to be proved by whom."

"And it will be proved," she returned, with an air of confidence. "Mr. Curtis, the detective, assures me that he has a clue to the mystery, though, to be sure, he told me that in confidence, and I ought to be whipped for betraying the secret. But, at any rate, Edgar, I feel certain that you will not say more to criminate poor George than you can help."

"Is it likely? But, Lydia——"

"Well?"

"You said that Mr. Curtis told you he had found a clue leading to the detection of the alleged conspiracy against George; will you tell me the particulars?"

"No, indeed, Edgar, though, for that matter, I could not if I would. But I leave the case trustingly in your hands."

"You may do so safely, Lydia."

"And now, good-bye. You need not tell George that I have seen you on this business, for he entreated me not to move in the matter, as he wished his enemies to be allowed to do their worst, confident that his innocence will be made patent by a fair trial and that their malice will be foiled."

"Does he include me amongst his enemies?"

"Yes; I tell you so frankly, but I feel sure he does you wrong."

"Ha!"

"But Mr. Curtis is sure that he can lay his hand upon the real culprit."

"Did he tell you so?"

"He implied as much."

"I hope he may not be mistaken."

"And I, with all my heart."

"Tell George, from me, that if he distrusts me he does me bitter wrong, and that I would gladly change places with him so concerned am I for his misfortune."

"Well, Edgar, I hope that all will end well, and that this strange and sad affair may have at least this good result: that it will lead to your re-union with us, for our estrangement has lasted too long, Once more, good-bye."

Miss St. Clare shook hands with Wenlock, and took her departure.

Left alone, the guilty young man seated himself upon a couch and buried his face in his hands.

He groaned in the anguish of his remorse.

"I cannot play out this tragedy," he muttered; "I shall never live to see the end of this trial. To stand in a court of justice to bear false witness against my best friend—I, who should be set in the dock to answer for my life against the bloody charge of murder! I will make what amends I can; I will give Renshaw a chance of escape, though he has been my evil genius, and has brought about my ruin; I will write a full confession of Aubrey's murder, as far as I was concerned in it; I will prove Grant's innocence; and then——I will bury my shame in the quiet grave!"

Wenlock drew a chair to the table, and, taking his desk, commenced writing hurriedly.

"Hulloa! Neddy, what are you doing?"

Wenlock hastily thrust the papers into the desk, which he closed and locked. Dandy Jack stood by his side.

"Ha! it's you?" he said, holding out his hand, while his face grew as white as the paper on which he had been writing. "I did not expect you so early. What news?"

"Golden; the counsel for the prosecution are cock sure that Grant must be convicted. I have found no difficulty in getting a passage for us both to America; the crack at Hall, Marks and Co.'s the jewellers' went off safe, and to-night we are to share the plunder."

"Where are you to meet?"

"At the Lummy Cove's."

"At what time?"

"At midnight."

"And when does our ship sail?"

"The day after to-morrow."

"Did you find that fellow Short a skilful hand?"

"Wonderful! But then he knew the premises; he holds possession of the swag till we meet to-night, when of course we shall go regulars."

"Sit down, Jack, I want a word with you; I think we are playing an infernally dangerous game."

"Perhaps so," returned the robber, sullenly; "but we'll play it out; that cursed Grant shan't escape me."

"But don't you think, Jack—come, you are not a fool nor yet a woman to sacrifice all to a miserable feeling of spitefulness—don't you think that you are risking too much for a mere fad? Grant has never injured you, and though you might wish to indulge your enmity against him under ordinary circumstances, don't you think our present position is rather too ticklish for such fool's play?"

"No; I won't leave the country till I can leave him fast in prison, a convicted felon," returned Dandy Jack, ferociously; "besides, we have gone much too far to retract now; we are watched."

"Ha! and by which of the traps?"

"Joe Curtis."

"Humph! I have heard so too."

"From whom?"

"Grant's sweetheart, Lyddy St. Clare, has been here; she told me that Curtis assured her he had found out that the books had been tampered with, and that he could form a shrewd guess as to who is the real culprit."

"The devil she did?"

"Aye; she wanted me to use my best endeavours to save her lover. I promised to do so; and upon my soul, Jack, I have not the heart to confront him in the open court."

"Pshaw! We can fix him safely, I am sure of it; besides, I repeat, we can brave it out," returned Dandy Jack, "and s'truth we must do so, for if we attempt to move, the crushers will clap hands on us. Once get him convicted, we can take our time; there will be no pursuit."

"Yet consider, he will be ably defended; the burglary at the jewellers' may get blown; we can escape to-morrow, and the next day he will be convicted for all our absence; it will be thought that I have absconded merely to save my friend. After all, Jack, I trust you will concur with me, that it will be mere madness to carry our game any further; let us throw up the cards and make off with the stakes; you have done Grant sufficient injury to glut a devil's vengeance, for there is nothing, even in a sudden shameful death, so terrible as in a lingering ruined life. Our flight will not establish his character—a good name once wounded is seldom made whole again—he has lost his reputation, let that suffice. I tell you, Jack, I mean to act resolutely for once; I shall not move further in this business; I shall go on board to-morrow, and remain close under hatches till the ship sails."

"It can't be done, I say," cried Dandy Jack, fiercely. "I say we have gone too far; we must brave it out, and whatever nonsense Curtis may talk, with the praiseworthy purpose of consoling a pretty wench in distress, there is nothing can save George Grant from transportation. Have you seen the fighting man?"

"No; he has been away from town."

"Aye, starring in the black country. But I hear he has been sent for."

"His evidence will upset the whole theory of the prosecution," said Wenlock. "George, of course, will try to prove an *alibi*, and though we have the evidence of the landlord and the barman of the 'Fighting Cocks' on our side, the Bethnal Big 'Un will be able to turn the balance in the prisoner's favour, unless we can bribe him to swear according to our directions."

"That won't be a hard thing to do," returned Jack. "Let us go to him at once. All men of his class are reckless blackguards, and would sell their souls for a handful of silver. I know where to find him; he puts up in Long Acre; he is ours; his evidence is all we want for our purpose, and that we shall have for a price; and what is there in this world that can not be had for paying for it?"

CHAPTER XXXIX.

A STRANGE STORY.

OUR scene changes to the home of old Beamish and his wife.

Shem and his sweetheart, with our old friend Hogan, are present.

The supper has just been removed from the table, and the old tar produces a black bottle of "real Jamaica," while Kitty puts the kettle on.

The party are very jovial.

Old Mr. Beamish is called upon to twist one of his famous yarns.

The experienced old salt complies with the request, and amuses his hearers with the following

TRUE AND THRILLING STORY.

"Well, as I have told ye often, I was the only soul saved in the wreck of the 'Clio,' and, being picked up by the 'Alert,' and not feeling inclined to volunteer into the Royal Navy just at that time, I was landed in Jamaica, and consigned to his Excellency the Governor. The time of my arrival was just at the breaking out of an insurrection among the negroes.

"Tired of the sea, I had thrown off the blue jacket, and mounted the scarlet, and was about to commence active service.

"The day was beautifully fine; the sun's intense heat was moderated by a refreshing sea-breeze. The stores were filled with loungers relaxing from the fatigues of business, and all anxious to receive and communicate the intelligence brought out from England by the 'Alert.'

"Newspapers were handing about from one to another, passages from letters were read, and the large sangaree glasses were frequently replenished, when the strains of martial music awoke the town from its lethargic confidence and quiet, and to the great astonishment of the inhabitants, who had no conception of the actual cause, the regiments of the line from the different out-station barracks marched in from all directions, bands playing, colours flying, and their entrance appeared to be the signal for the drums and bugles of the Colonial Militia to sound to arms.

"Such a display of military movements, together with the sudden summons of the militia, created considerable excitement, which was greatly heightened by seeing the officers of the police actively engaged in seizing certain slaves and conducting them before the chief magistrate for examination.

"Rumours of the most alarming nature were circulated—every one trying to exceed the other in exaggeration.

"In a very short interval, to increase the astonishment of every class, the river was crowded with boats pulling steadily for the quays, and the marines of the 'Alert,' together with a body of seamen from the same ship, and as many as could possibly be spared from the merchantmen, all armed with muskets, bayonets, and cutlasses, were landed, and with a Union Jack in front proceeded to the great square, where the whole of the troops were already formed in admirable order, and were undergoing inspection by the general, attended by his full staff.

"The arrival of old Harll's batallion occasioned much merriment, from the manner in which the seamen attempted to keep something like a regular step, and the mode in which they shouldered their arms, as many being on the right shoulder as the left.

"To bring them into anything like a dress-front was impossible, till an old boatswain's mate, taking one of the carpenter's crew with him, chalked a line before them, which they toed with great precision, and presented a very fair face."

"Having inspected the troops, the general called the officers around him, and communicated the intelligence of the insurrection.

This, on returning to their companies, they imparted to their men ; and the news was soon quietly but effectually diffused through the ranks.

"The spectacle had attracted a numerous assemblage of slaves to the spot, who, unconscious of its meaning, were much gratified at the show, and passed their humorous remarks upon the awkwardness of the seamen.

"But this disposition to mirth was checked by the operations of several workmen in the centre of the square, which drew the attention of the more thoughtful, and when they saw a lofty gallows erected with rough timber, a supposition naturally prevailed that it was for the purpose of a military execution, and a deep silence succeeded.

"The number of spectators rapidly increased ; indeed, it seemed as if the whole black population of the town had collected together to witness the proceedings, and, except in some few instances, their conduct was most orderly.

"A buzz through one part of the crowd directed the attention of all eyes to the approach of a party of dragoons, surrounding a body of police, who were supposed to be escorting the unhappy criminals on foot.

"The troops opened to receive them.

"Scarce a noise was heard, beyond the sound of the horses' hoofs, and the clanking of the chains that manacled the condemned, as they moved slowly along to the centre, where a long table had been placed, and martial law having been proclaimed, a military commission was sitting to try those who should be brought before them.

"The negroes were kept at some considerable distance back from the soldiers, and, consequently, were unable to ascertain with any degree of precision, the character or rank of the culprits, though they could distinguish two persons ; but this was not the case with those near whom the prisoners had passed, for they at once knew that the men in fetters were Philip Augustus and Louis Deseigne.

"At first their names were murmured among the negroes who had witnessed their degraded situation ; but the fact rolled onward till it had passed round the square, and every one was made sensible who were the individuals beneath the fatal tree.

"Those who were connected with the conspiracy became immediately aware that their plots were discovered by the awful position of their leader Philip, whilst the imposing force before them was a convincing proof that efficient means had been adopted for crushing the rebellion.

"Still the slaves moved not from the ground ; they seemed, as it were, spell-bound with a degree of fascination that prompted them to witness the worst their fears could suggest.

"This was not the effect of accident ; the whole had been foreseen by the Governor and Mr. Wray, who hoped—indeed, felt convinced—that the tragic scene which was to follow would make a deep impression on every mind.

"Louis Deseigne was arraigned before the commissioners.

"Philip was allowed to give evidence against him ; and his testimony was corroborated in all the essential particulars by other witnesses ; the whole was, indeed, a strange, wild scene to me.

"I have already said the afternoon was beautifully fine, and the air was unusually temperate for a trophical climate.

"The great square was a vast area of many acres, having only two sides completed with villa-like buildings, that were detached some distance from each other, and also concealed by lovely foliage and flowers that grew in the gardens that surrounded them.

"A broad and commodious road passed within the houses, and along each side of the square ; inside of each a dyke was dug, but at the time contained no water. This dyke formed the boundary over which the negroes were not allowed to pass ; and the troops were drawn up, forming another square, whose sides were transverse to the angles of the great square, and at each extremity was a field-piece with the attendant artillery-men, flanked by cavalry.

"The general and his suite were moving along the lines, and the officers of his staff were galloping about with orders.

"The dark mass of human faces that formed the border was strongly contrasted by the sallow countenances of the whites drawn up in the interior, the whole resembling a huge picture in an ebony frame, the middle being occupied by the gibbet ; and the commissioners, some in scarlet, others in deep black, who surrounded the table ; the officers of the police in their grey coats with black collars, each armed with pistols and a hanger ; and the prisoners, with several negroes at a short distance, who had been brought as witnesses against them : for so well had the arrangements of the chief magistrate been made, that nothing was wanting which could tend to criminate the accused.

"Deseigne was an elderly, and rather insignificant-looking being ; but there was a peculiar expression that betokened low cunning and a propensity to mischief.

"He was plainly attired in the working dress of a carpenter, but remarkably clean.

"He stated himself to be a free man, and produced papers to prove his statement.

"Philip, still dressed in the first style, stood opposite to him but his proud and independent look was gone. The spirit which had actuated him whilst he supposed his secret was safe, was crushed down by the sense of his immediate danger. He made a voluntary confession of his guilt, and impeached his accomplices, without any promise of mercy having been extended to himself.

"The examinations commenced.

"It was fully proved, on the testimony of several witnesses, that Louis Deseigne had landed from St. Domingo, having obtained a passage in a colonial schooner ; that he was a secret agent from the people of colour in that island to incite the slaves to rebellion ; the whole of his proceedings were traced from the period of his landing—the secret meetings he had attended and the language he had used ; in short, the evidence was so conclusive that after a little more than an hour's trial, sentence of death was passed upon him, and preparation made for carrying it into immediate execution.

"The governor's chaplain approached to offer the last consolations of religion ; but Deseigne was a Catholic, and as no priest of that communion was present, he peremptorily declined the counsel of any other.

"His manner was bold, firm, and even gay.

"He strongly protested against the legality and justice of his trial, declaring that he was a murdered man, and disdained to supplicate the mercy of those he knew were thirsting for his blood.

"'Me quite content for die,' said he. 'De soul for me go to glorio, for I good man in sight o' Goramighty ! Wharra for me fear deat ?'

"And he sang in a loud voice that passage of Pope's Ode—

"'Oh, grabe, wherra be dy wictory ?
Oh, deat, wherra be dy ting ?'

"He then turned to Philip, and, with a look of scorn and contempt, exclaimed,

"'Traitor to you God and to you bretheren—d——d rascal for me ! Look at de tousand witness to you shame, and tens of tousand nigger slave shall cuss you black heart to unborn generations down to de last ancestor ob you race. Hark !' he shouted, whilst a smile of triumph animated every feature of his face. 'Hark ! dere be de voice of freedom cry aloud, and de tunder ob him shout shake off de fetter ob de slave.'

"He threw off his handkerchief and jacket, unbuttoned the collar of his shirt, and walked steadily to the bottom of the ladder, where he knelt down.

"The spectators had at first behaved with becoming decorum —at least, as far as silence went ; but, as the time grew tedious, and the solemnity wore off upon their minds, so did impatience and excitement increase, till the voice of Deseigne, which could be distinctly heard, and the movement round the foot of the gallows, had wrought them up to a pitch of phrenzy, which threatened to manifest itself by desperate acts.

"Deseigne passed a few minutes in prayer, and then, without noticing any one, he ascended the ladder, and became conspicuous to every soul in the square.

"He stopped about half-way up, looked round him, and, waving his hand, exclaimed—

"'Farewell, my broders ; me go peak to Goramighty for you all ; make you free men. Good bye ;' and he pointed to the necessary height, where the hangman was awaiting his victim.

"At this moment, from sullen silence which prevailed during Deseigne's address, the whole heaven's echoed again with execration, and shrieks and groans, and the immense crowd of negroes seemed waving to and fro, as if the mass were acted upon by one convulsive impulse, and were preparing like the panther to make a rush upon the prey.

"'Rear rank, right about face ; make ready !' were commands that were obeyed as soon as uttered. The soldiers faced round upon the negroes, and brought their firelocks to the required position.

"The cavalry pricked their horses into mettle, and seemed eager for the word which should loose them to the charge.

"Such a prompt demonstration had its effect ; and, just as the wretched Deseigne was writhing in the last throes of mortal agony, the negroes were running from the ground in scattered disorder, using the utmost speed to hasten to their respective homes.

"A few, however, remained, seemingly regardless of the consequences ; and their lowering looks and daring deportment were indicative of what they would have done if they had possessed the power.

"As soon as the execution was over, the body hung a lifeless corpse on the gibbet ; a regiment of the line, of the colonial rifle corps, and some horse artillery, proceeded on the main road by which it was expected the revolters would approach, for nothing was accurately known relative to their movements ; the rest took up various positions for the night, and the sea brigade was turned over to the sergeant of marines, who undertook the unenviable task of drilling them into something like the manual exercise.

"This in the course of time might probably have been effected, but the marching and countermarching, wheeling into companies, and then again into line, was a work of utter impossibility—at least in anything like order.

"But few eyes were closed in the colony that night, and the regulations against slaves being out of doors after a certain hour was rigidly enforced.

"About nine o'clock I was directed to take orders to one of the outposts, and, accompanied by an orderly sergeant to show me the way, I felt no small degree of confidence at being thus entrusted.

"The night was dark, and there were no lamps to illumine the streets or to direct our steps, nor was there any sound to break the solemnity of silence, but the 'who goes there?' of the sentinel, and the corresponding rattle of his fire-lock as he brought it to the poise ; no star shed its scintillating light on the atmosphere above ; the cold dews clung to the earth below and wetted the garments like rain ; and, at the same time, there was a sort of clammy heat that almost stifled the breath, and depressed the spirits into moody melancholy.

"'This 'll be something new to you, sir,' said the sergeant, with a patronizing air. 'The West Injers is a ticklish sort of place ; what with the niggers, and what with the fever, why there's not more than one in ten as gets over it, and you are as like to be that one as another. Temperance, sir, is everything ; never drink intoxicating liquors—this is a shivering dew though, and a drop of brandy would keep the damp out.'

"'Have you been long in the colony?' I inquired, for his one in ten had excited no very pleasant sensations, and, true to human nature, I could not resist questioning him as to his experience, by way of self-torment.

"'Fourteen years — equal to two apprenticeships, sir,' he replied ; and then, as if anticipating my motives, he went on, 'Have seen many a gallant fellow—aye, sir, and many a fine young man, like you, for instance, rubbed off the roll at a very short warning. Come out from England fresh as a bear's cub just caught—red faces, that looked amongst the old islanders like cherry-cheeked apples in the midst of snow balls—hearty in health—move about like grasshoppers — drink the new rum, sir, teeth begin to chatter, then burning fever—physic and bleeding — blisters and purges — a few pieces of deal nailed together—a grave dug—put him out of sight—all over in a few hours, and then hey for a fresh meal for the landcrabs.'

"'Land-crabs !' said I, shuddering with sickly fears. 'What are land-crabs ?'

"'Oh, you'll see 'em by and bye, sir, if your life is spared,' answered he, 'and as we shall have to pass the burying ground in our route, it's not at all improbable that you'll hear 'em to-night. Very unwholesome though the 'fluvier from such places, particularly after sundown. But them land-crabs are, as I may say, hangfibious—living on the land or rather under the land ; for nature's lent 'em powers to burrow the earth, and they get down to the dead bodies and have a jolly tuck out, and then they marches off to the water to drink. You may hear the rattling of their claws for half a mile. Some of 'em are big enough to carry off a man's head in their clippers, and I have heard of their walking off with a young babby. This insurrection will be quite a God-send in their way, and the Ingins will have some glorious rich stews, when they catches 'em, for them chaps seems to like the creatures the better for feeding on the dead—I wish I had some brandy though.'

"Such a combination of horrible events, though only in narrative, produced the most dreadful agitation in my mind. I felt the heavy mould of the charnel house pressing down upon my breast, and a cold clammy perspiration oozed out at every pore ; land-crabs were crawling over my body, and fighting for the fleshiest portions ; and then I was translated to the boiler of the Indian, who was cooking me up literally into twice-laid.

"'Is the colony healthy just now?' I ventured to ask, struggling hard to assume a composure that was very foreign to the mental anguish I was suffering.

"'Why, no great shakes, sir,' replied the sergeant, as he stumbled over something in the road. 'Halloo, what the devil is this ?'

"He groped down with his hands.

"'Aye, here's a proof of health, sir—another dead carcase, by all that's abominable, and one of the sentries too, as I may guess by the cross-belts. Well, we must let him be till we

(*To be continued.*)

CHAPTER VII.

THE LONE INN—AN INDEPENDENT MAN—THE EFFECT ON THE STUDENTS OF THEIR NEW POSSESSIONS.

FAINT, weary, travel-worn, and exhausted, the students flung themselves upon a plot of grass by the way-side, for both were now quite exhausted.

Jasper was unquestionably the more powerfully constitutioned man of the two, and, although he seemed to have suffered more personal violence than St. Leon, was the sooner recovered sufficiently to speak.

"St. Leon, are you much hurt?" asked he.

"I fear, sadly," said St. Leon, in a low tone; "there is not a limb of me but aches—not a joint but is racked with pain."

"No matter; think of what we shall be, not what we are. There are no princes, no kings, no emperers, that shall come near to us. We will outvie in magnificence the wealthiest, and, blessed by eternal youth, the choicest existence will be ours."

"All of which," said St. Leon, "I would now give for one cup of wine to put some life into me. I look around me in vain, Jasper, and I see no human habitation."

"Then I have better eyes," said Jasper, "or the slight difference in our situations enables me to see, what you cannot, an old inn sign swinging in the breeze by the way side, not a quarter of a mile from where we are."

"A welcome bit of news," said St. Leon, "a very welcome bit of news!"

There was a remarkable fir-tree in the front of the inn, around the trunk of which a bench was placed, whereon there sat one individual—a fat, somniferous-looking man—smoking a pipe, and with his great, sleepy eyes fixed upon a jug of ale that was on the ground at his feet. He took no notice of the travellers whatever.

There was a doorway leading to the right, which led into one of the best rooms of the establishment, if it might be judged exteriorly, and into this apartment they immediately went. There was a comfortable fire, and the room had rather a pleasant appearance; but why do the two students start back in amazement, and then look at each other with surprised eyes?

Seated very comfortably by the fire-place, and rubbing together his little, old, shrivelled hands, was the stranger who had bestowed upon them the gifts of immortality and invisibility!

"Ah, my young friends!" he said, "so you have got here at last? Well, make yourselves at home and welcome; it's very cold!"

"I do feel chilly now," said Jasper, "but it was not so a few minutes since."

"And how the wind howls!" said the little old man.

"But you are weary," said the little old man; "remain here a moment, and I will get you some of the canary and some glasses."

He was out of the room like a shot, and before Jasper could open his mouth to make a remark to St. Leon, he was back again, with a bottle of wine under each of his arms, and a couple of glasses in his hands.

"Now," he said, "we shall enjoy ourselves, and be merry."

Once or twice, the students talked of moving; but whenever they did so, he directed their attention to such a roar of wind, or to such a dash of hail, rain, or sleet, that right glad were they to get an inch or two nearer the fire, and bless their stars that they were within doors.

Suddenly the little old man started up, and exclaimed,

"By-the-bye, how thoughtless!"

"What is thoughtless?" said both the young men together.

"Why, I am thoughtless, to be sure. There was a man of the name of Digby, who remained in this inn a fortnight, and, not having money to pay his reckoning, he left behind him a valise, a large chest of clothing, in liquidation of his bill."

"Oh, did he really?" said Jasper.

"In a room above," continued the stranger, "are these things of Digby; they'll fit you both; he was near of a size to both of you. Come with me, and I'll show you where they are."

They followed the little old man up the winding staircase of the inn, and, after going a considerable distance, he paused upon a landing from which opened a great number of doors. Selecting one of these, he flung it wide open, and they all entered a gloomy-looking apartment, in which there was an ancient, faded bed. That room did not seem to have been entered for a long time, for black dust lay thick upon everything, and the footsteps of the young men were noiseless in consequence of the thick layer of dust on which they trod.

The mysterious stranger went direct to a trunk, which he emptied upon the floor, and to the surprise of the students they saw a profusion of the most costly apparel.

"Choose ye a coat each! choose ye a coat each!" cried the little old man. "We will soon repair the mischief the rascally mob has

made. How well they fit! As well as if they were made for you. Such as you should be bravely dressed, for are you not wealthy?"

The students assisted each other to put on some of the apparel, and the change it made in their appearance was indeed remarkable.

"Go to London," continued the little old man; "the riches and the luxuries are there concentrated. Go to London, and if ye have wealth, as you have, not the most sacred idol in the most sacred niche of the richest temple shall receive more worship than your fellow men will bestow upon you. Good day, I'm off."

While he had been speaking the little old man got nearer and nearer the door, so that, when he came to the last words he uttered, he quickly passed out of the room, banging the door after him.

An uncomfortable sensation came over the minds of both the young men that, perhaps, they were fastened into that room for some purpose. Simultaneously they walked to the door, and it was a great relief to their minds to find that such was not the case.

The door yielded in a moment, and they both issued from the room into the corridor without, but their mysterious friend was not to be seen. They descended the staircase, and looked into the room where they had so recently been seated; the fire was out, and there were the remains of the wine they had been drinking.

"Where can he be gone?" said St. Leon, "I suppose he must have left the house. But, Jasper——"

"Well?"

"Have you forgotten the conditions upon which we hold these gifts? We were told that we must pass through the gates of death first, before the revivifying liquid will restore us to a new existence."

"True—most true! And that death must be accomplished without injury to this mortal fabric. I must confess I do not like the ordeal, and, besides, how can it be accomplished?"

"In faith, I know not. Like yourself, I do not choose the pang of dying. The gift of immortality that we have saddled with such a condition loses half its value."

"And yet, St. Leon, we know of a subtle poison that in an instant stops life's progress—a poison without pain strikes the individual dead as by a stroke of lightning. We might manage the affair easily by that means. Suppose, now, that you first took the poison, and I revived you? You could then perform the same good office to me."

St. Leon paced the room uneasily; he appeared to be in deep thought, and after a time it seemed as if he had made up his mind most suddenly, for he turned sharply to Jasper, and said,

"Well, let it be so. I will be the first to pass through the pang of death to that new existence which you shall bestow upon me by one drop of that liquid, the wonderful effects of which we have already seen."

CHAPTER VIII.

THE TREACHERY OF ST. LEON—MUTUAL DISTRUST—THE FIGHT.

ST. LEON sat in the old arm-chair; he was evidently much excited; to his perceptions the room and everything it contained seemed to whirl round in a mad dance.

"Now, Jasper, now, Jasper," he said, "quick! quick! If this thing is to be done, let it be over quickly!"

"I am ready," said Jasper.

From a secret pocket the student produced a small packet containing a whitish powder, which sparkled as the light fell upon it; between his finger and thumb he took a small portion, and placed it between the lips of St. Leon. There was a sharp, shrill cry, and St. Leon was a corpse!

Even Jasper staggered back for a moment, and turned of a death-like paleness as he looked upon the work which he had done; death was before him in all its aspects, and, but that he flung his arms around him, St. Leon would have fallen from the chair.

Jasper found that, to support the pallid form of his companion, and likewise to take the small phial from his pocket, were two things not to be done at once, so he took St. Leon from the chair, and laid him on the floor. The phial was produced, and in his eagerness to witness its effects Jasper let more than a drop of it pass the lips of St. Leon. There was a shivering motion through the limbs, and the eyes of the dead man opened; a visible perspiration broke out upon the body.

"St. Leon! St. Leon!" cried Jasper, "can you speak?"

"Heaven! where am I?" said St. Leon.

"Sit down," said Jasper. "Most wonderful, strange, and inexplicable gift! 'Tis done! he has passed the gates of death! he has returned to life, and is immortal!"

"Oh, this is heaven!" said St. Leon. "The sweet spring-time of earliest youth has come again; the blood bounds freely through my veins; my heart beats with the full rapture of perfect healthfulness, and a thousand glorious images of things to come crowd my delighted frame! Ah! this is joy! this is joy, indeed!"

He sprang to his feet; the hues of health bloomed upon his cheek; his eyes sparkled with a light that was before unknown to them.

"I remember, I remember!" he cried. "Jasper, memory has come back to me; eternal life, eternal health, and eternal youth are mine!"

"And shall be mine also!" cried Jasper, who was enraptured at the effect which had been produced. "St. Leon, I charge you to be quick; the poison I will take myself; take you the life-giving mixture, and leave me not another moment in the arms of death!"

Jasper placed some of the poison on his lips; St. Leon caught him across his arm; he saw the last breath pass his lips, and he felt the listless weight of the dead. He paused a moment, and then let Jasper's body sink to the floor.

St. Leon carefully placed the wonder-working phial in a pocket in his vest; then, folding his arms across his breast, he looked upon Jasper, saying,

"Lie there and rot, ere I shall be guilty of the folly of raising you from the dead. If you, Jasper, forgot, I did not, that condition which imposed a change of forms each ten years upon us both. I have now the glorious gift without its trammels! I am free, rich, and immortal!"

He turned to the door, but as he did so it was flung open, and the little old man stood upon its threshold, his countenance looking dark and angry.

"What is this?" he said; "what is this?"

St. Leon started back, and the flush of conscious treachery came across his face.

"You here?" said the student.

"Yes; I gave the gift to both, and both must share it."

St. Leon was silent for a few moments, and then he said, in a low tone,

"Had it not been trammelled by that one condition of the exchange each ten years of persons, I should not have hesitated."

"I repeat," said the mysterious stranger, "that I gave the gift to both, so both must share it. You are unwilling to restore your fellow student to life; I will do so."

St. Leon felt that he dare not interfere with what the mysterious personage was about to do, although, to look at the two persons with an eye to their physical attributes, it would seem as if St. Leon could have exterminated the little old mysterious stranger by one blow; but, then, he knew not what more than mortal means of defence and offence he might have, and the young athletic man prudently, therefore, desisted from any interference with the old man's proceedings.

Producing another phial from his pocket of similar size and appearance to that which he had given to the young students, the old man stooped over Jasper, and administered a drop of it. The return to life was instantaneous, but before Jasper could observe the presence of a third party, the old man left the room, saying to St. Leon as he did so,

"Keep your counsel, and I will not betray."

A feeling of great mortification came over St. Leon. He felt all those disagreeable sensations which may be well supposed to come on any one detected in any flagrant act. Of course he would now much rather that he had himself restored Jasper, than that he should be at the mercy of the little old man to assert to the contrary; an assertion, which, if made, his consciousness of its truth would enable him to deny but poorly.

And now, Jasper, with similar feelings to those which had animated St. Leon, rose with all the delightful sensations of perfect health.

He grasped the hands of St. Leon, and shook them warmly.

"'Tis done! 'tis done, St. Leon! We have not been deceived, nor have we deceived each other. The advice of him who has made us what we are still rings in my ears. We will go to London, St. Leon; we will go to London! Come on, my friend; come on!"

CHAPTER IX.

THE FIGHT—THE DEATH OF JASPER—ST. LEON'S CONGRATULATIONS CHANGED TO DESPAIR.

NINE years have passed away since the two became possessed of their marvellous gifts.

They were rich, marvellously rich, and every enjoyment that wealth could procure, was partaken by both.

But in the breast of St. Leon, there was a feeling of deadly hatred against Jasper. The time was approaching when the change of forms was to take place, and St. Leon, contrasting his own handsome person with that of his companions, felt that the change would be a loss to him.

Moreover, they had both fixed their affections on one object—the beautiful Linda—and each pursued his suit with an ardour that was embarrassing to the fair girl, who at last, to end the strife she saw rising in the bosom of the rivals, pronounced her decision in favour of St. Leon.

He was elated, and his countenance beamed with happiness; but Jasper only smiled as he whispered to St. Leon.

"It matters not, my friend; you will enjoy her for one short year. I shall be in bliss for the next ten. Remember our compact."

St. Leon turned deadly pale. His lips quivered, and the blood seemed stagnant in his veins. At last he recovered himself, and turning fiercely towards his companion said,

"Never shall she be yours. I have long dreaded this, and the question must now be settled between us. If you are not a coward, meet me in the park in one hour, where one of us must die."

The moon was high in the heavens, as St. Leon, enveloped in the massy fold of a rich cloak, entered St. James's Park, by the courtyard of the old palace, and glided along beneath the shadows of the majestic trees of the Grand Mall, towards the appointed place of meeting.

St. Leon walked over the green turf, and strode noiselessly from tree to tree; and more than once he thought that Jasper would not come—that he had not come there to meet him.

"And yet I thought him not a coward; moreover, he has been heated by more causes than one—he surely meant to come."

He looked around him, but saw him not, and his disappointment was great, and he thought of how much he had lost by his chance of laying Jasper low, and seizing, by his death, the fairest prospects of pleasure and power that ever man yet possessed.

"Jasper, Jasper!" he said, half aloud, for he feared to exert his voice, lest he should alarm any of those who kept guard in or near the park during the night.

"Jasper, Jasper! why come ye not?"

"I am here!" said Jasper.

St. Leon turned, and saw Jasper within a very short distance of him.

They stood face to face for a moment or two without speaking, until at length St. Leon said,

"I feared you were too late, Jasper, and could not get in."

"My fears were of the same character as your own. I saw you not, and I believed you were not coming. I took care to be here in time."

"I am glad of it," said St. Leon; "we shall now conclude that which our tongues begun with our swords, and to that end have I come."

"And I," replied Jasper, "I am come, and my good sword beside me : to that will I trust, and the merits of my quarrel."

They both turned from the trees where they were and proceeded in silence together towards a small clear spot where there was no interruption of any kind experienced from trees or shrubs.

The two young men paused and looked around them for a moment or two, and then Jasper said to his adversary,

"Here, then, we decide our quarrel, if it suits you. To my eye a more favourable spot for our purpose could not have been made."

So saying, he divested himself of his cloak, which he carefully folded up and laid under a tree.

St. Leon also divested himself of his cloak, his hat, and other superfluous vestments, which he carefully and leisurely folded up and placed beside those of Jasper.

It would have been a strange sight for any one who could have seen these two thus divesting themselves of their upper clothing in the cool hour of night, under the pure silver light of the moon.

They both looked somewhat like beings of another world—beings who flitted about in the glimpses of the moon.

"And now," said St. Leon, as he bared his breast, and walking up to Jasper, "satisfy yourself. I fight fair, and seek no undue protection from the danger that may await me."

"And I," said Jasper, doing the like, "am equally free from such meanness—nay, such cowardice. See!"

As he spoke he bared his breast, and St. Leon saw that they were both on equal terms; and then, taking his sword, he unbuckled the belt by which it was secured to his waist, and, drawing his weapon, he flung the scabbard upon the heap of clothes belonging to himself.

There was a pause of some moments; it seemed as though some thoughts had taken possession of their minds for a short space of time; they stood motionless, and gazed at each other.

"Jasper!" said St. Leon.

"St. Leon!" returned Jasper.

"Are you ready?"

"Quite; come on, and meet with the chastisement which your engrossing and unfair spirit deserves; for you or I quit not this sod a living and breathing man."

"So be it. And now may the star of St. Leon prosper!"

(Continued from page 96.)

THE JOLLY DOGS OF LONDON.

get to the next post, and send some one to relieve him. No doubt an attack of cholera that'll soon sweep off half the population, and leave the other half like ghosts of their former selves. Well, well, I shall see it out if my life is spared.'

"Shocked as I was at such an occurrence, and with my mind harrassed by the most alarming apprehensions from the language of my guide, I yet could not help kneeling down, and feeling the pulse of the fallen soldier. There was a slight, very slight, palpitation, a gentle tremor, or quivering of the muscles.

" 'Let us raise him up, sergeant,' said I; 'we must not leave a fellow-creature to perish like a dog.'

" 'If it is the cholera, sir,' answered he, 'we shall be doing wrong to meddle with him; besides, sir, we have no time to spare for the purpose.'

"He approached, however, to feel his face, and then eagerly ejaculated in an undertone, 'Oh! God! what's this? Here has been murder done, sir!—horrid murder! The poor fellow has got his throat cut, and, as I live, here's a knife sticking in the back of his neck. I see it all—he has been drowsy in his post, perhaps, from the effect of intoxicating liquors. Some of the niggers have despatched him, and stolen his firelock. We must move on, sir, for the assassins cannot be far distant, and to make a noise would only be giving them a signal to escape. Come, sir, come.'

"And he rose up, and was nearly lost in the gloom, before I pursued his steps.

"Such a continued series of horrible adventures almost overpowered my reason, and I experienced such dreadful tortures that I was ready to commit almost any act of extravagance that the sudden impulse of my terror should have prompted; indeed, my terror and agony were nearly insupportable, and as I followed the sergeant in silence, it was with much difficulty that my legs were able to sustain the weight of my body.

"At length we arrived at an open area that seemed particularly dreary, and the darkness deepened to apparent palpability; the ground, too, was uneven, and it was evident that the sergeant himself was somewhat alarmed. Still there was a dim light on the face of the sky, like that which would glimmer through a funeral pall; and the wind howled and moaned in fitful gusts, bearing to the distempered imagination the vision of some suffering wretch, whose groans were eddied in the blast.

"We had cleared a portion of this space, when my attention was drawn to a huge undefined mass, that appeared against the heavens like some enormous bird of prey, which, fearful of the exposure of daylight, had come through the dense gloom to look for human food. It was in motion, and seemed to be hovering over an object which it had destined for an attack. Still the sergeant strode on, and still, half-maddened, I followed him, till, as we advanced, the figure in the air assumed more of the human form—gigantic in its proportions, and terrific in the threatening attitude of its long arms, extended to grapple with its victim. My fancy pictured it the prince of the powers of the air contemplating the mischief which his machinations had projected. It was moving to and fro as if uncertain where to descend. I thought it aimed at me, and my senses were becoming bewildered, when the sergeant suddenly halted, and looking up, exclaimed,

" 'Ah! there he is!'

" 'Who?—what?' shouted I, my feelings wrought up to the highest pitch of desperation. 'Tell me at once what it is, for I care not should it be the very devil himself."

" 'You've hit the right nail on the head, sir,' returned my companion. 'It is, indeed, the father of all mischief, though I should recommend you not to halloo quite so loud; but had it not been for his infernal plotting we should all have been snug in bed just now, instead of bush-fighting old nick in the dark.'

" 'But you certainly don't mean to say, sergeant, that the figure we see there is the ——. I was going to add 'the devil,' but I was hastily and somewhat pettishly interrupted by the sergeant exclaiming,

No. 14.

" 'Indeed, I do though, and if your life be spared you'll see a few more of e'm before many days are ended. That's the fellow they called Deseigne, a name which I take to have its proper meaning, for there,' continued he, laughing at his own conceit, 'there he hangs sure enough.'

" 'Is it usual to allow the bodies of criminals to remain so long on the gallows?" inquired I. 'In England they are not more than an hour suspended.'

" 'It is the governor's pleasure, and, I suppose, it is done to terrify the niggers.' answered the sergeant. 'You'll get none of 'em to pass this spot after dark for the next twelvemonth to come, for fear Jumber should catch 'em.'

"I had no time to ask further questions, for we had now got close to the place of execution, where a sergeant's guard was posted to prevent any molestation to the gallows.

"The soldiers, to screen themselves from the weather and from observation, had passed a piece of rope from one upright of the gibbet to the other, and spread mats over it in the form of a tent, beneath which some were sitting and others lying down, whilst pieces of hoisted cotton, burning in an earthenware pot, filled with fat and oil, gave a flaming light.

"Having answered the challenge of the sentinel the sergeant went under the cover to request that some of the men might be sent out to the murdered man to bring away the body, and one to take the post.

"The corpse of the condemned was swinging violently to and fro in the wind.

"I was gazing at it with the most intense eagerness, when suddenly it fell from its exalted position, and descending on the matted roof of the tent forced it down, carrying my companion the sergeant with it to the ground, whilst at the next moment the sentry, who had run to the assistance of his comrades, was struck to the earth by a heavy blow, but by what hand given, or how effected, I could not see, though something large did for a moment pass swiftly downwards before my eyes.

The scene of confusion that ensued is almost indescribable; shrieks, yells, and shouts, cursing and praying, entreaties for help, and struggling to get from under the cover, produced the most horrible sounds, when, to heighten the wildness of the event, the matting was ignited by the lamp, and being of very light and dry materials the whole was soon in a blaze, and the flames rising high, cast a terrific light upon the spectacle.

"As soon as the terrified soldiers had freed themselves from the burning materials, one of the most courageous went to the assistance of the sentry, who lay stretched at full length, insensible; but without rendering him the smallest aid, the fellow ran off to a considerable distance, shouting at the top of his voice,

" 'It's the devil! it's the devil! He's got two heads!'

"And, sure enough, on looking towards the spot, it was fully evident that there were two heads to the same body, one showing a white face, the other a black one.

"It was too plain to be the effect of a delusive vision; every one saw it, and I own that the accumulation of such strange circumstances made me doubt whether I was not labouring under the infliction of witchcraft.

"Crack, crack, in all directions went the reports of the muskets of the chain of sentinels, whilst the loud bellowing of a nine-pounder resounded through the stillness of the night like the continued rolling and rattling of thunder.

"In an incredible short space of time we had a troop of cavalry on the ground, and the *heroes* of the guard, recovering their animal courage, once more attempted to drag away the sentry, whose clothes were singed, and himself much scorched.

"The mystery of the heads was instantly explained, for on removing him away, the head with the black face was left behind, and some of the cavalry, dismounting, pulled out the body of Deseigne, which appeared to be headless.

"The fact was he had been left hanging by the neck, decomposition had rapidly taken place, the constant motion to and fro in the wind assisted the operation, the body was too heavy for the neck to support it, and the consequence of the whole was a separation, and it was the head, following the trunk, which knocked down the sentry.

"The fire was extinguished.

"A hole was dug in the ground immediately under the gallows, and the last mortal remains of Louis Deseigne, the agent of revolution from St. Domingo, was thrown into it like a dog.

"The general having come to the spot at the head of the troops recalled his order, which was, through some cause connected with the disturbance, rendered unnecessary, and I received directions to return to the Government House."

As old Beamish concluded this long but enthralling story, which we have translated from his own peculiar, semi-nautical style that it might be more easily understood by our readers, a tap was heard at the door, and the landlord popped his head into the room.

"There's two gentlemen below enquiring for you, Mr. Beamish," said he. "They wish to see you alone."

"Which on us—young Beamish or old Beamish?" asked the father, laying down his pipe.

"Yourself, Mr. Beamish."

"Go to him, Shem," said the old man. "My old hulk lies stiff on the stocks, and there can be no business that consarns me that don't consarn you also. What sort o' chaps are they, messmate?"

"Quite the gentlemen," returned the landlord: "One is dark and foreign-looking—appears to be a soldier officer; the other not so well-dressed, but still a smart-looking fellow."

"Don't know 'em. What can they want? Go to 'em, Shem, my boy."

His absence was somewhat protracted.

At length he returned. His looks betrayed much surprise and agitation.

"Well, my boy, and who are these strangers?" asked the old man, while all eyes were turned upon the young sailor, with a glance of curious inquiry.

"Shiver me, father, if this isn't the queerest thing that has happened a long while; one of the fellows is—guess who?"

"Dam'me, let's have it," rejoined the old man. "I bean't so shrewd as I used to be; p'raps it's my old friend Corporal Stiff."

"No, father, it's—Renshaw! the convict chap that you and Hogan rescued on the river."

"Tell him to sheer off!" cried the old man, sternly. "Let him brush! I want to have no truck with such a pirate rascal."

"But his business is important," returned Shem, excitedly. "He comes to make enquiries about our lost Elfie. He knows where she can be found, and he wants to get hold of the handkerchief, and of some of her poor mother's things—the scarf, the brooch, and the pocket-book, you know, with the photographs—"

"But you won't let him have 'em, surely, my boy?"

"I don't know, father, what to say," returned Shem. "It may be for Elfie's good; of course, I won't trust the relics out of my possession; but they want me to accompany them to a place where we are to meet some of Elfie's relatives."

"And who is the pirate's consort?"

"Renshaw's companion? Ha, I think, dad, he must be the same fellow who called to see our queer supercargo; but he had left us, don't you remember?"

"Aye, aye; looked like a poor author afflicted with a paralysis of the brain, as the scribbling chap that lives in our garret remarked. Poor soul, if he was an escaped convict, I should think he got out of limbo pretty easy like, for he was as thin as a dried herring, and might have squeezed through the bars of a gridiron; wasn't his name Darrel?"

"Aye, that's the chap; he seems honest and well-meaning. He asked me to let him see the few things that belonged to Elfie's poor mother, and I promised to show them to him."

"So you shall, my dear," said Mrs. Beamish, going to a little wardrobe and taking therefrom a neatly-folded bundle.

"There surely can be no harm in that; but don't let them pass out of your hands."

"All right, mother. It appears that our little foundling is of high birth, and I believe these fellows are sincere in their wish to see her righted; at all events, I'll keep my weather eye open you may be sure."

Shem took the bundle, and, descending the stairs, entered the little parlour where the two visitors awaited him.

Darrel rose and eagerly opened the bundle.

With trembling fingers he took the brooch, which was an ornament of opal, set in gold.

"It's strange that the poor girl did not part with that to supply herself with the necessaries of life in her bitter penury and distress," said Renshaw. "She must have possessed other jewels. Why did she esteem this more than them? You say that even her wedding-ring was gone from her finger."

"Aye, it was so," returned Shem.

"I think I can show you a reason for that," said Darrel. "Yes, 'tis as I thought."

He touched a spring. A little oval gold plate flew back and displayed the miniature of a handsome, but cold and proud-looking man.

Darrel frowned, then with a sickly smile held out the little picture for Renshaw's inspection.

"The Earl of Lindenwold!"

"Yes, but the picture is reversible; here is another spring," said Darrel.

The portrait turned upon a small pivot, and its reverse showed another picture—the likeness of a beautiful girl.

"It is Mabel!" he murmured. "This was the earl's gift, and there is no wonder that the poor murdered girl prized it so dearly; but now let us look at the pocket-book."

"Here it is, sir," said Shem; "but as you see, it contains no papers."

"Don't be too sure of that," said Darrel.

Taking the pocket-book in his hands he pressed it tightly.

He then closely examined the lining.

He produced a pen-knife and running the blade across the seam cut open a little silken pocket.

From this he drew out a piece of parchment and a letter sealed with black.

"Eureka!" he cried triumphantly. "Look, Mr. Beamish, here is the certificate of her marriage with the scoundrel nobleman, and I have no doubt this letter contains an account of her history from the time of her abduction from her grandmother's house; no link in the chain is now wanting; her cousin, Miss Angeline Lablonde, has found her diary in a desk which belonged to the wretched old faggot Margaret Herbert, who treated her daughters' children so cruelly."

"And can you tell me, Darrel, what became of that cursed old hag?" asked Renshaw, fiercely.

"Yes, the half-witted beldame is now in prison."

"On what charge?"

"Strange to say, for attempting to carry off little Elfie herself, from the people to whose charge I committed her."

"Why—dam'me, yes—I have been staring at you all this while with a notion that I knew ye," cried Shem, in amazement, "you are the scamp that stole our little pet on the night of the illuminations! you are Mr. Smith, the pleasant-spoken, lawyer-like shark that I've been seeking to overhaul for the last three months!" Shem, in his excitement, took a step backwards and began to pluck off his coat.

"Well, Mr. Beamish, I can make you no better reparation than to restore the treasure I robbed you of; little Elfie has been well cared for, and I will see her righted at any cost to myself. Do you believe that I am lying? Is it peace or war?"

He extended his hand.

"Avast, if you put it in that way, I don't know how to take it," said Shem, rather sheepishly; "but I can but accept your challenge—tip us your flapper, my hearty, but take care your future conduct is ship-shape and seaman-like, for, dam'me, Shem Beamish is not such a lubber as he looks."

The men cordially shook hands.

"And Margaret Herbert is in prison, eh?" said Renshaw, thoughtfully. "Who arrested her?"

"Inspector Curtis."

"Phew!"

OR, THE TWO ROADS OF LIFE. 107

"Have you heard the news about the earl?" asked Darrel.

"No."

"His wife is dead—she died of fever at Naples. At least, the poor lady will be spared the shame that will attend the disclosure of her husband's perfidy. The earl is in London; I and Shem Beamish will seek him at once and compel him to acknowledge his child and avow his marriage with Mabel."

"Go, then," said Renshaw; "for me, I have other business in hand; good night. I don't know whence comes the presentiment, but I cannot help feeling that our parting will be a long one. Darrel, we have been friends, at lea-t, we are bound to each other by mutual good serv ces; I have been a great villain—my life has been one fell mistake; yet the charitable might find some excuse for me; but let that pass; I have a parting favour to ask."

"Name it."

"If you do not see me before to-morrow night go to my chambers; take this key and open my bureau; you will find in it a secret drawer, in that there is a letter, it is my last testament; read and believe it, send it to the person to whom it is directed, and then forget me. Will you swear to do this?"

"Freely and faithfully."

"Enough; it is an oath, remember. Good night, good night!"

CHAPTER XL.

THE TEMPTER FOILED.

THE Lummy Cove was sitting with a clique of choice spirits, Corinthians, patrons of the ring, pugs, touts and cads, in the tap-room of the "Fighting Cocks."

The hands of the old case clock were meeting at twelve, the room was hazed with the bluish fumes exhaled from a parterre of long pipes, and rung with the buzz of conversation, occasionally interrupted by horse laughter, by outbursts of mirth, or fierce and foul oaths in quarrel.

His "right-hand supporter," as the snobbish phrase goes, was no less a personage than the illustrious Bos Hammers, champion of the heavy wets—nay, weights.

"I tell ye vat it is, Bethnal," said Bos, with a malicious grin, "arter your encounter with that 'ere swell feller as is lagged for doin' a cove's mark—vot's his name? Grant, ain't it? In course, Grant. Vell, I sticks to it, and am ready to make a bet with any gent, and 'll take vot hods yer like, that arter your little mill vith him, and the conseqvence of it, yer defeat, you ain't vorth that!"

And Bos knocked the ashes out of his pipe and pointed to it derisively; not with his index finger, but with the little one, his thumb being placed upon the rubicund extremity of his nasal organ.

The Big 'Un burst into blasphemy.

There was a general laugh.

"More's yer shame," growled the Bethnal.

"Mine!"

"Yours, yer blessed cur!"

"Mine! you sveet-tempered lap-dog?"

"Yes, yours."

"My shame?"

"Your shame! Am I a—vot you says I am?—a cur, a coward?"

Even the Bethnal Big 'Un's dull face looked bright and almost handsome at that moment, the flush of indignant scorn lighted his eyes, and the glow of self-conscious courage, shamed but not degraded by defeat, flushed his sallow cheek.

"Vell, I never insinivates; if the cap fits vear it, my pal."

"Then I am a cur?"

"As you vishes; I defers to your judgment, and vouldn't say you vern't for a fortin. Have yer own vay."

"Vhy, then, if I'm sich a coward as you says, how vos it you cried a go in the fourth round at Whackem Downs?"

Another laugh; this time at the expense of Bos Hammers.

"Pluck up, Big 'Un, you must have another set-to with the flash cove; he'll get a ticket, such as he always do," said a Corinthian. "Perhaps you weren't in good fettle when you met him last time."

"Sprained my foot," said the Bethnal.

A laugh of derision.

"I vanted to save my backer's money."

The company howled and hissed at the defeated champion as fiercely as roughs on the gallery benches of an east-end theatre might do at an unpopular actor, or as Tories on the opposition benches at a popular minister.

"At any rate, the next time you meet I hope you'll force the fighting."

"I'll smash him!" growled the Bethnal, with an oath, bringing his fist down upon the table with a blow that made the glasses dance and ring again.

At this moment the pot-boy entered the room, and whispered something in the Big 'Un's ear.

"All right, my kiddy, I'll vait on him," said the Bethnal, rising and following the boy from the room.

In the passage he encountered Edgar Wenlock.

"Vell, guv'nor, vot's up? Vot do yer vant?"

"A word or two with you, old boy," said Wenlock, clapping him on the shoulders. "What will you have?"

"Vell, rum's my drink. A go o' rum 'ot!"

"Good, and a glass of brandy for me, landlord; and can we have a room to ourselves, I and the Big 'Un have a little private business to settle?"

"Walk upstairs, sir."

Wenlock and the Bethnal Big 'Un retired to a small apartment meanly and scantily furnished.

They sat down at a rickerty table, and for some moments sipped at their glasses in silence.

"How are you up for cash, Bethnal?" asked Wenlock.

"Cussed hard up, that's vhot I am," returned the other.

"I thought so; your defeat in that bout with Grant has gone against you."

"Gone agin me? I'm a ruined man, that's vhot I am."

"Well, you can have your revenge."

"Don't know so much about that. Now, jes' look you here, there's many a cove as don't belong to the P.R. as can fight like a lion; George Grant's one o' that kidney. There ain't von of the fancy as I vouldn't rather toe the scratch vith than him; he's vhot I calls quiet and dang'rous."

"I don't want you to fight him."

"Oh, I'm game! Vill yer back me? I'll do my best; better luck mayhap nex' time."

"No, no; you know where he is now?"

"Yes; along o' that 'ere crack at the bankers."

"Yes; he's guilty."

"Dam'me if he is. Vhy, on that werry night he were——"

"Hush! Don't be a fool. Don't you fall to my meaning?"

"Fall! I never had sich a fall in my life as I had under his right mawley; he felled me down like a hox."

"What would ye do, now, for a consideration of fifty pounds?"

"That don't want no 'consideratin;' jes' anythink."

"Well, you can have that sum; you can win that, I say, Big 'Un, easily."

"Yes, if you'll back me agen Bos Hammers. I don't see how elsewise."

"You hate that fellow Grant, don't ye?"

"Well, dunno, it were a fair fight."

"But the fifty pounds?"

"Yes, stick to that, that's the word."

"You'll do anything to earn it?"

"Ain't uster hard work—ain't in trainin'."

"I tell you the trick is to be done as easily as—lying."

"Ho! perhaps it is 'lying?'"

"Not exactly so, neither. You remember the night of your fight with Grant?"

"Rayther; I carries a mementer of it," returned the Big 'Un, unconsciously raising his hand to his scarred cheek.

"Well, listen. Where did George Grant sleep on the night of the burglary."

"Well, then, he spent the night here, in this very room, attendin' on me, for the cussed people downstairs vouldn't come anigh me, and all my pals left me in the lurch; so that if he hadn't a done the needful, it might have proved a 'grave' case with me."

"But the landlord and the pot-boy both swear that they

saw him leave the house a little before twelve, with his friend Puffy."

"So he did; that's right."

"And are you prepared to give evidence to that effect?"

"Yes; I'll take my 'davy it fell out as you say; him and the t'other cove left the house a little arter twelve."

"And yet Grant said at his first examination that he had spent the whole of the night here."

"So he did, or werry near it. He left with Puffy at a little before twelve, and came back a little arter, say twenty minutes; the landlord were drunk and gone to bed, the pot-boy were closing the shop. Grant came upstairs to me; he passed through the side passage and hadn't been seen, p'raps; howsomever, he didn't leave till the morning broke, and then I were so far recovered as to be able to let him out myself."

"At what time?"

"'Bout five."

"Humph! the people at his house will swear that he returned home at half-past five. Now, I'll give you fifty sovs, Bethnal, if you'll just give evidence to this effect: that he left at twelve, did not return, and that the last time you saw him was in the company of some well-known thieves."

"And you'll give me fifty quids?"

"On the nail! here they are. They make pleasant music, don't they?" said he, chinking a bag of money. "Here's the golden balm that will heal your broken pate and wounded honour; only do what I tell ye, Big 'Un, and they're yours."

"Hark ye, Master Wenlock," said the fighting man, folding his arms upon the table, and fixing a steadfast glance on his companion's face. "You don't consider me a over scrup'lous indiwidual, not one o' them 'ere saintified, Methody customers as is altogether too good for this 'ere sinful world—them blessed critturs as seems to be vandered down from some 'igher and better sp'ere, and lives here in a perpet'al state of disgust at the vickedness of their feller critturs, and is allers engaged in contemplatin' their own diwine perfections? You don't consider me von o' that 'ere kidney?"

"Not exactly."

"Nor nothin' near it?"

"No."

"You knows as I'm a poor devil which can't afford to be too pertick'ler as to any ways and means as may offer for turnin' a shillin'."

"Of course I do; that's why I make you the offer."

"'Cos you thinks I'll accept it?"

"Surely, my boy, you would never be fool enough to refuse it?"

"Hark ye here, my tulip: p'raps I may be *fool* enough for anythink, but, smash my eyes, if I'm infernal *rascal* enough to back your nice little game by takin' a false oath agin one of the best and straightfor'ardest gen'lemen as ever fought a fair fight accordin' to the rules o' the ring. B——t ye, do ye mean to insult me?"

"Why, my good fellow, insult ye? Is the offer of fifty pounds an insult? You are beside yourself. Just consider; your evidence is wanted only to complete the case against Grant; whether or not you give it it will affect him little either way, for the case against him is too strong to admit of the slightest chance of his escape."

"Why, you sneakin', crawlin', treach'rous, wile and wenomous, slimy sarpent!"

"Come, come, no abuse."

"Do you think that the Bethnal Big 'Un, as once held the champion belt of this blessed united Hempire agin all comers, any nation, age or veight, vould bemean hisself by jinin' in a foul and filthy conspiracy to swear away the liberty and repitation of a hinnercent man, like any blood-sucking wulture of a perjured peach, or are yer jokin' now?"

"Oh, it's no joke."

"Not anyways it ain't."

"I only thought——"

"Cuss me, if yer'd on'y *thort*, it wouldn't a bin so unbear-able; thorts is free, and such a black heart as yours is sure to breed reptiles; but you did more than *thort*, yer act'lly had the outrageous inserlence to perpose to me——"

"That's enough; I have your answer."

"Not yet, you gory traitor; take it—take it, and if yer ain't satisfied, take it agin."

And he incontinently kicked the scoundrel downstairs.

CHAPTER XLI.

THE END OF THE JOLLY DOGS' CAREER.

"I WONDER if she'll come," muttered the Lummy Cove, as leaning from the window of his squalid den, he peered through the dank fog in the direction of the black archway, into the filthy back alley where he dwelt. "Vhat's the time?"

He consulted a magnificent gold repeater, which he took from his jacket pocket.

He threw himself moodily upon a chair, and kept an anxious watchful eye upon the door.

"Things is so 'fernally quiet," he muttered; "there arn't been any kinder shine, either about the clerk's case, nor yet about the crack at the jeweller's. I don't half ways like it; there's allers a storm arter a carm. I thought, vhen I slummed that ken as it vere a cussed piece of folly to take Dandy Jack into the job; him and t'other cove on'y thinks of theirselves, though that's but nat'ral; 'tain't by any means impossible that they'll be sneakin' off, and leavin' me to the mersey of the crushers. Curtis is hard down on this lay; he's a dog as don't bark, but bites. I wish I were landed safe o' t'other side the herring pond."

He paced about nervously for some moments, and then resumed his seat.

"I a'most vish I hadn't writ that letter to Ang'line Lablonde; and as for tellin' her as I'd finally square up accounts, and give her that precious dokiment—her written confession of that guv'ness gal's murder—I orter be squelched for bein' sich a fool; but all as I vanted vere to get her here; and then—vell, I ain't in no humour to stand no cussed nonsense. Hillo! vhat's that? I'm as narvous as a stray cat. Hist! that's her fairy-like futsteps and no error."

A timid knock was heard at the door.

Angeline appeared on the step.

She looked shudderingly into the foul den.

She hesitated to enter.

"Come in, can't yer; vhat are yer 'feared on?" growled the burglar, savagely seizing her by the wrist, and dragging her down the steps.

Angeline screamed.

Uttering a dreadful oath the burglar clapped his broad, hard, and dirty hand over her pale lips, and hurried her forward.

The door jarred to.

The bolt clashed into the lock.

Angeline cast a wild and despairing look around.

"Oh, why did I come—why did I blindly trust this villain?" she exclaimed.

"Because, my beauty, you knows as I'm a man o' my word, and that if yer hadn't a bin here to-night, you'd a been in the Detention 'Ouse to-morrow."

"Oh, let me begone."

"Why yer've on'y jest come! What's yer blazing hurry? Don't like the look o' the ken; this yere humble style don't soot yer fine drorin' room notions I s'pose; nothin' less than a fine serloon 'll please yer. Well, don't grumble; I s'pose you've heard talk o' love in a cottage, you'll soon get used to it, bless yer. Any ways it's better than a condemned cell in Newgate, if not quite so light and cheerful."

"You wretch!" panted Angeline, "I came—I came, because you assured me that this was to be our last meeting—that you would give me the papers—that you were about to leave the scene of your crime and cruelty for ever."

"Blow me! cruelty! But, come, things has turned out ockward. I expex company to night, and I don't want to be hindered with any more pulin' rubbidge. Have yer brought the stuff?"

"The—the money; yes," murmured Angeline. "One hundred pounds, to which I have added twenty of my own free will. Take it, and give me the papers and let me begone."

The burglar snatched the bag which Angeline held out to him, and then said, with a leer,—

"Since we're partin', my charmin' Ang'line, leave us summut by way of a keepsake, jes' for the sake of remembrance, now. Some little locket or trinket; that 'ere watch would be a purty present, now."

"Take it," said Angeline, detaching the chain from her dress with trembling fingers.

"And, raaly, a ring or two vould look slap-up on my delikite fingers; but I'm afeared they're a little too small; let's try 'em on, jes' for the cur'osity of the thing."

Angeline tore the rings from her fingers and threw them to him.

"Hulloa! there's another chain a glitterin'; under yer shawl; let's look at it."

He seized her arm, and rent the shawl from her bosom.

She struggled and screamed.

"Ho, my! how affectin'! A lock of 'air and little locket, a reg'lar ' affections gift' as they writes on the young un's china mugs."

"Not that!" shrieked Angeline, "Not that! Oh, as you hope for mercy, if you have one spark of feeling left, give it me back! I will sell all I have, to the last pennyworth, and give you the sum total of all my poor possessions if you will give me that. Look now; the chain is of value; just the chain; indeed, indeed, the portrait is valueless to any one but me; you shall have the chain, but leave me this one kind remembrance of you when you are gone, that you granted me this great favour. Oh pray, pray, give me that locket; I will pardon you then for all the injury you have done me. I will wish you God speed; will think of you without bitterness, even with gratitude. Doubt it if you will, but there is one who avenges the cause of the weak and persecuted; do not bring the curse of my broken heart upon you. You will—I know you will, give me back the only thing that I prize in all the world."

The girl threw herself upon her knees, and raised her hands imploring.

The robber grinned, and opened the locket.

He started back with a melo-dramatic gesture.

"Powers of 'Ivin!" he ranted. "Here's a romance in raal life! Here's a hinterestin' hincident! ' The lovier's portrait,' vhy, that's a name for a novel in three wolumes. Oh! cry! what a pretty bloke! A orsifer too—blue uniform like a crusher's, a cocked hat, and a silver star on his coat collar—and what a killin' look to be sure! Oh! my! sich a duck of a man!—

" 'And the captain vith his vhiskers
Took a sly glance at me!'

"Raally, my sveet Angerliner, I'm werry sorry to disoblige yer, I'm sure; but part with this hinterestin' relic, I raally can't, so don't let's have no more vords about it."

"I will have it, villain!" cried the girl, rising proudly, and advancing towards him with flushed cheeks, flashing eyes, and dilated form. "I will not part with it though I lose my life."

"Cuss yer! take care, or you'll lose both. I ain't in the humour to be played vith," growled the burglar, rushing upon her.

He fixed a grip upon her slender throat.

Bending down her golden brow upon his arm, she seized his hand with her strong white teeth, and bit his fingers to the bone.

The ruffian howled and danced in anguish.

Then uttering a torrent of awful oaths, he snatched up a heavy bludgeon, and was about to dash out her brains.

A sharp click caused him to turn with a start.

A man stood by the now open window with a pistol in his hand, which, with deadly aim, he levelled at the robber's head.

Angeline threw herself into his arms.

"It is you, my Arthur!—my deliverer! Oh! thank God you have come!"

But Aubrey did not return her fervent clasp.

A cold shudder ran through his frame, and he gazed on her with a look of unutterable remorse and agony.

Angeline looked timidly and wonderingly up into his face.

His eyes were turned away from her, and were fixed with a deadly glare upon the face of the burglar.

The Lummy Cove slunk away with a subdued and currish air, quelled by the blushing glance of the stern-faced Aubrey.

"Let us fly from the dreadful place, Arthur," murmured Angeline. "Why did I trust such a villain?"

"Why did you not trust me, Angeline?" said Aubrey, in a quivering tone of tender reproach. "Did I not tell you that I would at once sweep away the filthy web which has been weaved about you by this designing villain, and which you have so foolishly taken for a mesh of iron? You are free, Angeline, free!—I have made all clear. Your cousin Mabel did not die from the effects of the poisoned rose-leaves, though perhaps it would have been well for her, for she was preserved only to perish by even a sadder fate. Her child, however, lives, and is acknowledged by her rich and titled father. George Grant is set at liberty through the means of the detective, Curtis, and he is here to take you away."

At this moment George Grant entered the room.

Angeline greeted him warmly.

She looked with amazement, however, from his serious face to the calm but despairing countenance of Aubrey.

"But—I am so bewildered—have I lost my senses? Are all these strange events but the fantazies of madness?" cried Angeline. "Why do you shrink from me, Arthur? Why, George, do you look so sadly and chilly upon one who has just rendered you such inestimable service—one who you know is my betrothed?"

"Dear Miss Lablonde," said George Grant, taking her hand, and speaking in a broken voice, "do not seek to fathom this mystery. I implore you to cleave to the bliss of your ignorance of a too cruel truth. But come, let me escort you homewards; for yonder ruffian, he shall not escape punishment, you may rest assured; but my chief anxiety at present is to bring you home."

"To take me away—away from Arthur?" said Angeline, in a voice of wonder. "Speak to me, dear Arthur; in this hour of my great deliverance have you not one cheerful word for me? Why do you stand looking on me so strangely?"

"Angeline, if Arthur's name were ever dear to you, grant this request: leave me—we must part for ever. There are reasons why it must be so. To Mr. Grant I appeal to confirm what I have said."

"George, speak: what does this mean?"

"Simply, dear Miss Lablonde, that it is imperative that you should part with this man for ever—that you should efface his name from your memory."

"Arthur," cried the poor girl, flinging herself at his feet, and holding up her hands appealingly, "tell me, am I to be thus torn from you? Can it be with your consent? Can you wish that we should be irrevocably separated? No, no, it cannot be! I am your own, and you are mine—no power but death shall ever part us! Is it not so? Answer me?"

Aubrey did not speak, though his face grew rigid with mortal agony.

He took the miniature of Angeline which he wore around his neck, and placed it in her hands.

As the chain fell upon her quivering fingers she uttered a loud and piercing shriek, as if she had been stung by a serpent.

Then she sank back, and fainted.

"It is well," muttered Grant, hoarsely; "she will enjoy at least a few moments of oblivion, and will escape the last and bitterest pang of this agonising parting. Wretched man, you are the author of all this misery!"

"Hush! do not reproach me," said Aubrey, drawing a long breath. "Bear her away; and now, give me your hand; let us part in charity."

But Grant recoiled with a shudder.

"He who dies pays all debts," said Aubrey, with a ghastly smile. "I have just one hour to live."

"Surely you will not add to your crimes one that is the most awful and profane of all offences against the great Creator? You do not contemplate self-murder?" asked Grant, sternly.

"My hand is stained; more blood will not make it fouler," gasped Aubrey. "Mine is the crime of Cain—I have slain my brother! I was an accomplice in the dreadful act that has blighted the life of her I could have loved with all the passion of a strong and fervent nature. But away! you who are so careful of my wretched life would not see me dragged to the gallows? Every moment you linger is an age in peril to me! Away! teach her to forget me! I dare not plead for forgiveness; my crime has placed me out of the reach of God's mercy or man's forgiveness. Once more, away, unless you wish to betray me!"

Grant bore the fainted girl from the house.

A carriage was waiting at the entry of the court, in which they hastened to Angeline's residence.

Left alone with the burglar Aubrey seemed suddenly to rouse himself from his deep apathy, and to recover somewhat of his native elasticity of spirits.

"You hound," he exclaimed, menacing the robber with his pistol, "I have half a mind to lodge the contents of this in your wolf's throat; but there'll be time enough to settle our quarrel anon. Is all ready for the start?"

"Yes; I knew ye at first, Dick Renshaw; dam'me, don't let's fall out. What has been yer little game since you broke out o' the jug? What's the meanin' of the little scene as just been acted? What's up? Are we blown on?"

"Dog! if you question me I'll give you an answer from this iron mouth-piece. Get everything ready for our escape; Jack and Wenlock will be here on the instant. Hark! they are coming!"

At this moment the door was burst open and Wenlock and Dandy Jack rushed in.

"Egad, Dick, we must show a fair pair of heels," panted Jack, "the crushers are after us."

As for Wenlock he was too terrified to speak.

"Quickly, but steadily; there is a passage through the next house, do you still hold the right of way, you Lummy Cove?" asked Renshaw.

"Aye, I've the freeman's key. Shall us go that way?"

"Yes; 'tis not for myself I care one jot," said Renshaw, "but this murderous hound must escape," he added, pointing to Wenlock, "if he is brought to the gallows my reputation will suffer, for I was with him when the deed was done."

"A gentle way of putting it, Dick," returned Wenlock, with a weak smile. "But why revert to the past at all? In the new world we shall forget all these."

"In the new world we shall forget," sighed Renshaw; "ah! that remains to be tried. If it were sure that death is but oblivion who would live? But that's a hackneyed theme. Now, my pals, look sharp. Take no weapons, Lummy; you'll find 'em more dangerous to yourself than to others. Heave along that swag box; don't forget the tools. Now, you awkward swab, take care with that chest, it contains a set of Sèvres, every dish and cup worth twice its weight in gold."

The men carried such of their booty as it was possible to remove through the adjoining house, and placed it in a cab.

All was ready for the start.

The men lingered for a moment in the burglar's den.

"Here, Ned, take care of this for me," said Richard Aubrey, handing a pocket-book to Wenlock; "it contains notes for a thousand. It's better to divide the spoil as much as possible, lest either of us should get nabbed; and now, pals, let's have a stirrup cup before we start, and let's drink to a fair voyage and a safe land-fall!"

"Hurrah!"

The Lummy Cove produced the black bottle.

The three criminals filled and clinked their glasses.

"A merry voyage and a safe land-fall!"

"Come, Dick, you have not drunk," said Dandy, stamping his foot impatiently, and turning an uneasy look towards the door.

"Here it goes, then," said Aubrey, holding aloft the glass. "'Tis the right colour and the right spirit, and yet the curse of uncertainty lingers to the last; for 'tis but as you take it; the fire-water is a burning draught from some hell stream, or it is the sweet water of forgetfulness, the *nepenthe* of care, crime, and remorse! Be it what it will, here goes! I drain it to the dregs to lose Angeline!" and, having quaffed the contents of the glass, he dropped it upon the ground with a clash, and it was shivered to atoms.

"What the devil does this mean? what mummery is this?" asked Dandy Jack, fiercely. "Come, Dick, not a moment must be lost; come, or we shall be nicked after all."

But Aubrey made no answer.

He stood with a strange fixed smile on his haggard, but fine dark face.

Then he raised his hand and pushed back the elf locks from his pallid brow.

He reeled a little, and then fell flat on his face.

"Good God! he has poisoned himself," cried the three confederate villains, as they stooped over him and raised him in their arms.

His face was livid pale, and his features worked convulsively.

"Warehawks!" suddenly shouts the Lummy Cove.

"Yes, yes, the crushers are down!" shrieks Dandy Jack. "Run, run, for your lives!"

The door was burst open.

A crowd of policemen, headed by Curtis, and a number of gentlemen, rushed into the place.

Wenlock was seized.

The Lummy Cove was about to make his exit by a trap-door, when a huge blood-hound, which accompanied one of the gentlemen who had entered with the police, sprung like a lion upon the burglar and pinned him to the ground.

Wenlock wrestled with the policemen and broke away; before they could stop him he had escaped by the window.

"After the villain!" cried one of the gentlemen, a tall, handsome young man, whose face bore the traces of recent and severe sickness, whose brow was scarred, and whose arm was bound in a sling. "Seize the wretch! a hundred pounds to him who takes him! It was he who struck me down, and not my brother!"

Curtis clambered out of the window, and on to the roof.

Wenlock was running along the narrow ledge of a parapet at a reckless rate, and at dire peril.

Curtis sprang after him.

Wenlock turned.

The two men grappled each other.

Backwards and forwards they swayed over the fearful brink.

"Let me go!" whispered Wenlock, fiercely. "I do not want to have your blood upon my head!"

"One or both of us," was the stern reply.

Once more they wrestled madly.

Wenlock is forced over the brink.

He draws a pistol from his breast.

Before he can draw the trigger, Curtis, who has gained a foothold on the roof, hurls him forward into mid air!

Down!

The next instant a dark and mangled mass lies on the blood-spattered pavement far below!

Within the robbers' den the policemen are busy handcuffing Dandy Jack and the Lummy Cove.

A group of gentlemen surround the prostrate body of Richard Aubrey *alias* Renshaw.

His head is supported by the pale and wounded gentleman, in whom our readers have, doubtless, recognised the resuscitated Arthur Aubrey.

Richard Aubrey is dying fast, but he retains perfect consciousness, and clasps the hand of his twin-brother.

He murmurs faintly, but it is scarcely possible to catch the import of his dying words. At last the accents grow clear, though weak—

"Cherish her, brother, and when you speak of me speak kindly. Mine has been a wild life, but my temptations have been strong. Where are you now? If she were at my side —if she might say a parting word of forgiveness; but I do not deserve that grace. Brother, I loved her, guilty as I was; madly, yet proudly I loved her. Now it is come! Lift my head a little. Aye, thanks. Where are ye—near me still, brother! O, God forgive me!"

With awe struck faces the bystanders watched the brief struggle and sudden parting of that restless, guilty, but not ignoble spirit of the felon, Richard Aubrey; and

Thus ended the career of the three Jolly Dogs of London.

[THE END.]

They now approached each other in slow and measured steps until they were almost within arm's distance of each other.

Jasper was evidently anxious to begin the fray, and St. Leon was cautious and wary in his motions.

"Come on!" said Jasper, "come on and take your thrust at me, I stand fearless! Break your ground."

"No," said St. Leon; "I never follow an enemy's counsel in preference to my own. Do you follow the advice you give."

Jasper returned no reply, but made a desperate plunge at St. Leon, who parried, and returned the thrust with admirable skill and coolness.

They had now crossed their swords, and had no other thought save what was centred in the fight. The first desperate thrust of Jasper being so well parried, checked his haste, and made him cautious and wary also.

The clash of the swords rang clear in the night air, and it was strange that it did not attract the observation of some of the parties who paraded the park, for it must have been distinguishable a long way off.

The fight continued, and Jasper got pressed; he seemed to retire from before the force of St. Leon's thrusts and parries, for he followed Jasper up close; but the merest slip in the world caused him to be almost too late in his parry, and a slight wound of the arm was the consequence.

The two combatants could hardly see their swords, so quick were their motions; and they could not read in each other's eyes the stroke or thrust that was next intended.

The fight continued. They crept closer to each other—retreated alternately—and another wound was given to St. Leon, who, maddened, pressed quickly upon Jasper, and wounded him desperately in return.

Jasper, feeling he was hurt, staggered back, placed his hand upon the wound, and then, gazing upon St. Leon, rushed upon him, regardless of himself, but with the intention of sacrificing himself and his adversary at the same moment.

St. Leon stood upon the defensive, watching the effect of his thrust upon his adversary. He well knew that, in a moment of desperation, when a man knows that he has been sacrificed, he often rushes forward, impaling himself upon his adversary's sword, if he can but succeed in securing his savage object—the certain death of his until then fortunate adversary.

St. Leon retreated; Jasper followed; it was a moment of breathless interest. Jasper continued to follow St. Leon, who retreated from before him, and contrived to parry most carefully every thrust, without making one in return.

Fortune had now declared for St. Leon, for Jasper's foot caught in a tuft of grass or sprout from the root of a tree, and he stumbled forward to meet the ready sword of St. Leon, who ran him through the heart; then, placing his foot against the breast of his adversary, he withdrew his blade, and Jasper fell back a corpse!

St. Leon saw him fall. He turned away; but, horror! he saw a man stand close to him! Their eyes met within a few inches of each other; the recognition was complete; it was the mysterious little old man!

The astonishment, and even terror, of St. Leon was great, and for some minutes he neither spoke nor moved, but stood gazing at the little old man with starting eyes and parted lips. There was, too, an expression on the little old man's countenance that by no means spoke favourably for his mood of mind.

one, who had the knowledge that he had, and probably possessed power, too, as he had every reason to suppose, might be dangerous.

The silence was broken only by the little old man, who said—

"Well, you have done something at last; power has been ill bestowed on you, young sir; your skill of fencing has scarce done you the service you believe it has. You are wrong."

"He is dead," said St. Leon, looking around hastily at the body of Jasper, for he thought the little old man meant that he had not, or could not, kill Jasper.

"Yes, he is dead," said the little old man; "he is dead; but wherefore?"

"Because I killed him," said St. Leon. "It was a fair fight, and he had the same chance for life as I; but the day is mine."

"Yours?"

"Yes. Do you not see it is?"

"Do you know that you have broken your compact?"

"I wished it at an end, and am in no way grieved that what I desired is accomplished."

"You must recover him; give him some of the liquid to recall life to him. He must be recovered," said the old man.

"Not I. I will not give him any, though I could recover him ten times over. I would rather he continue as he is."

"You think, then, to escape the change of form every ten years by his death?" said the little old man. "But you are mistaken—quite mistaken."

"How! change forms with a dead man? You must make some

mistake, my worthy sir—some very great mistake. Yonder inanimate and lifeless piece of clay will have rotted away in its grave long before that period shall have passed over my head."

"It may be so."

"And can a living body take the form of that which has rotted and become shapeless?" asked St. Leon. "No, no!"

"But I say you shall. I will restore him, if you will not, and at the appointed time you change your forms."

"And can this be?"

"Yes. Listen. He cannot be recalled to life in the body, for, as I have before told you both, you were released from the power of death upon renewal and change of forms every ten years."

"Yes, provided we suffered from no mortal injury to our bodies."

"That is correct."

"And yonder lies one who has suffered those mortal injuries which has caused his death."

"But you killed not the spirit, young man; you have destroyed the body, but the spirit remains, and that immortal part will claim its share of the compact, and you will find yourself assume the shape and form of your fellow student, Jasper."

"Do I hear aright? can this be possible? I'll not believe it. Jasper will no longer be here; he will have no shape, no form to exchange with me. Away, away! it's all a delusion—a mockery—a midsummer night's fancy!"

"It may be strange to you, I admit; but I know all these things; they are old, very old truths to me. Your age is but a span to mine, which has lasted for ages."

St. Leon looked hard at the little old man, and thought he had never before seen such an expression of great age in all his life before. He had never noticed it, and was particularly struck with the look of the old man.

"And yet," said the mysterious stranger, "I am a perfect juvenile at my age to what some people are. I could do many things that would yet astonish you."

"But that dead body?"

"That form will be yours when the ten years are expired, and you will assume that shape; the voice, and look, and all will be yours; and none shall know you, but deem you Jasper."

"And what becomes of my form? Will that be assumed by——but it is impossible; he will have nothing that can be moulded to anything like such a shape."

"Yes, he will bear your resemblance—he will be as you yourself; but he can only mix with the world between sun-set and sun-rise."

"Ah!"

"Yes; he can, when the sun sinks below the horizon of that part of the world you are in, assume your form, and you will become as he is now in appearance. When the sun's first rays pass over the eastern line, then he must vanish."

"And I resume my shape?"

"Not until the ten years have expired, and then you become what you are now, St. Leon."

St. Leon staggered in alarm and horror.

"Will you aid in his recovery?" said the little old man.

"I will not."

"But he must be recovered. Pour between his lips one drop o that life-giving liquid, for it must be done."

"He may perish, and must perish, for not one drop shall pass his lips from my hands," said St. Leon.

"Then since you will not save him, I must," said the old man "and the ten years when expired will bring its change with it."

He made a motion to walk towards the body of Jasper, which was yet warm; indeed, the blood still oozed out of the gaping wound St. Leon's sword had made; but, before the stranger had touched it, St. Leon made a rush from the spot, determined that he would not witness the resuscitation.

CHAPTER THE LAST.

THE CHANGE OF FORMS.

GREAT was the horror of St. Leon at this unexpected defeat of his dearest hopes. The compact he had striven so hard to dissolve was renewed in a manner ten thousand times more horrifying to his feelings.

He pictured to his imagination the beauteous Linda denying his identity, and clinging with loving fondness to a being unnatural, and released only during the hours of darkness from the grave; and the thought almost drove him mad!

"Oh, cursed, cursed gift!" exclaimed he, "what dreadful penalties has its possession caused me! And doubly cursed be my slain rival who first tempted me into the paths of such unholy study."

Again the thought of Linda recurred to him, and he said,

"Can I—dare I make her a sharer in this fearful compact?

Shall I expose her whom I so love to such dreadful contamination? Would it not be better for me to fly to some lone part of the world, and endure my fate away from the presence of civilized man?"

But twelve months would soon roll away and might not Jasper, in the form of St. Leon, claim her.

Whichever way he sought to consider the subject the same black impenetrable cloud impeded his view, and at last, in utter despair, he determined to claim his bride, and leave the future to fashion its own ends.

But here many delays occurred; first the marriage settlements were, upon completion, most strangely lost, and the marriage was postponed to allow of other deeds being prepared; then Sir Michael was summoned to attend the death-bed of an only brother; and when, at last, all these obstacles were removed, St. Leon himself, overcome by mental agitation, fell into a fever that prostrated him and rendered a further postponement of the marriage necessary, so that when at last the ceremony really took place St. Leon remembered with terror that it was the last day of the tenth year.

The incidents that took place on that day up to the time of the disappearance of St. Leon and the entry of his resemblance has been given in the beginning of this story, and we must now, previous to concluding our story, fill up the blank that intervened.

It will be remembered that St. Leon was summoned away by a tall personage, who had mysteriously gained admission to the wedding party.

Upon reaching the exterior of the premises, however, this stranger suddenly disappeared, and St. Leon, falling into a kind of stupor, felt himself lifted from the ground and carried through the air at a great speed.

The journey seemed to last but a few seconds, but when St. Leon's feet again touched the ground he found himself alone in a strange, wild spot.

It was a deep, rocky dell, through the centre of which ran a foaming torrent of dark water; a few trunks of trees, with branches destitute of leaves, were scattered here and there by the water's edge; not a blade of grass was to be seen, nor, save the horrid cries of some vultures, could St. Leon discern any sign of life.

For a moment St. Leon remained still, but the turmoil in his mind was too great for endurance, and he walked rapidly towards a cleft in the rocks that he fancied might give him egress from the place.

A few paces brought him to a pool of water, clear as crystal, and a thought flashed through his mind.

Was he still St. Leon, or had he taken the form of the dead Jasper?

One glance satisfied him. The change had not yet taken place.

Onward, then, he took his way, and in a few minutes reached the cleft, but no sooner had he done so than he started back in terror, for he perceived that he had only gained the entrance of a dark and gloomy cavern, and a terrible foreboding possessed him.

He turned to fly; but at that moment there issued from the cavern the sound of mocking laughter, and a voice exclaimed,

"Welcome, St. Leon, the rites await you."

And then gaunt forms that seemed to rise from the ground surrounded St. Leon, and bore him struggling to a spacious chamber within the rock.

At the instant of his entrance this chamber became illuminated as if by magic, and St. Leon found himself in the midst of a conclave that filled him at once with despair and horror.

On a seat at the far end, elevated some feet above the level of the chamber, was seated the withered form of the old man from whom he and Jasper had received the fatal elixir, but oh! how changed.

At the time of the gift he had borne the appearance of an aged man, but one who still possessed the activity of youth, indeed he looked not more than sixty, but now he seemed like one in the last stage of decay, like one who has outlived every function of the human body; the eyes were bleared and sightless, the cheeks, resembling a thin piece of white skin, were drawn tightly over toothless jaws, the body was emaciated, and the arms and legs seemed more like sticks than members of a human body.

Beside him, drawn up to his full height, and contrasting most strangely by the youthfulness of his figure, stood Jasper, his face pale as when St. Leon saw him lying dead, but his finger pointing emphatically to the wound in his side.

Ranged down either side of the chamber were a number of other men, bearing much the appearance of him who acted as their president, varying only in point of apparent age.

The president spoke, and his voice struck a deadlier chill to the heart of St. Leon.

"Brothers," said he, "another ten years has passed away, and, faithful to our compact, we again meet to exchange our forms. Let us not forget that time is brief—that we have laid down for one hour the magic spell of immortality, and endure for that space the evils of humanity, and that, should we but overstep the time but one second, the gift passes from our hands to return no more. I have to introduce to you two new brothers, one of whom has joined our order in spirit and truth, the other with deceit and for selfish ends. What say our laws on this subject?"

"That he shall sow, but shall not reap," was the response, given in a solemn tone.

"Enough!" said the president. "The law is just, and will be carried out. St. Leon slew Jasper that he might possess immortality alone. By a subtle essence I have preserved the dead man from decay, and he is here to renew for ten years the life he was deprived of, while St. Leon fills his place in the grave. St. Leon has wedded a fair wife, but Jasper will enjoy her love!"

"Hold! hold! for mercy's sake!" shrieked St. Leon. "Do what you will with me, but spare my Linda!"

"Your Linda?" laughed Jasper, mockingly. "In a few minutes she will be my Linda!"

"No, Jasper, no! Great God! what is this?"

"'Tis time!" shouted the voice of the president, and the tones of a deep bell echoed throught the cavern.

St. Leon writhed on the ground in fearful spasms; the whole assembly seemed in commotion; the lights died out and a dense darkness enveloped the place.

The sound of the bell ceased.

A laugh sounded in St. Leon's ears, and a voice said,

"Farewell, for ten years, I go to embrace Linda!"

*   *   *   *   *   *   *   *   *

"Why, St. Leon, St. Leon, what means this? Come, rouse you, man; do you intend to sleep all your wedding-day away? Shame on you, man! turn out. What will Linda say?"

And the young man laughingly sprinkled some water over the face of the half-awake bridegroom.

"Well, I declare, you look quite scared. What, in the name of all that's unfortunate, have you been dreaming about?"

"Is—that—you—Jasper?" asked the other, in a low, impressive tone. "Yes, yes, I see it is." Then, passing his hand two or three times across his brow, he said, "Heaven be thanked! the past is BUT A DREAM!"

THE END.